Bruce Aiken was born in Kent but
has lived and worked for most of his
life in a small village in the Exmoor
National Park, Devon, England.

LIFE AFTER ALISON

Bruce Aiken

To everyone who had, and still has,
unending patience with me.

Chapter 1
Friday 16th August 1991

There was nothing extraordinary about that first morning, or nothing of which I was immediately aware. I was sitting at our kitchen table, both hands palms down on the waxed pine surface. I did feel slightly lightheaded, but nothing that worried me unduly.

I should tell you that my name is Alison Walker because I am not mentioned in this story as often as I might have hoped – my best friend, Hayley Boyd, pops up more frequently than I might have expected her to. I am, or was, Richard's wife and also Claire and Martin's mother.

There was a thump from upstairs, which made me jump, closely followed by Richard calling to the children. His voice echoed from the hall and reverberated up the stairs. I remember thinking that he should be in the garden, lighting the barbecue.

"Hurry up Claire, breakfast is ready, we're running late."

Breakfast? That didn't make any sense – we'd had breakfast hours ago. I was in the middle of preparing food for the barbecue.

I turned to check the microwave. The interior light was off, but I could see that it was empty, no longer defrosting a brick of frozen sausages. Then I realised other things were missing – the bowl of salad I'd just put on the table, a plastic tub of tomatoes, bread rolls for the burgers and sausages, plates, forks – everything had disappeared.

Richard's footsteps echoed on the bare boards of the staircase. We had taken up the carpet prior to the school holidays to strip the dark mahogany stain from the banisters.

1

"I'm choosing for you if you're not down here in thirty seconds," he called..

To one side of the door to the garden was a framed cork panel that we had named our clutterboard. A new photograph was pinned to it. It was of me, Martin and Claire, a picture that Richard had taken earlier that summer. But I was sure it hadn't been there before.

It was as if I was in a dream, or maybe a nightmare, where everything is both familiar and slightly skewed at the same time.

Next to the photo was a calendar, which also doubled as the family diary. About half the days had a red diagonal line struck through them – Richard's daily routine. The first unmarked day was Friday the sixteenth of August, but it should have been the fifteenth of June, I was certain of that as we were having a barbecue to celebrate the first anniversary of moving into the house.

Everything was wrong. Only a few minutes ago I had spoken to the children, they should still be outside, not upstairs. It had sounded like they were trying to drown each other in the paddling pool. Richard had been oblivious to the commotion, fiddling with the barbecue, a bottle of lager in his hand.

He appeared from the hall. I was so confused that I couldn't find my voice for a few seconds. When I did manage to speak, it came out as a croak.

"Richard..." I hesitated for a moment, worried that I might be going mad. "What day is it?"

He was carrying a giggling Martin upside-down. They both ignored me. In fact Richard looked straight through me as though I wasn't there. He was in his customary teaching uniform of white shirt and dark grey slacks, not the shorts and polo shirt he had been wearing in the garden. A tie was hanging loose around his neck, not yet knotted. Why would he be dressed smartly if it actually was August? It would be the school holidays.

It was at that point that I became aware of what I was wearing – my old red cord jeans. They had been ripped when we were moving in and relegated to gardening duty, but they looked like new. Running a hand down my thigh I could feel the nap bristle against my fingertips. There was no sign of the sewn-up tear over the left knee.

Richard took two bowls from a cupboard and put them on the table while Martin giggled and claimed that the whole world was upside down. He wasn't far wrong as far as I was concerned.

The chair wouldn't move when I tried to stand, even when I pushed so hard that it should have tipped over backwards. It was like someone had nailed it to the floor. Sliding sideways I managed to extricate myself and moved nearer to the back door. Neither Richard nor Martin had acknowledged my presence, it was almost like they were pretending they couldn't see or hear me, playing some sort of stupid game.

Keeping out of their way, I checked the calendar again. According to those ticked off days I had somehow forgotten or lost two months.

Richard flipped Martin over and put him on the same chair I had been sitting on a few seconds earlier. When he pushed the chair in, it slid across the floor with no problem at all. It must have been caught on something – that was the only explanation.

"Richard, please, what day is it?"

I knew I sounded desperate, almost pleading. Neither of them gave any indication that they had heard me. Richard blew a raspberry on Martin's neck that solicited yet another bubbling giggle – I was losing my patience.

"Richard? Can you hear me?"

3

He was moving in my direction, towards the back door, a trailing hand ruffling Martin's hair.

I deliberately positioned myself directly his path. I folded my arms and planted my feet. I stared him down.

The lack of eye contact should have been a warning, but how was I to know what would happen next. Richard barrelled into me as though I wasn't there. The shock of the impact threw me against the door. Richard didn't break step. As he turned to say something to Martin he collided with me again and I ricocheted off the wall, ending up sprawled on all fours by the cooker. I lifted my head and looked straight at him. I spat my anger through gritted teeth.

"What the hell was that about you idiot?"

Richard ignored me. I wasn't injured as far as I could tell, but I was shaken, scared and definitely confused.

I didn't trust myself to stand up. I sat back on my haunches and stayed on the floor. I was far enough away – Richard was unlikely to walk into me again.

He was about to pour chocolate-coated cereal into a bowl, whistling softly to himself as though it was just another morning. We never bought that junk for the children.

"Have I gone mad, or is this a dream?" I asked, no longer expecting an answer. I knew that in a dream normal courtesies wouldn't apply.

Richard had gone to the foot of the stairs and was calling Claire. I huddled into a ball, arms wrapped tight around my knees, making myself as small a target as possible. When he returned he still gave no indication that he could see me. Claire flounced into the kitchen a few moments later, a self-assured eight-year-old, confident that the world revolved around her.

"I don't want cereal Daddy. I want pancakes, Mummy always made us pancakes."

4

"No I don't," I protested.

"Okay, as a special treat you can both have pancakes – I think we've got some in the fridge."

My manipulative children both cheered.

With yet another body in the kitchen, I felt too exposed and decided to take evasive measures. I edged around the table and tucked myself between the end of the cupboards and a wine rack. There wasn't much room, but somehow I managed to squeeze in. Even though I suspected that it was all a dream, it didn't hurt to be cautious. I was worried that I might knock the top bottles off the wine rack, but they appeared to be quite securely planted.

Martin chose that moment to catch his cereal bowl with his elbow and skitter it off the table. It skidded on the floor and spun on its rim without breaking, speeding up just before it came to rest. The sound produced a nervous giggle from Martin.

The bowl was one of a pair that Richard and I had bought when we moved in together, our first joint domestic purchase. Leaving the safe retreat of my corner I tried to pick it up, but my fingers couldn't even pry the edge of the rim off the floor. Richard bent down and retrieved it with no effort, but in the process his head hit mine and knocked me onto my back.

"Lucky that didn't break," he said. "We're running out of dishes and that was one of your mother's favourites."

"Lucky my head didn't break either," I muttered, retreating to my safe space.

Richard had just used the past tense when referring to me. He was an English teacher, always precise with language, to the point of being a pedant. That was the first moment when I wondered if this strange situation was real – or maybe it was just a very clever dream.

"Come on Claire, hurry up, you've only five minutes to

5

clean your teeth before Auntie Hayley gets here."

"Auntie Hayley?" I couldn't help but repeat her name out loud, but nobody was listening. What was Hayley doing here? She was in Japan teaching business executives the nuances of the English language. She had sent a postcard only last week saying how much she loved it there. But, of course, if the kitchen calendar was correct, that was now over two months ago.

I watched while Martin finished his breakfast, Claire was lagging behind as usual. Richard shepherded Martin out of the kitchen, chasing him upstairs to clean his teeth.

"It's okay mummy," Claire said. "The bowl didn't break."

I spun around to face Claire, but she wasn't looking at me. She had just speared the last piece of her pancake.

"Daddy doesn't like me talking to you, but I know you're listening somewhere."

A shiver ran over my whole body.

"So it's not a dream?" I whispered under my breath. "Am I dead? Am I a ghost?"

Claire didn't answer because she couldn't hear me.

Chapter 2
(ten minutes later)

A key turned in the front door. The familiar voice of my oldest friend was reassuring. "Come on kids, Auntie Hayley's here. Who's ready for the zoo?"

Hayley had spent most of the years since we had graduated in various far-flung places, but her accent hadn't changed in any way. We had grown up together in the city suburbs and shared dreams of travelling the world, but Hayley was the one who had realised those dreams. I wondered how she came to have a key to our house.

"Whoa, steady you two," she laughed. "Don't knock me over."

She kneeled down, gathering my children as they rushed into her arms.

"Okay kids, go get your bags." Richard leaned over Claire and Martin to exchange air kisses with Hayley.

Martin scuttled upstairs, Claire followed more sedately. I had to relinquish my position in the kitchen doorway when Richard and Hayley moved towards me. I retreated to my safe corner.

"Thanks for taking them today Hayley. Do you want a coffee before you leave?"

"No, they'll be eager to get going. Do you think you'll get everything ironed out today?"

"There's not that much to do. The insurance company has transferred the money so it's not much more than signing the trust fund documents. I don't see why they couldn't have simply mailed them to me. Then I've got the bank after lunch to change the mortgage and the joint account details. It all feels a bit final really."

I had forgotten we both had taken out life insurance policies.

"Well, time is no problem, I didn't have any other plans and I'm looking forward to showing them all the animals."

Martin made a noisy entrance to the kitchen, hands up front of him, fingers curled into claws and his mouth wide open. He was roaring like a lion, jumping up and down in his excitement.

"Can we go now please Auntie Hayley? I want to see the animals."

Hayley knelt down in front of Martin and straightened his collar.

"We'll see all the lions soon, and the zebras, and the snakes."

She tickled Martin's neck when she mentioned snakes and he giggled and escaped to hide behind Richard's legs.

My heart almost broke because it was Hayley making Martin giggle, not me. I wondered when she got to be so good with children. She had always said they scared her. Hayley claimed you could never be sure what children were thinking or even whether they liked you.

Claire had appeared in the doorway quietly. Her hair was tied in a high ponytail, the way I had done it for that barbecue – it felt like a lifetime ago. I gasped, covered my mouth with both hands. If I really was dead then it was a lifetime ago for me.

"I'm ready," Claire declared. "Bye Dad."

She offered her cheek for Richard to kiss and wrapped her arms round his neck when he bent down, but she didn't kiss him back. Martin came out from behind Richard's legs and took Hayley's hand.

"I should be back before four." Richard said.

"No problem, we have a lot of animals to see, and to

count. How many monkeys do you think there will be Martin?"

"A hundred and fifty two," he said confidently.

"Probably more like ten," Claire countered.

"Okay, let's see who's closest then. Are, we, ready, team?"

I watched Hayley depart, my children on either side of her, each holding one of her hands.

Once alone Richard returned to the kitchen and I slid into a chair at the end of the table; it was still immovable as far as I was concerned, but there was just enough room for me.

"So how long has Hayley been back?" I asked as he cleared the plates and glasses.

There was no response. Richard stacked everything in the dishwasher and wiped the table. I leaned back so as to avoid any contact.

"And when did Hayley get to be so good with children?"

Richard looked around the kitchen and, just to confirm my invisibility, I got up and stood right in his line of vision. I waved my hands frantically in front of his face, but he gave no sign of seeing me. All he did was give a big sigh and wander out of the kitchen to the foot of the stairs, but there he stopped. He checked his watch and went into the living room. I followed a pace or two behind.

"Hayley was in Japan wasn't she? How come she's here now?"

I spoke to Richard while he opened a drawer in the sideboard and fished around at the back of it.

"And, more importantly, what happened during the last two months? What happened to me?"

Richard had a video tape which he slid it into the mouth of the player. He perched on the edge of the sofa and I sat next to him, making sure not to get too close to his elbow in case he knocked into me.

"What are we watching at this time of day?"

I didn't expect an answer. I had recognised the video from its case. Richard punched the remote control with his thumb and the screen showed a flowing white script on a black background. It flickered a little, as it always did. We had laughed at the amateurishness of our wedding video, but wouldn't change those terrible caption cards for the world.

We both sat in silence and watched the familiar scenes play out, complete with wobbly, fast, pan shots and people going in and out of focus with every close-up. The many faults were all part of its unsophisticated charm. Hayley waved madly at the lens as it zoomed in on her. My mother's imperious demeanour remained immutable, until she winked at the cameraman. That woman had no shame. Geoff, an old friend of Richard's was behind the video camera. He must have been at least twenty-five years her junior

"Rewind that Richard? It's so bloody typical of the woman."

Richard stopped the tape and spooled it back to where Lydia looked knowing at the camera and gave a meaningful wink. I ignored the screen and turned towards Richard.

"Can you hear me?"

"You always found that so funny Alison. God I miss you."

Richard's words brought a lump to my throat.

The video moved on. But I couldn't bear to watch it. I saw the tears forming in Richard's eyes and the last lingering doubt that I was dead evaporated in that moment. It was not a dream. Richard wiped the back of his hand across his cheek and stopped the video.

"I'm still here," I whispered, "I know that you can't see or hear me, but I am here."

I remained on the sofa, my legs curled under me to keep out of Richard's way. He pushed the video to the back of the drawer again and left the living room. I heard him moving around upstairs. A wardrobe door opened and closed. His soft footsteps padded on the uncarpeted stairs that creaked at familiar intervals. Looking through into the hall I watched as he bent to tie his shoelaces. He stood straight, shrugged his shoulders and checked his tie in the mirror. The front door opened and closed and I was alone, more alone than I had ever been in my whole life.

I sat in silence, not knowing whether to laugh hysterically or cry quietly. This wasn't a dream. I wasn't about to wake up. My life was over. I was dead. I was a ghost.

I had been, I think, a good wife and a caring mother, but my life was best described as ordinary. I'd been a passable artist, competent illustrator and amateur maker of small, crafty things. My successes were minor, but only if you judge such things by financial reward or fame.

The room was pretty much unchanged, maybe a little bit tidier if I were to be honest. On the coffee table was a stack of photograph albums. It was unusual they were out like that. When I tried to open the top one it wouldn't budge. Like the kitchen chair, and everything else I had touched, it might just as well have been carved out of stone.

With Richard gone I wandered around the house by myself. He had left the living room door half closed and I automatically took hold of the handle to pull it open. Of course it didn't move. I realised then that if he had closed the door completely I would have been trapped in the living room until he or Hayley returned to release me. Getting used to the rules of being a ghost was going to be a steep learning curve and one I was struggling with.

The kitchen hadn't changed very much in the two months I had been gone. Maybe it was the state of perfect neatness that unsettled me slightly. The hall was much as it always had been, the stairs still without carpet, but now stripped back to the original pine. Richard must have done that himself because we hadn't started it before I had died. It still felt unreal to think of myself as dead when I was there, walking around our house. There was an unnatural silence, no muffled radio from the kitchen, no washing machine or dishwasher burbling away in the background. The house sounded as dead as I was.

The third and sixth steps always creaked when you trod on them, but not now, at least not for me. The door to our room was open, just wide enough for me to squeeze through. The bed had been made, the quilt perfectly straight, but one pillow was still in disarray. Richard's side of the bed had been slept in. On my side of the bed was Clarence, my teddy bear, named by my mother. He was the only remnant of my dysfunctional childhood that I had clung to.

Clarence had fallen over sideways and looked like he was sleeping – it was better than finding Hayley's nightdress crumpled on the pillow, always assuming she wore one. But if I had left my family motherless, I could imagine far worse women than Hayley to take my place.

I shook my head to clear the image of Richard and Hayley snuggling up together, on our bed, maybe more than snuggling. I blinked rapidly, shuddered and tried to think of something else to replace that thought. On top of the chest of drawers lay Richard's hairbrush, a pair of cufflinks and a couple of paperback books – nothing of mine remained. I stared for ages before turning back to the bed and to Clarence. He looked as sad as I felt, alone and abandoned.

The shock of sitting on the bed and finding it as hard as

nestling on a sculpture in a museum was something I would not get used to in a hurry. I'd wanted to snuggle down onto the quilt, feel it wrap around me, but all I could do was try to fit into the random contours left by Richard's bed making.

Closing my eyes I wondered how many other things I'd always taken for granted. My new life, or my death, was confined to an extremely limited tactile range. Everything was hard and unyielding. As I lay there I realised that the cotton covers didn't feel either cool or warm – temperature simply did not register on my senses. My eyes half closed and I allowed my body to relax and mould into the peaks and troughs of the quilt's landscape, something it did with remarkable ease. I could see, I could hear, but the subtle variations of touch were gone. It didn't appear to make sense to me – but why would it?

At school, at the first opportunity, I'd dropped sciences in favour of the arts, but still odd bits of information had lodged in my head – even if I didn't entirely understand them. There was something about sound and light being wave patterns. That was all I could remember, but maybe that was the answer. If I could have opened an encyclopaedia, or asked somebody who understood these things, maybe I would have been able to get a logical explanation of what was happening. I was exhausted, not physically, but mentally. I breathed out. Was I even really breathing or just remembering the sensation? I couldn't tell. I let my eyes close to escape reality.

A noise brought me back to the real world, or whatever this was. It was the scrunch of a key sliding into the front door lock. The clock on the bedside table showed almost a quarter to four. It must be wrong, either that or I had slept all day? I squeezed through the bedroom door and went to the top of the stairs to see what was happening.

"Come on kids, shoes off. We don't want to mess up Daddy's carpets."

"We don't have carpets in the hall." Claire pointed out.

"All right Clever Clogs. We don't want to mess up the floorboards."

"I think the tigers were the best," Martin stated seriously.

"What are you all doing back so soon?" I asked.

Nobody answered me of course; nobody even glanced up to where I was standing. Martin sounded happy but I could hear the edge of tiredness in his voice.

"Come on," Hayley mustered them towards the kitchen. "It's almost four, Daddy will be home soon, what shall we have for tea?"

"What happened to the day?" I'd often asked both my children and Richard if they thought I was talking to myself when I asked them to do something, now I really was talking to myself.

"I haven't been up here for more than ten minutes, fifteen at the most." Thinking out loud was strangely comforting when nobody else was speaking to you or listening to you.

I sat half way down the stairs, my chin in my hands, feeling more than a little sorry for myself. There was a burble of conversation coming from the kitchen. It sounded like a recounting of all the animals they had seen. Apparently the monkey count had to be abandoned because they wouldn't stay still long enough.

"All right, before we eat, you monkeys need to go upstairs and wash your hands."

Claire and Martin both came out of the kitchen, bent over, wide legged, arms hanging loosely by their sides and both making whooping noises. Hayley whooped in reply from the kitchen and chased them towards the stairs.

I was in danger of being knocked over if I stayed where I was. Running back up and hiding just inside our bedroom I

14

watched as Hayley bustled my children into the bathroom. She was more attentive and patient than I would have expected her to be, leaning against the doorframe and gently encouraging them to wash their hands thoroughly.

"We don't want any monkey poo getting all over our tea do we?"

Martin turned to look at Hayley.

"But I didn't touch any monkey poo."

"I know you didn't Darling."

"Auntie Hayley is joking," Claire explained, "but we may have touched things that were dirty. That's why we have to wash our hands properly."

"But we washed our hands at the zoo," Martin moaned.

"And we need to wash them again now we're home."

Claire sounded so grown up. I wanted to hug her, hold her fragile body in my arms and smell her hair. I knew that I wasn't going to be able to do that ever again and sank to the floor. All my strength sapped from me.

A few minutes after they had gone downstairs I struggled to my feet and followed them. Careful to avoid any collisions, I made my way back to my self-allotted corner and sat on top of the wine bottles in the rack, wrapping my arms round my knees to make myself as small as possible.

Hayley managed to get Claire and Martin sitting quietly at the table and recounting the day's highlights, while she prepared their supper – no mean feat by itself to keep both of them still. She looked very much at home in my kitchen and I wondered how many times she had performed this kind of service for Richard. And, come to think of it, any other kind of service.

While she was sharing chicken nuggets and skinny fries between their plates I imagined how involved she might be with Richard in those other, more personal aspects of their life. It was a depressing thought that domestic life was continuing so smoothly without me, but if it had to be someone, at least it was my best friend.

The front door opened and Richard's voice rang out – far too cheerfully for my liking, I'd only been gone a couple of months. Why was I being such a bitch? It wasn't their fault that I was dead. At least I didn't think so?

"Hello, anybody home?"

"We're in the kitchen Richard. I'm just feeding some animals I brought back from the zoo."

"Daddy, we saw lions and tigers and monkeys and giraffes and everything."

"Did you see them all?" laughed Richard and gave both the children a hug.

"It was neat," Claire added – ever the concise one.

Richard kissed Hayley on the cheek.

"Finish your tea first kids and then tell me everything you've seen and done. I want to hear all about it."

Hayley and Richard looked like a happily married couple but was I reading far too much into the scene in front of me?

Richard sat at the table with the children and Hayley joined him, bringing mugs of coffee for them both. Martin went into great detail about their day out, Claire corrected him occasionally and added some extra anecdotes.

I had seen Hayley flirt on many occasions and she wasn't dialling it up to ten at this moment, but there was definitely something in her manner that was more than platonic. Of course my point of view was skewed due to me being Richard's wife, albeit his dead wife.

"I'll get off back to my place once I've cleared up."

"You're not staying for supper? I feel I owe you that at least."

"Well, I suppose I could. I presume that will be pizza or Chinese unless you're offering to dazzle me with your culinary skills again?"

"Again?" I repeated. "How often are you here?"

"But you like Chinese, I would hate to disappoint you."

"Oh good heavens Richard," I muttered. "Could you be just a little less obvious."

I was no longer so certain that it was Hayley who was making a play for Richard, they appeared to be on the same page.

Both refrained from flirting any further when they noticed Claire paying close attention to them.

Hayley cleared the table while Claire and Martin showed Richard all the souvenirs they had brought back from their day out. Martin took time to explain that there hadn't been any actual dinosaurs at the zoo, even though he had a wooden construction kit of a stegosaurus.

I was still in my hiding place while I watched Hayley stack the dishwasher. Richard took Martin up to bed to read him a story – Martin's eyes were already trying to close of their own volition.

Claire was absorbed in a colouring book so her question caught Hayley out as much as it did me.

"Are you and Daddy sleeping together?"

Startled, I slipped off the wine rack.

"Um, no." Hayley answered cautiously.

"Okay. I just wondered."

Claire went back to her colouring, Hayley raised her eyebrows and I picked myself up from the floor.

"Claire," Richard called from upstairs. "How about an early night to give me and Hayley a chance to get our supper organised?"

Claire packed up her book and pencils and gave Hayley a hug.

"Night Auntie Hayley."

I could see that Hayley was still a little thrown by Claire's question, as was I.

Hayley checked in the fridge then headed over to where I was scrunched up. For a moment I thought she had seen me, but all she wanted was a bottle of wine. That wouldn't have been a problem if I hadn't been sat on top of the wine rack. When she pulled a bottle out from under me I did a kind of back somersault and tumbled onto the floor.

By the time Richard returned to the kitchen Hayley had opened the bottle and I had regained some of my dignity and my observation post.

"Wine?" she asked, holding out a full glass.

Richard emptied a third of it, almost in one swallow, and Hayley refilled it for him.

"Tough day?"

"I still can't quite believe Alison's gone. Dealing with things like today brings home the reality of it all."

"Richard, there's something I ought to tell you – something Claire just asked."

Hayley went on to report Claire's question and her own response.

"Where did she get that idea from?"

"She's growing up. She notices things."

"But we're not... we haven't..."

"I think I would have remembered if we had," Hayley smiled and raised her eyebrows.

"Oh come on Hayley, I've only been gone two months," I muttered. I'd seen her pull this sort of move before, in our youth and more often than not with a successful outcome.

Richard coughed and scrambled in a drawer for the Dragon Palace menu, our favourite Chinese restaurant. Presented with his back, Hayley shrugged. I wondered whether she had been joking or serious, sometimes it was difficult to tell with her.

Hayley remained leaning against the kitchen work surface, sipping her wine, while Richard phoned through their order.

"I'm going to pop upstairs and change," Richard said, avoiding direct eye contact with Hayley.

"I'll lay the table. Do you have chopsticks anywhere?"

"That's better Hayley, just concentrate on laying the table rather than my husband," I muttered – not very graciously.

"Er, they sometimes include them in the order, but I'm okay with just a fork if they don't."

Hayley put two plates in the oven to warm and arranged place mats on the table. She didn't hunt for anything, she knew where everything was kept. She looked over to where I was perched and I wondered if she could sense me, even if she couldn't see me. But all she wanted was a second bottle of wine, which went into the fridge. This time I was prepared and avoided a repeat of my previous acrobatic performance. Richard reappeared at the same time as the doorbell rang with their food delivery.

Once they were settled into their meal, it felt safe to leave my hideaway. The only remaining chairs were pushed in close against the table and I couldn't insinuate myself into any of them. In desperation, I climbed up on the table and sat cross-legged at one end.

"So," Richard hesitated. "Is there anyone in your life at the moment?"

"You mean apart from you?"

Richard, bless him, looked embarrassed and concentrated on the noodles on his plate.

"Just kidding," Hayley added. "There's nobody special, nobody at all really."

"Too busy travelling I guess?"

"Yes, there's that and I'm not really the settling sort."

"You can say that again," I added. Hayley frequently had more boyfriends in a year than I'd had in a lifetime. Then I

19

cursed, because I realised my lifetime's sexual adventures were done. There wasn't even going to be the frisson of an extramarital fling for me – not that I'd been planning one.

"I was never very domesticated, never felt the urge to have kids."

"Really? I thought all women got that ticking clock thing at some point."

"Urgh no, never could get my head round that whole thing about pushing out a baby. It's not natural, well, I know it's natural, but not for me."

"You get on well with Martin and Claire."

"Oh I love them. Other people's kids are okay, some of them anyway, Martin and Claire in particular. I just didn't want to produce any of my own."

This was a weird conversation to be part of, although I wasn't really a part of it, just an eavesdropper. There was definitely something going on between them and I didn't know whether I wanted to stop it or encourage it. Not that I could do either as far as I could tell.

"I'm not a good long term prospect," Hayley suggested, almost to herself.

"You were often a good one night stand though," I chipped in. "Oops, sorry Hayley, I'm turning you into a slut and you weren't. You were just good at enjoying life. I suppose we both were back then."

Richard smiled at her, that same smile that had won me over the first time I met him.

"I think you're being a bit harsh on yourself Hayley. Not everyone wants children, there's someone perfect for you out there."

She shook her head.

"I don't like being tied down, never wanted to settle."

Was Richard making a move on Hayley? Testing the water? Looking for a possible replacement mother for my children? I studied him carefully, trying to judge his expression, but I couldn't be sure.

"In fact the agency has lined up another job for me."

"Congratulations, a woman in demand, although I'll miss you being around. When do they want you to start?"

"I leave the day after tomorrow."

"That soon?"

"I'm flying to Ireland on Thursday afternoon."

"Where?" I demanded.

"Where?" Richard echoed. We had both responded at almost the same time, but I was the only one who noticed.

"Ireland, that big place just to the left of Wales."

"But don't they speak a version of English there already?"

"I'll be teaching immigrants you idiot."

"The kids will miss you. They've got used to you being around."

"I'll keep in contact, I get time off for good behaviour, it's not like the other side of the world – and I'll miss them too."

"Not me?"

"Of course I'll miss you. It's not easy to find a man who smells of sawdust, but can still correct your grammar."

"I think you mean 'Is able to correct your grammar', you only 'can' beans."

"See what I mean?

They both laughed and the tension eased. Over the second bottle of wine they actually got around to talking about me. It was really odd listening to them, but also infuriating as they gave no clue as to how I'd died. Hayley suggested that they might have a barbecue with the kids the next day as a farewell. I saw her bite her lip as she said it.

"I'm sorry Richard – bad idea."

"I don't know. Maybe it would lay a ghost to rest. It might be good for the kids too."

"And I assume I'm the ghost?" I said. Nobody confirmed my suspicions.

Chapter 3

Hayley left in a taxi quite soon after they had finished their meal; she didn't even stay for the coffee that Richard offered. He waved her off from the front door and then wandered aimlessly back into the kitchen. After topping up his wine, Richard took both the bottle and the glass into the living room.

Richard picked up the top photo album from the pile on the table. He was slumped in the middle of the sofa, leaving no space for me, so I perched on the arm and leaned in to look over his shoulder. On the first page his index finger gently stroked a close-up of my face.

"Why did you have to leave me?" he whispered.

"I don't know Richard. I wish I hadn't."

He turned over the next few pages. The album covered the year when we had first met. Hayley featured frequently, after all it was her who had been at university with Richard and it was her who had introduced us. Looking at those pictures now, I wondered whether she had secretly had a thing for him all that time.

"Did you fancy Hayley back then?" I asked.

Richard sniffed loudly and put his glass on the table. He leaned back on the sofa and his shoulder caught my arm, which had been stretched out behind him. My balance on the side of the sofa was lost and I fell head first into his lap, my nose hitting a picture of Hayley. Scrambling to regain a more composed position I banged my elbow against his wine glass. Not only did it not budge, even the surface of the wine remained undisturbed.

"Bloody hell Richard. Be careful will you."

I knew he couldn't help it, he couldn't see me. It was up to me not to put myself in vulnerable situations. I sat on the arm of the sofa again, feet on the cushion, leaning on my knees.

"Are you looking at me or Hayley now?"

My jealousy was unhealthy and unproductive. You can't be jealous of the living, well, you can, but it doesn't get you anywhere. In my heart I wanted Richard to be happy again. In my head things were more complicated.

"If you like her, then ask her out properly, don't let her run away to Ireland and end up losing her to some soft-spoken lothario."

"What would you have done Alison? Would you have moved on if I'd died?"

That was a question I had never had to ask myself. I wouldn't have moved on of course. I would have stayed true to Richard's memory for the rest of my life, eventually dying an old woman surrounded by her grandchildren with a photo of Richard in a locket round my neck. Who was I kidding? I would have moved on if I'd met someone, but maybe I would have waited more than two months. But then I was also a great believer in grasping opportunities when life offered them to you.

"Go on, go for it Richard. Don't let this chance pass you by. Hayley may meet someone in Ireland, then you'd be gutted wouldn't you?"

"I'll ask her. Tomorrow. At the barbecue."

Richard shut the album and put it back on top of the others. He looked at them for a second, picked up all four albums and stacked them back on the shelf where they usually lived. I hoped he wasn't putting me away forever.

Richard tidied up the kitchen before going up to bed. I watched from the kitchen doorway, stepping to one side as

24

he turned off the light and came through into the hall. I followed him upstairs, not sure what I was going to do for the rest of the night.

After looking in at the kids to make sure they were settled, he dropped his clothes on the floor and wandered into the bathroom. I sat on my side of the bed. I had no desire to share his nightly rituals tonight any more than I had when I was alive. When he crawled into bed and put Clarence on his back, I turned to face him.

"Goodnight Richard." I whispered.

"Goodnight Clarence. Goodnight Alison."

His words came so closely after mine that I gasped. At least, I think I gasped, it felt like I'd gasped, but of course no actual air was involved in the process. This I think I now know, but at that time I was concerned that Richard may have heard me and I clamped a hand over my mouth.

I lay down next to him, sharing the space with Clarence and looking into Richard's face. His eyes were closed so I leaned in and planted a small kiss on his lips. It was probably coincidence, but he rubbed his nose before he turned over, facing away from me.

When I pulled back I noticed Clarence looking at me as though I'd usurped his position. It felt so odd to be lying next to Richard, when I wasn't supposed to be there, that I got up. I thought I might spend the night in Claire's room. I could sleep just as easily on the floor – all surfaces were the same to me now.

"Goodnight Richard. Sleep well." I said quietly and he stirred slightly, then his breathing settled back into a steady rhythm.

My next problem was getting out of the room. Richard had left the door open an inch or two, nowhere near enough for me to squeeze through. I gripped the edge of the door, but couldn't budge it.

"Bugger-damn-bastard-shit," I muttered. I was furious with the whole stupid world. "Why can't I just drift through walls and doors like a proper ghost? What's the point of being a ghost if you can't do that?"

In the end I was shouting at full volume. It didn't matter much as I wasn't going to wake anybody up. Then Claire cried out and I froze.

Richard sprang out of bed and yanked the door open, flattening me against the wall in the process. Even though it didn't hurt, the sensation was quite unpleasant. I followed him into Claire's room once I'd recovered my senses. She was clinging to Richard, who was sitting on her bed.

"I dreamed that Auntie Hayley had died," she sobbed into Richard's neck. "Just like Mummy did."

I couldn't help but put my arms round both of them. It didn't really do them any good, or me, but I couldn't just watch.

"Auntie Hayley is fine. She's home asleep by now."

"Are you sure?"

"Of course I am. Do you want me to phone her so that you can talk to her?"

"No." Claire said quietly and more calmly.

"We were going to have a barbecue tomorrow, but we don't have to if you don't want to."

"No. It's okay. Mum's death wasn't really anything to do with the barbecue was it?"

"No it wasn't. It was just one of those things."

"One of what things?" I asked. "Was it something to do with the sausages?" Those sausages in the microwave seemed to be fixed in my head, although I had no idea why.

"I know. It was a brain anulism," Claire said, never had managed to get the word quite correct in her head.

"An aneurysm?"

"Yes. And it's not going to happen to Auntie Hayley, or

26

me, or you, or Martin."

"I died of a brain aneurysm?" But I was perfectly healthy. How did that happen?

"Mummy was just unlucky."

"That's a bit of an understatement," I said.

I was thrown by this news, although it was old news to everyone else. I retreated from the bed and leaned against the wall for support while Richard settled Claire. He left the door open slightly when he finally went back to bed, but I had no intention of leaving Claire by herself. I sat on the floor by her bed and tried to stroke her hair. The soft silkiness of her hair was gone, at least to me. I leaned in close to try to smell the sweetness of my daughter as she slept, but with no success. I could see, I could hear, but touch was limited and all sense of smell absent.

"I didn't want to leave you Claire," I said quietly, in case I disturbed her. "I didn't want to leave any of you. I loved you. I still do."

Claire murmured something that I didn't quite catch. It sounded like 'I know'.

"I wish I was still here for you." I said and kissed her hair as softly as I could.

"It's alright Mummy, I know you didn't want to leave us," Claire half-whispered, half-mumbled.

I held my breath, not daring to believe that Claire could hear me, knowing that it was coincidence, but wishing it wasn't. I couldn't stay there any longer. Being both that close to her and yet so far away was too painful.

Richard had left the door open some three inches, not enough for me to squeeze through. I looked at the gap and remembered what had happened when I was caught behind the door in our bedroom. The dressing gown on the back of door had squashed me flat against the wall; I was no more substantial than air in comparison to solid objects.

I only half-closed my eyes and leaned between the edge of the door and the frame. There was no sensation of being squashed or reshaped, or anything painful or uncomfortable, but somehow I slid through the gap and was on the landing before I realised.

Although apparently quite simple to achieve, I had no desire to repeat that experiment any sooner than necessary. Lying on the bed next to Richard while he slept was not the same as when I had been alive and not so appealing.

I wandered back downstairs, jumping a few times on the steps that should have squeaked in protest, but with no success. The photo albums were back in their place on the shelf, but I couldn't have opened them if they had still been on the table.

I looked closely at the framed pictures on the mantelpiece. One was of us on our wedding day. The other two were of us holding our newborn babies. Our life together had been so short, summarised in three pictures. Twelve years sounds a long time, but it wasn't long enough. Why didn't we put more pictures on the wall? I'd have more to look at now.

I sat on the sofa, staring at those three pictures, and closed my eyes for a moment, just thinking about what had happened to me.

When I opened my eyes sunlight was reflecting off the windows of the house opposite, it was morning, but I had only shut my eyes for a few seconds. I must have fallen asleep.

Chapter 4
Monday 21st October 1991

Something on the table caught my eye; it was a travel brochure about Ireland. It hadn't been there the previous day or I would have noticed it. I looked around for other signs of change, but apart from a sweater thrown over the arm of a sofa there were no other obvious clues.

"Come on Claire, hurry up and clean your teeth. Sally will be here any minute."

It was Richard's voice, but what he was saying didn't make sense. I assumed it was Saturday, that I had slept through the night. Sally was our neighbour, why would she be coming round?

It had been Sally and Mike who were coming to my last barbecue. Hayley was supposed to be here today, not Sally. I stirred myself from the sofa, made sure that the hall was clear, and hurried into the kitchen to check the calendar. Something was different there too, but I wasn't sure in what way.

"Has anyone seen Ronnie? I don't want him in your bedroom again Claire." Richard's voice grew clearer as he approached the kitchen.

"Who the hell is Ronnie and what's he doing in Claire's bedroom?" I demanded.

Asking questions was pointless, I knew that, but couldn't get out of the habit. As I moved towards the back door I tripped over something on the floor and caught my elbow on the work surface. I cursed, not because it hurt, but because it felt decidedly weird and I was confused. But when nobody can hear you it doesn't matter what language you use.

There was a litter tray and two bowls on the floor. Fortunately nothing was spilled. I had no effect on anything in the real world. Richard must have acquired a cat and I didn't even know he liked cats.

I don't know what made me do it, but I dipped a toe into the cat's water bowl. To be accurate my toe didn't penetrate the surface, the water didn't ripple, didn't even stir. With great care I moved all my weight onto that foot and stood on tiptoe, on top of the water. I, Alison Walker, could walk on water. A good trick, but not so impressive when you had nobody to observe your spectacular ability.

Richard was almost on me when I came out of my daydream. I jumped out of his way and he swung the back door open.

"Ronnie. Breakfast time Ronnie. Come in now or it's a one way ride back to the rescue centre."

A large, long-haired, ginger cat crept out from under a bush and sauntered across the lawn, stopping occasionally when some movement caught his attention. The lawn was strewn with mottled amber leaves and the cat was perfectly camouflaged amongst them.

"Dad, would you really take Ronnie back?"

Martin was sat at the table, elbows close together and chin resting in hands. Neither of us had noticed him come into the kitchen.

"Of course not Martin, I was joking."

Absorbed by what was happening around me I had forgotten to check the calendar. It was October, Monday the twenty-first. More than two months had slipped past since I shut my eyes last night. The autumn leaves should have been a clue of course. I wondered what had happened at that barbecue with Hayley? Had she gone to Ireland? There was a postcard on the clutterboard, a picture of a river with several bridges crossing it. The caption said

'River Liffey'. That was in Dublin if I remembered correctly. It was probably from Hayley, but of course I couldn't see the other side. There was also, in big bold capitals, the word 'PARTY' written on the calendar for the following Saturday.

I saw the cat looking at me. He gave a silent meow and I tried to shoo him away.

"What's wrong with Ronnie?" Claire asked.

"What do you mean?"

"He's staring at the calendar."

When I moved the cat's eyes followed me. Ronnie could see me, or maybe sense me. When I put a hand out to stroke him his body convulsed twice in quick succession. He threw up on the kitchen floor.

Richard swore, Claire took a step back and Martin's face scrunched up in revulsion.

"Yuk, Ronnie's eaten a mouse again."

Equally repulsed as Martin, I backed away, reclaiming my sanctuary on top of the wine rack – a ridiculous place for a grown woman to hide, but I felt safe there.

Their school lunch boxes were on the table and, while Richard cleared up the mess on the floor, Claire added a small chocolate bar to each container, plus an apple for her and a tangerine for Martin.

"Now kids, don't forget that Sally is picking you both up after school. I'll be back by six tonight, maybe a bit earlier."

"Thomas is a bully. Do I have to play with him?"

Mike and Sally had two children, both roughly the same age as ours. Thomas was a bully, or at the very least he was extremely physical in his approach to life. Jacqui, however, was Claire's best friend, not so intelligent of course, but gentle and considerate. Maybe a little too acquiescent, but who could blame her with Thomas as a brother.

"Hellooooo Richard," Sally called as she let herself in

through the front door. "Sorry. Am I late?"

"Have you given a key to every woman you know?"

"No it's okay, you're early if anything." Richard checked his watch. "These bloody interviews are nothing to do with my department, but I have to attend."

Sally had teetered into the kitchen on heels that were not designed for the school run. The girls immediately ran upstairs, while Martin and Thomas exchange sullen stares.

Sally accepted the offer of a coffee and settled herself at the table, crossing her legs and allowing her skirt to ride up and expose rather more thigh than was appropriate at eight-fifteen in the morning.

"Go on boys, off you go and play. Give us some peace." Sally shooed the boys away and turned her attention back to Richard. "Honestly, I have no idea how you cope with two kids all by yourself."

"It's not that hard, except for days like today. And thanks again for doing this."

"Mike would be useless by himself."

"Oh he'd manage I think."

"No, he wouldn't. He'd probably get an au pair, some skinny little foreign bimbo, all tight tits and short skirts."

"Then he'd shag her," I added.

"Then he'd play golf all weekend, not that he doesn't now. And he'd probably shag her if he got half a chance."

"Told you."

Richard didn't say anything for a moment or two. "So, Saturday? Who else will be there?"

The party must be at Sally and Mike's. Her cooking was usually a triumph or a calamity, rarely something in-between.

"Just Mike, me, Ben and Cora – you, of course and Jane. You remember Jane from our party last New Year?"

"Surely you haven't forgotten Jane have you?" I teased

Richard, without effect. "She introduced herself to us as divorced and looking for husband number three? You and all the other men couldn't keep your eyes off that micro dress she was almost wearing."

"Ah, Jane, yes I think I remember her."

Richard sounded embarrassed. Maybe he had heard me.

"She said she's looking forward to meeting you again. "

"Er, actually, I'm not sure I'll be able to make it. Sorry. Alison's mother is not going to get here until late Saturday afternoon now. It would be a bit rude to leave her in charge of the kids as soon as she arrives."

"My mother's coming here... to stay? Unbelievable."

"I'm not trying to fix you up with Jane if that's what you're thinking. We only invited her to make the numbers even. If I thought you were available I'd point Mike in her direction and nab you myself."

"Ease off lady, and that's my husband you're coming on to," I muttered, even though technically we were no longer married.

Sally re-crossed her legs and her skirt rose even higher. Now the choice of heels made sense. Richard looked uncomfortable. He checked his pockets for some unspecified item, passing his coffee mug from one hand to the other.

"Mike's always had a thing about her." Sally continued. "He's like a stag in rut whenever she's around."

Richard held his coffee in front of his face, making a show of taking small sips from what was probably an empty mug. He checked his watch.

"Um, I'd better get off. I hate these interviews."

"Is there an outstanding applicant?"

"No, not really. We're not the most favoured school in this area. Anyway, thanks for looking after Claire and Martin today, it's much appreciated and I'll be back as soon as I can this afternoon."

"It's okay, they practically entertain themselves. I'll see you whenever you get back. We can catch up on things then, Mike's away on business, he won't be back tonight, so I'm at a bit of a loose end."

Richard called to Claire and Martin that he was going. Claire responded with a cheerful 'okay' from upstairs, Martin rushed out and hugged Richard round his legs.

Once Richard had left, Sally helped herself to another mug of coffee and lifted the lid off the biscuit barrel. She looked inside and bit her lower lip in thought.

"Go on," I urged. "One biscuit isn't going to do you any harm."

Sally was on an almost constant diet and I knew that Richard didn't fancy chubby women. She picked out a shortcake biscuit and ate it in two bites. The smile of delight on her face was quickly replaced by a frown.

"Go on Sally, you might as well have a second one."

I couldn't believe how obvious she had been with Richard. I counted on my fingers – August, September, October, I had only been dead four months. Sally dipped into the biscuits again. I wondered if I really did have some way of communicating with the living, even if they weren't aware of it. It was fun being the devil on Sally's shoulder.

"So, how about a third biscuit, they do taste good don't they?"

Sally still had the lid of the biscuit barrel in her hand, but I saw her face scrunch up in determination. The second biscuit went back in the barrel and the lid snapped firmly back into place – so much for my supernatural powers of suggestion.

"Boys, can you make a little less noise in there."

Sally sat back at the table, kicked her shoes off, dragged a second chair out with her toes and put her feet up on it.

Her eyes closed as she cradled her coffee mug in both hands.

"Please be quiet boys, Mummy's having a little me time."

With Sally safely settled, I eased myself off the wine rack and edged round the table. I didn't think there was any way I was going to disturb her, but I was still not used to the constraints and effects of my new form.

The boys were in the living room, Martin on the sofa, clutching Ready Teddy, his favourite bear. Thomas was waging war with a selection of Martin's other toys.

"What do you think your doing?" I asked Thomas, but he didn't take any notice of me. Thinking about it, he rarely did take any notice of me when I was alive. "Why can't your mother do anything about you, maybe even tie you up?"

Nothing I could do was going to change things, but I went back to the kitchen, ready to give Sally a piece of mind. She was nibbling through another biscuit.

"Your bloody son is wrecking Martin's toys. Can't you get up off your arse and do something about him?"

It was refreshing to be brutally honest to someone face to face without having to fear recriminations. As I stood there haranguing Sally she opened her eyes, took her feet off the chair and stood straight in front of me. I swear that I thought she was going to say something to me, but she just stretched and yawned. Not an attractive sight when you're only a few inches away.

You would think I would have had the presence of mind to move before she walked into me, but I was distracted by Martin's problems with Thomas. I was still lying flat on my back on the kitchen floor when she put her mug in the sink and called to the children that it was time to go.

"You could at least have washed up the mugs," I grumbled.

Sally ignored me. She glanced at the biscuit barrel and took one more biscuit. "Cow. Hope you get fat." How come she managed to stay so slim if she kept dipping her fingers into the biscuit barrel? Some things in life are not fair.

I followed her into the living room. My life, or rather my death, had turned into a procession with me always taking up the rear.

"Come on boys, clear up this mess. I don't know what you two have been doing to make it this untidy."

"Martin hasn't been doing anything," I protested in his defence. "This is all down to Thomas."

Sally started to push all Martin's toys into a heap with her foot.

"Martin, you must know where they all go, but we haven't got time now. You can clear this lot up when you get home this afternoon."

I stood open-mouthed. Surely Sally could see who was to blame for all the mess.

"Girls," she called upstairs. "Time for school. Come and pick up your lunch boxes."

Martin skirted the jumbled pile of toys and ran upstairs. When he returned it was without Ready Teddy. I hoped he'd put him somewhere Thomas couldn't find him.

After Sally had left with the four children, the house was quiet again, all but for a distant meow from the kitchen.

I watched out of the living room window while Sally's car pulled out of her drive and turned towards the school. Another meow from close behind made me jump.

"Hello Ronnie. So tell me honestly. Can you see me?"

"Meow."

"I'm not sure whether that's a yes or a no. I don't speak Cat."

"Meow."

"So, I don't suppose you could tell me what's happened in the last couple of months? I don't even know how long you've lived here."

Ronnie stared at me and then turned his back.

When I followed him into the kitchen he sidestepped out of my way. I sat on the chair that Sally had left out and patted my lap. Ronnie hesitated, wiggled his bottom and jumped. Except it wasn't quite as he or I expected.

Ronnie made a clumsy landing on the chair, both of us having misjudged my solidity. He instantly leapt down without pausing, like a scared cat, quite reasonably so as he was.

For me the experience was equally unsettling. When Ronnie met my thighs they gave way, or squidged out of the way somehow. There was no sensation, no pain, just the disturbing sight of my thighs distorting to avoid Ronnie and then reforming as soon as he had left. It was all so fast I wasn't quite sure what had happened, but I didn't want to try it again. One look at Ronnie told me that he felt the same way.

A shiver ran through my whole body. "Time to sort out this time skipping thingy," I muttered. "There is something comforting about hearing my own voice even if nobody else can."

"Meow."

"Okay, except for you Ronnie. I know you can hear me."

I stood in front of the calendar and, to fine tune the experiment, I checked the time on the kitchen clock. I guessed that time skipping was something to do with closing my eyes. I blinked deliberately. Calendar and clock, both remained unchanged.

Steadying myself I shook my arms, like an athlete about to attempt a new level on the high jump. There was no logic to this, but it made me feel more prepared for whatever might happen next.

I closed my eyes and counted to three. Snapping my eyes

wide open I noted the calendar hadn't changed. It was the same day. I checked the clock and double-checked the clock. Just over 4 hours had zipped past. If I shut my eyes for any length of time would I lose another two months, three months, a year? It was now past lunchtime. The children should be back in about three hours.

A count of two should be about right. I shut my eyes again. One, two... I was about to open them anyway when I heard a key in the front door. I looked down and Ronnie's bowl was empty.

"A whole day? Gone in two blinks of an eye."

"Meow."

Turning quickly I saw Ronnie strolling out of the kitchen towards the front door. As soon as he saw Sally accompanied by four children he bolted for the back door and was through the cat flap without breaking step. There were too many people in the house and I knew exactly how he felt. It was time to get back on top of the wine rack. Sally threw her bag on the kitchen table.

"Why don't you boys play in the garden, it's nice and sunny out there – go on."

The girls didn't follow Sally into the kitchen. They must have gone straight up to Claire's bedroom. When Thomas and Martin went out they left the back door open, just enough for me to squeeze through. Thomas kicked a football into a large shrub. Ronnie shot out from under it and scaled the fence to a safer place on top of Mike and Sally's summerhouse.

It must have been quite chilly, given the time of year, but I was no longer aware of such corporeal matters. It was just as well because at some time my cord jeans had switched for a summer dress. I wasn't even sure when, but thinking back it might have been when Sally was displaying her thighs to Richard. Was I that competitive, even when dead? The dress was one of Richard favourites. He had mentioned as much on more than one occasion.

I sat on a bench positioned to catch the last light of the day. Although I couldn't feel the warmth of the sun I still stretched out my legs and draped an arm along the back of the bench.

Thomas was on the swing, riding as high as he could, twisting the seat so that the chains groaned and snapped in objection. Martin was examining the dead flower heads on our hydrangeas.

A blackbird, probably Billy, the one we had been feeding, flew straight through me. My body rippled and reformed in the time it took for Billy to reach the end of the bench. He sat on the arm and held his head on side as though expecting something from me.

"Is that what I get for putting out all those raisins for you Billy? You flew straight through me you ungrateful bird."

Billy adjusted his position and cocked his head to the other side.

"Don't tell me you can see me too?"

He flew off as swiftly as he had arrived. While I had been distracted Martin had selected three dried flower heads and managed to break them off the bush. I followed him back into the kitchen, dodging in front of him before the door swung closed. Sally had her feet up again, settled with a cup of coffee and yet another biscuit. The woman was definitely letting herself go today.

"Can I put these in a vase please Mrs Cooper?"

"Of course you can Martin, they're lovely. They were your mummy's favourite flowers weren't they?"

"Can we put them in water?"

Sally didn't object even though the water was unnecessary.

"You can call me Auntie Sally if you want to Martin."

"That wouldn't be right because you're not my auntie."

"But you call Auntie Hayley auntie."

"She's Daddy's friend."

I felt bad about the way I had been judging Sally. She was okay really and just trying to help. Maybe she didn't deserve such brutal honesty from my son.

Sally put the vase in the middle of the table.

"They'll be a nice surprise for Daddy when he gets home."

"No, he probably won't like them. Daddy doesn't really like dead things, even flowers. But I think they're pretty. Mummy was pretty too."

Sally didn't finish her biscuit and I wasn't sure whether to laugh or cry. I covered my face with my hands and shut my eyes. A stupid thing to do given my new understanding of how time in my new life functioned – or more accurately, time in my afterlife.

Chapter 5
Saturday 26th October 1991

I took a deep breath and exhaled, my hands still covering my face. When I lowered my hands I found that everyone had gone. The kitchen was quiet, except for Billy at the back door, tapping on the window and expecting currents.

"At least you're still here Billy."

The sound of a lawnmower kicked into life and scared Billy. He flew away. Richard came into view a few moments later behind the mower. I turned to check the calendar, five more days had been checked off. The clock showed that it was almost ten-thirty on a Saturday morning.

I heard Claire's raised voice from upstairs, her self-assured bossy mode.

"Just sit still Martin, I've almost finished."

I could not hear his response as it was mumbled.

Jumping months, even days, was unsettling. I was left trying to play catch-up every time it happened, but learning not to close my eyes was almost impossible. Claire and Martin's conversation became clearer as I climbed the stairs.

"I'm going to use two ribbons on each side. We need to make a proper fashion statement."

"Okay, I don't mind, but it's taking you ages."

"Well if your hair was longer it would be easier."

Martin's hair was quite long already. Richard really ought to have taken him to have it cut months ago, probably without the green and blue ribbons, with which Martin's hair was now adorned.

"Do you like the ribbons?" Claire asked him.

"I think they're pretty. Do you think Daddy will like them?"

"Daddy doesn't have any fashion sense so his opinion's not that important."

"Cruel, but true Claire," I agreed.

I sat on the bed and watched. Claire had managed to secure Martin's hair in bunches just behind each ear. He also had one of my old costume necklaces round his neck.

"Okay, I've finished. We can show Daddy now if you want."

Martin leapt up, ran to the top of the stairs and I just managed to flatten myself against the wall as he went past. I probably did literally flatten myself, but was unaware of it at the time. Claire followed more nonchalantly and I took up the rear – again. She left the back door open so I was able to go out into the garden with them.

Richard didn't notice the children immediately. He turned the mower at the end of the lawn and was half way back towards the house before he spotted Martin and the ribbons in his hair. The mower engine spluttered to a halt.

"That's a new hairstyle Martin."

"Do you like it Daddy?"

"It's certainly different," Richard chuckled. "Though I'm not sure everyone could carry off such a... an individual look."

"Do you think I look funny?"

"I'm sorry Martin, I wasn't laughing at you. I think you look very nice."

Martin pulled the ribbons out of his hair and it fell back into its familiar long mop top. Claire harrumphed at all her careful work being undone.

"So what do you two fashionistas want to eat for lunch?"

"Not hungry, don't care." Claire responded unhelpfully.

"How about lunch at the mall?"

Martin's face lit up.

"Can we go to McDonald's Daddy, pleeease can we?"

Martin repeated saying 'pleeease' until Richard gave in. That was another thing that had changed since my departure. I would never have acquiesced to that particular demand.

"And we have got to do some shopping of course."

This time it was Martin's turn to sulk, Claire always having been easy to get into any shop.

"Do we have to go shopping?" Martin whined.

I wondered whether it might be possible to squeeze into the car somehow as there would be a spare seat, but the thought of dodging all those people on a Saturday shopping spree made me shiver with fear. I remembered how Richard had batted me from one spot to another before I placed myself out of harm's way. It was enough to make me decide to stay and wait for their return.

Richard ruffled Martin's hair.

"Stop it. And what's funny about having ribbons in my hair?"

"They were the wrong colours for you. Maybe red and pink would be better."

"Is there a correct colour combination for hair ribbons for our son?" I asked.

"Why not green and purple?" Claire asked.

"We could look for some at the mall." Richard suggested.

"You're both being horrible. I'm not wearing them any more."

"Good decision Martin," I was on his side. "Don't let them bully you."

The three of them were in a good mood when they left, which was more than could be said for me. I was left alone to while away a couple of hours. There wasn't much you could do as a ghost other than hang around waiting for people. I could see why they always appear to be in a bad mood in stories.

My family would be two hours at the mall, nearer three if they were having lunch. I went to my usual spot where I could see the calendar and the clock.

"So, one second equals about one hour?" I mused out loud.

I did a prolonged blink, not very long, maybe just over a second. The clock jumped an hour and a half. The calendar was still showing Saturday, same month, same year – so far, so good.

My eyes fell on an envelope on the clutterboard. I was fairly sure it hadn't been there earlier in the week. In fact it overlapped the postcard from Ireland, so logically it must have been pinned there later. The envelope was in Claire's handwriting and just said 'Mummy'. There was no address. I couldn't open it, but I couldn't help but wonder what Claire had written and why Richard had put it there.

I did another deliberate, slow blink, but slightly quicker this time. Forty-eight minutes. I was getting pretty good at this time travel stuff, but one more blink and I could miss their return. Ronnie brushed past my legs and almost unbalanced me. He went through the cat flap and I had an idea. Could I fit through the cat flap as a means of escaping the house? I knew my body could squeeze through small spaces. I'd got through that door that had been left open only a couple of inches. This could be my way in and out of the house without having to rely on somebody leaving a door open. I got down on my hands and knees before realising the flaw in my plan. I couldn't move the flap.

While on my knees I missed the front door opening. Claire staggered into the kitchen with two bulging carrier bags that she dumped on the floor. Martin had one, which he was carrying with both hands.

"Come on kids, we need to get this lot packed away so we're nice and tidy for when Granny arrives."

"She likes to be called Grand-mere," Claire corrected.

"My mother's lucky to be welcome at all," I muttered. "She wouldn't be so welcome if I was here and I know just what I'd call her. Grand-bitch would be more appropriate."

"I know Claire, just Daddy's little joke."

"Don't let her take over Richard. She'll desert you once she starts to miss her life of leisure. She deserted me often enough. I've told you before, you can't rely on her."

"Why does she live in France Daddy, she's not French is she?"

"Come on Richard, let's see you explain this one."

"Well Martin, her best friend is French."

"Do you mean Louis?" Martin asked.

"Yes, Louis."

"Louis is her paramour," Claire explained.

Where on earth did Claire get a word like that, not quite accurate in this context, but I couldn't help but be proud of her vocabulary.

"Louis is her toy-boy Claire," I explained. "Not her paramour. You'll understand the difference when you're older."

"Or is he Grand-mere's toy boy?" Claire words echoed mine.

My voice appeared to resonate with people at times, even though I could not be heard.

"Best not use that term Claire, Granny would consider it derogatory and... it is a bit rude. Anyway, she's coming over to help us for a few days, or maybe a few weeks? She wasn't very clear when she rang."

"Do we need her help?" Martin looked puzzled.

"Absolutely not Martin, you don't need her, nobody

45

needs her – she's poison. She was the definitive example of an absent mother when I needed her most."

Richard sent the kids off to tidy their bedrooms, threatening that Granny might want to make an inspection.

"How many times have I told you Richard, don't trust her, she couldn't tell the truth if her life depended on it. When Daddy died it took her less than a month to get both an au pair and a boyfriend. She has no interest in children, they irritate her."

The doorbell rang, interrupting my rant, which could probably have gone on for a considerable time.

"Kids, Grand-mere is here," Richard shouted up the stairs.

When he opened the door there she was, upright, elegant and almost entirely without charm, managing to look as though she had been waiting for hours.

"Lydia, how lovely to see you. Did you have a good journey?"

"Terrible."

"Oh, I'm sorry to hear that. But come in. Let me take your coat?"

My mother took one look at the bare boards of the stairs and sniffed.

"And how is Paris?"

"Dull."

Lydia shrugged her coat off her shoulders and shook it to make sure the sleeves hung neatly. She asked Richard if he had a suitable hanger.

"I'll, er, hang it upstairs in a minute."

He draped it over the end of the bannisters. Lydia stared at him as he did so and sighed deeply as though the coat was already ruined.

"My cases are in the taxi Richard. I only have a few francs with me as I haven't had time to acquire any British currency. Would you be so kind as to settle up with the driver. And don't tip him, he is such a vulgar man."

"It's not the third world Mother. Surely you kept some currency from when you were here last? I presume you came over for my funeral?"

Lydia appraised the hall with a quick glance and strode into the kitchen. She brushed the back of one chair with a finger and sniffed again. Richard returned from paying the driver with a deep frown carved into his forehead.

"You took a taxi Lydia? All the way from the airport?"

"How else was I supposed to get here?"

The airport was almost two hours drive from us. It must have cost a small fortune. I saw Richard shake his head in exasperation behind Lydia's back.

"I don't like to say I told you so Richard, but I told you so."

"And how is Louis?" Richard asked politely.

"He's French. How would you expect him to be?" she snapped.

"I think you knew he was French Mother when you first picked him up."

"My grandchildren are here somewhere I presume."

Martin and Claire were peeping in from the hall. I, naturally, was squatting on top of the wine rack. Lydia glanced down at me and sneered. At first I thought she could see me, then I realised she was checking the wine labels. Martin hiccoughed and both Lydia and Richard turned to see my children staring at her.

Richard gestured for Martin and Claire to come into the room. "Come and give your Grand-mere a kiss?"

"Go on, give Granny a hug kids, and a nice big wet kiss. She loves close physical contact with children."

Lydia accepted their embrace with open arms, which surprised me and she took one in each hand to lead them into the living room.

"Now, in France we don't greet honoured guests in the cuisine, we prefer to entertain them in the salon."

I never believed my mother could become more insufferable or pretentious than I already knew her to be, but I was wrong. She ushered the children in front of her and took station in the centre of the sofa, perching rather than sitting. My mother instructed Claire and Martin to sit either side of her.

"Richard darling, would you get my bag for me, I left it in the kitchen I believe, on the table."

I had to duck to one side when Richard came out of the living room. We had never possessed a salon, not even a sitting room. While he was gone I slipped into the room and settled myself on top of the television. It was the most out of the way place, but not the most comfortable as I had to balance with my heels on the edge of the television table.

Lydia opened her bag, a smile playing over her face that I found quite unsettling. She produced two tiny, but very smart paper carrier bags. One was deep burgundy, one buff coloured, both with the Galeries Lafayette logo in white. She handed one to each of my children and glanced up at Richard.

"I'm sorry Richard, I had no idea what to buy you."

Her attention returned to Martin and Claire as she watched them open their gifts.

Claire peeled layers of tissue paper back to reveal a bottle of Chanel No 5. It was not only far too expensive, but quite inappropriate for an eight-year-old. Martin was puzzling over a Montblanc fountain pen.

"Bloody typical," I muttered under my breath.

My mother had no idea what children liked or needed, just what she thought might make an impression. But she failed spectacularly as neither Claire nor Martin showed any sign of excitement.

"A simple thank-you would be appreciated," she said, managing to look quite put out.

"You still have no idea do you? All the presents you sent me that remained unused. How can you not have learned anything?"

"Thanks Nanny," Claire mumbled, lifting the stopper and taking a tentative sniff.

Martin was still turning the pen over in his hands as though it might explode.

"Grand-mere please. Nannies are female goats. Unless of course that's how you see me."

"Sounds about right to me," I couldn't help but add – especially as she couldn't hear me.

"So, Lydia, how is Paris," Richard was being tactful as ever. "Exciting and full of life?"

"It's fine," my mother snapped. "How much would you like to know about my private life? You've never been to visit me, even before Alison..."

Richard interrupted her before she could finish her sentence.

"Actually, I thought we might be able to visit in the spring, during the Easter holidays. Paris is said to be beautiful at that time isn't it?"

"I suppose it is, if you say so."

This was not my mother as I knew her, something was wrong. She was far too spiky, even for her.

"I thought maybe I could take the children to Disneyland Paris while we were there. You could join us."

Suddenly my children came to life, presents forgotten. They swarmed over Richard who fell backwards in his armchair with an arm round each one.

"Whoa there, I only said maybe. But I'm sure Grand-mere would love to show you around Paris."

49

"There's not enough room in my apartment," she countered quickly. "Much as I'd love to accommodate you I simply don't have the space."

"That's the way to deal with her Richard, call her bluff."

I confess that I poked my tongue out at my mother at that point, something I'd done only once as a child. On that occasion she had her back turned to me but she had still known. 'You can desist from that vulgar expression this instance young lady.' was all she had said. I never did work out how she knew what I was doing.

My mother looked directly at me. And although I knew she could not see me I retrieved my tongue and swear I blushed, even though I'm not sure that's possible for a ghost.

"I would love nothing more than to have you visit, but it's simply not possible at the moment, or in the foreseeable future. I'm sure you will understand without my having to go into unnecessary detail."

"That's okay Lydia, we can book into a hotel."

I punched the air, got down off the television and did a little dance in front of my mother. I'm not proud of my performance. I tripped over the edge of a rug, dived for the sofa and missed. I ended up flying over the top of it, hitting the wall and sliding down the . I can't claim that it hurt anything other than my pride.

"I hate being a bloody ghost," I grumbled as I clawed my way up the back of the sofa.

My only solace at that moment was seeing my children on Richard's lap and my mother alone. The presents she had bought still lay, wrapping discarded, on either side of her.

"Am I to understand you are going out tonight Richard?"

"Er, yes, couldn't get out of it really, sorry. But I won't be back late."

I could still 'read' Richard. Faced with an evening with my mother or a possibly uncomfortable supper party next door, Richard was going to choose the it's-not-a-date evening that Sally had arranged. I couldn't blame him. I would have done the same.

"And what time do you expect to return?"

"I don't know exactly, but not too late. You don't need to wait up for me. You must be tired after your journey."

My mother bristled. Even Richard could see the warning signs.

"In that case, could you show me my room so that I might at least freshen-up. I presume I will be eating supper with the children."

"If that's all right with you."

"It will have to be."

"You're going to sleep in my room," Martin informed her solemnly. "And I'm sleeping in the attic."

"In the attic?"

"It's a very special room, perfect for me, because the ceilings aren't very high and neither am I. You're not very tall either but Daddy said I was better at climbing the stairs because they're quite narrow."

I could see my mother confounded by this logic and covered my mouth as I giggled uncontrollably. An unnecessary precaution, but my mother looked in my direction and I stopped laughing immediately.

Chapter 6

Martin took my mother's hand and led her into the hall. He was explaining to her that they had moved his clothes and toys out of his room, but left her his bedside lamp so that she could read her trashy novels.

"Oh really Martin?" My mother spoke loud enough for Richard to hear her. "You must tell me what other special preparations have been made for my visit."

"I don't think we made any other special preparations Grand-mere."

"So it was simply a consideration that I might not be able to squeeze up a narrow staircase?"

"Oh no, it wasn't that, Daddy said you were a skinny old bat, but I don't think you look anything like a bat, they have big leathery wings. But he did say you would have been out of the way up in the attic."

I saw Richard wince and exchange a quick glance with Claire. She, wise beyond her years, responded immediately.

"Grand-mere," she called out, skittering out of the room to follow them. "I think Martin's got confused with Auntie Hayley. Daddy said she reads the worst possible books considering she teaches English to foreigners and he said she's skinny and quite batty."

Richard slumped into one of the armchairs and mouthed a silent 'thank you' to Claire.

"How long is she here for?" I asked.

"A whole month," Richard sighed. "How do I cope for a month?"

Once again it was as though Richard could hear my question. I put it down to coincidence in that we were both thinking about the same thing. That shared wavelength that we'd always had from the first time we met. I smiled remembering how Hayley had said she felt excluded from half our conversations because, according to her, we spoke in a special secret code.

"Are you really going to leave them in her custody tonight? She'll poison them, not literally, but she'll poison their minds if you give her half a chance."

Richard didn't answer. He picked up the bottle of perfume that Claire had left on the sofa, opened the top, sniffed at it tentatively and frowned. Picking up the pen he wandered out into the kitchen and put both presents on the table.

I watched him prepare supper for my mother and the children. I couldn't wait to see what her reaction would be to pizza and salad. His saving grace would probably be the rather good bottle of wine he had taken out of the fridge.

Claire appeared while Richard was making a salad dressing that I doubted would be to Lydia's liking.

"It's okay Dad, I think I've covered your arse."

"Where did you pick up that expression?"

"Everyone says it Dad, even Mrs Bowen."

"The school secretary?"

"I heard her say it to the headmaster."

"Well, I don't think either Mrs Bowen or Mr Govern would like to hear it repeated, so best not use it again. But, thank you anyway."

I heard Martin padding down the stairs, humming to himself, and moved nearer to the back door to be out of the way. Martin was still holding my mother's hand, but she had changed from her customary black trouser suit into jeans and a polo shirt. This was not the mother I knew.

"Grand-mere has moved into the attic room and I have my own room back, she said it's perfectly adequate for her. Oh, and can we make her a cup of tea," Martin looked up at her. "Grand-mere says she'll even suffer the builder's dust we usually serve."

And there she was, back again, a smile of pure innocence gracing her face.

"I think we can offer you Lapsang Souchong Lydia, or there's Earl Grey, or raspberry and Echinacea if you'd prefer that?"

For a moment I wondered how Richard came to have such a selection of teas so readily on hand? The answer of course was Hayley. She went through fads and fashions the way most people go through paper hankies.

"I really don't mind Richard, whatever you're making."

She cast a glance down at Martin, but rather than displaying the malevolence I expected, she smiled and asked him if he could find her a biscuit. There was definitely a change in my mother, but I also suspected there was an ulterior motive behind her behaviour.

"So Richard, at what time do you have to depart for this party of yours."

"Oh, not until seven-thirty, I'm only next door if you need me for anything."

"What could I possibly need you for? I'm looking after my grandchildren, not taming a herd of wild tigers."

"Tigers don't come in herds Mother, and you don't have much practice with children if my memory serves me correctly."

I watched while Richard made a dressing for the salad, ran a cutter through three small pizzas, artfully arranged the slices on a ceramic cheese plate that he had heated in the oven and presented the array to two very happy children and one emigre from Paris who raised an eyebrow, but allowed a smile to play across her face.

Lydia stared at the table for several seconds before she helped herself to salad and sniffed inquisitively in the direction of the pizza. The bottle of wine in the fridge might have saved Richard any criticism, but then I realised that it was intended for the party next door.

My mother relaxed when Richard joined them at the table with his mug of tea, she even nibbled at the thin end of a slice of pizza. Try as she might to disguise her pleasure, she was obviously surprised by how much she enjoyed it and ended up eating the whole slice in delicate bites.

The children were much more attentive to her than I thought she deserved and even dragged her upstairs to help with Martin's bath. I followed and, with some disbelief, saw a side to my mother that I had never experienced as a child. She read to both of them, and while Claire changed for bed, she indulged Martin with a second and then a third story.

I watched from the doorway and it was only when Richard bumped into me from behind, sending me sprawling into Martin's bedroom, that I remembered I wasn't really there as far as they were concerned. Watching and hearing were things to cherish, but I couldn't hold, cuddle or interact with my children. Apart from a few coincidences where Claire or Richard appeared to respond to me, my life was now one of observation. I didn't count Ronnie or Billy as their conversation lacked a certain sophistication.

I huddled in a corner of the room, my legs drawn up, my arms wrapped round my knees, my face hiding behind them, peeking out to watch my family. I was left alone with Martin as he drifted into sleep. The sound of Claire reading to my mother and Richard fussing around in our bedroom barely penetrated my consciousness. I wanted to lay next to Martin, feel the warmth of his body snuggle into me, smell the sleepy little boy that I'd left behind.

When Richard left for the dinner party next door I let him go by himself. The thought of being a fly on the wall at that dinner held no attraction for me. He would have to cope with Sally and Jane by himself. I couldn't watch and not be involved, I'd prefer to watch my children sleep.

Being in the house alone with my mother was strange. It hadn't happened that often when I was growing up, in fact most of my memories are of her wafting out of the house to attend some party or function, or hearing her arrive home in the early hours of the morning. She rarely surfaced before I went to school and whatever au pair was in residence collected me in the afternoon. Daddy had died when I was only one year old and left her wealthy, independent and bitter. By the time I was a teenager she had virtually disappeared from my life.

But now she was moving around downstairs, probably picking apart our life. The television had been turned off and her every action echoed through the silent house. The thought of her nosing around our personal possessions annoyed me. I dragged myself to my feet and plodded downstairs. How could I feel so weary, I didn't have a physical body to tire out?

The lounge was empty. I found my mother in the kitchen, a glass of wine in one hand, peering at the calendar on the clutterboard. But it wasn't the calendar she was looking at. She reached out and unpinned the letter that was addressed to me.

"Don't you dare read it Mother," I hissed.

She pulled a chair out from the table and settled herself with the envelope laying in front of her, her hands palm down on the table either side of it. I hoped she was going to leave it unopened, but I should have known that was not a possibility. After taking a sip of wine, she huffed at the flap and inch-by-inch managed to peel it open. A single sheet of paper folded in four was tucked inside.

Part of me wanted to read it over her shoulder, but that would make me as guilty as her, even though the letter had been addressed to me. I sat on the wine rack staring at her expressionless face.

"You bloody bitch." I spat the words out. A lifetime of venom released in three small words.

She turned the page over to check that there was nothing on the back, folded it up again and put it back in the envelope. With an ease that suggested a certain amount of practice, she licked her finger and ran it along the gum on the flap, pressing it down firmly to reseal the envelope.

Her hands rested either side of the letter and I noticed a tear trickling down her cheek. My mother lifted a hand and elegantly wiped it away with her middle finger, but it had been there. I'd seen it.

Lydia went to sit in the lounge while I stood at the table, looking at that envelope, willing it back onto the clutter-board. I don't how long I'd been there when I heard the door open behind me. Even without closing my eyes time was playing tricks on me. Richard leaned against the closed door looking up at the ceiling.

"Never again," he said quietly, assuming everyone was in bed and asleep.

"Never again what?" asked Lydia, who had materialised in the hall doorway.

"Oh it's nothing," he replied. "I thought you'd be in bed Lydia, especially after your long day."

"My mother had snooping to do," I told him.

Richard tried to evade any further digging into his evening by my mother, but he wasn't a match for her.

"Spare man syndrome my dear Richard. No husband likes a free, good-looking man in the neighbourhood. Too much temptation for bored wives."

"It was Sally who arranged the party actually."

"Ah, with a free, good-looking woman?"

"I suppose so."

"Same syndrome, just other way round. Removing the temptation to stray herself."

"Not everyone wants sleep with every good looking man they meet. We're not all like you Mother."

"Well I think I'll head for bed if that's okay with you Lydia?"

"Don't mind me, I never have been early to bed."

"I think you mean early to sleep," I sniped at her.

Richard spotted the letter on the table. He picked it up and turned it over, presumably checking whether it had been opened. My mother's technique was not as good as I assumed, the flap was lifting away from the envelope.

"It fell off that silly board when I was looking at the calendar."

"Fell off and opened itself?" I asked.

"I'm sorry Richard, I didn't know what it was."

For once my mother sounded flustered.

"You read it?"

My mother just shrugged, in a manner that I expect she learned after many years in Paris.

"Why did you read it?" Richard muttered. "It's a private letter from Claire to her mother."

"Maybe you should read it too. I'll have an early night after all and Richard, I mean that, you really should read it."

A warm smile flickered across her face, barely more than the edges of her mouth turning up a little. She turned and left the two of us alone, Richard more alone than me.

"What would you do Alison?"

"It's open now Richard, Claire is going to know somebody has read it."

Richard sighed, turned the envelope over in his hands, looking at my name on the front. He sat at the table and slid the letter out, unfolding it slowly. I moved round behind him, leaning on the back of the chair to see over his shoulder.

Dear Mummy,

Auntie Hayley said I should write to you even though I can't actually send this letter to you. She has been staying here a lot. She likes Daddy, but they are not 'a couple'.

We all miss you. Daddy tries hard not to cry, but he cried quite a lot at first. Martin doesn't say much about you, but I know he misses you as much as I do.

I'm sorry I didn't kiss you that morning you died, I was angry about something that I can't even remember now. I will write again soon.

I love you, Claire xxx

I had to turn away. There was a lump in my non-existent throat and my eyes were filled with ghostly tears. I wanted to tell her that I missed her too, so much, and that she had given me so many kisses over the last eight years that I had plenty to last me a lifetime. I heard Richard catch his breath. I couldn't bear to see him cry. I closed my eyes tight shut.

Chapter 7
Thursday 19th December 1991

When I opened my eyes it was dark, really dark. There were no lights on in the house and, when I looked out the window, there was no moon or stars. Only faint outlines of trees showed against the distant glow from street lighting. When I turned from looking out of the kitchen door I could just detect a faint glow in the hall.

The rest of the kitchen was comprised entirely of abstract shapes in varying shades of almost black. I put a hand out to find something solid, to confirm my position. Once I had located a corner of the table with one hand and the end of the cabinets with my foot, other outlines become discernible.

The calendar was unreadable, even though I peered for ages at the place where I knew it was. There was no way I could operate a torch, turn on a light switch or strike a match to light a candle. I felt my way out of the kitchen towards the dimly lit hall doorway, catching my knee against a chair that had been left out from the table. It didn't hurt, but threw me off balance when my leg bent and slid around the obstruction. I was getting used to my amorphous body and caught myself from falling by grabbing at a tea towel that was on the table. It didn't slide off when I grabbed it. The tea towel was as immoveable – as if it had been carved from the same piece of stone as the table.

The house opposite had left on an outside lamp and shafts of light broke through the stained glass on the front door, painting splashes of colour on the wall.

I glanced into the lounge. That same lamp shone through the front windows and sparkled off the decorations on a

Christmas tree. It had to be December. But was it still the same year? How long had I shut my eyes? A blue light from the video was flashing the time, 04:05, but gave no clue as to the date.

I crept upstairs, cautious for some reason, although why I was exercising such care made no sense, I'd not managed to make any noise so far that could wake anybody.

Claire's door was slightly ajar. I pushed my way through the impossibly small gap into her room, squishing my body as I did so. It didn't hurt, it wasn't even uncomfortable, just slightly disturbing that I could distort myself enough to pass through a gap of no more than a couple of inches.

Claire was fast asleep. Her digital clock showed 04:08. I tried to stroke her hair, but it was like stroking a statue, there was no soft silky sensation. Sitting cross-legged on the floor I watched her fidget and turn under the covers as she dreamed.

"You know I love you," I assured her. "I only wish I was still here for you. Here for real, not like this."

Claire mumbled something. I didn't quite catch what she said, but it sounded like 'I love you too Mummy.' I put it down to wishful thinking on my part.

I stayed there for almost an hour, watching as she slept, wondering what sort of woman she might grow into and how much she would remember of me. I wasn't going to be there to guide her through her teenage years, share secrets with her or even disapprove of her boyfriends. To see her and not be able to feel her hair or smell the warmth of her sleeping body was almost too much to bear.

"Will you miss me?" I whispered. "What will you remember about me?"

The red numbers on her clock flipped over to five o'clock. I levered myself off the floor and back onto my feet. The door was still in the same position so I had to squeeze myself out of her room suffering the same mental discomfort as when I'd entered.

I eased myself into Martin's room in much the same manner, although his door was open a few inches more than Claire's, so less concentration was required. In fact the process produced no after effect in me and I wondered how small a gap I could squeeze through if required. If I set my mind to it could I squeeze myself through a keyhole? I wasn't ready to try that nor was I sure how to go about it.

Martin was restless in his sleep, tossing and turning every few minutes. I sat on the end of his bed wanting to sooth him. All I could do was to talk to him softly, hoping that in some way he could hear or sense me.

"Shh, Martin, everything's okay. Try to sleep my beautiful boy."

He appeared to settle a little when I spoke, maybe it was coincidence or maybe there was some way that he could sense my voice. A book lay open beside him, one I recognised. The story was about a lost mouse. I must have read it to him a hundred times and the simple plot was forever lodged in my memory. The first line came easily to me.

"Peter was a small mouse living in a small cosy hole at the bottom of a very large oak tree."

Martin shuffled slightly as though getting into a more comfortable position. I continued the story from memory.

"Every morning Peter looked outside to check the weather and see if he needed his umbrella or his sunglasses. One morning he looked out and decided he needed both because there was a large bright rainbow stretching across the sky from the hills to the sea."

Martin mumbled something in his sleep. It sounded like 'rainbow colours'. I carried on, listening much more carefully for anything else he might say.

"The rainbow had every colour Peter could imagine, red,

orange, yellow, green, blue and violet."

Again Martin mumbled a single word, 'grey', and at that moment I knew for certain that he could hear me. He shuffled in the bed pulling the covers around him. It wouldn't have been a problem if I hadn't been sitting on them. The covers went one way and I went the other, pitching face first onto the carpet. After I had struggled back into a sitting position, still on the floor, but now with my back resting against the bed, I tried to remember where I was in the story.

"Why am I so grey? Peter asked, not expecting anyone to answer."

It wasn't just a coincidence. Every now and then Martin would murmur something else that was pertinent to the story, but his responses got quieter and less frequent until eventually he drifted into peaceful sleep.

I sat there for some time listening to his faint breathing and continued the story, until I got to the last line.

"Peter closed the bedroom door and snuggled under his big, colourful, rainbow striped bedcover."Martin didn't stir when I kissed the back of his head.

Back on the landing I noticed a glimmer of light coming from the narrow staircase to the second floor. The stairs were now carpeted – they hadn't been in the autumn. Light was coming from under the door at the top. It caught in a draft and creaked as it opened a couple of inches. Whatever else Richard had done, he hadn't mended the door latch.

I climbed the stairs and was about to shut my eyes and slip through the tiny gap between door and frame, when I remembered that shutting my eyes was not a good idea. It would make time jump and I didn't want that to happen again, at least not yet. I looked up at the ceiling, not wanting to watch the process of my body distorting even if it wasn't painful. In fact I hadn't been aware of any physical sensation when I'd done it before, but what I'd seen looked decidedly strange. Without any discernible effort I found myself inside the room.

"Mother? What are you doing here?" I didn't expect her to answer even though she was sat on the edge of the bed looking straight at me. "How long have you been living up here?"

"It's time to sort things out," she said quietly, but with a certain determination in her voice.

"I thought you'd have already gone, back to Paris, back to your lover."

"I'll sell. I'll get a small apartment in town, or a little cottage in the country. It's time."

"Something's happened hasn't it? Something you've not told us, I mean not told Richard."

My mother sighed, a sound she had employed throughout my life to signal her disappointment in me. This time though I couldn't be the subject of her disapproval as she couldn't see me, even though she was staring straight at me. I even turned round to check. There was only the door behind me.

"Can you see me?"

There was no answer.

"Can you hear me?"

I knew the answer was implied by the lack of response to my previous question, but I still felt the need to ask. My mother rose and walked directly towards me. I moved quickly to avoid her and she opened the door. Its hinges didn't make a sound. It wouldn't dare to squeak for my mother.

"Where are you going? Don't wake the children, it's far too early."

She walked elegantly down the stairs, head held high, eyes focussed straight ahead. There was no hesitation in her step; no swollen knee joints or stiffened hips affecting her movement. She hardly made a sound.

"God," I muttered. "I hope I'm half as agile as you when I'm your age."

Hearing what I'd said, and knowing that I would never get to her age, made me close my eyes in exasperation for a few seconds, only a few short seconds.

When I opened my eyes it was light and my mother was nowhere to be seen. "Noooo," I moaned, angry to myself. "When am I going to learn not to do that?"

There were voices downstairs. My mother's usual strident, commanding voice had softened to more measured, lighter tones. It was difficult to catch what she was saying. I crept down the stairs, careful not to make a noise and shook my head at my stupidity. I hurried down the last few steps.

My first instinct was to check the calendar. It was five days before Christmas, still 1991. I assumed that I hadn't lost more than a few hours when I closed my eyes just then, but there was no way of telling for sure. At least it was still the same year. Could my mother have been here, sleeping in the attic, for almost two months or was this a return visit?

"Are you sure?" Richard said.

"Yes, I'll put my Paris flat on the market in January and find somewhere suitable over here."

"I'm sorry to hear that Louis has been..." Richard left the sentence hanging.

"Pft," my mother dismissed Richard's concern with a exhalation of air through pursed lips. "He is of no conse-quence."

"But you've been together for a long time."

My mother stared out of the window for a few moments before turning back to look Richard in the eye.

"He has been having affairs for several years now, merely *cinq à sept* was his explanation. No apology. He is no longer of any consequence. The foolish man either thought I didn't know or didn't care and then claimed my English prudishness to be the problem."

Richard's lips parted as though he was going to ask what *cinq à sept* was and then he appeared to think better of it. He nodded as though he understood and empathised with her situation.

"I have had the most awful month with him and I've told him to find someone else to keep him before I return to Paris. It's time to put myself first for once in my life."

"You've never done anything other than put yourself first Mother."

She had chosen to share her life, and the fortune Daddy had left her, with a man more than twenty years her junior, a man who never had a real job in his whole life as far as I knew. How long had she thought the attraction would survive once she tightened the purse strings? I knew this was slightly unfair, that my mother looked and acted nothing like her age, but I had only met Louis twice and he had made a pass at me on both occasions. He was not even very subtle in his overtures.

"If there's anything I can do to help..." Richard left the offer hanging. "Um, what sort of place are you looking for?"

"Oh, something simple, not too expensive, but I would value a second opinion."

Richard nodded. It looked like he had set a trap and caught himself in it.

"Your father knows a little about property I seem to remember?"

This was a move I should have anticipated. My mother always had an ulterior motive, but surely she couldn't be interested in Richard's father as a potential partner. At least Anthony was her generation, in fact he was a few years older, but he was also normal, pleasant, kind, easy going. I realised as I thought this that he would be like putty in my mother's hands.

"What are you after Mother? If you hurt Anthony I will haunt you forever. I will never let you rest in peace."

"I just need some advice really, maybe another pair of eyes to save me from making a mistake. I can be quite naive in matters of property."

"My mother is devious Richard, not naive, you might want to suggest your father goes on a cruise to avoid her. A long cruise."

"I'll ask him," Richard said. "I'm sure he'd be glad to help. He often says he retired too early."

"Ah, I had forgotten that he had retired." Lydia managed to sound surprised.

"I doubt you forgot that detail mother, or that he made a substantial sum of money when he did retire."

Anthony had still been an accountant when Richard and I first met, a partner in quite a large firm. His property portfolio had started with a house for Richard when he went to university, but it had grown over time. He had a health scare a couple of years back and decided to sell everything and retire. Richard's mother had died when he was just seventeen and Anthony had been alone ever since. Anthony was an almost perfect target for my imperfect mother.

"I'll write his number down for you." Richard scribbled his father's home and mobile number on a scrap of paper and slid it across the table to my mother. "I'll tell him you might call. I'm sure he'll be happy to help you."

My mother tucked the paper into her purse and thanked Richard. I had seen enough of her and went in search of my children. I found them both in Claire's bedroom, one at each end of the bed.

Martin was propped up by a pillow and reading a book. Claire was at the other end with the other pillow. She was leaning against the wall and writing on a pad propped against her knees. They looked perfect, the bookends of my life. I felt a tear come to my eye, but when I raised my hand to wipe it clear there was nothing there. I sat on the bed between them. Neither of them stirred.

"What are you writing?" Martin asked without looking.

"Just a letter to Mum."

"Okay."

I felt like I was prying into something very private when I leaned towards Claire to read over her shoulder, but the letter was to me so I reasoned that it wasn't really invading her privacy.

Dear Mum,

Grand-mere is going to be here for Christmas. She has asked me to call her Lydia as she says the term Grand-mere is now making her feel too old. I like having her here but she can be a bit bossy.

We all still miss you and it won't be the same having Christmas without you. Auntie Hayley was going to stay, but I heard Daddy on the telephone to her saying it might be a bit difficult with Lydia here. I suppose we don't have enough bedrooms unless she shares with Daddy. So she is just coming for Christmas day.

Daddy says we have to look forward as well as back because you wouldn't have wanted us to be sad forever, but I think I will always be sad without you.

Love and kisses, Claire

I watched as she gingerly tore the sheet from the pad and folded it carefully, making sure the edges matched precisely. Claire sprang off the bed making Martin wobble and me fall over sideways.

When I righted myself Claire was kneeling on the floor, tucking the letter into an envelope. There was an old Terry's 1767 chocolate box next to her, one of the boxes my mother sent every year. My children fought over the contents when it was new, and again for possession of the box when it was empty. It looked to have several envelopes in it already, in an assortment of colours and sizes. Claire added the newest to the pile and replaced the lid with its red rosette band. She pushed down gently with both hands. The lids were always a satisfyingly snug fit. I managed to lean over the edge of the bed and touch the ribbon on the top of the box before she slid it back into its dark hiding place.

"I'm going downstairs," she announced

"Okay," Martin mumbled in reply, still engrossed in his book and pretty much oblivious to what was going on around him.

I stayed with Martin, leaning closer to see what he was reading, but the cover was partly obscured by his knees. As he turned a page I saw that it was called *Bill's New Frock*. I had heard of the book and presumed Richard had bought it for him.

I leaned closer and read with him, seeing his lips move when he stumbled over a difficult word. When Martin reached the last page I moved away, not wanting to turn somersaults again when he finally scrambled off the bed.

I stood at the top of the stairs, leaning over the banister rail and could hear Claire and my mother talking downstairs. Martin sauntered out of Claire's room.

Although I heard him, he was humming a tune that I couldn't quite place. There was barely time for me to turn before he walked into me.

I defy even a ghost not to shut their eyes and wince in fear when tumbling head over heels down a whole flight of stairs. I landed spread-eagled on the hall floor.

When I opened my eyes Martin was nowhere in sight, but then he wouldn't be. I had closed my eyes again. I tried to think how long it had taken to fall down fourteen steps, or how long I had waited to open my eyes before I was sure I wasn't hurt. There was no way of calculating either.

Chapter 8
Thursday 16th April 1992

It was daylight. The ceiling gave nothing away apart from a cobweb swaying gently in a draught. Richard never noticed them. He did run around with the vacuum cleaner occasionally, put the washing on and even knew where the dusters were kept, but things like cobwebs often escaped his attention.

There was a deathly quiet to the house, a poor choice of words considering my situation, but you know what I mean. No radio or television was mumbling away in the background, no sound of children or of Richard. I turned my head to check out what clues there might be. Halls don't change much from day to day, but there were no winter coats draped over the end of the bannisters. Either everyone in my family has acquired tidier habits, or some months had passed by.

I rolled over onto my hands and knees, still bemused, but grateful for the fact that I wasn't able to break bones because I didn't appear to have any, nor could I feel any bruising. There were not many advantages to being a ghost, but I would definitely put these two on the plus side of the list. I stood up, checking again that I was intact.

A car hooted outside, which made me jump, but silence returned immediately afterwards. The lounge was bare of festive decoration. The Christmas tree had gone, not even leaving a scattering of pine needles to show that it had been there the day before, or at least my day before.

The calendar of course would give me an answer to the date, but even as I walked into the kitchen I could see a collection of drooping daffodils in a vase on the table. It looked like I'd skipped the whole of winter, or possibly more than one winter. The calendar was opened to April 1992, only a four-month jump into the future.

I was getting used to missing chunks of my life, not my life if I'm to be accurate, but my family's life. The cat's bowl was empty, wiped clean by a tongue or a cloth? There was no sign of Ronnie, but cats operate to their own schedules so this was no great surprise. The days were crossed off up to Saturday the eleventh, but if it was the weekend where was everyone? Out for the day, off on holiday? Then I remembered mention of Paris, Disneyland Paris, Richard had promised the children a trip there in the spring. Claire's birthday was on April the seventeenth. Had fate brought me back in time to be there for her ninth birthday, or was that just a coincidence?

A key turned in the front door. My first impulse was to hide – an unnecessary precaution. It was my house, so I had every right to be there, but also because nobody could see me. The clock showed it wasn't quite midday yet. There were no voices, so it couldn't be Richard and the children, they would bring a babble of chatter with them.

I backed off to my familiar safe space on top of the wine rack to avoid being pushed and tumbled around. The face that appeared in the kitchen door was Lydia, my mother, and my heart sank at the sight of her. In a lifetime's experience I knew that no good ever came from my mother turning up by surprise. She was carrying a supermarket carrier bag, a very non-Lydia accessory.

She heaved the bag onto the table as though it contained a week's shopping, but it didn't look like it had more than a few items in it. My mother looked around the kitchen, appraising it, an expression on her face that had been applied to my bedroom as a child, my exam results, my choice of clothes, boyfriends, in fact, practically every aspect of my life.

Lydia made a disparaging noise in her throat and walked across to the calendar, taking the felt tip pen that was hung on a string, she crossed off days with a diagonal line through each one. I thought for a moment I had missed Claire's birthday, but the last day she struck out was Wednesday the fifteenth April. My mother disgorged milk, eggs and butter from the carrier bag and put them in them all in the fridge.

"We don't put the eggs in the fridge," I grumbled.

To my surprise she stood with the fridge door open, letting all the cold air out, and picked up the egg box again. She stood with it in her hand for what seemed like ages and then looked around for the egg rack that Richard and I had put on our wedding list and that she had bought us. It had seemed a mean present at the time, but several days later we received an anonymous bank transfer that allowed us to put a substantial deposit down on our first house.

My mother always denied that it was from her. I think it was a gift driven by a guilty conscience, therefore one she did not want to explain. Richard's father had helped us with the cost of the wedding and would not have been secretive if it had been from them. She denied it so vigorously that we doubted our suspicions, even though there was no other possibility. We never mentioned it again.

My mother also left a loaf of bread and bottle of wine on the work surface. It was artisan bread and would be stale by the next morning – Parisian habits die hard. Lydia dug a pen out of her shoulder bag and looked around for a piece of paper. She shrugged and wrote in the small space on the calendar for that day.

'Essentials in the fridge. Hope you enjoyed Paris.'

She drew a large circle round her inscription, but then I saw her attention switch to a postcard pinned lower on the board. It was a cartoon picture of two people in a downpour and simply said 'and then it rained'.

She pulled the pin out of the postcard and turned it over to read it. I scrambled out from my position, eager to see what was written and knowing that this would probably be my only opportunity. As it happened, I needn't have rushed as my mother read it out loud in a mocking tone. I saw Hayley's scrawled signature and she had drawn a smiley face and put three kisses under it.

Have a great time in Paris.
Wish I could have been there with you.
See you soon. xxx

"Three kisses," my mother snorted. "Who puts three kisses on a postcard sent to children?"

"Er, someone who loves them Mother, and doesn't mind admitting it."

Then I realised that the message could as easily have been intended for Richard. My mother pinned the card back where it had been before I had a chance to check the addressee. She took a long lingering look at the image.

"What a stupid postcard," my mother sneered. "Totally pointless. There must be so many pleasant views in Ireland."

She squeezed in another four words in the box for Thursday. I couldn't see what she was writing until she moved away.

'Anthony has been wonderful.'

"What does that mean Mother? What's he wonderful at? Buying houses? Making money? Making love?" I shuddered at the image that sprang into my head.

Lydia took a last look around the kitchen, sniffed loudly, and left the way she had come in. I heard the door click shut from where I was, still looking at the calendar for clues as to what had happened during the last four months – not very much from the evidence of the few words under the crossed out days.

I had nothing to do until my family returned home and I had no idea when that would be, except that it would probably be later today or early tomorrow morning based on Lydia's delivery of essentials.

I took the time I had to explore my house, or at least those rooms with open doors.

The lounge offered no clues about recent life in the house. One of Martin's socks was half hidden under the sofa, but that was not unusual. Martin's bedroom was tidier than I would have expected and Claire's was more of a mess than it usually was. Clothes had been strewn around in what was probably a late packing frenzy.

I had just knelt on the floor to see if the box containing Claire's letters was still under her bed when the front door lock rattled again. From the top of the stairs I saw that it wasn't Richard and the children, as I had expected. It was Hayley, carrying a cardboard box with holes pierced in it. That explained the absence of Ronnie – he had been on holiday too.

"Everyone and their mother has a front door key to this house." I muttered.

Hayley disappeared from my sight in the direction of the kitchen. Instinctively I checked behind me before descending the stairs. I was certain there was nobody up here, but I wasn't ready to lose another four months.

"There you go Ronnie, a nice bowl of tuna chunks, I bet you haven't tasted anything that good for the last few days?"

The way Ronnie was wolfing down his food it didn't look like he had been fed at all while he had been away. He paused for a moment and looked at me as though his enforced separation from home had been my fault.

"Don't look at me Ronnie, your holiday had nothing to do with me."

Ronnie meowed and went back to his bowl of tuna. Hayley had left a small suitcase in the hall, but brought a carrier bag into the kitchen and was now unloading it onto the table. More milk and bread, white sliced this time, and two boxes of cereal, one being chocolate coated. She saw the calendar with the circle round Lydia's note, read it and giggled.

"Priceless," she said. "Lydia and Anthony, he didn't stand a chance?"

"What do you know?" I demanded. "What's happened?"

She saw the card she had sent pinned on the board, touched it with her fingertips and smiled.

Ronnie had finished his bowl and was trying to wrap himself around my legs, but every time he tried to lean his weight against me he stumbled sideways as my legs sort of squished away. Not daunted by this reaction Ronnie kept trying. He was a persistent kind of cat.

"What are you doing Ronnie? I'm not really here."

The phone rang, interrupting any possible answer Ronnie might have provided, even if he could have talked. The phone call was one of those conversations where you have no trouble imagining the unheard party.

"Okay... About four... Did you have a good time?... Great... See you then... Have you eaten?... Okay, I'll sort something out ... Bye... Looking forward to seeing you."

Hayley blew kisses down the phone as if I wasn't even there. I know that to her I wasn't there, but it still rankled with me that little-miss-never-going-to-settle-down appeared to be quite comfortable settling down with my husband and family – and in my house too.

"Why don't you just move in?" I suggested, somewhat

ungraciously.

Okay, I know I was not being totally fair, but in my own defence I had just mislaid four months and learned that my incorrigible mother was probably having an affair with my all-time favourite father-in-law. I wasn't in the most forgiving mood.

The newly domesticated Hayley put the shopping away, then went out into 'my' garden and cut fresh daffodils from 'my' border to replace the ones in 'my' vase in 'my' kitchen. This was a new Hayley. I barely recognised her. She opened windows to air the house, even spotted and picked up Martin's sock. She took her own suitcase upstairs, left it on the landing and then put Martin's sock in the wash basket in the bathroom.

By the time Hayley had cleared the dishwasher and wiped down the sink and draining board, I was more than ready to surrender my house, my family, my husband and whatever might be left in my wardrobe to this new version of my old friend. The woman had become unrecognisable, but somewhat more suitable as my replacement.

Hayley had only just settled down with a mug of coffee when a clunk and click from the front door announced the return of Richard and my children.

"Hello," came Richard's familiar voice. "We're back."

Without hesitation I was up on top of the wine rack once more. At least, thanks to my mother there was an extra bottle there that stopped my foot slipping between the struts and making an uncomfortable lopsided perch.

"Auntie Hayley," my children cried, almost in unison but not quite.

They started babbling, talking over each other so it was impossible to follow either of them.

"Whoa," said Richard. "Auntie Hayley can't listen to you both at the same time."

"We've been to Disneyland," Martin said solemnly.

"Euro Disney," Claire corrected.

My children bundled in to hug Hayley and then started listing everything they had seen and done.

"And there were trams and a spaceship," Martin gushed. "And we went on a steamboat and saw Mickey Mouse and there were shops selling sweets and..."

"Let your sister tell Auntie Hayley some of it."

"It's okay," Claire said. "I don't mind."

"And we had to queue for ages to get in and there was lots and lots of cars waiting in front of us."

I saw Richard mouth 'less than an hour' over the top of Martin's head.

"And I drove a real car."

"Actually the car was on a track with a rail to guide it," Claire added, then saw the disappointment in her brother's face. "But it felt very real and Martin was very good at steering it."

Between them they regaled Hayley with a detailed description of the big parade and every Disney character they had been photographed next to.

Richard leaned against the work surface and mouthed another message to Hayley without the children seeing him do it. 'Four rolls of film.' He pulled a huge smile and gave her a thumbs-up.

Hayley returned his smile and laughed. It was her special laugh, from low in her throat, flirtatious, slightly dirty. I had heard her use it so many times in our university days.

"You've slept together already haven't you?" I was practically shouting at Richard. "When was it? Was it at Christmas? Was it while my mother was here? Do the children know?"

When Hayley had gone upstairs earlier she had taken her bag with her. I was now wondering in which bedroom it had ended up. I got off the wine rack and slid round the kitchen table, dodging between everyone. This was made easier by the fact that Hayley had picked Martin up and Claire was cuddling her from the other side. It would have been nice to be missed a little more, just a few words would have done, 'Wouldn't Mummy have enjoyed Paris' or 'I wish Alison could have been with us'. Not much to ask when you're dead.

As I left the kitchen I turned and saw them all there together. To all intents and purposes they looked like a complete family unit.

"You could have at least waited a full year before sleeping together," I muttered to both of them.

Hayley's bag was nowhere to be seen in our bedroom. The door to the attic was open. I was not even half way up the narrow staircase when I saw it on the floor at the foot of the bed. I turned and sat on the stairs wondering what I was doing, how I fitted in to everyone's life now that I couldn't be seen or heard.

I sat there the whole afternoon, just feeling sorry for myself. I'd had enough of the happy family scene downstairs for the time being. When Martin came up to clean his teeth and get ready for bed I was still there. Nobody needed the attic room at that moment so I remained on my step and watched as first Martin and then Claire were settled in bed. Richard turned Martin's light off after reading him a story and Hayley spent ages in Claire's room before reappearing. She skipped downstairs like a seventeen-year-old eager to meet with her date for the evening.

I didn't feel like watching my children sleep, but was even less enamoured by the prospect of sharing an evening in the lounge with Hayley and Richard. I slunk back to the kitchen and stood where I could see both the calendar and the clock. It might work out okay for my children if Richard and Hayley became a couple, but that didn't mean I had to watch them courting. I closed my eyes for a beat or two.

"Same day, two hours," I said, checking both the calendar and clock. "I'm definitely getting the hang of this."

The news was on the television when I looked into the lounge. Richard was in an armchair, Hayley on the sofa. At least they weren't cuddled up together like teenagers. There were two coffee mugs on the table.

"How long can you stay?" Richard asked without taking his eyes off the television. "The kids were so excited when I told them that you were going to be here when we got back."

"A couple of nights at least, maybe three. I have to go and see my parents at some point – do all the daughterly stuff. I just couldn't face them straight away." Hayley sighed. "All those hints from my mother about settling down, pictures of her friends with their grandchildren."

She shuddered. If you didn't know her you would have thought the problem was her mother, but I knew her and knew that Hayley had never planned to have a baby, not for one moment, not even for a nanosecond.

"Okay, maybe we could do something special while you are here."

"I'm all yours for next few nights," she said. "And thanks for the excuse to stay. My mother can't really take offence at me helping my best friend's family in their continuing time of need."

"You make me sound like a basket case, but I am glad you're here."

Hayley stretched her legs out, sinking into the sofa as she did. Her skirt rode up revealing even more of her thighs to Richard. Hayley knew she had killer legs and had often used them to her advantage.

"I'm just about ready for bed," she cooed. "How about

80

you? You must be ready to drop after four days with the children in Paris."

I turned my back on the room, put my fingers in my ears and shut my eyes, just for a moment. When I opened them the television was no longer on and neither were any of the downstairs lights. A toilet flushed upstairs and I glanced into the kitchen to check that I was still on the same day. The clock showed just past eleven.

Upstairs Richard was sat up in bed reading and there was a light showing from under the attic door. Maybe I'd misread the situation. There was plenty of space on the bed for me. I climbed on next to Richard, who was still on his usual side. I snuggled up to him, although it was more like snuggling up to a statue, not his fault, but not exactly comforting.

"So, what are you reading?" I asked, looking directly at him.

There was no answer. I almost closed my eyes to try to imagine I was still there for real, but caught myself just in time. Richard sneezed and I bounced right to the edge of the bed, almost falling off.

"Bless you," I said.

"Thank you." Richard replied, letting his book drop onto the bed. He looked up at the ceiling. "When am I going to stop imagining you're here Alison?"

"Never I hope."

At that very moment there was a soft tap on the bedroom door. Richard and I both turned towards the source of the sound at the same time. Hayley's face appeared.

"You're not asleep yet?" she whispered.

"What are you doing in here?" I moaned. "As if I can't guess."

"Er, just catching up with some reading."

"Not you Richard, I was asking her."

Hayley edged into the room. She was wearing a t-shirt with a Ghostbusters logo on it. The t-shirt was not long enough, not long enough by several inches.

"Not a good idea Hayley," I muttered. "This really isn't the right time with the children in the house."

"This isn't a good idea Hayley," Richard said quietly.

I turned to look at Richard. Once again surprised that maybe he had heard me, even if only subconsciously.

"I just thought... me up there alone... you down here, also alone... it seemed a pity not to get together."

"I like you Hayley, you know I do, but I don't think I'm ready for a relationship yet."

"I wasn't thinking about a relationship Richard, just two friends, both alone, sharing a night together. Nothing more complicated than that."

"It's always complicated when you sleep with your best friend's husband," I muttered. "Even when she is dead."

Hayley was being Hayley, standing there looking vulnerable, shy, virginal, although how she managed that was beyond me. I knew for a fact that Hayley's virginity was ancient history, she had told me the details when we were still at school.

Richard closed his book and I saw that Hayley had won. She slid down into the bed. I was sandwiched in between the two of them and on top of the duvet, bobbing around like a cork in a stormy sea.

"You are sure Richard?" she whispered. "I don't want to come between you and Alison."

"Er, I think you'll find I'm the one in the middle here."

Hayley leaned towards Richard and, in the process, tumbled me over the top of him and onto the floor.

I had two options. I could crawl under the bed or try to make a hasty escape. I chose the door, but Hayley had closed it. I hadn't heard it click shut so she must have shut it quietly when she was leaning against it, posing for Richard. At least she had the sense to ensure that the children wouldn't stumble in on them, but I was trapped.

I turned back towards them and Hayley was kneeling astride Richard, they were kissing, one of his hands was behind her head. He wasn't exactly resisting. I tried to hide in the corner of the room, hands clasped over my ears, singing to drown out any noise.

Singing Whitney Houston's *I Will Always Love You* was not the best choice, not by subject matter nor vocal range. My voice was never exactly high octane in life, and death hadn't improved it. When I ran out of lyrics, which was surprisingly quickly, I had to resort to humming in order not to hear anything that might be happening behind me.

While I was trying to concentrate on the tune, I inadvertently closed my eyes. I often did when I was trying to remember something.

Chapter 9
Saturday 18th July 1992

When I opened my eyes again the bedroom was flooded with light. I turned back towards the bed, but it was empty. There was a nightdress half concealed on my side of the bed so I presumed that Hayley must have stayed with Richard all night. I hoped the children hadn't seen her in bed with him. They needed to be introduced to that sort of change carefully, slowly, not as a surprise first thing in the morning. The bedroom door was closed, but a window was open. My mistake was in assuming I'd only skipped one night.

Even before I moved closer to the window I realised I had skipped months. The light was too bright, too warm. A breeze was moving the edge of the curtain. Trees from the garden behind ours were in full leaf – the pale greens and deep shadows of full summer. I had missed Claire's birthday, missed Easter and missed spring.

I wondered what would happen if I simply jumped out of the window. What did I have to lose? Would I squish when I landed or bounce? At least I knew could not die because I'd already done that. A familiar voice drifted up from somewhere below.

"Richard, what time are you planning to light the barbecue?"

It was Hayley. I looked down out the window, but couldn't see her. She must have been in the kitchen. What I did see was Martin, laying face down in a large, rectangular paddling pool. He was wearing a pair of goggles and a snorkel. His shorts were new, I hadn't seen them before, they were blue with yellow polka dots. He had a suntan, but he didn't look significantly older.

Claire was lying on her back on an airbed, arms out-stretched on the grass, palms face upward. She was wearing a bikini and sunglasses. The pose made her look older than her years, but her body was still that of a girl.

It was as though I was looking at a photograph with neither of them moving, until Martin suddenly lifted his head. He yanked the snorkel from his mouth, spluttered and shook his hair furiously. Water sprayed over Claire who screamed at him.

"Martin, you idiot, you've soaked me."

"I think you'll survive my dear." It was the voice of my mother, an unexpected mediator. "He didn't mean to splash you and I'm sure he wants to apologise."

"Sor-ry," Martin mumbled, splitting the word in order to demonstrate that he didn't really mean it.

Richard's voice, slightly muffled, joined in from the shed at the bottom of the garden. "If you're going to say sorry at least say it like you mean it Martin."

I noticed Richard inside the shed, wrestling with the lawn mower, trying to manoeuvre it back into position. Mowing the lawn was never Richard's job – I always did that. When he came out from the shed Hayley was just visible below me.

"Sorry Richard, I forgot to put it away."

Hayley mowed the lawn? I wondered if there was any aspect of my life that she wasn't willing to take over?

"No problem," Richard answered. "Oh, do me a favour, can you shut the bedroom windows before I light the barbecue?"

If Hayley was going to come up to close the window, then I wasn't going to have to find out, first hand, what happens when a ghost jumps out of a window. I could sneak out of the door when she came in.

In the garden the climbing rose was in bloom, the one that always attacked me, but the azaleas had finished flowering so it had to be mid summer.

A gentle breeze blew the curtain against my face at the same moment as the door opened behind me. The two events may have been connected, but I was less concerned with the door than I was with the curtain, which landed against my face like a plank of wood. The blow from the curtain spun me round and deposited me sprawled on the bed. I scrambled off the other side to avoid Hayley.

"I suppose you're living here now?" I asked her. It was more an accusation than a question expecting an answer.

Hayley looked out of the window and smiled at the scene below her, she pulled it shut and straightened the curtain. She didn't answer me of course. As she turned I realised that I could easily get trapped in the room without an open window to leap from. I scurried to the door and just got through it before her, dodging to one side before she could walk into me. I followed her downstairs still asking her questions that I knew wouldn't be answered.

"Do you ever talk about me Hayley?" I stopped half way down the stairs, leaning over the bannisters. "Do you ever wish I was still here? Well I am here. I am here, and it's horrible watching you steal Richard away from me one day at a time."

I was in an uncontrolled rage. Everything I'd bottled up was spilling out all at once. It was hard for me to reconcile the fact that, for me, it had seemed like only a few days since my death, whilst in Hayley's world I had been gone for almost a year. Last night I had witnessed her climb on top of my husband to seduce him, but it hadn't been last night for her, it was weeks or maybe months ago.

When Hayley reached the kitchen I followed close behind her.

"So, is this it?" I asked, calming down a little. "Are you finally settling down, with my family, or are you going to get itchy feet and disappear abroad again?"

Hayley ignored me and moved towards the back door with a plate full of sausages and burgers. I pressed my back against the wall to give her plenty of room to pass.

"You've never put down roots Hayley. What happens when you've had enough of playing happy families? Will you simply move on?"

My words were delivered to her back and had no effect other than to make my whole body slump, even though technically I didn't have a body.

Alone in the kitchen I glanced at the calendar. The days were still crossed off with diagonal lines. It was the eighteenth of July, but I had to count off the months on my fingers from mid April to May, June, July. Hayley and Richard had been together for three months, assuming she'd been here all that time and not in Ireland.

"A year and a month." I spat my words out angrily, but nobody was listening to me. "That's all it's been, just thirteen months and you're living my life. It's not fair."

I followed Hayley into the garden and saw that Lydia was sitting with Richard's father on a bleached wooden bench, shaded by a large sun umbrella that I hadn't seen before. The message Lydia had left for Richard on the calendar had been ambiguous, but the two of them looked suspiciously close – as though they might be a couple. It wasn't just the sun umbrella that was new – our old barbecue had been replaced by a rather elaborate gas version.

"What happened to our old one Richard? You always said that getting the charcoal to light was half the fun?"

"See, I was right wasn't I," Hayley said triumphantly. "No fuss, no trouble, instant heat and no smoke."

"I know," Richard replied. "You were right. It's so much

better."

"Where did my old Richard go?"

She started to put sausages on the barbecue, but Richard bumped his hip against hers, just hard enough to unbalance her.

"Not so fast lady, this is my domain," he said jokingly. "You've already hijacked my lawnmower today, I refuse to relinquish any further ground without a court order."

"What am I doing here?" I mumbled and turned only to see my mother holding Anthony's hand. She was saying something to him and her head was inclined towards his.

"And what are you two cooking up?"

I kneeled in front of them, leaning on Anthony's legs in the hope of hearing what my mother was saying. Anthony didn't seem to mind, but my mother had finished whispering her secrets and was now smiling at me, or through me, it was very difficult to tell which. Her head was still close to Anthony, as though she was about to rest it on his shoulder.

"Are you two a couple now?" I asked Anthony. "I hope Richard warned you about my mother. She's not to be trusted you know."

Billy flew from behind me and landed on the end of the bench. He passed so close that the tip of his wing rippled through my shoulder and chest. The encounter, if that's the right word, lasted for a microsecond, but made my whole body shiver. I didn't really feel it, but there was certainly a reaction in whatever I'm made of. Billy looked back at me from his perch and angled his head in a parody of my mother's pose.

"Oh look Anthony, don't move too quickly, it's Alison's blackbird. I expect he still misses her."

"You didn't miss me just then did you Billy, even though you can see me."

I stood up, kneeling in front of my mother was like being

88

a supplicant, and that was never going to be the relationship between us ever again. I'd had too much of that when I was young.

Retreating to the end of the lawn I slid onto the seat of the swing. It didn't move. Even though I was used to being a ghost I still wasn't used to the immutable state of the real world. I wanted to swing gently, to feel that comforting, predictable motion, but the stubborn apparatus wouldn't budge an inch.

Richard was turning sausages on the barbecue and I was lamenting that smell was yet another missing feature of my life after death when Hayley re-emerged through the kitchen door. She held a bottle of fizzy wine in one hand and a cluster of champagne flutes dangling from the other.

"Ah, champagne. What are we celebrating?" Anthony asked

"You two of course. A fortuitous partnership and a great result?"

I jumped at those words and almost fell off the swing. It was only because it was solid as a rock that I managed to maintain my posture.

"Richard, come and pop the cork will you."

Hayley set the glasses on the table and held the bottle out to him.

"Can I have some Daddy? Pleeease?" Claire drew out the last word and I knew that Richard wouldn't refuse her.

"And me please?" Martin echoed her words but not her emphasis.

"And why not?" Lydia asked. "All children in France learn the beauty of wine when they are barely out of the nursery."

"I wish you'd let me drink Mother. It might have made my childhood more bearable."

"Just a half glass then," Richard conceded, "and only

because it's a special occasion."

I had slumped on my swing. Even Ronnie was looking away in the disinterested manner that all cats effect with effortless ease.

Billy was the only one watching with me when Richard poured the wine. My children were going to grow up as alcoholics if my mother had much say in the matter.

"Better be just the one for me," Anthony said, turning to Lydia. "Got to drive you home this afternoon."

"We have some apple juice," Hayley suggested.

"I should be fine with just the one glass, we won't be leaving for quite a while yet."

The thought of my father-in-law canoodling with my mother made me shudder. Billy took flight.

"Sorry Billy, I didn't mean to scare you."

Ronnie turned to look at me and, without changing expression, managed to look reproachful.

"To Anthony and Lydia," Richard announced, holding his glass up.

"To the new house," Hayley added.

They all took a sip of their wine. My mother raised one eyebrow, Anthony frowned and Claire pretended to like it, but didn't take a second sip. Martin drank most of his glass before Richard managed to wrestle it off him.

"Steady on, we're only toasting the purchase of a house, not the launching of an ocean liner."

A house – only a house purchase. I punched the air with joy. That was when I fell off the swing. It was inevitable really. My face ended up only inches from Ronnie's.

"Meow."

"It's alright for you, she's not your mother."

Billy tweeted. I looked up. He had returned to the swing, happily perched on the seat I had vacated so ignominiously.

"You two don't understand. I thought my mother and

Anthony had become a couple, tied the knot, mated, paired up, done whatever cats do." I looked at Ronnie "Do cats fall in love Ronnie?"

I doubted that they did considering the noise they made. Ronnie meowed again and Claire saw him looking at Billy on the swing. In fact he was looking at me, but Claire couldn't know that.

"Don't you dare Ronnie, shoo, go away you bad boy, that's my mummy's blackbird."

Ronnie slunk away and Billy, startled, flew off so suddenly that he left a feather behind. It drifted down and through my leg to settle on the grass. Claire turned back to the others. I was left alone again.

I watched all of them chattering while Richard turned sausages and started on a second glass of champagne. Claire was looking so grown up, still sipping at her glass, pretending she was enjoying the wine. Martin had lost interest in proceedings and was laying on a rug on his tummy, reading a book.

I couldn't smell the food cooking, didn't feel in any way hungry, but still wanted to be a part of it all. I sat on the rug next to Martin, making sure there was a buffer zone between us in case he moved suddenly. Hayley whispered something to Richard and he topped up all the glasses, including Anthony's.

"I have another toast," Richard said. "Oops better just move that sausage."

"I'll do that," Hayley said.

"Right, well, it's concerning Hayley actually."

"Please no Richard. You could have waited a bit longer."

"Hayley has a new job. She's given up her globetrotting and will be staying here for the foreseeable future."

Hayley did a curtsey.

"Does Ireland count as globetrotting?" My mother added,

her sarcasm had never been overly subtle.

Claire tilted her head to one side. "Here, with us you mean?"

"Yes, quite literally with us," Richard added.

"Hmm," my mother snorted loud enough for everyone except Martin to notice.

Hayley saw Claire looking down at her glass.

"Yes," Hayley added. "The lodger in the attic is back, just until I find a place of my own that is."

"In the attic?" my mother asked of nobody in particular, glancing towards a shrub as though it held the answer to her question.

"So what's your nightdress doing in my bedroom? I mean in Richard's bedroom?" I fixed her with a stare. "You know what I mean."

Hayley and Richard exchanged glances and she studied her wine glass, as though she had just found something interesting at the bottom of it.

Anthony saved any further embarrassment by standing up and raising his glass. "Well, congratulations," he said, smiling at Hayley. "Glad you've decided to settle down, in a job that is, here. What is this job then?"

"It's the local college, languages department, nothing dramatic."

"You'd be good in the drama department," I grumbled. "You're performing rather well today."

"You could always live with me," Lydia offered. "I have two spare bedrooms now. Just until you find somewhere to settle permanently."

Richard cleared his throat. "I think Martin and Claire will enjoy having Hayley around."

"I will," Martin piped up, having finally laid down his book.

"That attic room has very narrow stairs, you won't find

them awkward will you?" Lydia suggested.

"Aunty Hayley could have my room if she wants. I like the attic."

My mother gave Martin a withering look that was completely wasted on him.

"You've got your house Mother, you've obviously got your hooks into Anthony, why can't you let other people have their lives without you constantly interfering."

I realised that I was supporting my best friend moving in with my husband. But at least my children would have a substitute mother around, even if it was someone who had always claimed not to have a motherly bone in her body.

"Well I think it all sounds splendid," Anthony brought a sense of celebration back with those few words. "I shall look forward to being invited round for family suppers in the very near future."

He had taken hold of my mother's hand. It looked something more than a friendly gesture to me.

"And Hayley might also protect you from that awful predatory woman next door," Anthony laughed.

Richard put his fingers to his lips. "Not so loud Dad," he whispered.

There was a rustling sound from just the other side of the fence. I thought it was probably a bird, or maybe Ronnie on a hunting expedition, but I wandered over there anyway. I didn't need to stand on tiptoe to see over the top of the wooden panels. My new status allowed me to clamber on top of the plants and, although precarious, I perched on the highest stems and leaned right over the fence panels. Sally was there, half crouching, listening to every word.

"Eavesdroppers never hear good about themselves," I whispered, hoping she might be able to sense what I was saying.

Sally looked up, startled me, and my foot slipped off the

fuchsia on which I had been balancing. It took some scrambling and a degree of body distortion to get back to the relative safely of the lawn. I preferred not to think about how it would have looked to anyone who could see me. Only then did I notice Ronnie. He had obviously been watching, with some concern, as his tail was completely fluffed up. He spat in my direction.

"Thank you for your support Ronnie – do cats get sarcasm? Anyway, I thought we were friends."

"What have you seen Ronnie?" Claire came over and stroked him in an attempt to restore his equilibrium.

Fortunately Ronnie couldn't talk or the rest of the afternoon might have been even more stressful for everyone. Tensions were running high enough thanks to my mother's continued questioning of Hayley.

"So when are you moving in... to the attic?"

Richard and Hayley exchanged glances, but it was Richard who answered.

"Hayley has moved in already, yesterday in fact."

"Oh really?" I muttered, "I got the impression you moved in on Richard a few months ago."

"You don't have to return to Ireland for your belongings?" Lydia looked slightly flustered.

"Everything I own fits in two suitcases Mrs Anderson."

"Lydia, please. If you are taking my daughter's place you may at least refer to me slightly less formally."

"I'm not taking Alison's place."

"Yes you are." I said, finding myself on my mother's side now. It was a slightly unnerving and novel position.

"Mummy wouldn't mind," Martin said quietly, almost to himself. He was back on his tummy, ostensibly engrossed in his book, but obviously following everything that was being said. "She liked Auntie Hayley."

"I did, I still do," I said. "And you're right Martin. If

anyone is going to take my place I'd choose Hayley."

"Do you think Mummy can see us?" Martin added. "My teacher says when people die they go to heaven and watch over us."

My mother was ready to say something, but Anthony squeezed her hand again. I saw her wince slightly and turn to him.

"I'm not in heaven Martin. At least I don't think I am. Not quite that far away."

"I think…" Anthony paused for a beat, "that we should always behave in a way that we hope Alison would approve of. In so far as we can."

"I'm not sure Mummy is watching us," Claire spoke rather solemnly. "But I think sometimes she can hear us if we ask her a question."

I was standing so close to Richard that when Hayley leaned towards him and whispered in his ear I heard every word she said.

"I hope she couldn't hear us last night."

Richard tried to suppress a laugh, but instead he sprayed half a mouthful of champagne over the lawn. He coughed a couple of times and only recovered when Hayley slapped him on the back quite hard, twice.

"Sorry, went down the wrong way," he managed after clearing his throat.

"The champagne or Hayley?" I asked.

"Right," Anthony said, diplomatic as ever. "Are those sausages cooked or are we all on a diet?"

The afternoon moved on. Sausages, burgers, salad and a large bowl of fresh fruit and cream were consumed. More wine was opened and drunk, by everyone other than my children and Anthony.

I was back on the safety of my previous perch, glumly swinging my legs as I couldn't get the actual swing to move.

Ronnie sat next to me on the grass for a time and even Billy made a fleeting appearance, until Ronnie looked at him and licked his lips.

There was nothing for me to do. I'd had enough of listening in to conversations in which I couldn't take part. I blinked my eyes deliberately and everyone jumped into a new position. Another long blink saw Hayley and Lydia in the kitchen, looking like they had formed some sort of alliance, or at least a compromise. One more blink and only Anthony and Martin were left, Martin now on the bench, leaning in with his grandfather's arm round his shoulders while Anthony read from Martin's book.

I realised that my presence was superfluous to the future life of my family. I sighed and Ronnie meowed, in sympathy I hope.

Chapter 10
(twenty minutes later)

Lydia came out from the kitchen and walked behind the bench seat. She looked over Anthony's shoulder as he read the final chapter to Martin.

"That sounded like a nice story."

Martin was almost asleep.

"Are you ready to go home Lydia?"

"Only when you are. I'm not in a rush."

Martin yawned and stretched.

"Will you read me another story Grandpa?"

"I have to take Grand-mere home soon Martin."

"Are we both so old that we don't have names any longer Anthony, just epithets noting our antiquity?"

"It's not so bad Lydia. I'd feel a little odd being called Daddy now that Richard is forty. And I rather like being Grandpa, I feel I've earned the title."

It was only Anthony's throwaway comment that made me realise I had missed Richard's fortieth birthday. It was last September, almost a year ago. Richard and I had been planning to go away for the weekend, just the two of us. Hayley was going to look after the children. Anthony lifted Martin up to carry him indoors.

"My goodness you're heavy young man, how much did you eat?"

The three of them disappeared through the kitchen door and it swung closed after them. I was still on the swing and realised that I was now stuck in the garden unless someone opened the door again.

The barbecue wasn't covered, there was the rug Martin

had spent the afternoon on and various other items scattered around. Someone was bound to come out to clear up and I didn't want to spend the night in the garden completely alone. I sat on the ground right next to the back door, leaning against the wall.

I looked at the detritus of the afternoon and there was nothing to suggest that I'd been there at all, but I suppose that was how it was in reality.

A car gently coughed into life and purred somewhere outside the front of the house. I recognised the note of Anthony's Jaguar as it pulled out of our drive, murmuring softly as it drove away.

The door opened. Richard appeared, whistling to himself. Hayley and Claire followed him out and the three of them started to tidy up the garden. I took the opportunity to slip inside and go in search of Martin.

The sound of running water in the bathroom led me upstairs. Martin was already changed for bed and brushing his teeth. His pyjamas were new, pale green, I wondered who had chosen them as they did not look like something Richard would have selected.

When I heard footsteps on the stairs I panicked, looking for a safe place to watch from. The bath was my only option. Richard put his arms round Martin from behind and lifted him off the floor. Martin giggled and slotted his toothbrush back into a holder fixed above the sink.

"Mummy would be proud of you and what a big boy you are now."

"I wish she was still here."

"We all do Martin, we all do."

I remember not feeling I could breath at that moment. Richard swung Martin over the bath so that his feet were on the rim. I leaned back against the tiles.

"Now, have you washed properly or should I give you a

quick shower in your jim-jams just to make sure?"

"Hayley gave me a bath Daddy," Martin giggled. "She said I was clean as a whistle."

"Did she now? And how clean is a whistle?"

"Very clean. Like me."

"Okay, I believe you. Let's go read you a story – but just a short one because it's been a long day and it's way past your bedtime. Now you go and pick a book, I'll be there in a minute."

Martin scurried out of the bathroom and Richard turned to the mirror over the sink and sighed.

"Why did you have to go Alison?"

"It wasn't my choice."

"I don't know what to do."

"Do you mean with Hayley?"

"The children like her."

"Keep her here Richard. If you like her, keep her here. If it's right for you, it's right for Claire and Martin."

"Ready Daddy."

Richard closed his eyes. "Okay, I'm on my way." He stared at himself in the mirror, took a deep breath and his face lifted into a smile for Martin.

He left the bathroom, but I stayed where I was. Richard's voice carried to me from Martin's bedroom, but I didn't recognise the story. Looking down I saw that I was dressed for bed myself. Not in the way Hayley would probably choose, I was in a plain cotton nightdress and dark green dressing gown. It was one I'd bought when Richard and I first lived together in a cold and draughty terraced house. I pulled it tight around me and stepped out of the bath.

I stood in the doorway to Martin's room and watched as Richard straightened his quilt. It was decorated with a large dinosaur and it looked like Martin had been pinned to the bed by it.

The room was almost unnaturally neat and tidy. Martin had always taken care of his possessions – a trait that he hadn't inherited from his mother. I moved back into the corridor when Richard stood up.

"I'll leave the door open a little for you."

"Thank you Daddy."

"Don't read for too long. Night-night."

I heard Martin scrambling around for something, but couldn't see him. Richard leaned against the wall, shook his head and headed downstairs. I followed after I had pushed an arm into Martin's bedroom, just to check I could get through the gap later if I wanted to.

The sun was low in the sky and Hayley was sitting on the bench in the garden, eyes closed, her face absorbing the warmth of the late summer's evening.

"Well I think that all went well." Richard said as he sat next to her.

I stood watching them from a distance in the kitchen doorway.

"Mmm." Hayley sounded content. "What would they have said if we'd told them the truth?"

"We did tell the truth... sort of."

"So what is the truth Hayley?" I asked.

"Everyone will be okay with it once they get used to the idea Richard."

"I guess so."

"Lydia could have been a bit more gracious."

"My mother?" I scoffed. "Gracious? Don't hold your breath."

"So, you sure that you're ready to settle down? I mean, a proper job, a family life?"

"Yes. It's time I think."

"To stop roaming the world?"

"As Lydia said, Ireland is hardly globetrotting."

"The wanderlust has gone?"

"It's wandered off somewhere."

"And it's never going to wander back?" I asked. "These are my children you're messing with. They don't need any more disruption."

"When do you think we ought to tell them?" Richard asked. "When should we make it official?"

"Oh they all know Richard, I'm sure Lydia and Anthony do, and Claire definitely does. I don't think Martin is interested. None of them are dumb, it's like a game isn't it? How long do you have to wait before you can officially sleep with someone else after your wife..." Hayley stopped.

"After your wife has died?" Richard added.

A silence fell over their conversation and Richard put his arm round Hayley's shoulder, pulling her closer to him. I had seen enough for the time being. Hayley would make my family the correct shape again. I really could not have felt more comfortable with anyone else in that role, but I also wondered whether that relationship had always been there, simmering under the surface.

I turned away from the scene before me and walked back through the kitchen. Everything was familiar, but a year had left everything slightly skewed. The kitchen scales had been moved, the kettle had been plugged into a different socket, a salt pig had appeared from somewhere and a string of garlic bulbs hung from the end of the cupboard.

Either everything else was out of place, or maybe it was me.

Upstairs I paused at Martin's door. For a moment I worried because I couldn't hear him breathing, but then he snuffled and moaned a little. I heard him move under the bedclothes before he settled and went quiet again.

I leaned against the wall outside his room and wondered what I was doing there. Why was I there at all? Claire sneezed and I walked along the corridor to her room. It was half open and I slid inside without any fuss.

Claire was sitting cross-legged on her bed writing again, the paper resting on a book on her knees. I sat next to her on the bed and rested my head on her shoulder. It was not my intention to read her letter, but I could not help myself.

Dear Mummy,

Daddy and Auntie Hayley are an item now. I think it's good that Daddy has someone although Auntie Hayley will never be the same as you. Grandpa and Grand-mere know but don't say anything. I'm supposed to call her Lydia now but it sounds wrong when I try.

Auntie Hayley is pretending to sleep in the attic bedroom, but spends most of the night in Daddy's room. I hope she stops pretending soon because it's hard for me. I have to get up quietly in the morning to make sure she has gone upstairs before I go in to see Daddy.

We had a big barbecue today and it was okay. I drank champagne. I thought about you a lot. Grand-mere and Grandpa are very friendly now too, I think they should live together and keep each other company. I'll write again soon. I miss you Mummy.

Love Claire xxxxxxxxxxxxx

I wanted to laugh and cry in equal measure. Claire had seen through all the charades that were being played for her and Martin's benefit. She folded the letter neatly, kissed it and sealed it an envelope. The letter went in the box with all the others.

Instead of getting back on the bed, once the chocolate box

was safely stowed, she turned on her heel and left the room. I couldn't move for a moment or two, but when I heard her in Martin's room I went to investigate.

The gap between the door and frame was slightly wider than before and I slipped into the room with no problem. Claire was reading Martin a story. I watched, leaning against the wall until she had finished. Martin snuggled down under the covers.

"I'll go down and tell Auntie Hayley to pop up and say good night."

Martin stifled a yawn and nodded at the same time. I stayed with him until Hayley had come upstairs and given him a cuddle. His little arms wrapped round her neck and squeezed her hard, his face nuzzled into her. My legs weakened and I slid down the wall onto my haunches.

After Hayley had left I stayed scrunched up on the floor, watching Martin as he shuffled under the cover, turned once and settled into sleep. I envied him the simple act of closing his eyes and waking up the next morning.

Once I was sure that he had gone off to sleep, I struggled to my feet and walked over to his bed, touched my fingers to my lips and then to his head.

"Good night sweet boy, good night and sleep tight."

Martin mumbled something in his sleep that sounded like 'Night Mummy'. My breath caught in my throat. I swallowed hard and turned away.

Downstairs in the kitchen Claire was sitting with her elbows solidly planted on the table and her fists under her chin, watching Hayley and frowning as she emptied the dishwasher. Richard was in the garden, I could hear him singing.

"Do you love Daddy?"

Hayley stopped and turned towards Claire, a set of clean

plates still in her hands.

"Yes I do Claire, and you and Martin."

"But not Grand-mere? Sorry, I mean Lydia."

"It doesn't sound right does it?"

"No. She's always been Grand-mere. Ever since I can remember."

"Let's call her Lyddy, just between us shall we?"

"Okay, that's cool."

"Or you could just call her the old mare," I suggested.

Nobody picked up on my suggestion.

"But do you love Daddy the same way Mummy did?"

"Hmm," Hayley put the plates away in the cupboard before replying. "I think we all love people in slightly different ways. You can't really make comparisons."

"Why not?"

"Well, you love Martin don't you?"

"Yes."

"And you love Ronnie?"

"Yes."

"But you don't love Ronnie in quite the same way you love Martin – and not the way you loved Mummy?"

"I still love Mummy. You said it like I don't love her any more."

"Thank you Claire," I whispered. "You are definitely your father's daughter."

"I'm sorry Claire," Hayley gave her a long cuddle. "I didn't mean you don't love Mummy any longer. I still love her, and Daddy does too."

"It's okay Auntie Hayley, I know what you meant."

Claire looked fine, but Hayley's eyes were moist and I could see she was holding back the tears by the way her lips were pressed together so tightly.

She rested her fingers on Claire's back and turned away from her, wiping her eyes on the tea towel that was draped over her shoulder.

"Are you sleeping with Daddy?"

Hayley froze. Fortunately her back was to Claire so she didn't give anything away by the fraught expression on her face. Her teeth were clenched and her eyes screwed up as she wondered how to get out of such a direct and unexpected question. Fortunately for her, Richard came in from the garden and saved her from answering.

"I think it's your bedtime Miss," he said.

"Okay. You'll come up and say goodnight to me?"

"Of course I will, now scoot."

"And you too Auntie Hayley?"

Hayley didn't turn to face Claire and had to clear her throat before answering.

"I'll be up in a minute."

Claire sauntered out of the kitchen.

"Well dodged Hayley." I said, my sarcasm at its sharpest. "But of course you are sleeping with Daddy aren't you?"

"That was close," said Hayley.

"We're going to have to come clean soon. We can't go on playing musical bedrooms can we?"

"How do you think they'll react?"

"Honestly? I think Claire's got us sussed already and I doubt Martin will think it a big deal."

Hayley put her arm round Richard's waist and gave him a quick kiss on the cheek.

"So Hayley," I asked. "Just what are your plans with Richard? Is this love or is it just a passing fad – another one?"

"I always liked you Richard, ever since we first met."

"You just wanted me to buy you supper if I remember correctly."

"I was an impoverished first year student and my grant hadn't arrived. You were my knight in shining armour. I'd have starved if you hadn't taken pity on me."

"It was a coke and a pizza, a quattro stagioni I think. Hardly the traditional fare of valiant knights."

"Well, you were my knight."

"Oh my god, just get a room why don't you?" As I said it I realised that they already had a room, my room, well, Richard's room.

"But then you went off with that idiot surfer with long blonde hair."

"Tony. Yes, sorry about that. Not one of my best life decisions."

Richard had told me the story years ago and how he didn't mind because that was how he came to meet me. Hayley brought me along to her college a few weeks later as his consolation prize, and I consoled him on that very same night. I smiled remembering how we had been almost inseparable ever since – until my death separated us permanently.

"I wouldn't do that to you again." Hayley hung her arms loosely round Richard's neck.

"Not even if you get wanderlust and are offered a job in Japan, or Singapore, or China?" Richard asked.

"You never did get to China did you Hayley? Good point Richard."

"I wouldn't leave you for a stupid job in China."

There was something in the set of her eyes, a kind of distant look. I recognised it right back from when we were children. Hayley was thinking about foreign lands, places she had never been.

"How about a really good job in China Hayley?" I was posing as the devil on her shoulder – and maybe she heard me.

"Penny for your thoughts?" Richard asked.

"I wasn't really thinking." Hayley gave Richard I light kiss on his lips before moving away.

I still wasn't convinced, but I had heard enough for now.

I went back upstairs to see my children, to say goodbye to them. Weariness had crept over me during that day, watching lives move on without me. There was no role for me in their world.

Martin was sound asleep, not moving apart from the barely discernible rise and fall of the bedclothes as he breathed. There was so much I wanted to tell him, but he wouldn't hear, or if somehow he did hear I doubted that he would remember.

"Bye bye baby boy," I whispered and kissed the back of his head.

He snuffled and rearranged his body. I wanted to believe he had said something to me, but it was probably my imagination. I lingered at the door before slipping out through the narrow gap.

Claire was on her back, hands laying on the pillow either side of her head, her hair framing her face like a dark halo. I sat on her bed and brushed the back of my fingers against her cheek, knowing she wouldn't wake.

"Bye my darling. I hope to return at some time in the future. Please keep writing to me. Keep my memory alive."

Claire did not stir and I sat there for ages, knowing what I was about to do and delaying it for as long as possible.

The stairs still didn't creak for me as I descended. My hand trailed down the banister rail, remembering the silkiness of the wood that had been polished for almost a hundred years by other hands doing the same as mine were now. Only the sensation was of nothing, not warm, not really cold.

Richard and Hayley were watching a travel programme on the television. Views of Venice from a motor launch travelling at speed across the lagoon.

"Better not let her watch too many travel programmes Richard. Not if you want her to stay."

"Have you been to Venice?" Hayley asked.

"No, never, Alison and I almost did before Claire was born, but it never happened."

"We should take them some day, they'd love it."

I turned away from them and their plans for a future in which I had no place. In the kitchen Ronnie was picking at leftover food in his bowl. He looked up at me.

"I'll miss you Ronnie."

"Meow."

"I know you'll miss me too, but maybe not in the same way. When I'm gone promise me you won't chase Billy?"

"Meow."

"Not sure whether that's a yes, but I hope it is."

My trusty calendar was there for me, the only reliable way of marking my passage through time. I took a last sweeping glance around the kitchen, trying to fix everything in my memory. It might not be the same when I next saw it.

I closed my eyes, but snapped them open again after a very short time. The lights in the house were all off, but there was enough starlight coming through the back door for me to see that the date hadn't changed. I'd only jumped a few hours. I needed to be with my children when I did this, or with Richard – it wasn't something I wanted do all alone.

There was no sound anywhere upstairs other than a light snoring coming from Richard's room. I looked in on both my children and blew them each a kiss before slipping into my old bedroom.

Hayley was there of course, but both were asleep and mercifully not snuggled together. Richard lay on his side facing away from Hayley and she was on her tummy, hair in disarray, snoring lightly. I smiled, grateful that they weren't the picture perfect couple that I had expected to find.

I chose a corner of the room where I could see Richard, but not Hayley. Leaning against the wall I sank slowly to the floor, drawing my knees in and wrapping my arms round them. I had already died so this was no more than drawing a line under my life.

"Goodbye Richard." I whispered, closed my eyes and trying to think what sleep, or oblivion would feel like.

I don't know how long I managed to keep my eyes closed. Maybe I was trying to end the kind of half-life I was living. I probably was, but it didn't work. Instead I drifted into some semblance of sleep myself. When I opened my eyes I was met with sunlight flooding through an open window and the summer chorus of a lawn mower changing note as it turned at the end of a run. Part of me was disappointed that I was still trapped in this silent prison of my family's life.

The bedroom had hardly changed at all. The walls were a different colour, a pastel mustard, the duvet cover was pale grey and there was a picture on the wall, one I recognised, but not one that had been there before. It was a print of a knight and a lady on a horse. Richard must have bought it – he knew how much I liked Kay Nielsen's illustrations.

The door was open, so I wasn't trapped this time. When I stood and crossed the room to look out of the window I discovered that the sound of the mower had been coming from next door. There was nobody to be seen in our garden. The room was still our old room, but nothing felt the same. It was like I was trespassing in someone else's house. On the bedside table, on my side of the bed, was a paperback book. It was open, but face down, preserving the reader's place. Bridget Jones: The Edge of Reason. I hadn't heard of the book or the author, but it looked and sounded like the type of thing Hayley would read.

The hall was newly carpeted, as were the stairs. All the walls were painted off-white. Downstairs the kitchen still looked familiar. The cupboards, the table and chairs were still the same, but almost everything else had changed. One wall was painted deep grey and our clutterboard had been replaced with a larger, darker, corkboard. The calendar, a new one, showed that it was June, but no days were crossed off and no year was identified – most inconsiderate of the printer.

There were three bowls on the floor for cat food and, while I stood there puzzling over them, the cat flap rattled and two tabby cats made a hurried entrance. One, slightly more ginger, ignored me completely and went straight to the remnants of its food, the other, the greyer one, spat at me. Its fur stood on end and its tail trebled in size. I took a step back.

There was another 'meow' from behind me. I turned to find Ronnie looking up at me.

"Ronnie, you're still here. Are these your friends?"

"Meow."

"That sounded like a no?"

That was when I noticed an academic year diary laying open on the work surface. It was the type Richard always used. The month and year were clearly visible – it was June 2001. Nine years had passed since I had closed my eyes, ten years since I had died. Each day in the diary had a neat line crossed through it, except for Friday the fifteenth. It was ten years to the day since I had died.

"That's strange."

"Meow."

"You think that's strange too Ronnie? It can't be a coincidence."

Chapter 11
Friday 15th June 2001

Returning on the tenth anniversary of the date that I had died seemed to be an unlikely coincidence. But then of course everything about being a ghost was slightly strange.

The clutterboard, the new one, had various pieces of paper pinned to it as well as the calendar. A shopping list half covered a photograph. It took a heartbeat for me to realise that the woman in the picture was Claire, an eighteen-year-old Claire. My daughter was no longer a child. Beside her in the photograph was someone else, only half visible. It had to be Martin, but his face was almost totally obscured. My fingers automatically went to the paper to move it, so I could see Martin too, but I couldn't move it.

Jumping so far into the future was not only unsettling – it was confusing. The physical structure of the house was unchanged, but almost everything in it now looked unfamiliar. Even Ronnie had changed. My sleek, agile, friendly pussycat was now fat. There was no kind way of putting it.

"How old are you now Ronnie, you must be at least eleven years old?"

"Meow."

"And how much have they been feeding you? You've put on a lot of weight."

Ronnie looked hurt, or hungry, I was not sure which. Cat expressions are very difficult to read.

"And who are your two friends?"

"Meow."

His tone was lower and quieter. "Okay, so they're not really your friends."

Ronnie turned away from me and walked slowly back out into the hall. I followed him.

"Sorry Ronnie, about what I said. I didn't mean to offend you. I think you carry your... weight very well."

I knew he could see me and I was fairly certain he could hear me, but I didn't know whether he could understand me. Ronnie headed into the lounge and I'd like to say he jumped up onto the sofa, but it was much more of a crawl than a spring. It was also a new sofa – at least it was new to me. I sighed and looked at Ronnie. I knew he wouldn't answer me, but he was the only one there.

"I suppose everything changes in time?"

Nine years is quite a long time in the history of a family and a house. I was being a little unfair on both Hayley and Richard. I didn't even know for certain if she was still part of the picture. She could have left long ago and Richard might have found someone new, someone who had similar tastes in fiction.

Although the lounge was familiar, the sofa and chairs had been replaced, as had the television and the table it sat on. There were more pictures too, on the walls and along the mantle over the fireplace. In fact, framed pictures stood at angles on almost every available surface. It was a gallery of my children growing up.

I found one that showed Claire and Martin as I last remembered them, both with ice creams, standing in front of a very American looking parade of shops. It must have been taken in Disneyland on that Easter holiday. Various other pictures showed different stages of their life, things I'd missed and could only guess at. There were pictures on beaches, in woods, opening presents at Christmas and one of Richard and Hayley in what had to be Venice. Richard looked older, with small attractive wrinkles at the edges of his eyes and a softening in the intensity of his dark hair. It must have been taken fairly recently for him to have visibly aged that much. Hayley looked almost as she always had, maybe there was something more mature about her eyes, less frivolous. I assumed that she must still be ensconced in Richard's bed. I found that I was quite relieved to discover my children had a stable home life.

The most recent one of Martin, at least that was what I presumed, showed him with hair that was almost shoulder length and I wondered why Richard let him grow it that long and also what the school was thinking to allow it. Martin didn't look anything like Richard. Maybe he took after me. His hair had the same hint of auburn to it as mine and he had my eyes.

I traipsed up the stairs. Maybe weariness was a side effect of jumping so far into the future. My old bedroom showed the telltale signs of Hayley's presence. I don't know why I had failed to notice them before. A hairbrush on the dressing table, a pair of shoes by the side of a wardrobe, the edge of a nightdress showing under the bedclothes. On the back of the bedroom door was a kimono style dressing gown, probably a memento of Hayley's time in Japan. She was still very much in residence.

The digital clock by Richard's side of the bed showed 10:17 in glowing red figures. One second equals one hour – I closed my eyes, counted to twenty and opened them again. It was pitch dark. I could hear breathing from the direction of the bed. The clock said 02:12. Maths was never my strong suit, but even I could work out that I'd jumped about sixteen hours. I must have counted too fast, but I didn't want to reappear when they were getting up or, even worse, not quite getting out of bed. I would aim for mid morning. I shut my eyes and counted to eight. This time I counted too slowly. It was now daylight outside, but the clock said 12:32. As long as I hadn't got this completely wrong it was

113

Saturday afternoon. There was no sound anywhere in the house.

The door to Martin's room was still closed. Even though I knew it would have no effect I leaned against it, half hoping it would move. Claire's door was wide open so I wandered in, not expecting to find her laying face down on the bed, a portable CD player on the pillow and huge headphones clamped to her ears. She was singing along with whatever she was listening to. Sadly the evidence suggested that her voice was no better than mine had been.

Claire was wearing skin-tight blue jeans and a white spaghetti strap top. The vest had ridden up to show a ring of bare flesh round her waist. I had missed her teenage years. My daughter was eighteen – a young woman.

Claire had been writing something while leaning on her elbows, her back was arched. The pen in her hand hovered above a writing pad, waiting for inspiration maybe? Previous pages were neatly lined up on the top of the pillow.

As I stood there she pulled the headphones off, dropped the pen and twisted onto her back. She sprung off the bed and, before I could move, Claire had clattered into me. I was used to being bumped around. Knowing that I wouldn't be hurt made it easier to cope with the consequences.

From a crumpled heap on the floor I saw Claire disappear into the bathroom. By the time she returned I had composed myself and found time to read what she had written.

Dear Mum,

I'm going away to university this September, to study English Literature, but I'm not planning to be a teacher like Dad. They gave me an unconditional offer so, while I still plan to get good grades, my place doesn't rely on them. Maybe I'll write a novel, or become a celebrated poet, something that would have made you proud of me.

I haven't written to you so much over the last few years and I'm sorry, I don't know why I stopped, but I promise that I've never forgotten you. Hayley has been like a friend, but she says herself that she's not 'mother material'.

Sometimes I wonder what you'd think of us all if you were here and how different things would have been if you hadn't died. You would have been amused by Lydia and Anthony getting together, I know you didn't have a great relationship with Grand-mere, but Anthony has changed her. Lydia has taken up painting and is actually quite good. Of course she denies having any talent while secretly being pleased that we like her art.

Martin has promised me that he will talk to Dad this summer. I think the time is well overdue, but like I told you before it's up to Martin and he says he isn't quite ready for 'that conversation'. I don't know how Dad will react so I hope Martin tackles it before I leave.

It will be strange, but exciting, to be leaving home, to be leaving you. This house holds all my memories of you, but I will be back for Christmas. Some days I still can't believe you're not here, there's so much I want to talk to you about. I remember your perfume. Even now, when I walk past someone wearing it I have to stop and check that it's not you. I miss you. I will miss you forever.

When I get to university, instead of these letters, I am going to write a live journal. It will be a bit more public of course so I will have to be more careful about what I say. You wouldn't know about live journals, but they are a kind of online diary that everyone can read. It will be awkward that Dad and Hayley will be able to peep into my thoughts, although Dad is still a Luddite in respect of computers and may never read it. He is still using his trusty Filofax even though it's now the twenty-first century. I keep telling him it's time to throw it away.

115

I still miss you, but it doesn't hurt quite the way it used to when I think about you now.

The toilet flushed and I scuttled to the end of the bed where I would be safe. A lump had formed in my throat that felt like I had tried to swallow a whole hard boiled egg. I was also perplexed by some of those things Claire had mentioned – live journal and online? I had no idea what she was talking about.

When Claire returned and settled back on the bed I noticed a dark thread from some material had caught on her upper arm, probably a towel in the bathroom. My instinct was to reach towards her and brush it off. It would have been a futile gesture. As I leaned closer I saw that it wasn't a thread, it was a thin inked line, a tattoo, circling her arm like a wire bracelet. It wriggled on the outside of her arm, which is what had made me originally mistake it for a cotton thread.

Claire had her back against the wall, the last page of the letter she had written was propped on her knees and she was rattling her pen between her teeth while she studied it. I crept further up the bed on my hands and knees to get a closer look at her arm. It wasn't a random wriggling line. The tattoo included a word, my name.

"Oh Claire. Why did you have to do that?"

A key turned in the front door and she dropped her writing and pen on the pillow. With the agility of youth she propelled herself off the bed without any apparent effort. I was in the way again and ended up on the floor. She was out of the door while I was still on my hands and knees.

"Hi you two. You're back sooner than I expected," she called from the top of the stairs.

"He's been doing his grumpy old man act today."

It was Hayley's voice, unmistakeable because it still

116

hadn't changed since we were at school.

"Dad's always been useless at shopping, you should know that by now."

"I'm an optimist. I always think this might be the day he starts to understand that fashions change and clothes wear out."

I had caught up and was standing to one side of Claire, but not the side the stairs were, I had learned that much.

"It's never going to happen Hayley," I said, laughing. "He was like that before we got married."

"It's never going to happen." Claire echoed my observation.

"Stop talking about me like I'm not here." Richard tried unsuccessfully to sound affronted and mooched off towards the kitchen.

"Well, you're not here, at least not in the twenty first century," Hayley joked. "And your wardrobe is definitely last century, if not the one before," she added as he disappeared out of sight.

"There's nothing wrong with my clothes, leave me alone," came the muffled response.

I heard the tap running and the rattle of mugs being taken out of a cupboard. Hayley smiled and winked at Claire before she followed Richard into the kitchen. This all sounded like a well rehearsed routine for the three of them.

"I'll be down in a minute," Claire called and headed back to her room.

I stood in the doorway while Claire put her letter in the drawer of her bedside table. I squatted down so that I could see under her bed. The chocolate boxes were still there.

Claire slid her feet into a pair of cream espadrilles. When she headed my way I deftly dodged to one side, then followed her downstairs and into the kitchen.

"So did you get anything at all Dad?"

117

"He bought two polo shirts."

"And a pair of shorts," Richard added.

"Identical to the pair I made him buy last month."

"I'll make the tea," Claire volunteered. "Everyone want one?"

Richard picked up one of the bags off the kitchen table.

"I'm going to go up and change."

"Are we getting a fashion show?" Hayley asked.

"Very funny."

Claire giggled and I had to step quickly to one side as Richard brushed past me. The wine rack was still in its usual place, but with a box of beer on top of it, so when I climbed up my viewpoint was even more elevated and more precarious. One of the new cats, the grey one, sat directly in front of the wine rack and looked up at me

"This is my spot, shoo, go away."

He, or maybe she, blinked slowly at me.

"You're not wanted up here. You wouldn't like it anyway. You can't sit on me."

Hayley bent down to stroke the cat.

"What's wrong Angel?"

"Angel? Why did you call that aggressive little beast Angel?"

The cat responded to Hayley's voice, diverting its attention from me. Angel moved over to its bowl as soon as Hayley stood up.

"Now, why don't you just eat your tea and behave more like your nice little sister."

Angel meowed loudly, but was ignored. Claire called up to Richard from the hall door.

"Tea's made Dad."

I heard Richard come down the stairs – at least one thing hadn't changed. The third and sixth steps still creaked as they always had. When Claire and Hayley disappeared through the door into the garden I jumped off my perch and hurried after them, just in case Richard closed the door when he came through and trapped me inside the house.

Nothing much had changed in the garden other than the swings being replaced by a large wooden box with a thick plastic lid. It took me a while to realise that it must be a hot tub. Probably one of Hayley's mad ideas, I couldn't see Richard suggesting something like that. What it did provide was a perfect seat for me. My legs dangled over the edge when I levered myself onto it, not reaching anywhere near the ground, but there was plenty of room for Ronnie if he decided to join me.

I looked around for Billy, but of course he would probably be long gone, off to bird heaven if such a place existed. I had no idea how long birds lived but suspected ten years was way beyond a blackbird's life expectancy.

"So, how's your revision going Claire?"

Richard had appeared in dark blue shorts and a white polo shirt. He had his mug of tea in his hand. The mug was blue and white too. It was a familiar choice of colours for Richard.

"Those the new shorts Dad, or the old ones?"

"Don't change the subject."

"I've only got history left. I think I'm okay."

"Leave her alone Richard, she works quite hard enough. Much harder than we used to."

"Much harder than you used to Madam."

"Oh come on," I chipped in. "You missed plenty of lectures and I should know, I was in your bedroom for a lot of them."

"Alison used to say that you and her…"

"Yes, well, times were different then," Richard interrupted her. "Where did you say Martin was?"

"Swimming," Claire didn't offer any further details.

"With?"

"Andrew, who else?" Claire replied.

"Ah, yes, of course." Richard nodded thoughtfully.

"I'll take my tea back upstairs to revise. Yell if you're cracking open the tub and I'll join you – as long as I won't be intruding on your together time?"

"I'll get Mister Grumpy in there sometime," Hayley smiled. "And you're more than welcome to join us."

Hayley waited until Claire had gone. "Andrew is a nice lad, you don't need to worry about him."

"I know, it's just..."

"Nothing like that problem we used to have living next door," Hayley snorted.

"Are you talking about Sally or Thomas?"

"Sally was never a real problem for you was she? I know Thomas was always 'difficult', but neither of us ever expected him to be involved with guns did we?"

Richard and Hayley both stopped to take a sip of tea.

"What?" I shouted at them. "Guns? You can't leave it there. What do you mean guns? What happened?"

"I still find it difficult to believe it really was his." Richard said, frowning.

"It had to be. They found the ammunition in his bedroom."

"It could have come from one of the other cars he stole."

"What did he do?" I shouted, fruitlessly. "Did Thomas shoot someone? Stealing cars? I can't believe you're both so bloody calm about this."

Hayley raised her eyebrows. "But it was a match for the gun wasn't it?"

"It still might have been a coincidence," Richard said, sipping his tea again and staring into the distance.

"He was in your class. You said any number of times that he was uncontrollable."

Richard nodded. One of the good things about Richard was that he had always wanted to give everyone the benefit of the doubt. But on something like this I hoped he might have been a little more judgemental.

"Still, two years in jail?" Richard said with a questioning tone of voice. "It seems harsh."

"They could lock him up forever if it was up to me," I suggested. "An armed teenager living next door to our children? Come on Richard, you need to be a bit less reasonable sometimes."

"And anyway it's not jail, it's a juvenile detention facility," Hayley corrected him.

"So he'll probably be out in less than a year," I was in despair at their complacency. "And back here. Aren't you two worried at all?"

"Well it's not our problem any longer," Richard sighed. "Not now Sally has put the house on the market."

"It's sad though isn't it? A life wasted almost before it's begun."

"Sally's life wasn't exactly just beginning," Richard joked.

Hayley turned towards him, her face screwed up in puzzlement, but Richard was grinning, barely suppressing a laugh.

"I meant Thomas you idiot," she said, punching him on the arm.

They fell into a comfortable silence and I tried to piece together the last nine years from what they had said. Thomas had always been a bully – he had shown a complete disregard for Martin's toys when they were both small. It must have escalated dramatically as he grew up.

"Have you heard from Mike lately?" Hayley asked.

"Not really. I get the odd email. He doesn't mention Jane so I've no idea if she's in the picture now. But Claire and

Jacqui are still pretty good friends of course."

"I don't think Jacqui ever got on with her brother did she?"

"No, she's always been a quiet girl."

"At least when Sally leaves you'll be safe. No more unsubtle approaches."

"But I've always got you here to protect me."

"That's something I wanted to talk to you about."

"About you protecting me?"

"No. About me being here."

Chapter 12
Saturday 16th June 2001

Richard looked hard at Hayley. Both of us realised she was about to say something important because she was looking down, biting her lower lip, not even able to meet Richard's eyes. He hesitated before asking.

"So, what is it you want to talk about?"

"I've had an offer of another job."

"Another job? You've applied for a second job?"

"No, not exactly. Lucy contacted me. You remember her from uni?"

"Difficult to forget her."

"You remember I used to work with her in Japan."

"I also remember she had a huge crush on you."

"That's not the point Richard – and she didn't, don't you think I'd have known something like that."

"Come on Hayley," I said, agreeing with Richard. "She couldn't take her eyes off you. Even I noticed that and I only met her a few times."

"Anyway she's been with Penny for years now, so don't go reading something into this that's not there."

"So," Richard cleared his throat. "What sort of a job is this?"

"It's an overseeing role, they need to restructure the whole setup over there."

"You've got itchy feet haven't you?" I suspected this hadn't all been Lucy's idea.

"Okay, but not your old job?"

"No. It's an admin role, not teaching."

"How's that going to work? You don't have much more

spare time than I do."

"I know." Hayley took a deep breath. "I've given in my notice."

I knew when Richard didn't raise his voice that he was hurt by her decision.

"You didn't think it was worth discussing this first?" he asked quietly.

"It's a great job, an opportunity that's not going to come up again. I'm in a rut at school. Anyway, it's only a short term contract."

"So how is it going to work? You're planning to commute into town from here?"

"It's not in town."

"You're working from home?"

Hayley left a long gap before she replied quietly.

"I'll be based in Japan."

Richard didn't say anything. Hayley was still looking down, concentrating on pulling at a loose thread on her jeans. When he did respond I could hear the resignation in his voice.

"So, how often will you have to go over there?"

"It's only short term, just to sort out a few problems."

"How long?"

"Yes, come on Hayley, how long are you deserting my family for – or more accurately, your family . You have responsibilities, you can't just run away when the whim takes you."

Hayley didn't answer.

"How long?" Richard repeated quietly but firmly.

She looked up at him. "Three months." She said it so quietly that I could barely hear her.

"You're going over there for three months?"

"Come on Hayley, there's more to it than that isn't there?"

"I'll be back by December latest, in plenty of time for Christmas."

"That's six months, not three." Richard corrected, but his voice had hardened. "You're leaving us for six months."

Hayley didn't respond.

"You are planning to come back?"

"Of course I am, I love you, and Claire, and Martin. It's just that… this might be my last chance."

"Last chance for what? I don't understand."

"Her last chance to run away and have an adventure," I explained. "What she's been doing all her life."

I was ignoring the last ten years, during which I presume she had helped bring up my children. Ten years had gone by in the blink of an eye for me.

"It is only a short term contract," Hayley protested. "Not permanent. And I won't be away all that time. Lucy needs someone she can rely on to sort things out over there."

"Why can't she do it herself?"

"She can't leave Penny right now."

"But you have no problem leaving Richard and my children?"

"In what way is Penny more important than us?"

"She's seven months pregnant."

I was lost for a suitably sarcastic and biting response. Both Richard and Hayley fell silent. Even Ronnie, who had been sleeping in the shade under the bench, crept away and hid under a bush. He must have sensed it was time to lie low and I have to admit that I felt similarly inclined. The truth was though, always has been, that I was too nosy to walk away. And, to be fair, I did have a vested interest in the future of my husband and children.

"It's only for three months," Hayley repeated.

"You said you might not be back until December."

"The salary is amazing, more than I get paid for a whole

year at Highfield Road."

"We don't need to chase money Hayley. I know you feel uncomfortable about it, but Alison's life insurance means we will never have to worry on that front."

"Yes, Alison's money." Hayley sighed. "I want to help though, contribute more than I do now. Maybe I could help cover some of Claire's university costs."

"Don't you dare use my daughter's education as an excuse for your wanderlust," I fumed. "This is about you not her."

"Are you unhappy?"

"No." Hayley shook her head. "I love you, you know I do. I couldn't be happier."

"So you're bored? Is that it?"

"I just don't feel like I'm doing anything important with my life, I'm not going anywhere."

"Like Japan?" I added helpfully.

I had definitely become more sarcastic since I'd died. It was probably being safe in the knowledge that nobody was going to hold anything I said against me. I had total immunity.

"I want to do something that counts."

"Helping to bring up Claire and Martin counts."

"As much as I love them, they're not my children are they?"

"You never wanted children, you were quite adamant about that."

"I know, I didn't, I still don't. But then you never wanted to marry again did you?"

"I never said that."

"Alison has never really left has she? I still feel her in the house, even in the garden. She's still here."

"Don't look at me," I spluttered. "It's not my fault, I've tried leaving. In fact I've not been here for the last nine years."

It was only then that I realised I'd been playing with my wedding ring all the time Hayley and Richard had been arguing. Had I been wearing it ever since I had come back as a ghost? I had no recollection of it being on my finger. When I looked down I was wearing a rather short, brushed cotton dress with a jacket over it. It was my going-away outfit. Even as a ghost I instinctively pushed at the hem. That dress had always had a mind of its own, trying to reveal more of my thighs than my mother considered appropriate. She mentioned it several times at the evening reception.

I laughed at myself. Who did I think was looking at me? I was a ghost. I noticed Ronnie peeking out from under the bush where he was hiding. He stared straight at me and managed a questioning look while mouthing a silent meow.

"Stop looking at me like that Ronnie. I don't have any control over what I'm wearing. At least, I don't think I do."

"I'm sorry," Richard said. "It's like I can almost feel her around here still."

Hayley kissed him on the cheek.

"I'm sorry too. I should have talked to you about it before I said yes to Lucy."

She leaned against Richard who put an arm round her, his hand gently rubbing her shoulder, just like he used to do with me. They were staring straight at me.

"Don't look at me," I mumbled. "It's not my fault. All I did was die, and I didn't plan to do that."

"It's hot," Hayley said. "I'm going to go in and change into something more comfortable."

Richard kissed her forehead. She untangled herself from his arm and kissed his fingers before walking towards the back door.

"Hayley?" Richard called after her. "Do Claire and

Martin know – about the job?"

She turned to look at him and shook her head. "I haven't said anything to them. I was always going to tell you first."

"Martin idolises you. He's going to miss you."

"He's growing up fast Richard, he'll survive without me. And I am coming back."

"For Christmas?"

"Yes, probably before Christmas. I'm not leaving you forever."

Hayley turned and left Richard in the garden by himself. There was something in Hayley's tone of voice that made me suspect she hadn't told Richard the whole truth. I followed her in, knowing I couldn't interrogate her, but I wanted to see what she did once she was alone.

She stopped at the clutterboard and unpinned a postcard that showed a lake surrounded by tiers of trees in full autumn colour. I looked over her shoulder as she read the message on the back.

I remembered how much you love Daigoji Temple. Thought you might like a reminder. Lucy x

It was a not very subtle message designed to persuade Hayley to take the job, but that subtext was only apparent now that she had told Richard about it.

"Why are you really going away Hayley? It's not about money or that old 'finding yourself' thing is it?"

She couldn't hear me, so didn't answer. Hayley moved a couple of other items around to mask the gap left by the postcard, maybe hoping Richard would forget that the incriminating evidence had ever been there.

Her finger brushed the faces of Claire and Martin, now fully revealed. Her touch was so gentle, almost as though she was making contact with them for real, saying goodbye.

She took the postcard from Japan with her when she left the kitchen. I heard the steps creak as she went upstairs. As I'd thought earlier, some things never change.

The picture of Claire and Martin was completely uncovered, revealing a third person. A boy was standing close to Martin, taller than him by an inch or two. It was most likely Andrew, the friend he was off swimming with today.

I peered closer at the picture. Martin had his right arm round Claire, his hand draped over her shoulder. Andrew was almost leaning into Martin, standing so close that I couldn't see where his right arm was. Both the boys had one arm raised, waving at the camera. Claire was acknowledging the camera with her right hand raised a little, her elbow still tucked into her ribs.

They looked so relaxed together, so innocently intimate, that it would be easy to assume they were all siblings. Andrew as the eldest, and Claire and Martin could almost be taken for twins as they were so well matched in stature. Something in the picture made me uncomfortable, but I couldn't have put it into words.

I followed Hayley upstairs – of course they didn't creak for me. Martin's room was still inaccessible, but I leaned on the door with a forlorn hope of it swinging open.

Claire was on her tummy on her bed, headphones in place. Snatches of some melody escaped her lips every so often. A book was open in front of her. It was a Shakespeare play, one that I was vaguely familiar with. I sat on the bed next to her, resting a hand on the small of her back. Claire didn't move or respond to my touch.

When I stood up again, my fingers slid off her back. The sheets on the bed had the same unyielding texture as her skin, the same undefined temperature, neither hot nor cold.

"Do you want me to take a towel down for you Claire?"

The voice came from directly behind and startled me.

Claire looked back over her shoulder and lifted her headphones from one ear. She was looking at Hayley, but she seemed to be staring straight at me.

"No, it's okay, I'll pick one up."

I turned towards Hayley. She was stood in the doorway barely decent in a skimpy bikini – she was adjusting the halter neck behind her head. Her figure was almost as good as when we were at university, maybe better as she had lost some of the rounded beer belly that we had all acquired during those years. She shared a birthday with Claire, making her forty-six, the same age I would have been were I still alive.

"I'll see you down there, just going to put some sunscreen on. I am totally lacking any sort of tan this summer."

"I want to finish reading this, then I'll join you. Is Dad going in too?"

"If I tempt him with a beer he can probably be persuaded to jump in."

"Okay, I'll be about twenty minutes or so."

Hayley turned back down the corridor and Claire slipped her headphones into place again and went back to reading her play. It was Macbeth, not a cheery tale from the little I knew of it – and didn't it have a ghost in it?

I wandered out onto the landing and heard Hayley's voice coming from our room. At first I thought Richard had come up to change, but it was only one side of a conversation. Hayley was on the phone.

I paused just outside the door, being careful to remain out of sight. Remembering that hiding was a somewhat redundant precaution in my condition, I slipped into the room so that I could hear more clearly.

"I just told him... Well he wasn't that happy... Yes, I can start whenever you need me to... The twenty-second? That's what..." I watched Hayley counting days on her fingers. "That's next Friday?"

There was a long pause with Hayley nodding every so often and offering the occasional 'Mm' and 'Okay'.

"So, next Friday? ... And you'll bring the paperwork here? ... Tuesday afternoon? ... I'd better get my skates on."

There was more nodding from Hayley and she blew out a huge breath that sounded like relief.

"Japan. I can hardly believe it's happening... Oh, sorry, I forgot to ask, how's Penny?"

I caught a movement from the corner of my eye. It was Claire. She had been listening too, but had melted back into the corridor when Hayley turned towards her. By the time I got to the door she had disappeared back into her own room. I felt like a yo-yo, permanently attached to my old life by a piece of string and spinning madly, with absolutely no control of my own destiny. I went back downstairs and out into the garden.

Richard hadn't moved, sitting at one end of the bench with his eyes closed and face tilted up to the sun. I sat at the other end, leaving a space between us – immediately occupied by Ronnie. He looked at me then raised his head towards Richard as though smelling something in the air.

"Meow."

"Hello Ronnie." Richard said opening his eyes. He scratched him between his ears. "I hope your day has been better than mine?"

"Meow."

"You'll miss a lot of pampering what with Claire going to uni and now Hayley announcing she's off to Japan. You're going have to share me and Martin with your two friends."

"Meow."

"I know, Willow and Angel aren't really your friends are they?"

"What about Andrew," I asked. "It sounds to me as

though he's a bit of a fixture around here?"

"Shame Andrew is allergic to cats, because he's a nice gentle lad."

"Meow."

"Hayley says she'll be back by Christmas, but I'm not sure."

"You too?" I snorted.

"Meow."

"You thought that too Ronnie? Reminiscing about her travelling has become a bit of a feature of our conversations just recently."

"Are you saying that you saw this coming Richard?"

"I'm surprised it took this long to surface if I'm to be honest."

Someone called from the side of the house.

"Yoo-hoo, anyone home?"

It was Sally. I thought she was history from what had been said earlier.

"Richard, I'm glad I caught you," she said, wandering through uninvited and sitting on the edge of one of the sun beds. "I just wanted to say that we've sold the house, or at least accepted an offer. Mike has to approve it of course."

"Ah, okay. That's good. I mean it's probably time for a fresh start – for you."

Sally cleared her throat and looked at her feet. An uncomfortable silence followed.

"I just wanted to say I'm sorry again, about everything."

"There's no need to apologise Sally. It wasn't your fault that… things turned out the way they did."

"That's very generous of you Richard. I can think of many other outcomes I would have preferred."

"Snagging Richard for yourself being one of them?"

Richard said nothing and Sally fiddled with her wedding ring, now worn on her right hand I noticed.

"I hope we can keep in touch Richard?"

"Don't go along with her Richard, especially with Hayley going away, you'll be like catnip to the bitch. And we don't want Thomas anywhere near Martin from the sound of it."

"Of course we can Sally. And I can't see Jacqui and Claire losing contact."

"I couldn't help overhearing Hayley saying she was going away?"

"Overhearing?" I laughed. "You've probably got this garden bugged. You could always get a new career as a spy."

Once again Richard didn't respond.

"Sorry, but you were talking rather loudly. I didn't intentionally eavesdrop."

"They weren't talking that loudly," I said.

"I just thought, well, if there's anything I could do to help..."

Richard still didn't respond and I could see Sally was getting slightly uncomfortable with his silence. She had taken the ring off and was slipping it on and off other fingers, but avoiding the ring finger on her left hand.

"Thanks for the offer Sally, but I think we've got everything under control."

"Just get on with your move, as soon as possible," I urged her.

"I won't be away for long." Hayley had appeared without any of us noticing. "I think Richard can cope for a few weeks by himself."

"Oh, I was under the impression you were going to be away until Christmas?"

"Just three months," Richard reverted to Hayley's original statement.

"It's not forever – and I'll be back every few weeks."

"Will you?" Richard looked at her for confirmation.

"Of course I will."

Hayley was standing behind Richard now, her hand resting proprietorially on his shoulder.

"Okay," Sally said. "Well you've got my mobile number if you need me."

"I think we've all got your number Sally," I joked.

Sally started to confirm her number. Both Richard and Hayley finished it for her. She looked embarrassed, but slid the ring firmly back on its original finger on her right hand and stood up briskly.

"I'll leave you to your afternoon then. I don't want to be a nuisance."

Richard stood and gave Sally a friendly hug.

"I hope things work out for you Sally."

Hayley turned it into a group hug and I saw tears forming in Sally's eyes. It may have been Hayley's figure that was the final straw for her. She had obviously succumbed to the biscuit packet quite frequently over the last nine years. I wondered if my subliminal messages had precipitated the decline of her figure.

A wave of guilt swept over me, but as waves do, it faded quickly once Sally had left.

"So, she's found a buyer at last." Richard said.

"For the house or her body?" Hayley quipped quite acidly.

"I wouldn't put anything past her," I chipped in.

"For the house," Richard confirmed.

"I was joking."

"She's had a difficult year."

"No reason to come poaching here," Hayley mumbled. "I have first dibs on you."

"And yet you're moving to Japan."

"I'm not going to be in Japan forever and it doesn't make you a free agent while I'm away Richard Walker."

It was tiring to listen to Richard and Hayley bickering. I knew when Hayley made up her mind to do something she

134

wouldn't budge. After ten years of living together Richard should have learned that too. I chose to leave them to it and go back upstairs.

Claire had finished reading. She was laying on her back on the bed, headphones still clamped to her ears. She had her eyes closed, her head was moving from side to side and her lips were syncing to whatever she was listening to. Only the occasional grunt or strained phrase escaped to the outside world.

Scattered over the floor were letters from the boxes that lived under her bed. I knelt down, eager to read them, twisting my body and turning my head to align with each one in turn.

They were all folded, or half covered by others, thereby concealing the bulk of their contents. Only a last line or two with a variations of 'I love you', and 'I still miss you' were in clear view. My knees crumpled and I sank to a tangled jumble of arms and legs on Claire's floor. The letters were all for me but I would never be able to read them.

When I dragged myself into a kneeling position again I saw that Claire had another letter laying face down on her tummy. The envelope on the bed beside her was addressed to me, but would never be delivered. Maybe that was how things were meant to be. Hayley had suggested writing letters for Claire's benefit, not for mine.

I pulled myself up with the help of Claire's bed and looked out of the window, preparing to close my eyes again and see if my departure might be more permanent this time.

Hayley was stretched out on a sun bed, sunglasses on, paperback book held up in one hand. From here she could almost be taken for the same age as Claire. Ronnie was curled up in the shade under the head of the bed. Willow and Angel were nowhere to be seen. Richard had vacated the bench, maybe he was too hot or maybe not in the mood to discuss Hayley's plans any further.

There were footsteps on the stairs and the familiar complaining creaks accompanying them. Richard knocked on Claire's already open door. I thought I was in a reasonably safe position by the open window. If necessary I could always jump and discover the effects of gravity on a ghost. Claire opened her eyes and lifted the headphones from one ear.

"You okay?" Richard asked, looking at the letters strewn over the floor.

"Yeah, fine thanks Dad. Just taking time to think about stuff."

Richard nodded. They looked at each other, but both appeared to be avoiding the subject of my death and the letters strewn over the carpet.

"The cats are going to outnumber the people in this house soon."

"I already know Dad. I heard Hayley talking to someone. I think it was Lucy?"

"Ah, okay."

"I think I've guessed most of it. Hayley's going to Japan?"

"Yes."

"For good?"

"No," Richard's voice snagged. "She said it's just until Christmas, but..." He shrugged.

Claire rolled of the bed and hugged Richard in almost one continuous movement, a trick only a young body with a perfect sense of balance can perform with ease.

Her headphones still lay on the pillow, squeaking intermittently.

Chapter 13
Saturday 16th June 2001

I felt that I was intruding, even though I was invisible to Richard and Claire. I made my way back downstairs and into the garden. Richard appeared a few minutes later and called to Hayley from the back door.

"You ready for the hot tub?"

"Ready if you are. I put some beer in the fridge earlier. I'll get you one if you take the cover off."

Richard unclipped the four fasteners on the cover of the hot tub and, when he folded it back, steam rose that had been lurking there, waiting for a chance to escape. The water appeared hot enough to simmer vegetables. I watched as Richard sunk into the tub with a sigh, half-closed eyes and a blissful smile on his face.

Hayley returned with a bottle of beer in one hand and a glass of wine in the other. Her hair was now tied up with a red ribbon. She looked even younger like that and it was difficult to believe she was forty-six, assuming my calculations were correct – maths never had been one of my strengths. Hayley gave both drinks to Richard to hold while she slipped easily into the water.

"I'll be back from Japan before you know it Richard," she said, taking back her glass. "Every three or four weeks I have a long weekend back here. I made Lucy write that into the contract."

"The flight must be ten or eleven hours, not to mention the cost."

"You're worth it, and it's actually twelve hours on a direct flight. I can fly home on a Thursday night and then go back late on a Sunday afternoon. I have it all worked out."

"Why doesn't that surprise me?" I muttered ungraciously.

"That's a rather generous deal. What does Lucy get in return?"

"A six-day week while I'm out there."

"Isn't the change of time zones going to mess with your head? Not to mention making you grumpy?"

"You'll just have to be especially nice to me when I'm here then."

It sounded horrendous to me, but Hayley had always taken travel in her stride. Jet lag had never appeared to affect her.

I moved closer to the hot tub with some trepidation, but I realised that at least I was now suitably attired in a bikini – one I remembered from when I was at uni – and it fitted. It was a small consolation for not being alive. I wasn't aware when I had changed and I didn't think I had any direct influence over it – not at that time.

I wasn't sure about the hot tub though. There was a sort of triangular platform in one corner of the tub, so I eased myself onto it and swung my legs over the edge. I tried to dangle my feet into the turbulent bubbles. I should have known that it was a mistake from my early experiments with Ronnie's water bowl.

The bubbles bounced against the soles of my feet and I lost my balance, just about managing to grasp the edge of the tub with my fingertips before disaster struck.

"I'll put the air on," I heard Richard say as I was struggling to lever myself back into an upright position.

I heard a gurgling sound from under the water and saw the large bubbles rising just as I righted myself. It was far too late to take any evasive action.

The bubbles exploded around and under my feet. The

impact threw my feet in the air and tumbled me back off the side of the tub. I landed on the grass in an ungainly sprawl. Ronnie was there, watching the whole fiasco. He gave me a disdainful stare.

"Don't look at me like that."

"Meow."

Ronnie turned away from me, distracted by Claire emerging from the kitchen door.

"What's up with you, you big silly pussy?" Claire said as she bent down to ruffle Ronnie's neck.

"Do you want to grab yourself a glass and bring the bottle back with you?" Hayley suggested, holding her empty glass upside down to illustrate her point.

"And another beer please." Richard added, smiling sweetly.

When Claire was out of earshot Richard turned back to Hayley. "I expected the boys to be back by now."

He was frowning as though something was worrying him, but it was a sunny Saturday afternoon, not that late, so I couldn't think what problem he foresaw.

"You know what it's like at their age. They will have lost all track of time at the Lido."

"At the Lido?" I had been vaguely aware of a campaign to re-open it before I died.

"I'll be back at the end of July or the beginning of August, maybe we could all go there one weekend. A big family day out."

"Yes, I suppose so, that would be good," Richard replied quietly.

"Claire won't be starting uni until the beginning of September will she?"

I had retreated to the sun-bed. Hayley was looking up at the sky and smiling. She looked happy and relaxed, but I suspected it was the thought of going away and the relief of having told Richard rather than the planned weekends home that were responsible for her wistful expression. Claire returned and pulled a small table next to the hot tub.

"Wow it's warm in here," she exclaimed, sinking down into the water without worrying about her hair – it floated and spread over the now calm surface.

Even though I was in a bikini I couldn't enjoy the warmth of the sun or the gentle breeze as it wandered through the leaves in the garden. Stretched out on the sun bed I looked down at my body, the slimmer, fitter, more lithe version that I had owned when I was maybe eighteen years old.

"Meow."

Cats obviously have poor memories. Either that or Ronnie was getting senile. When he jumped up onto my tummy he squished me down and found himself on the canvas, surrounded by my now distorted flesh.

He yelped louder than if someone had stamped on his tail and he leapt off the sun bed to the safety of the lawn. Both Willow and Angel appeared from under some shrubs to see what the commotion was about.

Angel spat at Ronnie while Willow sat and contemplated the situation. Ronnie's fur expanded until he looked almost round and my body reformed into a more agreeable shape. I shuddered and closed my eyes without thinking.

When I opened them again I swore at my stupidity. The sun was lower in the sky, the lawn now in partial shade from a buddleia that had outgrown the garden.

The hot tub was covered, but at least it was the same day. Hayley's book was on the arm of the bench and Richard's beer bottles, now numbering three, were scattered on the grass by the side of the tub.

I was still in my old bikini, but as the temperature didn't register with me I didn't know how much warmth was left in the day and whether I should be feeling chilly. The back door was open, but there was no noise coming from the kitchen.

I ventured inside and found the table laid for supper for five people – two candle powered dish-warmers sat in the centre of the table. The clock showed six-forty. From upstairs there was the sound of a shower running. As I climbed the stairs I could hear singing in the bathroom. The song's main refrain was being sung endlessly and with gusto. It was the same one Claire had been murdering earlier in her bedroom.

I could hear an intermittent tapping and occasional strange buzzing sound from upstairs. The attic door was open. Richard was sat at a small desk. Bookshelves lined one wall and a sofa bed and low table suggested that the room was now more often used as a study rather than a bedroom. Angel was curled up on a cushion. The aggressive little beast looked up at me as if to challenge me to take her place. I declined the invitation.

The tapping was Richard on a computer keyboard. I was surprised that we had one at home and looked over his shoulder to see what he was doing. The screen had an article about Kyoto University, not the green type on a black background with which I was familiar, this looked more like a magazine page. As soon as I started to read what was on the screen the front door clattered open.

"Hi, I'm back," Hayley called, "and I've got the boys and the food with me."

Richard reached across the desk and turned the computer off at the wall.

"Just looking for a book," he called. "I'll be there in a minute."

I stood out of his way as Richard dithered, grabbed a book, pushed the chair he had been sitting on back under the desk and looked around the room again as if checking for some clue he might have left as to what he had been doing up there. I followed him down from the attic room, but paused on the bottom step when he called to Claire that Hayley was back with supper. Her reply was partially muffled by the bathroom door.

"Okay Dad, I'll be down in a minute."

The kitchen was a scene of industrious domestic harmony. Richard lit the tea lights under the warmers and opened another bottle of wine. Andrew, whom I recognised him from the photo, ran dinner plates under the hot tap. Martin and Hayley decanted containers of Chinese food into ceramic bowls and organised them on the warming trays. Everyone knew their task without having to ask, even Andrew.

I watched from the hall doorway, unable to get to my usual observation perch because of all the bodies moving around. Both boys were in shorts and tee shirts, barefoot, hair tousled – I assumed from chlorinated water. Claire's feet pattered on the stairs as she hurried down and I squeezed myself into a corner of the hall to allow her to get past me – not that I would have proved much of an obstacle to her progress.

"Okay to have a beer Dad?" Martin asked.

"I'm on it," Hayley answered for Richard.

They looked like a family. They were a family of course. They were my family, but not really mine any longer. I leaned back against the wall and let the air escape my lungs. The weight of being dead, being separate, lay heavily on my heart – or whatever I had in place of flesh and blood. My eyes closed with weariness.

When I opened them again the kitchen had fallen silent, but the television was murmuring in the lounge. Some remains

142

of the meal were still in evidence so I hadn't lost too much time – unless this was a later Chinese meal. A quick glance at the calendar confirmed it to be the same evening.

The back door was open and I could hear a soft bubbling in the otherwise silent garden. The sun had set, but there was enough ambient light for me to see that the two boys were now in the hot tub. Steam rose in wisps around them, evaporating in the twilight. Underwater lights cast strange shadows over their faces, flickering from the movement of the water. Andrew was in one corner, his arms draped along the sides of the tub.

At first I stayed by the back door, watching, not wanting to intrude on them. I pulled my cardigan round my body and a shiver ran through me. I wondered when I had changed into a pair of jeans, a tee shirt and a long cream cardigan that I had worn for years and still cherished when I had died.

Martin lifted an arm out of the water and traced a line with his index finger from Andrew's shoulder to his wrist. Andrew opened his eyes and turned to face Martin. There was a burst of bubbles and steam and I missed what he said.

I moved closer and sat on the edge of the sun bed, huddled into myself, watching my son and his friend.

"So... you're going to tell them soon?" Andrew asked quietly.

"Soon, maybe not tonight. How do you think your parents will take it?"

"Mum will be okay. I think she's pretty much on it already."

I told myself not to jump to conclusions. The water, the twilight, my constant state of change – they might all have distorted my view, maybe I was imagining everything. I stared up at the stars closing my eyes for a second and expelling the breath that I hadn't realised I was holding in, but I couldn't be breathing as I didn't have a body in that sense. I swore when I realised I'd closed my eyes yet again.

The cover was on the hot tub and the boys were no longer there. It crossed my mind as to where I went when I shut my eyes? Was I still there, unseen, unheard? Those questions helped me to avoid asking others – questions about Martin, about Andrew, and about their friendship, their relationship.

There were lights on in the kitchen, but the door was closed. The remains of the day had been cleared from the garden and there was no reason to see why anyone would come out again. I wandered down the side of the house to the front garden. I was tempted to simply keep on walking, away from the house, away from my family, away from everything I knew, everything I had known.

The front door opened behind me and I turned to see Andrew already on the first step down to the drive, framed by the light spilling from the hall. Martin was leaning against the edge of the half-open door, fingers of one hand curled round it as though he was hanging on to keep himself from falling. The other arm extended across the open doorway and rested on the windowsill just inside the door.

Andrew reached up to cover Martin's fingers – a gesture so tender that it couldn't be mistaken for anything other than what it was. There were footsteps on the pavement behind me.

"Hello Martin, and you Andrew, did you have a nice day at the Lido?"

Sally always had the ability to appear when she wasn't wanted. Andrew withdrew his hand from Martin's. He slid his fingers into the pockets of his shorts and suddenly found something interesting about his own feet. Martin looked straight through me to where Sally had stopped at the end of our drive.

"Yes, it was all good, thank you Mrs Cooper. How's Thomas doing?"

Whether Martin's intent was to distract Sally or whether his concern was genuine was difficult to discern.

"He's... doing okay thank you Martin." Sally was already moving on as she spoke. "But thank you for asking. I'd better be going... I have to... anyway bye Martin, bye Andrew."

Sally hurried away and Andrew managed to suppress his laughter until she was out of earshot, then he practically exploded

"You are priceless Martin," he said, a broad grin animating his face. "Like you give a toss about Thomas."

"Well," Martin smiled. "It's only polite to ask isn't it?"

Andrew stepped back up to Martin's level and kissed his fingers where they gripped the door before turning and sauntering down the drive towards me. I couldn't move. Andrew walked through me, knocking me onto a flowerbed, which I managed not to damage, but not for the lack of trying. I thrashed angrily at the plants, but only succeeded in unbalancing myself with every futile gesture. It was like trying to stand up while being entangled in an abstract wrought iron artwork. When I eventually scrambled to my feet the front door had closed.

With no hope of success I pushed at the door and knocked on the stained glass panel. It didn't move and nobody answered. I sank to my haunches in the porch and sighed.

"Meow."

"Oh, hello Ronnie. I suppose you like being out at night?"

"Meow."

"Well it looks like I'm locked out for the night. You have a nice little cat flap that lets you get back in – no such luck for me."

I did wonder whether a window might have been left open and made a quick circuit of the house, but with no luck, so I returned to the porch to keep Ronnie company. When I sat down I instinctively pulled my cardigan tight around my body. I wasn't cold, but I was depressed, I had a right to be depressed. I was dead. Enough for one day I thought and closed my eyes – this time on purpose.

Chapter 14
Sunday 17th June 2001

After every time I closed my eyes it felt like I had just woken up, but without that drowsy stage in between asleep and awake. Whether it was a new day or a new year didn't make any difference, it all felt the same to me.

A whisper of light summer rain was falling through the trees in the garden. High up in the sky, translucent clouds were making a half-hearted attempt to dampen the parched earth. Each drop that hit the drive dried almost before another had a chance to join it.

I was sheltered under the porch as there was no breeze to scatter the rain my way. Ronnie was sitting opposite me, staring. It was impossible to know whether he had been there all the time I had been away or whether he had anticipated my return.

"Meow."

"Good morning Ronnie. I don't suppose you can tell me what day it is can you?"

Ronnie looked away, sharing no interest in my obsession with how much time had passed or what the date was. There was no sign of activity in the street, no revving of engines, no slamming of doors, nobody wandering past. I could sense the silence and the stillness of an early suburban Sunday morning.

I stretched out a hand to let the raindrops kiss my open palm, but they drilled straight through, leaving tiny holes that healed almost immediately. I was aware of a sharp contact when they first touched my skin, no more than that, but made a mental note not to get caught in a thunderstorm.

"Do you know if there's anyone in?" I asked Ronnie.

He looked at me and blinked, twice. Was that a message or indifference? I stood up and tried to peer through the stained glass on the front door. Although it offered only a distorted view of the hall, I caught sight of a movement, a flash of something pale that could have been Claire's blonde hair. I rapped my knuckles on the glass, but the effort failed to make any sound.

Ronnie meowed again, much louder this time, and the blonde blur stopped and came towards the door. As she got closer I could see that it was Claire. She opened the door and squatted down.

"What are you doing there Ronnie? Don't you want to get wet going round to your cat flap or is Angel harassing you again?"

Claire stood up and opened the door wider. Ronnie looked up at me and I took the hint and squeezed through into the hall. He followed lazily, rubbing himself against Claire's legs.

"You are a silly old puss aren't you," she said, and bent down to ruffle the fur on the back of his neck. "You're lucky because Willow and Angel have had their breakfast already, so I'll get you some now and you can eat in peace."

Ronnie purred in appreciation, doubled back and rubbed against Claire's leg again. I took that opportunity to make my way to the kitchen. The calendar and clock confirmed that it was Sunday, ten o'clock in the morning. I'd only jumped one night.

Nobody else appeared to be up yet and I watched while Claire spooned cat food into a bowl for Ronnie and made three mugs of tea, one was left on the work surface, the other two she took upstairs. I didn't follow her, as I had no desire to see Richard and Hayley snuggling up together in bed.

I tried to assemble my thoughts, to form a plan of action in a world where I couldn't really make any substantive difference. Nobody would be drinking wine on a Sunday morning so I looked over to check my familiar perch – at least I would be out of the way if the kitchen was busy with bodies later.

A line of five white wine bottles, labels neatly turned face up, filled the top row of the rack – not that it mattered to me what colour they were. I levered myself up on top of them, still nervous that they might topple, and sat cross-legged, my hands resting on my knees. Satisfied that I was as safe as possible I closed my eyes – briefly. I only wanted to jump forward and hour or so and was ready to check the clock when I opened my eyes again, but I didn't need to.

Richard and Martin were each working their way through plates of bacon and eggs. Judging by the lack of any plates, crumbs or cutlery where Claire and Hayley were sitting, they had restricted themselves to coffee.

"What's everyone doing today?" Richard asked while he smacked the base of the ketchup bottle with an open palm.

"Revising," Claire said a little wearily.

Hayley held her coffee mug up so close to her lips that when she spoke it would have been easy to miss her completely.

"I have to read through the notes Lucy sent me."

Richard didn't acknowledge Hayley's plans. I sensed the continuation of a disagreement that had not yet run its course. Martin came to the rescue by breaking the silence

"I was going to the Lido with Andrew, but probably not if the weather stays like this."

"It might clear up," Richard turned to look out the window. "I was hoping to cut the hedge – you could give me a hand if you're free."

Claire excused herself and said she was going to start

work, but would take the afternoon off.

"Good plan," Richard said. "You need to take some down time, you can't revise every hour of every day."

"I might follow her example," Hayley said. "I'll be up in the study if you want me."

The two women left a silence behind them that Martin tactfully filled.

"You want any toast Dad?"

"Better not, I've been piling on the pounds recently."

"I've noticed," I added. "You don't want to end up like Sally."

"You've got nothing to worry about Dad, you ought to see Andrew's father."

Martin puffed his cheeks and stomach out and arched his back to demonstrate.

"Idiot," Richard joked, poking a finger into Martin's extended tummy and making him splutter back into his usual shape. "With Hayley going away I don't want to get into bad habits."

"You okay with her going off to Japan Dad?"

"Well... it was a bit unexpected, but it's Hayley's life. Happiness is learning to accept that which you cannot change."

They had both finished their breakfast. Martin cleared the plates and started to stack the dishwasher while Richard wiped the table.

"There was something I wanted to talk to you about Dad. I don't know if this is the right time, but then I don't know if there is a right time."

"That sounds serious."

Richard leaned against the work surface watching Martin re-arrange the contents of the dishwasher. He still had his face almost inside the cabinet when he spoke, so his voice echoed slightly.

"I think I'm gay Dad." He paused and I could see his

shoulders tense and release. "What I mean Dad is that I am gay. There's not really any doubt."

On top of my perch I hugged my knees to me. I wanted to hug Martin to tell him it was okay, to ask how long he had known. I wanted to be there for him, but I could do nothing other than listen and watch. Richard reached out a hand and rested it gently on Martin's shoulder.

"It's okay," he said softly.

Martin stood up and turned nervously towards his father. Richard held both arms out. Martin moved towards Richard who hugged him and whispered in his ear.

"All I want, all your mother and I would have wanted, was for you to be happy. If you're happy then so am I, and your mother would be too."

"It still feels like she's here sometimes Dad. Do you really think she would be okay with me being gay?"

"Of course she would. She loved you."

"I did love you Martin. I still do. But I am worried for you and I can't protect you."

"Sometimes I wonder if I even remember her at all or whether it's just what you and Hayley, and Claire, tell me about her. Would it sound crazy if I said that I think I can hear her sometimes?"

"It's not crazy Martin. I think sometimes that I can hear her too."

I couldn't speak. I wanted to but I couldn't even swallow. I had never felt so close to them since I had died, but I had also never felt so far away, so hollow. There was nothing I could do or say. I gripped my knees even tighter.

"I love Hayley, but it's not the same as having Mum here is it?"

"Have you told anyone else about this - not about Mum, but about... you know, coming out?"

"Claire knows. She says she's sort of always known,

even before I did I think."

"Okay. Well, is there anything you need me to do, any help, any advice?"

"So you're suddenly an expert Dad?" Martin laughed and straightened up and wiped the back of his hand across his nose. He pulled away from Richard.

"Good point. You're probably going to have to educate me on this one."

"I'll sort you out a reading list."

Martin laughed and Richard smiled, but it slowly turned into a frown. I could see the practical side of Richard taking over.

"What about Hayley? Have you told her?"

"I haven't said anything to her. I wanted to tell you first."

Richard nodded. I could see him thinking it through.

"So where does Andrew fit in all this – assuming he does?"

"He knows," Martin shrugged. "We're both kind of in the same place. We were going to talk about it again today, about how to break the news to 'the parents'."

"Do you want to phone him? To tell him you've done the hard bit."

"He'll be round later. I don't want to interrupt if he's in the middle of... you know..."

"Ah yes, I see what you mean, in the middle of telling his parents?"

"Yes precisely Dad."

Even though I had witnessed Martin and Andrew together the day before and seen the way they were with each other, I still hadn't been certain in my assumptions.

My nose was running, tears were falling from my eyes, or at least it felt that way. I reached for a tissue – I always had one tucked in a pocket or poked up a sleeve.

Why I was back in the red cord jeans made no sense to

me, maybe it was Richard mentioning hedge trimming, maybe they were a comfortable reminder of when life was simpler – when I had a life. There was a tissue in the pocket of my sweatshirt. I blew my nose on it and then didn't know what to do with it. The waste bin was open so I tossed it in that direction. The tissue disappeared almost as soon as it left my hand. I shook my head. There was no point in trying to make any sense out of anything any more.

"I have about a hundred questions," Richard said.

"Shoot," Martin replied. "But I doubt that I have a hundred answers."

"You and Andrew? Just friends?"

Martin swept his hair back with one hand, his fingers running through it before he answered.

"Just friends Dad. Good friends, close friends, but just friends – at the moment."

The phone rang right next to me. I jumped at the noise and fell off the wine rack, cursing loudly as I hit the floor. Scrambling on all fours I retreated under the table.

Richard picked up the handset, said hello, and handed it over to Martin.

"It's for you," he said and mouthed 'Andrew'.

Martin took the phone and Richard opened the back door and wandered out into the garden, looking to see if the sky had cleared, or just being tactful. I crawled out from under the table, but was undecided whether to follow Richard or listen in to one side of the boys' conversation. Fear of impending rain kept me in the kitchen.

"You okay? ... Yes I told my Dad this morning ... actually he was pretty cool about it ... sure – what time?"

Martin made a couple of positive grunts and then hung up. He followed Richard into the garden. Fortunately he left the door open so I was able to join them – after checking to make sure the rain had stopped.

"I'm going to meet Andrew at the Lido Dad. Okay?"

"Yes sure. I was going to ask you about Hayley."

"What about her?"

"Should I tell her or do you want to?"

Martin thought for a moment. "Could you Dad?" he finally said.

"Leave it with me."

Martin nodded, turned on his heel and ambled back through the kitchen door.

"Well, is that it?" I asked Richard. "You're just leaving it like that?"

He didn't answer. He sat on the bench and then cursed and stood up quickly, brushing the seat of his shorts. The bench was wet. It served him right.

I heard the front door slam. Martin had wasted no time, but I assumed that he and Andrew had notes to compare. I followed Richard upstairs to the attic bedroom. Hayley was sitting on the sofa bed, her legs curled under her. She was reading through a sheaf of papers. Laying on her back against Hayley's thigh was Willow, content to have her tummy tickled by Hayley's free hand. The computer screen had some sort of abstract pattern playing over it.

"Mind if I interrupt for a minute?"

"Er, no, that's okay. You sound serious?"

Richard sat on the swivel chair at the computer, hands clasped together on his lap. His knuckles went white as his fingers tightened, then the colour returned as he relaxed a little.

"I was just talking to Martin. He had some news, some information of sorts."

"Something connected with Andrew?"

"Sort of, but not really. It seems Martin is gay."

"Ah. I wondered when he'd tell you."

"You knew?"

154

"Well, not for certain, but it was pretty obvious."

"Not to me." Richard frowned at Hayley. "Why didn't you say something?"

"It wasn't my place to bring it up."

"But you could have said if you suspected."

"I didn't want to interfere."

"Interfere? I thought we were a family?"

"I don't know Richard. Martin is your son, I'm just Auntie Hayley, a friend – I'm not even a real Auntie."

They were only a couple of feet apart, but Hayley might just as well have been in Japan already. Richard sniffed and looked down at the floor. He stood up, walked to the stairs and left the room without looking back at Hayley.

"I'll be in the garden if you want me," he muttered as he shuffled down the stairs.

"Richard, I'm sorry," she said, but Richard had gone. "Shit. How is this my fault?"

"It's not your fault Hayley. It's not even about you."

"Why can't I just be happy with the way things are?"

"I don't know Hayley. Why can't you? I would have been."

I left Hayley sitting on the sofa bed in the attic. There was nothing I could say that would help her, even if she could have heard me and if I'd wanted to comfort the selfish bitch. Downstairs, in the kitchen, Richard was standing framed by the back door. He had his hands in his pockets and was staring out into the garden.

"What happened Alison?" He spoke so quietly that I could easily have missed his words. "Why can't it all be like it was – like it should have been?"

"Maybe this is just the season for goodbyes Richard. Hayley is leaving for Japan, Claire is leaving for university and Martin is leaving childhood behind. You have to be here Richard. They will all need someone to return to."

I was standing close behind him, resting a hand on his shoulder. It was no more comforting to me than it was to him and I let my hand fall away. I backed away from the stone statue that was my husband and leaned on the table. My own head dropped, focussing on the pattern on the floor tiles.

"We'd all like to wind time backwards Richard, nobody more than me, but we can only go forward. All any of us can do is go forward."

And that was all I could do too – move forward. My life had ended all those years ago, yet I was still in their life, held by memories, tormented by what might have been. I let my eyes close – for how long I didn't know or care. When I opened them again Richard was still there, but he was staring out through the back door at a white carpet of powdery snow.

Chapter 15
Saturday 5th January 2002

Richard was wearing a pale blue pullover, but not one I recognised. There was a dusting of snow on the lawn with tufts of grass breaking through the grained white surface. The garden cast a cold stark light through the door and made me shiver. Martin and Hayley were doing a jigsaw puzzle on the kitchen table and from the patch they had already completed it appeared to be a brightly coloured cartoon of holidaymakers on a tropical beach.

"Have you heard from Andrew recently?" Richard asked without turning round.

"He should be online soon," Martin glanced up at the clock. "In about twenty minutes."

It was just past two in the afternoon. The calendar showed that I had moved on about seven months, skipping autumn, Christmas and the New Year – my favourite season. It appeared possible for me to control jumps of an hour or even a day or two, but attempting anything longer resulted in a seemingly random leap forward. I had no idea what Martin was talking about when he said Andrew would be 'online soon'.

"Is he doing okay up there?"

"He's alright I think," Martin shrugged, "given that he's practically a prisoner."

"The prisoner of Loch Ard," Hayley muttered, not looking up from the puzzle. "Sounds like the title of a terrible novel."

"Not one you would want to read?"

"Nope," Hayley said emphatically as she fitted another

piece of the puzzle. "Okay, who wants a coffee?"

"Not for me thanks." Martin straightened his back, stretched and yawned.

"Okay to use the computer Dad? I don't want to miss Andrew."

"Are you sure they don't know you two are chatting online?"

"No way. They wouldn't let him out of the house if they knew."

"Well, say hello from both of us. Tell him we miss him."

"Will do Dad."

Martin pushed back his chair, but just before he got up he tested another piece of the puzzle in the area he'd been trying to fill. It didn't fit and he tossed it over to Hayley's side of the table.

I eased myself off the wine rack, noticing that the top row of bottles were now predominantly red. I presumed that I must disappear completely when I shut my eyes otherwise someone would have knocked me off my perch when they took out a bottle. So where did I go? I shuddered at the thought of being somewhere else that I couldn't even remember.

"Say hello from me too," Hayley added as Martin left the room.

Martin headed upstairs, all the way up to the attic room. I followed and watched, fascinated, as the computer screen lit up with a green-blue background and lots of little symbols on it. I was familiar with computers before I died, but had never used one. Seeing Richard on this one last summer I knew that technology had moved on a huge amount in my absence, it was over ten years now.

Martin clicked on a symbol on the screen. I was startled by a strange twittering and shrieking noise that came from a small flat box beside the computer. A panel appeared on

158

the screen entitled 'Yahoo Messenger'. Martin typed in two of the spaces in the panel, I didn't understand the meaning of anything he typed, it looked like gibberish to me.

The panel changed and half a dozen names appeared in a list. Martin clicked on 'ANDREW4685' and almost immediately a line of type appeared with a yellow background.

- *Hi Martin, you're there?*
- *What's up?*
- *Its all gone crazy up here. I'm coming back.*
- *Brilliant, but how come?*
  Thought you were stuck up there forever?
- *Angus told my Dad that he can't do anything with me.*
- *When will you be back?*
- *Soon. Not sure. I'm getting a train back from Glasgow.*
- *That's brilliant.*
- *I'm still not sure about Dad. I don't think he's happy.*
- *Have you spoken to him?*
- *Not since I broke the news and he went apeshit.*
  But how's it with you?
- *All cool here. I miss you though.*
- *Yeah, I miss you too.*

It seemed like their conversation might be going in a more intimate direction so I backed away, leaning against the wall and watching Martin's fingers flutter over the keyboard, pausing while he waited for Andrew's response. I was far enough away that I couldn't read what was on the screen, but the box next to the computer continued to twitter and screech spasmodically. After a few minutes I turned away and headed towards Claire's room.

She was on her bed, surrounded by books and with her headphones on. It was impossible to hear the tune clearly and it would be unlikely to be anything I recognised anyway.

I stood in the doorway looking at her for several minutes. She was half way through a book of poetry, marking lines with a pencil. She rattled the end of the pencil between her teeth while thinking.

I turned back towards the stairs, but hesitated, leaning over the railings, looking down into the hall below. Weariness overcame me and I let my eyes close for a moment or two, knowing that I would be shunted forward in time. It was dark when I opened them again.

The only sound I could hear was the faint murmur of the television downstairs. I glanced back to Claire's room and her light was on. She was still laying face down on her bed, her back arched and her head resting in one cupped hand. With the other she was writing on a ruled pad. The book Claire had been reading earlier was face down on the carpet, still open. I walked over to the side of her bed expecting her to be writing notes on the poems, but she was writing a letter, to me.

Dear Mum,

Wow, it's so long since you left, so much has happened. I was going to write a live journal while I was at uni, but it was all too personal and seemed too public, so here I am again.

Not sure what to tell you first. Martin has come out as gay. I've known for years and I think you would have guessed too, but it came as a total surprise to Dad. He was brilliant about it, not like Andrew's family who packed him off to Scotland to be 'cured' by a sensible climate and physical work on his uncle's estate – like there's a 'cure'. But you don't know Andrew so that won't mean very much to you.

Uni is fantastic, you'd be proud of me I hope. I still haven't decided what I'm going to do when I graduate, but you'll be the first to know. I promise.

Hayley is still here, and still Hayley. She never changes, which is good, but also frustrating. I can see her itching to get away again. It's not that she doesn't love Dad. I know she does love him because we've talked about it, but I think she's like a bird that has some sort of migration instinct built into her DNA. I hope Dad doesn't take it too hard if she flies off again.

Oh, and I have a boyfriend, sort of, maybe, he's...

Claire stopped writing. She looked at the page, screwed up her face and started scribbling furiously. The pencil was almost tearing into paper because she was pressing so hard

...gorgeous, tall, frustrating, clever, untrustworthy, unfaithful, a bastard, and think I hate him, he's going to be history when I go back.

She broke the pencil lead when she banged the tip of it down to make the final full stop, then hurled it across the room in frustration. The pencil went straight through me. It didn't hurt, but I shrieked nevertheless. Claire ripped the page off the pad, screwed it into a ball, but managed to miss me when it followed a similar trajectory into the corner of the room.

With her head buried in her hands, a sob escaped her throat, quickly followed by a small angry shriek. Claire balled her fists and hissed between clenched teeth.

"I am not going to cry over you Henry. You can fuck whoever you want to from now on – it's just not going to be me."

My instinct was to sit next her on the bed and comfort her, even though offering effective physical comfort was beyond my ability. But I did sit next to her and I rested my hand on the small of her back.

"He sounds like you will be well rid of him," I said. "You deserve better than someone who cheats on you."

Claire swallowed and shrugged her shoulders as a shiver went through her body. She flipped over onto her back.

"I deserve better." She repeated after me and in such a determined voice that I wouldn't have wanted to be Henry when she next met him.

She closed her eyes and slowed her breathing until it was even and shallow. I touched her hand and stood up, backing out of the door, hoping she would stick to her intentions when she returned to university. I wondered what would happen if I tried to follow her, but the idea of navigating buses and trains with all those bodies jostling me was quite scary.

In the kitchen the jigsaw puzzle was still on the table, but now three quarters complete. I stood at the door into the lounge. Richard and Hayley were sat on the sofa, his arm round her shoulders and her head resting against his chest. The programme credits were rolling up the screen. Richard lifted the remote control and pointed it at the television. The screen went black.

"So what next?" he asked her, still concentrating on the dormant television.

"How do you mean?"

"Well, you said the job in Kyoto is just about done?"

"Yes, maybe a few weeks," Hayley sighed. "One more trip, just to tidy up some odds and ends and make sure everyone knows what they're doing."

She turned and gave Richard a small kiss on the cheek.

"You'll have no trouble getting supply teaching round here," he said, his hand stroking her arm.

"Actually I've already had an offer." Hayley's head dropped. She wasn't making eye contact with Richard. "Well, not really an offer, more someone sounding me out."

"That sounds good. I didn't think you'd have any trouble slotting back in round here. Is this back at Highfield Road?"

"It's a twelve month contract," she said so quietly that I almost missed it.

I knew something was wrong and wanted to nudge Richard to pay more attention, but he was being relentlessly positive.

"That's a better deal than supply teaching. A good chance they will make it permanent."

"It's in Brazil," Hayley whispered.

Richard didn't say anything. Even I didn't say anything. He looked down at Hayley but she wouldn't meet his gaze. I could see her biting her lip.

"But you don't speak Portuguese." Richard said flatly.

"I don't need to. They want the students to learn English not the teachers to brush up their own language skills. It's sort of their whole point."

"You've accepted it haven't you?"

"I haven't signed a contract yet."

"But you've said yes?"

"I wanted to talk to you about it first."

"And this is that conversation?"

Hayley shrugged, but still didn't look up. Richard's arm loosened its hold on her and rested along the back of the sofa. They were both staring in the direction of the black screen of the television.

"Why?" I asked Hayley, not even vaguely understanding what was going on in her head.

"Why?" Richard asked.

Hayley shrugged again.

"I wasn't looking for it. It was just that someone asked Lucy if she knew anyone suitable and she..."

"Bloody Lucy again," I muttered. "I should have known."

"But please don't blame her. It isn't anything to do with her."

"No, I suppose it's more to do with us isn't it?" Richard said quietly.

Hayley concentrated on a broken fingernail, picking at it and avoiding answering Richard.

"Is this it then? Are we over?"

"Of course not," she insisted. "I still love you."

"But not quite enough to stay with me, with all of us?"

"It's not like that."

"Sounds like that to me," I chipped in angrily.

Richard's arm settled back around Hayley's shoulders, his hand pulled her in towards him and he kissed the top of her head.

"I should have asked you to marry me."

"But you didn't, did you?"

"Will you?"

"Marry you?"

"Yes. I'm asking now."

I had been standing with my back to the opened door, watching them. The strength went out of my legs and I slid down until I was sitting on the floor.

"Can I give you an answer when I get back?"

"You are coming back?"

"I'll always come back Richard."

From where I was I could only see the back of Hayley's head. It moved away from me, towards Richard. Nothing was said and I assumed she was kissing him – or he was kissing her. Whatever was happening it didn't include me. Why should it? Nobody remembered me any longer. Richard wasn't kissing me. Hayley's head moved back.

"She is still here isn't she?"

"Yes I am. Thank you for noticing me at last." Impolite of me for butting in, but this was still my family she was toying with, and my husband.

"Alison you mean? I can't just write her out of my life

164

like she never existed."

"I know. And I wouldn't want you to."

"I know you have to do this. Maybe I wouldn't love you so much if you weren't so bloody frustrating."

"You do love me then?"

"I do. I just asked you marry me – remember?"

"You'll have me back?"

"There will always be a bed here for you Hayley."

"Your bed?"

"Of course my bed you idiot."

Nothing more was said for a while. They may have been kissing, or simply holding to each other. Whichever it was I couldn't see and didn't want to see. I didn't have the strength or the will to drag myself up from the floor.

"I spoke to Martin today," Hayley said out of nowhere. "While we were working on that bloody jigsaw."

"About you going away again?"

"No. About what he wants to do."

I hadn't thought until then about what Martin was planning in terms of a career or job, my attention had been entirely focussed on the other aspects of his life.

"He said he's thinking about sports physiotherapy."

"I didn't see that coming, but it's a fit with his subject choices."

"He said he couldn't face being a teacher."

"Have we set such a bad example?"

"Obviously I haven't," Hayley laughed.

"Well he didn't get the sports bit from me."

"That's Alison isn't it? She was so fiercely competitive when we were young. She used to beat me at everything."

"Did she?"

"That's because you didn't try," I suggested.

"It was never worth me trying that hard. She was a natural at all ball sports."

I'd missed so much of Martin's growing up that I hadn't realised he'd inherited anything from me. Martin had been too young when I died to know whether he took after me and was going to be sporty, although he did swim like a fish. We'd always had trouble getting him out of the water on holiday.

"What about you Richard? Isn't there anything burning in your soul that you desperately need to do?"

"I like teaching. I know that it's unfashionable to admit it, but I still like seeing the kids grow during their time at school. Well, most of them anyway." Then he added, almost as an afterthought. "But I do quite like gardening."

"So, you're going to become Mister Self-sufficiency while I'm away and grow all your own vegetables?"

"Why not?"

"I remember you had ambitions when we were at uni. You wanted to go into publishing and start your own imprint?"

"Maybe I'll write a novel then."

"One that I'd read?"

"I hope not."

Whatever Richard did next made Hayley giggle.

"Stop, stop, please stop," she cried in a strangled voice.

Richard stood up and I pulled my feet in close so that he wouldn't kick me as he left the room. Hayley leaned over the end of the sofa and tried to slap his bottom on his way out. He deftly avoided her hand and she rushed after him into the kitchen. I stayed where I was, my shoulders sagged and my head dropped onto my knees, but I didn't close my eyes. I wanted to think what to do.

There was a strangled screech close to me. I turned towards the hall where the sound came from and Angel was there. Her fur stood on end and her teeth were bared. She pulled back into a crouch, wiggled her bottom and sprang

166

straight at my head. If there had been time to think I would have known the evil little devil would have passed straight through my body and scared herself more than me – but I didn't have time to think. Turning away I curled up into a defensive ball and instinctively closed my eyes tight shut. It was quiet when I opened them again, but I was still curled up in a ball on the floor, still in the lounge.

Chapter 16
Sunday 13th January 2002

My first fear was that Angel was still there and prepared to shred me into small pieces, but she was nowhere to be seen or heard. The lounge was deserted, it was daylight and the only sound was a voice on a radio, burbling away in another room – probably the kitchen.

I felt slightly embarrassed, which was stupid because nobody had seen me cowering, nobody ever saw me doing anything other than the cats and Billy the blackbird. I used the end of the sofa to pull myself up. Willow was asleep there, curled up into a ball with her head tucked under a paw. I attempted to stroke her, but it was like caressing wire wool and I stopped after one pass of my hand. My shoulders dropped and I felt the air go out of my lungs - even though I didn't have any. Everything about being a ghost was a deception, and I was often the one being deceived.

I leaned out into the hall, to check that nobody was going to walk past and clatter into me, and made my way cautiously to the kitchen, trailing my fingers along the wall to keep some sort of contact with reality. At least the wall felt the way it should – solid, unmoving and naturally cool to my touch.

The trusty calendar was still there, displaying the same picture of a frozen lake with ducks walking across it in single file. Eight days had passed since Angel had scared me into closing my eyes. There was a deeper layer of snow outside, no grass was poking through the even white surface where the lawn should be, but the path was cleared.

A red light flicked on and off again on the oven control

panel. I moved closer. Through the glass door I could see a joint of beef in a roasting tray, just beginning to brown. I heard someone coming down the stairs and, skirting the table on the far side from the hall door, I retreated to my usual perch. I looked around the kitchen, trying to think of an alternative place from which to observe, but there was nowhere else that kept me out of harm's way.

Richard stopped in the doorway and called back upstairs.

"Martin, do you want to peel potatoes or lay the table? And whichever it is can you get down here soon, Lydia and Grandpa will be sure to turn up early."

The response was muffled which suggested that Martin was in the attic, probably on the computer chatting to Andrew. Richard changed channels on the radio and was humming to himself while he started to peel potatoes. Martin appeared and Richard didn't even turn round.

"So did you get hold of Andrew?"

"No not a word. Do you think I should ring? It's just that I don't want to talk to his dad."

"He was only coming back yesterday wasn't he? Maybe he's tired, having a lay in. I'd give it until tomorrow before worrying unduly. Dad and Lydia will probably be here soon."

Martin set out four places on the table so I assumed Hayley was away somewhere. Could she have left for Brazil already?

Richard and Martin worked easily together. When my son headed towards my observation post I stood up, balancing on the bottles with my hands raised against the ceiling to steady myself.

"Do you want a Sancerre or Muscadet Dad?"

I looked down at the labels on the bottles waiting for Richard's decision.

"Muscadet I think, it's one of Lydia's favourites."

I was on tiptoe, both feet on the Sancerre while Martin lifted the chosen bottle. He also took a red from lower down the rack and headed back to chill the white wine in the fridge. Richard had just put the potatoes on to boil when the doorbell rang.

"They're early I told you they would be."

Martin answered the door. I heard Lydia stamp the snow off her feet on the doormat before she bustled her way into the kitchen.

"We're not eating until two Lydia."

"That's fine. What do you want me to do to help?"

"I think we're about ready, nothing much more to do really."

"Nonsense, there's the rest of the vegetables, move over."

Was this really my mother, a woman who I could hardly remember boiling an egg when I was young? Anthony or age had changed her, or maybe I had never seen this side of her.

Anthony opened the red wine, Martin poured a dry sherry for Lydia and I sat there watching, hardly moving, realising that this could have been my life.

"I'm going in the lounge if that's alright with the rest of you." Anthony wasn't so much asking permission as stating intent.

"I'll help Grandpa – if you need any help."

"Another brain never goes amiss, devilishly complicated this crossword compiler."

"Do you miss her?" Lydia asked when they were alone.

Richard and Lydia had their backs to each other, she was peeling carrots while he was getting wine glasses out of a cupboard.

"She's only been gone two days."

"Not Hayley – Alison."

Richard put two glasses down in front of him and didn't

170

move or say anything for what seemed like an eternity to me
– I wanted to hear his answer and feared it at the same time.
What if he'd got over me, what if I was just a chapter in his
life and he'd completely moved on?

"There's never a day I don't miss her Lydia, never a day
I don't think of her."

That hard-boiled egg was lodged in my throat again. I
couldn't breath or move until a shuddering gasp released
me, I heard myself moan as grief for a life lost flooded
through me.

"I do too," Lydia said quietly. "But you have Hayley now
and I have Anthony and we have to go forward."

"That we do Lydia."

Richard had turned towards her and put a hand on
Lydia's shoulder. She sighed but didn't turn. I sniffed and
shuddered myself back to normality – as though anything
about my present state could be described as normal.

Moments like those are sent to test us, and I failed in the
next few seconds. Trying to descend from the wine rack I
forgot that Martin had removed one bottle from the top row.
My foot slipped into the empty space, I lost my balance and
pitched forward. My chin caught the edge of the table before
my hand was able to contact the floor to break my fall.

I think my neck must have stretched because I did
manage to get both hands on the floor while my foot was still
in the wine rack and my chin on the table. The salt and
pepper mills were inches from my nose. Not painful,
probably comical, maybe scary if anyone could have seen
me, but not comfortable. My foot eased out of the wine rack
at the same time my chin slipped from the edge of the table.
I ended up on my hands and knees promising myself that I
would never climb on that death trap of a wine rack ever
again.

I didn't try to stand up, just crawled into the hall on all

171

fours, hoping I didn't meet Angel on my way out of the kitchen. In the lounge Martin and Anthony were sat on the sofa with the newspaper resting on Anthony's crossed legs. Willow was curled up on Martin's lap, purring rhythmically.

"How are things with you and Andrew now?"

"He should be back now but I've not heard from him."

"Your father told me about Scotland and the wicked uncle."

"It's his father that's the bigger problem I think."

"Ah, a little bit of a dinosaur I understand?"

"Bloody huge dinosaur is more like it."

"It will work out – somehow."

"That's what Dad says, but he doesn't know Mr Stewart."

"Well, if there's anything your grandmother and I can do, you will ask won't you?"

"I will Grandpa, thanks."

"Now, that anagram, I think I might have solved it."

I was slumped on the floor, leaning against an armchair. The digital clock on the box under the television showed 12:58 in illuminated red figures. Whenever I jumped forward in time I returned invigorated – that was what I needed, a short escape. I breathed out, softly closed my eyes and opened them again. The clock clicked onto 14:07 as I looked at it.

Everyone was sat around the kitchen table, Richard was offering a plate of carved slices of beef to Anthony and Martin was dishing out potatoes to Lydia while she protested that she had hardly any appetite.

I left them to it and wandered upstairs with no purpose other than to leave them all to eat their lunch in peace. In the attic the computer screen was displaying an animated abstract pattern. I leaned on the back of the swivel chair in front of it and the screen lit up, making a small ping as it did so. At first I thought it had reacted to my presence.

"Meow."

"Angel," I whispered, startled and a little scared. "Can we make peace please? I'm not going to hurt you."

Angel had stood up and arched her back, stretching and trembling the sleep from her body. That was what must have disturbed the computer, the mouse had been left on the chair and Angel had been sleeping on top of it.

She blinked, twice, stared at me for a moment and curled herself back into a ball of fluff on the chair. She had obviously decided I wasn't worth the effort.

The now familiar box was on the screen and a line of type appeared as I looked at it.

"Coming round, hope it's okay, can't stay here. Will explain when I see you."

Scampering down the stairs as fast as possible I rushed into the kitchen.

"Martin, Richard," I babbled. "Andrew is coming round any..."

I stopped, what had made me think they would be able to hear me? Willow was patiently waiting by the table, hoping for a scrap to fall to the floor. We exchanged glances.

"Why can't you talk? It would make life so much easier – or rather it would make death so much easier."

"Meow."

"Okay, okay, you can talk, but I meant words, useful words."

"Meow."

The doorbell did a double ping. My complaint about Willow's lack of basic language could wait until a later date. Martin went to answer the door.

"Andrew, what are you doing here? I mean great to see you but why?"

"Long story."

"Is that Andrew?" Richard called.

"Yes Mr Walker, sorry is this a bad time?"

"Bring him through Martin, we can lay another place."

They shuffled around to make space for Andrew who looked slightly embarrassed by being seated at the table and helped to a full plate of roast beef, potatoes and greens.

"When did you get back Andrew?" Richard asked, passing him a jug of gravy.

"Last night Mr Walker, quite late. Sorry Martin," he said turning to my son. "I didn't know what to do, where to go."

"What's happened?" Richard asked.

Andrew closed his eyes and breathed out a huge sigh.

"My dad's chucked me out," he whispered. "He says I can't stay at home any longer. He said it was me or him, that I could stay last night but he wasn't having a..."

Andrew paused in his explanation, he had opened his eyes but was staring intently at the plate in front of him.

"He said he wasn't having someone like me staying under the same roof as him. He said I can go back when I've come to my senses."

"Bastard," Martin muttered.

"And your mother?" Richard asked quietly. "What did she say?"

"She tried to get him to change his mind, but he won't. He said she could f-off too if she wanted to live with a..."

I could see a tear slipping from the corner of Andrew's eye as he spoke. He raised a hand and wiped it away then sniffed.

"You have to stay here," Lydia announced. "Do you have your belongings with you? It doesn't matter if you don't, these things are trifles – easily dealt with."

"Andrew's bags are in the hall," Martin said.

"Excellent. Then that's settled, Andrew can stay here

174

can't he Richard?"

"I would have to let your parents know you are here – at the very least I'd need to talk with your mother Andrew."

"You won't have any luck phoning them. Dad smashed the phone last night when they were fighting about me."

"Andrew could stay in the attic Dad, we don't really use it that much."

"I can't see a problem, as long as I can clear it with your parents Andrew."

"I'm worried about my mum. I ought to go back and make sure she's okay."

Anthony cleared his throat. "What we need is a plan of action. I don't think it's a good idea for Andrew to go back home by himself."

"I can go round this afternoon Andrew, if that's okay with you?" Richard offered. "I can tell them you're staying here for the time being and check that your mother's alright."

"I'll go with you Richard," Anthony said. "Best to have a little back-up if necessary."

"Men," Lydia snorted. "I will accompany Richard, you will stay here Anthony. The calm of a woman's presence will be much more beneficial."

"My mother the calm mediator. That's a new one on me," I laughed. But I had to admit my mother had changed. Years ago she would have stayed out of family matters such as these and judged them from afar.

"She should stay in the house if at all possible," my mother ruled imperiously. "Possession is nine tenths of the law and Andrew and his mother can be reunited in the family home if that obnoxious bigoted man can be sent packing. I'm sorry Andrew, I know I'm talking about your father."

"And if that's not possible," Anthony added. "She must

come and stay with us."

It was agreed that Richard and Lydia would go to Andrew's house and, at the very least, let them know where Andrew was and check that his mother was safe.

I didn't know where Andrew lived, but it couldn't be that far. Would they walk or take the car? If so who was going to drive? My mother had the answer for that too.

"I will drive," she said. "I believe you've had too much wine Richard. What are your parents' names Andrew?"

Andrew hesitated and Richard answered for him.

"Thomas and Sarah I think? We've met on parents' evenings, bumped into each other occasionally in town."

"Another bloody Thomas," I muttered. "I might have guessed."

Chapter 17

During dinner Andrew explained what had happened in Scotland. His uncle's intolerance and determination to 'cure' him had turned out to be in complete contrast to the attitude taken by the local school. His uncle had stormed in to see the headmaster, caused a huge fuss and then declared to Andrew's father that there was nothing he could do to help.

Andrew had been sent back after a long and heated argument between his uncle and his father, only to be thrown out of the house the morning after his return.

Richard asked if his father was likely to be in on a Sunday afternoon and Andrew shrugged.

"He'll probably be asleep in front of the television."

"Lydia," Richard turned to my mother. "I think the earlier we go round there the better."

"Well I'm ready whenever you are Richard."

Andrew sighed. I couldn't tell whether he was relieved that something might be resolved or worried that there would be another confrontation.

"You don't have to go Mr Walker. I can go and see my Mum when Dad goes to work tomorrow."

"If you're going to stay here I think we should make sure everyone knows where you are."

Andrew's problems were not really that closely linked to my own family but I wanted to see what his ignorant throw-back of a father was like in reality. I decided to try and stow away in the car and join Richard and my mother's visit. To be honest I was also intrigued by this new selfless version of my mother and wanted to see her in action.

While Lydia put her coat on I lingered by the front door so that I could slip out as soon as it was opened. I hadn't worked out how difficult it would be to get in the car. Richard got in so quickly that I didn't have a chance to slide in first and scrabble into the back seat – my initial plan. Lydia's passenger door clicked shut only a moment later and I thought I had lost my opportunity. But when Richard wound the driver's window down to clear the mist on the wing mirror I dived impetuously, but rather gracefully, through the opening.

It's difficult to maintain one's dignity when sprawled across the laps of your husband and mother, but I did my best. When Richard's hand punched a hole through my tummy to release the handbrake I decided that sitting in the back might be less traumatic. I crawled between them and opted for a central position on the rear seats. I couldn't see that a seat belt was necessary and I couldn't have put it on anyway.

"So Richard," I asked. "What are you going to say to Andrew's parents?"

My mother released a huge sigh that ended with a pronounced hmmm. "Have you considered what will you say to Andrew's parents?"

Was she hearing me subconsciously or was her nearly identical question to mine a natural coincidence?

"Not very much. I think they need to know where Andrew is, his mother especially. I don't really want to pass judgement on them or the situation."

"Hmm, there are several things I'd like to say – to him in particular."

"I bet there are Mother. You've rarely been short of words when it comes to criticising people."

Richard appeared to know where he was going. I presumed if Martin and Andrew had been friends for a while he would have had to drop Andrew home on occasions. We pulled up outside a semi-detached house in an unremarkable but pleasant tree-lined street. I climbed into the front, crouched on my mother's lap, so that when she opened her door I was able to spill out of the car before she moved. I landed on a snow covered grass verge and was prepared to brush it off my jeans when I stood up, but none of it had stuck to me. In the drive was a car with the boot and a back door wide open, which was surprising given how cold it was.

Before Richard and Lydia reached the front door it opened, but nobody came out. Richard rang the bell and a man appeared almost immediately. I assumed it was Thomas, Andrew's father.

"You," he spat the word out angrily. "I suppose you're okay with those two little..."

"Can I stop you right there? I've not come to argue with you, just to let you and Sarah know that Andrew is staying with us tonight."

"He can stay where he fucking wants – as long as it's not here."

Andrew's mother was in the hall, a couple of feet behind her husband. Her arms were wrapped tight across her body and the knuckles of one hand were pressed to her mouth. With her hair in some disarray and eyes that were flicking wildly between Richard and Lydia, she looked worried and like she was trying to warn them.

"Thank you," she whispered, her voice cracking as she spoke.

Her husband glanced back at her, looked at Richard with narrowed eyes and grunted.

"I hope the little queers will be very happy sharing a bed.

179

Now, if you'll just get out of my way?"

Richard simply moved to one side. Lydia, surprisingly, held her tongue.

Thomas turned to pick up a large cardboard box. He pushed past Richard and Lydia and thrust the box into the back seat of his car, shutting the door on it with unnecessary force. He walked round the back of the car, slammed the boot lid down and climbed into the driver's seat.

The engine coughed into life at the third attempt. Thomas revved loudly and tried to back the car out of the drive. At first the wheels spun on the compacted snow, but the tyres suddenly found grip and the car lurched out into the road and stalled. Fortunately nothing was going past at that moment. Everyone heard Thomas swear again, even through closed windows. He restarted the engine and spun the wheels as he drove off.

"Good riddance," Sarah muttered under her breath.

"Are you alright?" Richard asked.

Sarah was leaning against the doorframe, the tension easing in her arms.

"Um, yes I'll survive, but how is Andrew? Is he okay?"

"He's fine, a little subdued maybe."

"Thank you so much for being there for him. I couldn't get Thomas to see reason."

"Where's he gone?" Lydia asked.

Sarah shrugged and said she didn't know, but probably gone to crash at his brother's flat.

"Change the locks," Lydia declared. "I'll get Anthony to pop round tomorrow, he will know someone who can do it quickly for you."

"I don't know." Sarah frowned. "I doubt he'll come back – and it's not like he's violent, not really – just an intolerant, bigoted halfwit."

I spluttered into laughter and suppressed it when I

realised that I was the only one who found Sarah's comments amusing.

"I think we were going to go our separate ways anyway. Andrew was just the excuse or the catalyst. God, what a mess – poor boy."

"Andrew can stay with us as long he wants, as long as it's okay with you Sarah."

"Thank you."

She turned to Lydia and asked who Anthony was. Lydia explained and Sarah nodded thoughtfully.

"It might not be a bad idea. Andrew could move back here safely then – if he wanted to."

"Will you be alright tonight?" Lydia asked. "We have a spare room."

"No I'll stay, probably best just in case he does come back."

"You have our number?" Richard touched Sarah's arm and I saw her flinch. Richard saw it too. "Call me if there's anything, anything at all I can do."

"Thank you. And please tell Andrew I'll ring him tomorrow, as soon as I get a new phone, tell him we'll sort this out, tell him I love him."

Sarah half closed the door, her face still showed through the gap and she mouthed another thank you before closing the door completely.

I had been standing a little apart from the three of them and had to spur myself into action when Richard and Lydia turned away from the house. This time I went round to the passenger door. Lydia always arranged her coat carefully before sliding into her seat and I had ample time to slip in front of her and scramble into the back.

I only half listened to Richard and Lydia on the way back. My own preoccupations were the possible consequences of Andrew and Martin living under the same roof.

From what I'd observed the previous summer, Martin was very fond of Andrew, maybe in a way that Andrew wasn't ready for. All this worrying was exhausting me. When the conversation in the front fell silent and the tyres swished on occasional patches of snow, I closed my eyes to rest them for a moment.

When I opened them it was much darker than it had been. Dusk had been fast approaching when we drove back but now there was the stillness of night. No moon illuminated the garden but a street lamp cast sharp shadows on the blue-white snow. I was alone in the car. I swore – then swore again, but it didn't help.

My first concern was how I was going to get out. My second thought was how much time had lapsed. Although there was still snow in the garden, that didn't mean it was the same week or even the same year. I felt panic growing in me. What if Richard had sold the car while I was still in it? I could have ended up anywhere – another part of town or even another part of the country. How would I have got back?

I frantically scanned the garden and house for any clues or signs of movement, anyone coming out to the car. I made myself calm down, took deep breaths, wondered how that worked when I was a ghost and immediately dismissed that enigma as irrelevant to the immediate problem.

I turned to look out the back window, to check whether there was still snow on the road, and saw a young man standing at the bottom of the drive, hands in pockets, staring at me. He looked to be barely more than a teenager and was dressed in shorts and a baggy t-shirt – completely unsuitable for the time of year and the weather conditions.

I crawled into the back seat and banged on the rear window, not managing to make any noise but at least catching his attention. We stared at each other, both stock-still for a moment before he started to walk up the drive towards me. He came up to the side of the car and tapped on the window. There was no noise, but he was looking directly at me. He could see me. He had those good looks I associated with confident public school boys who expect the world to be laid bare at their feet.

"Who are you?" I asked, not expecting an answer.

"Jeremy," he replied, his voice muffled by the glass

"You can see me?" I wondered if he was lip reading.

"Of course I can, and I can hear you too. What's your name?"

"Alison, Alison Walker."

He put his hands in his pockets and bent forward, his forehead resting against the glass.

"Are you trapped in there?"

I nodded – somehow words wouldn't come even though this was the first conversation, the first real conversation, I'd had since I died. Jeremy stood upright, his face disappearing from view, and I pressed mine against the window to see him.

He looked along the top of the car, pulled his mouth into a sideways thoughtful expression and walked round the front of the car. When he stopped at the driver's door I scrambled into the front seat. His fingers very slowly squiggled through a tiny crack where Richard hadn't quite closed the window.

"You can get out through here if you want to."

I looked at the gap he had indicated. It was tiny, barely a quarter of an inch.

"How?" I asked, frowning, not believing I could manage to negotiate so small an opening.

"Well, it's easier if you can't see what's happening, but you don't want to shut your eyes or you'll jump in time."

"I know."

"Turn your back to the window."

I did as he said, still not believing it was possible – even though I'd already squeezed through spaces much smaller than I could have when I was alive.

"Push your head against the top of the window."

I did as Jeremy said. He sounded confident.

"That's it, just keep pushing."

Nothing was happening – or so I thought. There was no sensation of my head being squashed, but one second I was looking at the interior of the car, the next my head was outside the car and I was looking at the roof.

"Look up at the sky. It's easier if you don't look at your body. Then just keep pushing with your feet."

Following his instructions I found most of my body and my arms free and outside the car. With my hands flat on the roof I wriggled the rest of me through. I didn't look down until my feet were firmly planted on the drive.

"There you go," Jeremy said. "You get used to it after a few goes."

"I'm not sure I want to get used to it, but thank you."

"No problem."

Jeremy had stepped a couple of feet away, he was staring in the vicinity of my waist and I looked down to see what was wrong, whether my body had remained distorted in some way.

It wasn't that sort of problem he was staring at. One thing I hadn't got under control at that time was my appearance. Whether I had reacted to his age and casual summer clothes or whether some part of my subconscious wanted to impress my rescuer didn't really matter. What did matter was that I had reverted in my appearance to being about seventeen years old. I was wearing a dress that had been judged a little on the short side even back then. At the time my mother had made her opinion quite clear with a withering look and a shake of her head.

"You're a ghost?" I asked in an attempt to get Jeremy's eyes to engage me a little higher up.

He nodded slowly, still looking at my legs. Okay, I was flattered, it had been a while since I'd been assessed quite so obviously and, although slightly uncomfortable, it was also a little flattering.

"How long have you been...?" I wasn't sure what the etiquette was when questioning another ghost as to when they had died.

"Oh, okay," he said and looked up at me. " It's January thirteenth isn't it?"

"Yes, I think so. I hope so." It sounded like I had only jumped a few hours.

"Two thousand and two?" He mumbled.

He looked up at the sky as he made a mental calculation – I could see his lips moving slightly.

"That would be thirty-three years seven months and about twelve days. I was eighteen, still am eighteen I suppose, or not. Sort of depends how you look at it."

"Do you know how...?"

"Nobody does," He interrupted me. "At least nobody I've met remembers. If you were ill, knew it was coming, then I suppose you could make a pretty good guess."

"You weren't ill?"

"No."

"So you have no idea what happened to you?"

Jeremy looked down, but not at my legs this time, he was studying his own feet. He spoke quietly without looking up.

"I have a twin brother. When I came back, or whatever you want to call it, he was still in hospital. Both his legs were broken, his pelvis, his right arm and several ribs. He still walks with a limp. My motorbike wasn't at home. I never saw it again."

He looked up, shrugged and I didn't want to ask any more questions.

"Thank you for rescuing me," I whispered.

"It's all right, makes a change."

He looked down at my legs once again, sighed and turned away, strolling back down the drive.

"Be seeing you Alison," he said without turning round.

I was rather sorry to see him go. A proper conversation made a pleasant change, even though we didn't have much in common.

"Do you walk past here often?" I called after him.

"Every so often," he replied, but didn't break his step.

Chapter 18

For several minutes I walked round the house searching for a way in. Although I shuddered at the thought of squeezing through a tiny gap again, the opportunity didn't arise. All the windows were closed tight and the cat flap had no discernible gaps. With my hands occupied with keeping the hem of my skirt from rising too high, I wandered away from the house and heaved myself onto the cover of the hot tub.

Light seeped through the curtains of one bedroom where they were not completely closed. I hugged my knees to my chest, unsure what to do. I knew I could close my eyes and jump forward in time, but I wanted to know that Martin was okay and how Andrew fitted into my family and into Martin's life.

Inside the house everything would continue without me, unaware that a passive observer and occasional prompter was missing. Someone entered the kitchen and the path close to the house was suddenly illuminated by light spilling through the glazed back door.

Richard came briefly into view, but moved again, out of my line of vision. I eased myself off the hot tub and wandered, without enthusiasm, towards the back door. I watched Richard fill the kettle and flip the switch on the back of it. He walked towards me, hands loosely buried into his pockets. I stood on the top step on tiptoes. We were only inches apart, me looking into Richards eyes, his staring vacantly at the garden and snow behind me.

He leaned forward until his forehead was resting against the glass and I did the same, stretching up to mirror his position. To steady myself I put both palms flat against the glass, willing Richard to be aware of me, to know I was there for him.

My breathing stopped when Richard took his hands from his pockets and placed them opposite mine on the glass. I missed the touch of his hands, the smell of him, the warmth of his body close to mine. It took all my will power not to close my eyes and hold that moment in my mind forever.

Richard pushed himself away from the door, but left his fingertips against mine, only the thickness of the glazed window separated us. I mouthed 'I love you' to him, but he couldn't have seen me even if he had kept his eyes open.

Tiredness showed in the fine lines of his forehead, the loose skin on his lower eyelids, and a greyed receding hairline. He must have shaved that morning but already his skin was roughened and lacked a healthy colour. The small scar on the side of his jaw, acquired while trying to do a handstand in the student's union bar, had softened with the years. I wanted to touch it, to feel the slightly raised line of pale scar tissue that stood out so much more in summer.

Richard's head dropped, his hands slid down the glass away from mine and he turned towards the cloud of steam that was billowing behind him. I wanted to believe that he had sensed me there and that we had connected in some way, but I knew it was a fantasy on my part.

The tension drained from my body, my heels settled back onto the concrete step, my hands released their pressure on the glass and I closed my eyes. Unconsciously I must have counted in my head, or I was getting a feel for the strange way time could slip past in my world. It can't have been more than seven or eight seconds before I opened them again, but of course Richard wasn't there. There was that strange half light before the sun has risen but after night had lost its hold.

The kitchen light was on. Evidence of breakfast was still on the table – a box of cereal, dishes with spoons resting in them and empty mugs, but there was no sign of Richard or the boys. I glanced to the side and could see both the calendar and clock. Only one night had passed, it was almost eight o'clock, they would all be leaving for school soon or may have already left – but Richard wouldn't have left the house without clearing the table. Two cats wandered into the kitchen from the hall. They both stopped to look at their food bowls – only two food bowls. I assumed that meant that I wouldn't be seeing Ronnie again, but I didn't want to believe it. Ronnie and I had bonded, he was my only constant companion in this new world in which I lived or at least existed.

Turning away from the door I noticed that a fresh layer of snow had dusted the garden, making the lawn sparkle in the low sunshine as though it had been sprinkled with diamonds. The cat flap rattled behind me. Angel and Willow emerged from the kitchen and picked their way up the path in single file, tasting the air, a hunting party always on the lookout for new victims.

I pulled my coat tight around my body. When had I acquired a coat? My short dress had changed to a calf length skirt and brown boots – items that I remembered were still in my wardrobe when I had died. I stared at my boots and willed them to change to a black pair that had predated them. There was a sort of shimmer and my boots morphed into the ones I had imagined – I realised I could control my appearance.

Feeling somewhat buoyed up by that success I walked round to the front door with a more positive attitude. The idea of accompanying my husband and son to school flittered across my mind, but the image of several hundred children rushing between lessons and the impossibility of finding a safe observation point made me shiver with fear. I decided to give that adventure a miss.

There were no footsteps in the snow on the drive and Richard's car was still there. I should have an opportunity to sneak into the house when they all left, then I could skip a few hours and catch up on events when they got home. Jeremy's voice made me jump.

"Hello. Still here then?"

He was at the end of the drive, hands in pockets, looking directly at me. At least he was now dressed more sensibly in jeans and a huge floppy mohair pullover.

"Have you been wandering round all night?"

"I like to keep my eye on the neighbourhood, see what's changed since I was last here."

"I cheated, closed my eyes for a spell."

"You look different. Is that more what you looked like when you died?"

I looked down at my clothes again.

"No, I was at a barbecue I think, in summer."

"You look older. I mean, not old, but not my age."

"Yes, sorry, this is more the real me I suppose. I don't know what happened yesterday when we met."

Jeremy smiled. It was a sweet smile, part friendly, part embarrassed young man.

"How old were you when you died?"

"Thirty-six."

"Married I suppose?"

I indicated the house behind me by pointing a finger over my shoulder.

"Husband, two children, boring old married woman I'm afraid."

"How long ago was it?"

I added it up in my head as best I could.

"Ten years..." I hesitated, smiling at Jeremy and counting

in my head, "seven months and eight days."

Jeremy laughed. "You'll be okay," he said.

"I think I probably will be."

We were standing some twelve feet apart. The thing that struck me as strange was that we were both surrounded by virgin snow, not a footprint in sight.

"Can I ask you something that's been puzzling me?" I said, leaning back against the car.

"Sure, anything, ask away."

"Why aren't there more ghosts around, more people like us? I mean, so many people die, everyone does eventually. The world should be littered with ghosts. We should be tripping over each other."

The thought had been hiding in the back of my mind ever since I had realised the truth of my own existence, but I hadn't wanted to confront it. Jeremy walked slowly up the drive and leaned on the car next to me. We didn't face each other but stared out into the tree-lined street. He left no footprints in the snow. Neither of us left any trace of our existence.

"I've met a few ghosts over the years. Mostly in the first few months after my death."

"But not since then?"

"I spent a lot of time hanging round the hospital – my brother was in there for a couple of months."

"Of course, I suppose there would be a lot of ghosts in the hospital?"

"No, not actually in the hospital, but I'd go for long walks, trying to make sense of it all. I didn't want to jump forward at that time. I didn't want to leave my brother in case something happened."

We both fell silent. On my part I didn't want to push Jeremy into talking about something he still obviously found difficult.

"They mostly disappear you know like fireworks burning out in the sky. We are the odd ones out – the ones that hang around."

"Why do you think that is? That we're still here I mean?"

"Some thing or some one to wait for I guess."

The snow was thawing in the early morning sun, dripping from the branches of the trees at sporadic intervals. We both looked down the street when we heard someone approaching, whistling, footsteps scrunching on the virgin snow.

"It's the postman," Jeremy said as he took my arm and gently pulled me to one side to keep me out of harm's way.

We watched as the postman paused at the end of the drive. His whistling broke into tuneless fragments. He delved into his bag, produced a small package and a couple of letters, did a sharp right turn and marched up our drive.

"Classic Elwin performance," Jeremy said.

"Do you know him then?"

"I was at primary school with him."

The postman was in the same school year as Jeremy? It was odd to think that the young man who had befriended me, would only be a few years older than I would have been – had he survived what I assumed had been a motorcycle accident. Richard was a similar age, maybe even the same school year. Had Richard grown up around here; Jeremy and he might even have been friends.

The postman knocked on our door and also rang the bell. I assumed that he required a signature for the package and that Richard, or one of the boys, would open the door. I turned to Jeremy as I moved away from him.

"I need to get indoors, but I want to see you again?"

"Who knows," he shrugged. "I hope we'll meet again, but it's a bit random."

"Do you count when you jump time?"

"Not any more, you get a feel for it after a while. You can

pretty much count if you want to jump a few hours or a day, but any longer than that and you have to sort of feel when you want to appear again."

"Okay, I'll try that. Midsummer day, at noon and right here?"

Jeremy nodded thoughtfully, but then the door opened behind me and I had to move quickly. It was Martin. I knew I wouldn't have much time to get indoors.

"Thanks for everything Jeremy."

I snuck past Elwin and, when Martin turned to call for Richard, squeezed through the half-opened door and into the hall. I had just managed to wave to Jeremy when Richard bumped into me, squashing me face first against the wall. I heard Jeremy's laughter, but couldn't see him. I managed to slide sideways and escape, but was then clattered into by Martin on his way back to the kitchen. Everyone is so inconsiderate to ghosts, just because you can't see us doesn't mean we're not here. To be fair, I don't know what Richard and Martin, or what anyone could do to avoid bumping into ghosts and knocking us all over the place. I was simply feeling a bit put out that morning, given that I'd been locked in a car and left out in the snow.

"What's in the mystery parcel Dad?"

Martin was clearing the table. Richard had sat down and was looking at the written address.

"It's Hayley's handwriting."

"So open it, it's not going to be a bomb is it?"

I was standing in the doorway, watching, and had forgotten that Andrew was not there yet. He must have been in the lounge because there were no squeaks from the stairs, no pattering of feet. When Andrew walked into me, square in the back, I effectively dived into the kitchen. I skidded on the floor and my body contorted as it encountered the legs of the table. Thankfully none of what followed had a serious effect on me or I would have been hospitalised for months – if there were hospitals for ghosts.

The legs of the table and chairs didn't impede my progress across the floor, they merely rearranged my body before I was finally stopped – when I slammed against the wall. It took me a moment to recover, not physically but mentally. I stood, brushed off my clothes, although nothing had actually stuck to them, and tried to strike a nonchalant pose – more for my sake than anyone else's.

"Are they Hayley's?" Martin asked.

Richard nodded slowly and unfolded a note that had spilled from the envelope along with a set of keys. I leaned across the table and read over his shoulder.

No point in lugging these all the way to Sao Paulo, I might lose them somewhere. Love H xxx

"Where is Hayley?" Andrew asked.

Richard looked up but it was Martin who answered.

"Gone off on another teaching assignment, to Brazil this time."

"Oh wow, I did wonder where she was last night. How long is she away for?"

Martin looked to his father to answer.

"It depends how things work out Andrew. Anyway, time to get to school I think. Are you both ready?"

Richard pushed the note and the keys back into the padded envelope. The table was clear of breakfast things and Martin and Andrew both picked up rucksacks and headed towards the front door. Richard gave the envelope one last lingering look before he followed the boys. The door clacked shut behind them and I was alone once again. At least this time I was indoors.

Upstairs Claire's door was slightly ajar. I pushed through

but nothing had changed in there. Andrew's attic room was neat and tidy, the computer was turned off – there was nothing to see. Already I was missing Jeremy. In a way we were so close in age, or would have been if circumstances had been different. If I'd met him when I was seventeen we might even have dated. If we had, I could have been on that bike when it crashed – Richard and I would never have met, Martin and Claire wouldn't even exist. Life can be so short and hangs on many small decisions. Death was forever, but at least I didn't have to stay through every minute.

I went into the lounge and made myself as comfortable as I could on the sofa – it was about as comfortable as sitting on concrete. My first decision was how far I wanted to jump. The boys would be taking their exams in a few months and I thought it would be good to know the results, even if I couldn't help them with revision. Maybe saying it out loud would help prepare me and get me to the right spot in the future.

"So, Alison," I said to myself. "Feel your way forward four months. You can do it."

But before I could close my eyes a familiar voice came from the hall. "Meow."

I turned, certain that I'd recognised that particular meow correctly. Ronnie was standing just inside the door looking up at me.

"Meow," he cried again and jumped onto the arm of the sofa.

"Oh Ronnie, I thought you'd gone. I thought I'd missed saying goodbye to you."

Ronnie gingerly stretched one paw down towards my lap.

"It won't work Ronnie, you can't sit on me. You've tried before."

Ignoring my advice Ronnie placed a paw on my thigh, transferred his weight to it and then put another paw down.

195

He didn't sink through me this time.

It took me a second to realise what was different. I carefully placed a hand on the top of his head and felt the silky soft fur under my fingers. Ronnie's head lifted and I ran my hand down his back.

Now confident of his ground Ronnie stepped onto my lap, turned round twice and curled his body into a crescent, purring enthusiastically. I stroked him gently, feeling the warmth and softness of his fur, the gentle rise and fall of his body as he breathed, but I knew he was no more real than I was. Ronnie had died too. He was a ghost cat.

We stayed like that for a few minutes. I remained perfectly still, not wanting to disturb him. The warmth and comfort of another body close to mine was almost unbearable after so long in a bland unforgiving environment.

Ronnie looked up at me and blinked slowly. He faded and reappeared when he closed his eyes. Then he tucked his head under a paw and, just before he disappeared forever, he seemed to glow slightly. His ginger fur became brighter, almost glowing, and then he was gone.

I leaned back against the rock-hard cushions, back in my concrete world. Four months I thought and closed my eyes.

Chapter 19
Saturday 22nd June 2002 (five months later)

The room was completely different when I opened my eyes again. The sun glanced off a passing vehicle and cast a pattern of shimmering shapes on the wall above the fire. A sudden movement in the corner of my eye made me start, but it was only a curtain blowing gently in the breeze through an open window.

The front garden had been transformed into the colours of summer. Deep shadows cast by the fence at the side of the drive contrasted with the delicate pale green leaves on a silver birch. A bird feeder hung from a low branch and two sparrows were arguing, but sharing the seeds it contained. It was a perfect day, the kind that makes you glad to be awake when you draw the curtains back in the morning – only that was something I could no longer do.

The windows were wide open but something was missing – it was that uniquely suburban bouquet of freshly mown grass and warm tarmac. Sound and vision had been granted to me in my afterlife, but touch, smell and taste were absent - their lack turned everything into a three-dimensional movie where you could watch but your senses weren't all engaged. I heard a key turn in the front door and a thump as something hit the hall floor.

"The prodigal daughter has returned," Claire shouted joyously and waited a moment for a response. "Is anyone in? Is anyone going to welcome the weary traveller?"

She walked past the lounge door, looked up to the landing and then spotted that the back door was open. I could see all this without moving. When she disappeared from my field of

197

vision I was galvanised into action. I moved fast, too fast, I caught my leg on the coffee table, spun, fell, got up but managed to catch up with her in the kitchen.

"Are you all out in the garden?" Claire called even before she got to the back door.

She stood framed against the light, one hand shielding her eyes from the bright sunshine. Claire was dressed in washed-out pale blue jeans and dirty pink trainers. Her cream cotton blouse was creased and crumpled and looked as though she had slept in it.

Careful not to get too close I looked past her and saw Andrew and Martin in the hot tub. I could hear the bubbles and the drone of the air pump, which I assumed was why the boys couldn't hear Claire calling them. They gave no indication that they had seen her either. She strode towards them and at the same time called loudly.

"Martin you lazy toad – aren't you even going to say hello to your long-lost brilliant sister?"

Both boys jumped as though they had been caught out, but were probably just surprised. I checked the calendar before following Claire into the garden. It was the twenty-second of June. I screwed up my face trying to remember when mid-summer's day would fall – I knew it was some-where around then, so had I missed my date with Jeremy? Following Claire across the lawn I propped myself on the arm of the bench – close enough to listen, not so close as to get in anyone's way.

"I didn't hear you come in sis. I thought you were supposed to ring us from the station?"

"And you'd have heard the phone?"

"Well you're not supposed to be back until later, but..."

Martin pointed to the cordless phone on a small folding table next to the hot tub.

"You don't drive."

"Dad left money for a taxi for you."

"Well, I got a lift."

Claire dipped her fingers into the water.

"Gosh that feels nice and warm."

"Plenty of room for one more," Andrew offered.

"I need a quick shower to lose the travel dust but I would love to, thank you Andrew, it's nice that there's one gentleman here."

"So how was your first year?" Martin asked. "Lots of parties I guess?"

"No idea what you're talking about," Claire responded in a playful tone.

She spun on her heels and ambled back towards the kitchen, but stopped suddenly.

"Where is Dad anyway?"

"Picking up Hayley," Martin raised his eyebrows.

The gesture meant something to Claire, but was lost on me. All three of them fell silent.

"What?" I demanded. "What's happened? Somebody say something, don't just look at each other like that."

"I thought he was picking her up yesterday." Claire said.

"He stayed over."

"Meaning?"

"They didn't finish with the agent until late afternoon and thought it easier to drive back today."

"What agent? Somebody give me a clue, please?" I begged.

"Is she selling or letting it out?" Claire asked.

"Letting."

"Hmm, okay, I'll go take that shower. See you in a minute or two."

I followed Claire. It would have felt like I was intruding on the boys if I'd stayed watching them – not to mention embarrassing if they were now a couple and I witnessed something not intended for public display.

"What is she letting Claire? Hayley doesn't have a house, what on earth are you all talking about?"

Claire lugged her rucksack up the stairs and practically threw it on the end of her bed. She looked around, a hint of a smile playing about her mouth.

"Hello Room," she said as though she were greeting an old friend.

Dropping onto her knees she reached under the bed and pulled out the ancient chocolate box. The ribbon on the lid had come adrift, the corners had suffered over the years, but the box still opened with a satisfying sigh. She took out the top letter and opened it up.

I couldn't bear to read it with her. The letters were part of her story, not mine. I leaned against the wall and watched her brush a few loose strands of hair back from her cheek and tuck them behind her ear. She let out a small laugh at one point.

The letter still in her hands, Claire flopped back on her bed beside her rucksack.

"Why aren't you here Mum? I miss you so much."

"I am here. I'll always be here – as long as you want me to be."

It was a rash promise. I had no idea how long I'd be there, no idea what my future held. According to Jeremy I was waiting for someone or something. At that point all I wanted to do was close my eyes again and jump as far as I could into the future. I was unconnected with them all – but I also wanted to stay. I could give nobody any comfort, any help, any advice, but I wanted to be with my family, if only for a few days. I sunk down the wall until I was sitting on the floor, my knees tucked under my chin.

Claire roused herself, replaced the letter in its box and swept out of her room and towards the bathroom. I listened

200

to her singing in the shower. Neither university nor time had improved her ability to hold a tune.

Returning with just a towel wrapped round her Claire rummaged through drawers until she found a bikini. The towel dropped and I watched my daughter, now a woman, wriggle into it. The tiny scraps of material joined with thin straps made me long for my own youth. I shuddered and thought of something else, I didn't want to find myself competing with my daughter as to who could wear the smallest bathing costume. She picked up the towel and swept out of the room. I took some time before I followed, my heart heavy with only being able to watch and not being a part of their lives. All three were laughing when I finally made my way out into the garden again.

"I'm going to miss all of your family," Andrew announced when the laughter subsided. "Even Lydia."

"What do you mean?" Claire asked, puzzled. "We're not going anywhere."

"But Andrew is," Martin added quietly.

"My mum has sold our house, we're moving nearer to my aunt."

"What about school?"

"There's a local sixth form college. It's not bad according to my cousins."

"I didn't know you'd be moving away," Claire sounded puzzled. "Are you okay about it? I mean you could stay on here couldn't you?"

"Nice idea, but it wouldn't be right. I need to be with my mum, she's been brilliant about... well, everything. Anyway, we're not moving until the end of August so plenty of time to get fed up with me before then."

"So, genius sister of mine," Martin asked, turning the conversation to Claire. "How was your first year – sum it up for us in four words."

"Well..."

Claire looked up into the cloudless blue sky for inspiration. I leaned forward, not wanting to miss her answer.

"Just four words?" she confirmed.

"That's three of them," Andrew joked.

She splashed him with water and Andrew pretended to be drowning.

"Okay then. Engrossing; fun; stressful; inspiring. How's that?"

"Sounds cool," Andrew said.

"What or who was inspiring?" Martin asked.

Had he picked up on something in Claire's voice? I too had noticed a change of emphasis on that last word.

Claire giggled. "Mind your own business."

"Come on Sis you can't leave us hanging like that."

"Well, I think I know what I want to do when I graduate."

"Already? My bet is journalism," Andrew guessed.

"Nope."

"Surely not a teacher," whined Martin.

They took turns and Claire enjoyed putting down each guess, laughing at some ideas, faking offence at others.

"An author," I whispered.

"You're going to be a famous author," Martin followed my suggestion.

"I don't think I have stories inside me."

"Poet?" Andrew frowned.

Like me he sounded unconvinced that you could make a living from poetry.

"One of the lecturers gave me an old paperback of his called 'Understanding Media'. I want to adapt novels for television and film. A script editor, a screenwriter, that sort of thing."

"Didn't see that coming," Martin said.

"I don't get it," Andrew frowned. "That's not really a career is it?"

"Well you have the story and the characters ready formed, but you have to make them come alive in a different way – it's a fascinating area. Terry has worked on several television programmes."

"Terry?" I queried the use of a first name only.

"Terry?" Martin echoed. Had I prompted him?

"He takes the module on creative writing. Everyone calls him Terry, don't go reading any sub-text that's not there."

Andrew interrupted any further analysis of Terry when he saw Hayley and Richard emerging from the kitchen door.

"Hayley. Hello."

Claire, Martin and I turned in unison. Richard was close behind Hayley. She looked older, maybe it was just jet lag, and she was dressed in a very un-Hayley-like formal trouser suit.

Claire had climbed out of the tub, her towel wrapped round her again. She met Hayley half way across the lawn and threw her arms around her.

"I'm so sorry I wasn't here Hayley, it was right at the start of my prelims, I wish I could have been with you."

"That's okay," she patted Claire's back. "I know you would have been there if you could. Anyway, look, you're making me all wet you silly girl."

Obviously something serious had happened but I had no idea what it might have been. Richard put an arm round Hayley. Claire moved back but took both Hayley's hands in hers.

"Can you stay for the whole of the summer? Please?"

"I'd love to, but I only have another week. I have to go back. They had to rearrange all my classes to let me have this time off."

"I still can't believe it," Claire said, her lips pressed together.

"I know. But mum was never the same after dad died. She didn't want to be here without him."

"Oh my god," I gasped.

Hayley's parents had practically adopted me after my father had died and my mother started playing the femme fatale. They hadn't actually adopted me, but they were there for me more than my own mother had been. And now they were both dead and I hadn't even known they were ill.

"Right," Hayley said. "Lots of stuff must have happened since I last saw you all."

"Exams mostly," Andrew groaned.

"Is Brazil as exciting as it sounds?" Martin asked. "It must be pretty amazing."

"You do know I'm working while I'm there. There's not been much time for sightseeing or exploring the jungle. Anyway, I need a shower and a bit of a rest, it feels like I haven't stopped for days. I think I'll leave you lot to your hot tub and catch up later."

It was the first time that Hayley's age had shown. In my head I was still thirty-six, but she would now be approaching fifty. We had grown apart, or I suppose Hayley had simply grown a little older and maybe a little wiser.

I felt out of place with my children, one adult among a group of teenagers, and I didn't want to follow Richard and Hayley who had retreated upstairs – to rest I presume, whatever that meant. There was going to be another Chinese meal tonight, or a pizza or Indian. Whatever it was I didn't want to watch, an outsider at a party again. But I wasn't planning to get shut out of the house, so I made my way into the lounge. My natural inclination was to choose the sofa or one of the armchairs, but what would happen if I came back and somebody else was sitting in it? Comfort was irrelevant as everything felt the same to me. I stood in the corner of the room, next to a lamp stand. It was late afternoon, twelve hours and a bit was what I needed to skip. I closed my eyes, thought what a count of twelve felt like and added a couple of beats.

Sunday 23rd June 2002

It was daylight, which was promising. It was also quiet, both in the house and, as far as I could hear, outside too – so it probably was Sunday. Under the television there was a new black box that I hadn't noticed before. It had a digital clock, which read 11:15 in blue glowing figures. I had overshot a little – I should have counted. The windows were closed.

I peeked out of the lounge door rather than marching straight out and triggering an unwanted collision. The hall and the kitchen were both empty, the back door closed. Upstairs was equally quiet. Richard's room offered no clues as to where everyone was. The doors to the other two bedrooms and the attic room were all closed.

"Bugger-dam-bastard-shit," I muttered under my breath when I had to accept that I was trapped and alone.

There was nothing to do but wait or make small jumps forward in time until they returned. For some reason I trusted the kitchen clock far more than that clinical digital display under the television. Before doing anything drastic I decided to check the calendar. Thankfully the habit of striking through each day was still in practice. There was small type in the space for the next day – midsummer's day – perfect. I climbed onto the empty kitchen table and sat dead centre, cross-legged, facing the clock. The time was just after half past eleven. I closed my eyes and counted to two. Twenty-two minutes past one – pretty good – but I didn't know where they had gone or when they might be back.

I jumped another hour, no change. My third jump took me to just before six and I opened my eyes to find myself surrounded by mugs, bags, a crumpled beach towel and a voluminous shoulder bag – Hayley's I guessed. The back door was open and there was laughter coming from the garden.

Forgetting that I didn't have any physical impact, I picked my way carefully off the table, stumbling at the last moment and swearing – only to realise belatedly that everything had stayed exactly where it was.

The washing line had towels and swimming costumes arranged neatly – Claire's work I suspected, Hayley would have been more haphazard. The hot tub wasn't in use so I perched on the lid and studied my family and the two additions.

Richard looked relaxed, wearing a polo shirt and long shorts and slumped in a canvas director's chair. Sunglasses, a panama hat, a bottle of beer hanging loosely from the finger and thumb of one hand gave him an air of insouciance. He looked older, but happy, which made me smile too.

Hayley was reclining on a steamer chair, a half filled glass of wine in her hand. The canvas seat covers matched the deep green of Richard's chair – the two seats must have been bought as a set. Her figure still looked amazing until I compared her to Claire who was face down on a towel on the lawn. Claire's arms were above her head and her lithe body still had that easy look of youth that no amount of diet and exercise could replicate. The boys were on each end of the bench, separated by a chessboard, which they were both studying.

My family were okay. They were surviving and flourishing without me. I hoped they still missed me, Claire had said as much in her bedroom, and that they all thought and talked about me from time to time.

Tomorrow was midsummer's day and I had a date with Jeremy. I relaxed and let my eyes close, feeling my way through to the next day.

Chapter 20
Monday 24th June 2002

The director's chair had been moved next to the bench, the steamer chair lay on its side, the back door was closed, the washing line was empty and I was alone in the garden. The sun was above the line of the houses behind us, the shadow from the buddleia crisp on the sparse, dried grass of the lawn. A sudden movement to one side made me start, but it was only a blackbird that had joined me on the cover of the hot tub. Head cocked to one side, he looked up as though waiting for an answer to a question that he had posed simply by being there.

"Billy?"

He looked away, looked back at me and his beak opened and closed a couple of times, but he made no sound.

"It is you isn't it? My goodness how old are you now?"

Billy didn't answer, but I was convinced that it was my old friend. I held a finger out to him and Billy looked up at me again. Maybe blackbirds were brighter than cats because he didn't attempt to make any contact with me, either by hopping onto my finger or pecking me.

"You've got more sense than Ronnie had."

In a sudden flurry of his wings, and leaving a feather behind, Billy flew across the garden and down by the side of the house. I was surprised at what I was wearing – high-waisted flared jeans and a long sleeved baggy shirt. I recognised the period I'd reverted to immediately. When I was seventeen years old I had been desperately trying to channel my inner Carly Simon. I played her music endlessly, dressed like her and, in my wildest dreams, I imagined myself to be her English half sister – the love child of a brief affair my mother might have had with Carly's father. Reaching up with one hand I touched my hair, it was long again, not as long as I'd wanted it to be at the time, but the longest I'd ever grown it. I lifted my feet expecting to see clumpy-heeled, bar shoes, but I was barefoot. Once again I found myself changed into an earlier, and slightly embarrassing version of myself.

Sliding off the hot tub I followed Billy's route down the side of the house to the front garden. Jeremy was waiting for me there, sitting on the low wall at the side of the drive. Billy was next to him. They were both looking at me and I felt the blood rush to my cheeks in a sudden flush.

"I thought you might have forgotten," he said, making no pretence about the way he scrutinised me.

As much as I was flattered by Jeremy's appraisal, the situation was ridiculous. Apart from us both being ghosts, I had made a date to chat with Jeremy, not a boy-meets-girl type date, not a how-can-I-impress-him date. I thought about trying to change my appearance, maybe I could think myself into a different outfit from a different period of my life, but that might have looked a bit rude. I decided to bluff it out.

I sat next to him, partly to be sociable, partly so that he wasn't looking directly at me.

"Can you control the way you look?" I asked while looking at my feet stuck out in front of me.

I had deep red varnish on my toenails and my little toe hadn't yet bent under its neighbour.

Jeremy was in the shorts and baggy shirt that he'd been wearing when I met him in the middle of winter – a choice that was now more appropriate in the summer.

"Yes, pretty much – you just think about it. But it doesn't make much difference does it? It's not like we're real."

"I feel real."

"I meant to everyone else."

I let my feet fall back down, not wanting Jeremy to study my feet, nor any other part of me. We needed a more serious topic than clothes to distract us both from the awkwardness of my apparently flirtatious appearance.

"Why do you think we're here? Sorry, I hope you don't mind me pitching straight into this stuff? It's just that you've been around a bit longer than me – as a ghost I mean."

"Ask away, but I don't have all the answers."

"You said before that you thought we were waiting for something or someone."

"That's just a theory I knocked up."

"Ronnie waited for me I think."

"Who's Ronnie? An old boyfriend?"

"The family cat," I laughed. "But he only arrived after I'd left so I never knew him properly, not when I was alive."

"It weird that some animals can see us, or sense us. I haven't worked that one out yet. Maybe they're just more open to using all their senses. There's a dog that barks every time I walk past him, but he never looks directly at me so I'm not sure if it's me he's barking at."

"None of it makes sense to me, even the fact that we're here and the time jumping whenever I close my eyes. You get that too don't you?"

"Yes, but I can't jump past August the seventeenth. Whatever I do, however much I count, I always open my eyes on the morning of that day."

"Why? Is it the day you... you know?"

"The day I died?"

I nodded, not able to look directly at him. Asking someone about their death is not something you get experience of when you're alive. It felt rude to keep reminding Jeremy that he was dead by asking him about it.

"Possibly. It would have been about then – and it happens like that every bloody year."

"I jumped almost ten years in one go."

"Wow, that must have been kind of weird?"

"It's all weird isn't it?"

"So what happened with Ronnie?"

"He jumped on my lap, hung around for a bit and then closed his eyes and sort of slowly disappeared."

Jeremy nodded as though it made sense to him.

"I got to stroke him though and he felt real."

A light breeze rippled through the trees lining the street and a discarded crisp packet fluttered towards us.

"Quick, lift your feet up," Jeremy exclaimed.

I reacted instantly and the crisp packet blew under our feet and came to rest against a dustbin.

"They don't hurt," he said. "But it's disarming when a shitty piece of litter tries to cut your leg in half."

We both relaxed, but I kept one eye on the crisp packet to make sure it wasn't going to attack us again.

"Do you think people can hear us sometimes?" I asked, still puzzled by the possibility and hoping he might confirm what I thought I'd experienced.

"My brother can – sometimes."

We sat in silence again for a few minutes. An unfamiliar cat prowled up our drive, stopped, looked at us, sat on its haunches and turned its head away from us.

"Not one of yours?" Jeremy asked.

"No."

He nodded as though this was significant, but I guessed he was just mulling something over in his head.

"I wish I could jump ten years, twenty years even."

"You don't like to keep coming back every year?"

"I want to get to the end, whatever the end is."

"You think there is an end then?"

"You up for another one of my crackpot theories?"

"Go on, I'm all ears."

I turned sideways so that I could see him better as he spoke.

"Okay, bizarre theory number two," he cleared his throat. "There are no ghosts that I've ever seen that go back more than sixty or seventy years."

"We're in the suburbs," I suggested. "Not many of these houses go back much further than that."

"The school does, some of the big old houses do. There would have been farms before that and cottages too."

"So, your theory?"

"We only stay around as long as there's somebody who remembers us, knows who we were as people, not just details about us written down in documents – or photos in a half forgotten album."

"Or on computers," I added.

"Do you understand computers?"

I only had to think for a moment before answering. "Not really."

"If there's nobody left to remember the real us, the living, laughing, swearing, farting us, then we disappear."

"Ronnie disappeared, and my children must remember him better than I do."

Jeremy's head dropped, he stuck his legs out straight in front of him and sort of sprung off the wall. He turned to face me and I was relieved to see he was grinning.

"I've been developing that theory for over thirty years and you and your cat have just blown it out of the water."

I laughed too. It was so silly talking about our existence like this. The relief of laughing was infectious and it quickly spiralled out of control. Jeremy doubled up holding his tummy and eventually had to sit on the brick pavers of our drive. I curled up where I was sitting. My ribs, which I wasn't sure I really had, hurt from laughing so much.

"Stop it," I gasped when I could catch my breath.

"It's your fault," he replied and started giggling again.

There were tears running from my eyes, I couldn't catch my breath properly. I tried not to look at Jeremy, but every time our eyes met it set us off again. It took a while before both of us managed to gain control again and at that point the postman came whistling down the street again.

"I bet Elwin remembers you," I said and couldn't stop a grin spreading over my face. "Maybe you're waiting for him."

"Oh fuck, I hope not," Jeremy laughed and frowned at the same time.

We watched Elwin sort through his bag, amble happily up to the front door, push the letters through the box and almost do a little dance as he came down the two steps and sauntered out of the drive.

"Would you really jump to the end – whatever it is?" I asked.

Jeremy pressed his lips together and then let a deep breath escape slowly.

"Yes, I think I would."

"What about all the things you might want to see, things that happen with your family on the way?"

"I don't think you can avoid them."

"What do you mean?"

"I think we come back when we're needed, summoned, however you want to describe it."

"That would mean my family didn't need me for almost ten years."

"Your husband must have done a good job. What happened when you did come back?"

I thought about it, all the stuff with my mother, with Anthony, with Martin coming out and Claire going to university. I didn't know what calamities and celebrations I had missed, but Jeremy could actually have a point – if there was any point to this strange existence.

"You don't think we can jump past a disaster or something momentous then?"

"I can't prove it, but as you know, my theories are always totally foolproof."

He was grinning at me when he said that. I smiled too and pushed myself off the wall.

"So, according to your theory, no matter how long I close my eyes for I will return when there's a crisis or something I shouldn't miss?"

"That's my theory, but don't quote me on it when we next meet."

"Do you think we will meet again?"

"I don't know – maybe. I'll wander past every August the seventeenth. But we don't have much in common, do we? I'm eighteen and you're an old woman of thirty-six?"

"You bastard," I muttered playfully. "And might I remind you that I was actually younger than you at one time."

"True, so maybe we do have something in common. I'll keep an eye out for you when I pass by."

"August the seventeenth?"

"Yes."

"Around midday?"

"Every year."

Jeremy had stood up by then, he was brushing off his shorts even though nothing had stuck to them. He was looking at me with a faint but friendly smile.

"It was nice meeting you again Alison."

"And you Jeremy."

He casually half waved with one hand and wandered down the drive, whistling softly.

"Don't let Elwin hear you," I called after him.

He raised a hand again without looking back. I watched until he crossed the road, turned a corner and walked out of my sight, perhaps forever.

According to Jeremy's theory I could close my eyes without fear of missing anything important, but it was a risk – I couldn't go back if he was wrong.

I lifted my legs up and stared at my feet. What did I have to lose? As a precaution, to keep myself out of harm's way I brought my legs up and wrapped my arms around them. The grass on the front lawn needed cutting – I would never have let it get that long. Looking up into the sky I focused on a single picture book cloud, isolated in a clear blue sky. I closed my eyes and wondered when I would open them again.

Chapter 21
Monday 24th July 2006

When I came back to life it was cloudy, not the heavy looming grey of winter, but high, translucent clouds that held a promise to burn clear during the day. The grass had been recently cut and was still a rich hopeful green. As I sat there looking for changes in the garden, an unfamiliar car turned into the drive. Richard was driving and Hayley was occupying the front passenger seat.

His hair had receded at the temples and the odd fleck of grey at the sides had whitened and spread. He had acquired the look of a distinguished professor rather than a middle school English teacher. Hayley had changed too, but carried her age with style. Her once tumbling hair was cropped short and looked like she had been caught in a strong wind. It swept in several different directions, flicking out at the ends as though repelled by some unseen force. The style suited her.

It was obvious that I had moved some years into the future of my family's life. Richard looked like he might be in his late fifties. Hayley's age would have been harder to determine had I not known she was only four years younger than Richard. She had a gentle even suntan that in no way resembled the fierce colour gained from a two-week holiday in the sun. A startling red shirt, open at the neck, revealed a delicate gold double chain. There was an exotic air to her and I presumed that she was still working in Brazil and had integrated into the local culture.

I pushed off the wall and landed slightly off balance, grasped the side of the car and steadied myself. Looking down I saw that I was wearing a pair of high-heeled sandals, that had usually been reserved for special occasions, and a black dress that was more suited to an evening out than a sunny morning in a garden. Staring at my dress and frowning intensely, I willed it to change into something more casual and suitable for the occasion. My trusty cord jeans slowly materialised along with an old gardening jumper that had holes in it and the odd splash of paint. The inappropriate high heels morphed into a pair of trainers.

"That's better," I mumbled, slightly disappointed that I couldn't have struck a more balanced look.

Following them after they got out of the car, I managed to slip through the door when Richard opened it and stood to one side for Hayley to pass.

Not very much had changed in the hall except for one wall, which was covered with stridently patterned paper.

"I'll get your bags," Richard said, still hovering on the doorstep.

"I'll put the kettle on. Do you want tea or coffee?"

"Tea please, I've given up coffee."

Hayley would have known that if she had been living at home – my home. That lack of knowledge suggested she had only just returned from Brazil. Claire emerged from the kitchen, holding an oven glove.

"Hayley, how are you?"

Claire looked so much older, not old, but she had an air of confidence, a difference in the way she moved. When she hugged Hayley she appeared to be looking directly at me.

"Claire?" I whispered. "Can you see me?"

"You must need a coffee after your journey?" she said, moving back a couple of feet. "And I love your hair."

I was in her line of sight, but she hadn't seen or heard me. I followed the two of them into the kitchen, not listening to their conversation. The calendar was still in its usual position, or at least its replacement was. I had landed in July 2006. That's what it felt like in my head, as though I had been on a flight, just like Hayley, except that I always landed in the same place I had taken off from. A little over four years had passed this time.

The wall clock had been replaced as well as the calendar. The new one looked old, as though it had been salvaged from a railway station, but it had a second hand, sweeping steadily round the dial. It was almost noon.

According to Jeremy I would have returned now because something was going to happen, or had happened already. Four years. I wondered how many of those skipped midsummer days Jeremy had loitered at the end of our drive, waiting to see if I would turn up. Would he have been disappointed that I wasn't there or envious?

"How was your flight Hayley?" Claire asked as she filled the kettle. "Only instant coffee I'm afraid."

"Oh, instant's fine. We were packaged like sardines, except no sardine ever got as fat as the woman sat next to me. She should have been charged double."

"Just as well it was only a short hop."

"An hour and a half sat next to a blancmange dressed in pink linen was quite long enough thank you."

Hayley couldn't still be working in Brazil if her flight was that short. Maybe Paris or somewhere in Europe? Her return couldn't be why I was here, she must have been back occasionally during the last four years. She sipped her coffee and looked at Claire over the rim of the mug.

"So, Richard told me you have a new job. How's it going?"

"Well, not so much a new job as an extra set of responsibilities. With all the cutbacks I'm lucky to still have a job at all."

"But you're enjoying it?"

"Not quite what I had in mind when I graduated."

"I did warn you that some people are not impressed by a First. I've heard it said so many times, 'academically accomplished but not suited to the real world'. Probably jealousy if you ask me."

"You got a First?" I spluttered happily. "Why couldn't I have come back for your graduation? So much for your theories Jeremy."

"I think they know by now that I can do the job – they did keep me on after all. But it's publicity, not what I planned to do."

Richard's feet drummed on the stairs. He must have taken Hayley's bags up to his room, or their room. I had no idea what domestic situation I had returned to. He breezed into the kitchen and kissed Claire on her cheek.

"Sorry I left you with lunch."

"No problem."

"What time did Martin go to pick up Dad and Lydia?"

Claire turned to look at the clock.

"Almost half an hour ago – he should be back any minute."

"I'm still not sure about Martin and that car," Richard sighed.

"He's fine," Claire laughed. "You worry too much Dad. Do you think Grandpa would have given it to us if he didn't think we'd be safe?"

Richard sighed again and I wondered what sort of car his father had donated to my family. I didn't have to wait long – the familiar purr and final rev of Anthony's Jaguar answered my question.

"Sounds like they're here Dad. See, nothing to worry about."

"He only gave it to ¬you two because he couldn't face selling it."

Hayley had been stealing carrots from a saucepan where they were waiting to be boiled – fishing them out and crunching them loudly.

"It must cost a fortune to insure?"

"It's in my name," Claire answered. "Martin is only a named driver and Grandpa pays for it anyway – as long as we act as his personal chauffeurs when we're around."

"Has something happened? Why can't he drive himself?"

After four years away, or in limbo, or wherever I had been, there was a lot to catch up on. If Jeremy's theory was right then none of it should be too dramatic, but it was like watching a television series where you'd missed an episode and nobody offered to get you up to date.

"How bad is Anthony's sight?"

"Thank you Hayley – at least somebody is listening to me. But what is wrong with his sight? Is it serious?"

Richard raised his eyebrows and puffed out a breath as though ready to offer a dismal prediction.

"It's not that bad," Claire said. "It's more about Lydia being such a nervous passenger – but I didn't tell you that and I'll deny it if you quote me."

Hayley laughed. "Okay, I will be tact personified."

"Since when?" Richard asked.

"How's Martin's course going? I haven't seen him since Christmas."

"Ask him yourself." Claire nodded towards the door where Anthony and Lydia had appeared. Martin was peering over Lydia. Had he grown that much taller or had my mother shrunk? Or maybe it was a little of both.

Anthony was sporting dark glasses. The sun was out of course and it was certainly bright outside, but dark glasses indoors? That wasn't Anthony's style and I wondered if his sight was more problematic than had been suggested.

"Hayley. How nice to see you again my dear girl."

Anthony's enthusiasm hadn't diminished. "You've stayed away far too long. We need to see more of you – and I'm sure my crotchety son does too."

Hayley gave him a hug and then held his shoulders at arms length and looked straight at him. "Why the dark glasses Anthony? Are we avoiding the paparazzi?"

Anthony laughed and took off his glasses to reveal a large purple-brown bruise under his left eye.

"Merely a little argument with a branch in the garden. It will teach me to watch where I'm going in the future."

"He couldn't see it when he was mowing the lawn," Lydia grumbled. "I've told him time and time again that we can get someone in to do menial tasks, but will he listen to me?"

"Nice to see you back to normal Mother. I wondered how long it would take."

Anthony ignored Lydia's comment and turned to Richard.

"It was just an accident, could have happened to anyone. Anyway, Martin has been telling us all about his course Richard. It sounds like he's doing splendidly."

Nobody had mentioned what course my son was taking. The last time I saw him he had been at school. Now he was a man, an inch or so shorter than Richard and his almost black hair fell to his shoulders in soft waves. I could see my mother in him and hoped that the resemblance was only physical.

The room was crowded. Six bodies and a ghost took up a lot of space in that kitchen-diner. I retreated to the wine rack, happy to find it still in place, although it was somewhat depleted. A quick adding up of the timescale on my fingers, confirmed that Martin was most likely taking a university degree course somewhere and, if so, he should be approaching his final year. What it might be was still a mystery.

"Ah, Martin," Anthony suddenly exclaimed. "The wine,

we've left it in the boot of the car."

"Okay Grandpa I'll get it."

Hayley had found two bottles of champagne in the fridge and handed one to Richard. "I think a gathering like this deserves a celebration, don't you?"

Martin returned with a box that probably held a dozen bottles of wine judging from the way he was carrying it. Richard popped the champagne cork and it bounced off the ceiling and through my thigh.

"Hey, watch out. That could have hurt."

It didn't hurt, not physically, but it was still disturbing when your body had a hole punched through it – even if it did self-repair.

Martin set the box in front of me and opened the top. My assumption had been correct. He started to transfer the bottles to the rack, ensuring that every label was facing upwards. Only when he had filled the lower spaces did I have to hop from one foot to another, anticipating where the next bottle would go on the top row.

"So, what are you studying?" I asked. "Can't you give me a clue somehow?"

He didn't answer, but Hayley handed him a glass of the fizzy white wine. "So what do you actually do in your third year Martin?"

"At last, the right question." Hayley had come to my rescue again.

"The most important module will be a dissertation. I've already narrowed it down to two possibilities."

"Will I understand them?" Anthony asked.

"Neither of them are complicated Grandpa, but I need to find a fresh approach so I might look at existing cohort studies and see how they correspond to individual cases."

"You've lost me," Lydia said shaking her head.

"I'm thinking of looking at either the effects of exercise on depression, or whether exercise can reduce the number of falls among the elderly."

"I confess I know nothing about physiotherapy," Hayley admitted. "And fortunately I've never needed to call on the services of an expert."

"I'll take care of you when you do need one Auntie."

"Cheeky sod – but I might take you up on that offer when I'm old and wobbly."

"Or depressed," Lydia added, emptying her glass.

Richard proffered the bottle in Lydia's direction.

"Would you like a refill Lydia?"

"I'll wait until lunch thank you. One of us has to remain upright, without the assistance of a physiotherapist."

Anthony had already taken a second glass and my mother cast a disparaging look in his direction. I wondered if the gloss had worn off their relationship and that was why I was here – to witness my mother destroy yet another episode in her life.

Anthony retired to the lounge, ostensibly to study the crossword in his newspaper. Richard and Martin followed to help him, leaving three women in charge of the kitchen – or four if you counted me. There was a detectable frostiness in Lydia's voice when she confronted Hayley. She didn't even look up at her, but pretended to search for something in her handbag – it was a technique with which I was familiar.

"How long are you here for this time Hayley?"

"I have to be back in early September, I can stay until then."

"Convenient having somewhere for a holiday isn't it?"

Claire stepped in as peacemaker, asking Lydia about the situation with Anthony's vision and whether the hospital had mentioned an underlying cause.

"He tries to pretend it's nothing," Lydia sighed. "I worry that he's not telling me the truth. It has become a bit of a contentious issue between us."

My mother took a paper handkerchief from her handbag and an old fashioned compact. She held the mirror up and wiped under the corner of her eye, harrumphed, and replaced both items. It had been a tear she wiped away. She had angled her head so that neither Claire nor Hayley could see, but she had faced me directly.

No matter how much trouble my mother had caused me when I was growing up, or how self-centred she had been all my adult life, I felt my heart soften towards her. She had revealed herself to be very worried about Anthony, maybe genuinely in love, but at the least deeply caring about him – possibly the only man she had cared for since my father died.

Wine was poured, everyone took their places for dinner and conversation rebounded from one minor subject to another until the meal was finished. Anthony and my mother were off to Paris for the first time since she had sold her apartment and Richard was joining an allotment group, located close to the park. Claire started to clear the table of empty dishes and plates when she announced, almost as an aside, that she had been invited to be part of a house share.

"Why?" Lydia asked sharply. "I imagine there is a man involved in this plan?"

"There are two men involved if you must know Grand-mere, but Janet from the office is the fourth person and, before you jump to conclusions, no we're not two couples."

Richard said nothing and gave no indication that any of this was news to him. My mother sat a little more upright in her seat, if that was possible, and dabbed at her mouth with a serviette.

"Sounds like fun," Hayley suggested, breaking the ensuing silence. "Closer to work I presume?"

"I could walk or cycle on a nice day – or take a bus if it's raining."

"Richard?" My mother's imperious tone had returned in full strength. "Have you given your blessing to this arrangement?"

"It's fine Lydia, maybe the time is overdue for Claire to fly the nest. She is twenty-four. If you think about it she's the same age as Alison was when we married."

Hayley picked up a bowl and delivered it to the dishwasher, turning away from the table at the mention of my name.

My mother grunted and I looked at Claire from a fresh perspective – she still looked so young to me. My own mother had prepared me for independence by abandoning me from an early age. I had effectively departed from my family life soon after my father died. Marriage had been a settling influence on me. I had been ready. I suppose I had deserted Claire too, by dying when she was at such a tender age, but it hadn't been by choice.

Richard chuckled. "And I will get to have the house to myself when you noisy brats finally clear out."

"I hope that doesn't include me?" Hayley said, still leaning against the work surface, away from the table. "I have to go back to Ireland Richard, I've signed a contract for another year. I wish you'd told me before that you'd be alone."

"I didn't know myself until the other day and of course I won't be quite alone. Angel is still here somewhere – unless you're planning on taking her with you Claire?"

"That vicious little tyke? No way."

I wondered if that was why I had returned at that juncture. If Jeremy was right I might be here to keep Richard company. Not that I was much company to anyone. I had slumped down onto my haunches on top of the wine rack and was taken by surprise when Richard turned in his chair and pulled out another bottle of wine.

Whether it was red or white was lost on me, as was the rest of that afternoon. A backward half somersault, an inelegant landing on my head and the sudden appearance of Angel under the kitchen table caused me to curl up in a defensive ball and close my eyes. I had always prized my ability as a fast learner, but this was definitely a blind spot on my learning curve – quite literally a blind spot until I opened my eyes again.

Chapter 22
Monday 11th September 2006

The kitchen was quiet when I returned. There were no legs or feet under the table and no Angel thank goodness. I could hear a murmur of unfamiliar voices from somewhere and for a moment I was worried that I'd jumped so far forward that Richard had moved and I was in a house full of strangers.

I took a deep breath and assessed what I could see. The table legs looked the same as before, there was a water bowl and a food bowl on a plastic mat, one that I recognised. If Richard had sold the house it would be stretching coincidence for the new owners to have a cat and the same bowls and mat.

Uncurling from my foetal position, I pushed off the floor and then used the edge of the table to drag myself upright. The kitchen was cleared of all signs of a meal, essentially unchanged, but tidy, Richard's sort of tidy.

The clock showed ten past ten. It was dark outside. The calendar was ticked off up to, but not including, September the eleventh. I gave a silent prayer that Richard had maintained the same system of striking a diagonal line through the previous day before he ate breakfast. It shouldn't have been a surprise as Richard had always been a creature of habit, not fanatical, not obsessive but definitely not one for changing a system that worked.

Tomorrow would be Richard's birthday, his fifty-fifth birthday. Maybe that was why I was here, why I opened my eyes on this day.

My clothes were still the same, those red cord jeans and

the jumper with unidentifiable stains and random holes. It wouldn't do. I needed to take control of what I was wearing, even though nobody but Jeremy ever saw or commented on my appearance.

The jumper had been one of those chance purchases that had become a favourite. With a little concentration the holes repaired, the stains faded and it became less baggy and disheveled. Why couldn't I have done that with my clothes when I was alive? As good as it looked, it was still a jumper and seemed to hold the memories of the blemishes even though I couldn't see them any longer.

What had been my favourite outfits? From sixteen to thirty-six my style had changed, but then so had my body. Although I was fairly sure my body would change to accommodate whatever outfit I chose, it felt wrong to go back too far. Meeting Jeremy in something resembling my teenage self had been embarrassing and uncomfortable - I hadn't known Richard back then so it would be wrong and strange to repeat that error.

I smiled and laughed to myself. There was one outfit that would be perfect for Richard's birthday. The February before I died we had celebrated my thirty-sixth birthday. Richard and I had booked our favourite restaurant and I wore an outfit that I had bought the previous weekend at Richard's prompting. It had been a rare extravagance at the time.

As I stood in the kitchen I pictured myself back then, checking my appearance in the hall mirror before we had left, giving our babysitter last minute instructions, or rather repeating instructions I'd given her ten minutes earlier.

Looking down I saw a calf-length dark blue skirt materialize, the one I'd been wearing that night. It was cut on the cross from heavy cotton and had angled pockets that could at best hold a single tissue. It was coupled with a brown belt, more decorative than functional, and a flannel shirt of pale blue and soft green stripes. My feet were once again in a pair of dark brown cowboy boots with a stitched pattern in tan thread - an outrageous, spur-of-the-moment purchase. Seeing them again made me feel young and mercurial, not that I'd had the opportunity to grow old.

I wanted to see myself in a mirror and repeat the final check I had made before our last romantic dinner together, but I knew that I cast no reflection. Ready to see Richard, I walked towards the lounge – disappointed that my heels didn't make those distinctive clicks on the floor that had drawn glances in the restaurant.

Richard was asleep on the sofa, the television wittering away about some local news item - they were the voices I had heard from the kitchen. All that effort and it was wasted on a man with his mouth hanging open, offering the occasional soft snore as commentary to the newsreader's concerns. I knew that he couldn't see me, but that wasn't the point.

I sat next to Richard, unable to wake him and not really wishing to. There was a photograph album on his lap, open to a page of the two of us on holiday in Brittany, camping. It had been the summer before Claire was born. We shared an old mini then and had stuffed our equipment into every nook and cranny. The tent was wrapped in plastic sheeting and secured on the roof rack with bungee straps. It had been all we could afford that year, but it had also been when we started our family as I had fallen pregnant with Claire on that trip. I forgave him for being asleep.

The television news held no interest for me, but I watched it anyway, happy to be sitting next to Richard. I rested my head on his shoulder. The local news contained the usual confection of traffic accidents, drugs and crime and ended with a weather forecast. Apparently it was promising to be the hottest September for fifty years. This should have been our life – children flown the coup, financial worries behind us, just the two of us, alone, together.

I eased my boots off, the toe of one pushing against the heel of the other. They fell to the floor in turn and faded from sight. I could always imagine them back if I wanted to.

"What do you think about when you look at us in those old photos Richard?"

He mumbled and adjusted his position, but didn't reply as such.

"I still love you, always will – whatever always means."

"Alison?" Richard murmured.

I would have liked to think he could hear me, but I knew he was probably thinking about the photograph album, mentioning my name was simply a coincidence - but it was nice to know he still thought about me. I tried to stroke his hair, where the flecks of grey had lengthened and acquired pure white ends. It was like stroking strands of wire.

The news programme ended with a few dramatic bars of music that roused Richard from his sleep. He woke up and the photograph album fell from his knees onto the floor. Richard cursed and tried to catch it but his coordination was still impaired from sleep and, as he lunged forward, knocked me sideways. Richard's shoulder spun my neck and I found myself face down on the sofa.

I swore, which should have been muffled by soft cushions but my words echoed off the hard surface that was common to everything I came in contact with.

"I am going to have to get that spine mended sometime."

"And what about mine?" I asked, rubbing my neck.

Richard closed the album, carefully squaring up the loose pages and interleaves. It went back into a drawer and he picked up an empty mug and turned off the television and the lights. I followed him into the kitchen and leaned against the wall while he washed his mug, dried it and put it back in a cupboard – on the same shelf where we had always kept cups and mugs.

Upstairs I lay on my side of the bed, listening to Richard as he cleaned his teeth. When he came back into the bedroom it felt slightly wrong, as though I was a voyeur secretly watching him undress – but he was my husband, or at least he had been.

My blue skirt and flannel shirt were inappropriate with Richard only wearing a pair of boxer shorts. Without any significant effort I changed into a nightdress, the one I had worn on our honeymoon – not that it had been worn for very long. That particular garment had become a private joke between us. I always retrieved it from the depths of a drawer or a cupboard on his birthday or any special occasion. It made us both laugh every time I put it on.

With Richard beside me, albeit under the covers and me on top of them, I was more content than at any time since I had died. He read for a while, but when he turned off the light and lay on his side, I let my arm fall across his waist. If I ignored the fact that the bedclothes weren't soft and that I felt no heat from his body, no familiar smell of fresh sheets and warm skin, we could have been a couple again, waiting together for sleep to overtake us.

I knew I couldn't stay in that position all night. Richard would move, turn over while asleep, and I would be pushed to the side of the bed or even end up on the floor. While we lay still, spooned together, my eyes gently closed and I counted to eight.

Tuesday September 12th 2006

I was awake before Richard. He had rolled nearer the centre of the bed and I found myself sprawled on top of him when I reappeared. His book was still on the bedside table, with the same paper ticket marking the place he had read to.

Worried that I might disturb him, I carefully moved one limb at a time until I was balanced on the very edge of the bed. Of course I couldn't have woken Richard if I'd jumped up and down on him, but even when you know that from experience, it's hard to believe it and hard to break old habits.

I leaned back towards him and kissed the tip of his nose. "Happy birthday," I whispered.

The phone rang somewhere behind me. Richard turned to pick it up and, naturally, I was in the way, but not for long. He reached out without opening his eyes properly, not that it would have made any difference, and virtually punched me on the shoulder. I was pushed off the bed and met the floor with my face. Hayley's voice squeaked from somewhere far away.

"Happy birthday Richard."

"I beat you to it," I mumbled.

Richard was hanging over the edge of the bed, directly above me, rubbing his eyes as he thanked Hayley and asked her what time it was. When he heard her answer he groaned.

"My alarm must have failed to go off."

"Did I wake you up then?"

"Yeah," he yawned. "I need to get a move on."

Hayley asked him what he had been dreaming about and he said he couldn't remember. After he'd hung up Richard flopped back on the bed with his hands covering his face and mumbled through his fingers.

"Oh god Alison, why do I dream about you as though you're still here?"

"I am here, whenever you think about me, I'll be here."

"Will I ever stop missing you?"

"I hope not, I still miss you even though I can still see you."

Richard rolled off the bed, fortunately on the other side otherwise he would have trampled all over me. I was on my knees watching him as he slid off his boxer shorts and wandered naked out of the room. A pump whirred, pipes hummed and the water, pressured through the shower rose, sounded like a sudden summer downpour. I lay back and crossed my ankles, waiting for his return.

He was still handsome, still reasonably fit at fifty-five. A slight loss of muscle tone, a hint of a paunch and considerably more body hair than I remembered, but I would have been happy to be there for real, making him even later for work. I couldn't help but wonder what I would have looked like at fifty-one? Would Richard have still fancied me? My mother had kept her looks and her figure well into her sixties, but I had no idea what regime she had followed in Paris to achieve that.

Richard only took time to slurp at a mug of tea in the kitchen while he gathered his briefcase and checked the contents. He locked the back door, ran some water into his mug in the sink, gave a quick look around the kitchen, as if to check that he hadn't left anything on, and he was gone.

There was nothing for me to do, nothing I could do. I made a tour of the rooms upstairs and was surprised to find the old chocolate boxes still in place under Claire's bed. Martin's room was like a time capsule of a life he would eventually leave behind. A poster for a movie called Harry Potter and the Philosopher's Stone took pride of place above his bed, it filled most of the wall and must have meant something special to him, but there were also toys and books from so long ago that I remembered some of them. The story he had read and I had finished when I first returned, about the small mouse and the rainbow, still had pride of place beside his bed.

When I climbed to the attic I found it still set up as a bedroom and study, the computer lurking darkly on a desk. The blank screen looked slightly sinister and made me shudder for no logical reason.

Downstairs nothing had changed dramatically. It was almost as the though curtains, wall paper, furniture and carpets could all be replaced over the years, but the house that Richard and I had bought remained underneath. Maybe he had never moved because he needed that link to a long-lost past as much as I now needed it. Presuming I could have followed Richard to a new house it wouldn't have been the same, part of me would have been left behind. I sat on the sofa in the lounge and stared at the blue figures on the box under the television, closed my eyes and counted to eight.

Richard's key clicking in the front door greeted me as I returned from my self-imposed exile. For the next few days I watched him make his supper, I sat with him on the sofa watching television programmes that made little sense to me, and lay with him on our bed until he finished reading and turned out the light. Every morning I remained on the bed while he showered and dressed, I even managed to imagine a mug of coffee in my hands while he ate his breakfast. When he left for work I would count to eight again and be waiting there for his return. I was a dutiful ghostly housewife, not a role I had envisaged when we married, but one I was happy to accept for a while.

Friday 15th September 2006

We were having breakfast on the Friday morning and I had a tomato juice held firmly in my hand. Rather frustratingly, the white wine I had magicked into existence the previous evening had disappeared the moment I put it down on the table. I wanted something more than simply to fade away while Richard was at school and decided that I would use the day to explore the area and see what had changed.

A clear sky, and that crisp light that autumn brings, made me want to walk in a park. Jumping from one month to another, or even one year to another, I had missed the slow change of seasons, the birth of new leaves and the drying death as trees fell asleep for the winter. I needed to fix myself in this month and this year, I didn't know when I would next return.

When Richard left for work I slipped out of the door in front of him and stepped sideways into the alcove on the porch. He reversed his car out of the drive and I looked up into an ice-blue sky. Although in my version of existence it made no difference, I wanted to be dressed for the season. Simple blue jeans, trainers and a pink pullover – I didn't want to stand out in a crowd if there were lots of ghosts sharing my excursion plan.

Setting off up the street I headed for the park, it wasn't far, Richard and I had been there often to feed the ducks or simply laze under a tree and read the Sunday papers on a summer's day.

The route took me to an area we would have liked to live and had planned to move to if and when we could afford it. The houses were grander, with larger gardens, but they were also closer to open spaces, tennis courts and the lakes that meandered through the park, all connected by artfully naturalised streams and traversed by small wooden bridges. Those houses had been way out of our budget.

Taking my time, I had lots of it, I studied each house, imagining what life might have been like if we could have bought one of them with their big curving drives and land-scaped mature gardens.

I had wandered up the drive of one particularly splendid detached house when a voice I recognised called my name. I turned quickly, confused and embarrassed at being caught in someone else's front garden.

"Have you been stalking me?" Jeremy asked, grinning broadly.

"No, certainly not. Have you been following me?"

"I can hardly be accused of following you when you turn up at my house – or rather my parents' house, or my brother's house I suppose."

"You live here?"

"I lived here."

"That's what I meant. Don't be picky."

"It's okay, I'm only teasing you."

"But this isn't your date, it's not August the seventeenth?'

"I said I can't jump past that date, not that it was the only time I came back."

"Do your parents still live here?"

"No, my brother inherited it when they died. Why don't you come round the back, there's a swing seat we can sit on."

"They always used to makes me feel a bit queasy."

"It's unlikely to now as it won't move."

I know, silly isn't it? Somehow you just forget. The back garden was enormous, in keeping with the house and the period it had been built. Sometime in the early nineteen-thirties was my guess.

We sat side by side on the swing seat, not swinging. The lawn was speckled with yellow and auburn leaves, breaking the two-tone stripes of the methodically mown grass. I didn't know exactly what our relationship was. We were friends of course, companions in a foreign land or were we simply strangers with a shared experience?

"What brought you back?" Jeremy asked.

"My children are spreading their wings. My daughter is moving in with friends, my son is at his last year at university and my husband is home – alone." I expected Jeremy to laugh at that last comment, but he would never have seen the film, or even heard of it. "They are at one of those turning points in life. They haven't noticed because they're wrapped up in the now and the new, not the then and the old."

Jeremy nodded as though he understood, but he was eighteen, he hadn't lived long enough to have any of those transformation points to look back on, or maybe one, the accident that he couldn't remember.

"I miss holding someone," I said as much to myself as to Jeremy.

"People are like stone," Jeremy said quietly. "It's like trying to cuddle a statue."

"You said you hugged someone once – another ghost?"

"Yeah, she freaked out. I didn't try it again."

Jeremy pushed himself off the seat and stood with his back to me, hands in his pockets, shoulders hunched.

"She was probably scared," I suggested. "I would have been too."

"No, it was something else. I don't know what it was."

I stood behind him and rested a hand on his shoulder.

"Would you try giving me a hug? Like a brother might – or a friend."

"You won't like it. I felt it too, what that woman felt."

He turned to look at me and I gathered him in my arms feeling his face burrowing into my shoulder as his arms wrapped round me. He was right. It didn't feel right.

There was an energy between us, a tingling sensation, keeping us apart, growing stronger the more we fought against it – like magnets repelling each other when they're not aligned properly. We both aborted the embrace.

"We're not really real are we?" Jeremy asked.

"I don't know. I thought you had it worked out."

"I was talking bollocks, trying to impress you. Nothing about us is real is it?"

"I feel real."

"Have you ever tried undressing, taking any of your clothes off?"

I thought back to my boots when I kicked them off. The way they faded out of existence.

"Yes, sort of."

"We're only here when someone else remembers us." He was tight-lipped, holding in his emotions. "I don't know what I am, who I am or what I'm doing here."

"You told me once that I'd be all right."

"I remember," he laughed. "More bollocks."

"Well, I think you will be too – all right that is. And I think you were correct about the other stuff. We are waiting for a time, a place – something, someone." I shrugged. "We just have to be patient."

"I've got to go," he said, sniffing and wiping the back of his hand across his nose.

"I hope we can meet again Jeremy."

He gave no explanation of where he had to be. My guess was that he simply needed to be alone. I sat back on the swing seat and watched him walk round the front of the house and out of my life for the time being and I wanted to be home, with Richard.

A sudden swirl of wind spun the leaves at the far end of the lawn. They twisted and turned a few inches off the ground as they danced closer to me. I lifted my feet onto the cushions to avoid them. As the leaves swept underneath me the wind caught the seat and set it swinging. I felt nauseous almost immediately, which was slightly unfair as I hadn't eaten or drunk anything for fifteen years.

I made a graceless dismount from the seat, stumbled on the lawn for a few steps, regained my balance and poked my tongue out at a bird that was stood on the grass in front of me with his head on one side. It was a song thrush.

Back home I waited in the porch for Richard, not risking shutting my eyes in case I missed him and had to spend the night outside.

When he did return, at gone six, he phoned through an order for an Indian meal, yanked off his tie, kicked off his shoes, poured himself a gin and tonic and breathed out a huge sigh after the first sip.

Maybe he'd had a tough day, maybe this was a Friday ritual, whichever it was I wished I had been able to hold him and make him feel relaxed and loved – because he was loved, by Claire, by Martin, by me and probably by Hayley too, in her own mangled manner. He drank half a bottle of red wine with his supper and watched an episode of a crime drama on television. It made no sense to me, but I was happy to keep him company.

When he went to bed Richard only managed two pages of his book before he reached out to turn off the light. I lay next to him, waiting for his breathing to steady and for sleep to settle over him. I leaned closer to kiss his cheek and then lay on my side, looking at the profile that I knew so well.

"Good night Richard. I love you. I'll see you soon."

Just as I shut my eyes, determined not to count, Richard mumbled something, it sounded like "Good night Alison. I love you too." But I suppose that might have been my imagination.

Chapter 23
Thursday 26th July 2007

When I opened my eyes it was light. The small shriek I heard came from my own throat as, startled, I jerked my head back away from my sleeping companion. Richard had metamorphosed into Hayley while I had been away.

My brain struggled to take in what had happened, but I should have been prepared for the possibility of Hayley being in my bed, our bed – Richard's bed. The shock had confused me. Edging away, careful not to disturb her, I couldn't help but take some satisfaction at the sight of Hayley's mouth, slightly open, a small drop of saliva wetting the edge of her lower lip.

There was no way I would have been able to wake her up, but instinct still made me withdraw stealthily. The side I had been on had the covers turned back, not neatly, but as though someone had just got out of bed. Obviously that would have been Richard, which also meant he had been sleeping on the wrong side. I found that more uncomfortable than the fact that Hayley and Richard had been sharing a bed for years.

The curtains were not completely closed, leaving a narrow slit through which I could see the garden. The trees were in full leaf and a row of tomato plants in black plastic tubs were lined up against the fence, the sun already warming their leaves to yield that sweet grass scent of summer. My head leaned against the hard folds of the curtains as I trawled through memories of gathering laundry dried outdoors in a fresh spring breeze, the zest of lemons as I pulled a knife across them and that first waft of ozone and salt when you wind down a car window near a beach.

"Beep-boop, beep-boop, beep-boop."

It was Richard doing an impersonation of an alarm clock and carrying a tray with two mugs of tea, a packet of aspirin and a glass of water.

"When did you ever bring me tea in bed - apart from my birthday?"

"Come on Hayley, time to greet the world."

"Or Mother's Day. You did make me tea on Mother's Day."

"I brought some aspirin up in case you needed them?"

"Or sometimes when I was ill and couldn't drink it anyway."

"I need a new head not aspirin," Hayley grunted. "What time is it anyway?"

Hayley's birthday was in April, I was pretty sure Mother's Day was in March and, from the sound of it, Hayley was suffering from a hangover, not an illness. Richard had no excuse.

"It was pretty much self-inflicted," Richard suggested.

"I know, I know, but we were celebrating weren't we?"

"Sounds like you were," I added grumpily.

"It's not every day I get to go to your son's graduation ceremony."

"Martin has got his degree? Why couldn't I go to the ceremony?"

"It was a good day wasn't it? I'm glad you managed to get over here."

"As long as you remember I'm poorly. You have to be nice to me."

Hayley pushed herself up in bed, fluffed her pillows, settled back against them and held out her hands for her mug of tea.

"Your back had recovered quite well last night," Richard suggested. "When we..."

"That doesn't count. I was on painkillers."

"I don't think gin is a medically approved treatment – not yet."

"If I hadn't feigned a back problem I wouldn't have been able to ditch my last three classes and get here in time."

"Don't you feel even a little bit guilty about letting your students down?"

"Um... no. They had a replacement for me, she's good, I trained her."

Richard climbed back into bed and they both sipped at their tea. Watching the steam rise from their mugs I could almost taste the fresh, leafy, rejuvenating qualities of a morning cuppa. Some of the simplest pleasures were those I missed most. Richard rested his mug on the bedcovers, both hands cupping it.

"I hope Martin didn't drink too much last night."

"You don't begrudge him a proper celebration?"

"I thought he'd covered that when they all got their results."

"Mmm, nice tea," Hayley sipped again and closed her eyes. "What did I drink last night?"

"Well, we're out of red wine if that's a clue, I'll have to pick up a couple of bottles for Sunday, something that will pass Lydia's scrutiny."

"Ah, the dreaded queen of the pregnant pause – she was on song yesterday."

"You're oversensitive, she's not that bad."

"Really? She didn't want me in the pictures did she?"

"That was as much you as her."

"Well she was right in a way. It was a family occasion and I'm just a hanger-on."

"That's not being fair on yourself. You were part of this

family, an important part."

"You just said 'were'. I'm not any more. And it should have been Alison there, not me."

"I know," I whispered, feeling sorry for the shadow I cast over their relationship.

"I know," Richard said. "But that wasn't to be was it."

They both sipped at their tea, looking straight ahead, not at each other. I was cross-legged on the end of the bed, but they weren't looking at me either, just staring into their own separate worlds.

"So, the interview, what time did you say it was?" Hayley frowned as though she had been told and couldn't remember the answer.

"It's at ten o'clock, but I don't suppose he'll hear today."

They both fell silent again. Hayley cleared her throat as though she was going to say something but I saw her mouth twist as she bit her lower lip and wrestled with it in her head.

"What would you say," she asked slowly. "If I told you I wasn't going back to Ireland?"

"I would say..." Richard paused, obviously choosing his words carefully. "...that it would be delightful to have you back with me on a more permanent basis."

"Ah, I didn't mean that. I meant I'll be here for the summer – if that's okay?"

"So where next? Back to Brazil, Japan, Timbuktu?"

"Hmm, Timbuktu? I've never been to Mali."

Hayley had that wistful faraway look at the mention of somewhere completely new. Richard had said the wrong thing if he wanted her to stay.

"Don't you ever get tired of not having a permanent base, a home?"

"But I do have one," Hayley said snuggling against Richard. "This is my home, you're my permanent base."

Richard closed his eyes, patient as ever, but he wasn't

smiling and Hayley couldn't see the slight downturn in his mouth.

"Anyway," she said. "There's plenty of time to settle down when I'm old and gray. Being in your forties is the new thirties."

"I'm fifty-five Hayley. I know I teach English but my maths isn't that bad."

"I'd prefer you didn't do the sums."

"You're fifty-two Hayley, I suppose that is the new forties whatever that means."

"So, how old do you think I look?"

"I'm not getting caught like that, but nothing like fifty-two, I'll grant you that."

"Shush, don't keep saying it out loud, you don't know who might be listening."

"Fifty-two, you're bloody fifty-two Hayley." My voice increased in volume with my frustration. "You might look forty-two but you're not, you're fifty-two."

To be fair, she didn't look much more than forty-two, but I was definitely on Richard's side in this argument.

"The only person who might hear is Claire and she knows you were the same age as Alison."

"I know," Hayley sounded decidedly grumpy. "I was her age once, and now she's still thirty-six and I'm... not."

"That's not my fault," I said.

And it wasn't my fault, but in a strange way I could see what she meant. My ageing process halted the day I died. There would never be a photograph of me with gray hair and rheumy eyes, nor one with grandchildren round me. I wouldn't shrink and shrivel with old age, I was forever preserved at thirty-six.

"You don't have to go away at all you know, there's always a shortage of good English teachers here. We have a vacancy at my school."

"I'm a bit out of touch with that grass roots stuff. You don't have to worry about classroom control in my job. And I haven't taught a curriculum for years."

"Shakespeare hasn't got any older than when you were last teaching – and he's not half as fanciable as you."

Hayley playfully punched him and he feigned pain, holding his arm until she offered to kiss it better. Their tea finished, their mugs put to one side, Richard and Hayley slid down under the covers. I had been here before, years ago for them, but only a few days ago in my memories. This time the door was left ajar from when Richard had returned with their tea and I was able to make my escape.

Out in the corridor I realised that I was still grasping a mug of tea in my hands. I let it go and watched it fall towards the floor, instead of spilling over the carpet it magically faded from sight before it landed. I shrugged and smiled – at least there was no washing up in the afterlife.

In the hall a rucksack lay awkwardly on top of a holdall, balanced against a large wheeled suitcase, the handle still extended. The three bags might well contain all Hayley's possessions – at university she had proposed a plan that her whole life's possessions should always fit in a large backpack.

The kitchen calendar confirmed that I had only been gone less than a year, but if I had returned only a day or two earlier I could have attended Martin's graduation ceremony. Life wasn't fair, neither was death.

I hoped that either the clutterboard or the calendar would have given me a clue as to where Martin's interview was or even what kind of job it was, but nothing was revealed there and I wandered somewhat aimlessly into the lounge. There had to be a reason to have reappeared at this time – surely it wasn't just to witness Hayley's fleeting visit.

Out of the window I noticed that the silver birch in the

front garden had gone. I walked closer to the window and from the corner of my eye I saw a motorbike leaned over on its stand at the top of the drive. I doubted that it belonged to Richard and Anthony's Jaguar was parked right up close to it – surely it couldn't be Martin's? My thoughts turned to Jeremy and the accident he didn't really remember. Whoever the motorbike belonged to was a mystery, but I was confident and grateful that it was neither of the men in my life. Maybe a neighbour had left it, or a recent visitor? A new voice upstairs brought me back to reality.

"Where's my tea then?"

I hadn't realised Claire was home and climbed half way up the stairs to see her leaning on the doorframe into Richard and Hayley's bedroom.

"Sorry, didn't realise you were awake."

"I wasn't."

Hayley giggled and I groaned at her coquettish manner. Maybe that's what happened when you were of no fixed abode, your mind failed to age or mature in the same way that everyone else did.

"I'll make my own. Anyone want more?"

Hayley giggled again. Was she putting on some kind of performance? Richard said he was okay and Claire turned to come downstairs. I flattened myself against the wall – I mean really flattened myself. I don't quite know how I did it and thankfully nobody witnessed my performance.

Once Claire had passed I relaxed and continued up to eavesdrop on Richard and Hayley, hoping that Claire had discouraged any more bedroom acrobatics for a while.

"It's nice to have you back, and Claire, and Martin. It's been awfully quiet with just me rattling round this house the last few months."

"Well I'm here for the whole summer, so make the most of me," she said, kissing his cheek.

"No chance of persuading you to stay longer?"

"What about Martin's interview? If he gets this job he'll be back living at home won't he?"

Richard waggled his head in a figure of eight acknowledging that it was a possibility.

"Probably, possibly, the starting salary isn't that great for a Grade 5 – and apparently he'll be on rotation for the first two years. But he has to get the job first."

"He'll get it. Who wouldn't offer a job to someone as smart and nice as Martin? You did a great job bringing him up."

"It wasn't just me."

"Are you paying me a maternal compliment?"

"And Alison of course."

"Of course."

Hayley's response was delivered in a flat unemotional tone, which carried more inference than if she'd made some sort of cutting remark about me. I couldn't defend myself and didn't feel I needed to. Hayley and I had shared Martin and Claire's upbringing and I was happy to recognise her part in that process. I suppose I was always the ghost in the background of their relationship, but there was nothing I could do about that.

I retreated to the kitchen where Claire was leaning against the work surface inhaling the fumes from her mug of coffee with her eyes closed.

"How is your love life Claire? Boyfriends? Lovers? Anyone special?"

Claire ignored me and rightly so, I wasn't in the mood for a empathetic conversation and if she could have heard me she probably would have avoided me. She put her mug in the sink and I had to dodge quickly when she walked out of the kitchen.

I heard the shower power on and another of Claire's

247

tuneless renditions while I sat on the bottom of the stairs. It couldn't have been more than ten minutes before she shouted her goodbyes to Richard and Hayley as she skipped down the stairs. I got out of her way and watched as Claire checked her makeup in the hall mirror. She was in jeans and a short leather jacket, not a style I associated with her, but when she reached down by the side of Hayley's bags and came up with a helmet and gloves it all made sense – horrible sense. The motorbike on the drive was hers.

"See you Sunday Dad, Hayley, don't stay in bed too long."

My mouth was still gaping when the front door closed on her. My body, or whatever served as my body, was trembling with fear for her. What on earth had possessed her to buy that machine and what was Richard doing to allow it. My body shuddered uncontrollably and I closed my eyes in fear for her safety.

Chapter 24
Sunday 12th August 2007

When I opened my eyes again, the door was still closed. There were voices in the kitchen, Claire's rising above the others. I said a silent prayer that she had returned without having had an accident and I moved towards her voice.

"When are Lydia and Anthony due back?"

Claire was looking at Richard, but Hayley was the one who answered - although not very helpfully.

"Maybe they'll rent a flat and stay for the summer. Lydia always said autumn was the best season in Paris – once the tiresome summer tourists have left."

"They're back Wednesday," Richard said. "Ignore little Miss Grumpy."

"I didn't mean Anthony," Hayley said defensively. "You know I love him, but Lydia has never had a good word to say about me."

"That's not true Hayley." I was defending my mother again. But when I thought about it, my mother had never been too keen on Hayley, even when we were teenagers, and with my mother the message always came through loud and clear.

"Is Grandpa okay now? He had some more tests didn't he?" Claire asked.

"With Lydia on his case he'll probably outlive me," Hayley mumbled.

"He's fine." Richard confirmed. "His cholesterol levels and blood pressure are better than mine and, as Hayley so subtly intimated, Lydia limits his alcohol consumption and makes him walk at least two miles every day."

"That's all good then isn't it?" Claire confirmed.

It wasn't just the three of them sharing a roast chicken in the kitchen. There was also a man, a total stranger, or at least he was a stranger to me. I was intrigued as Claire had moved her chair close to his.

"I'm looking forward to meeting both of them. They sound interesting," the man said.

Claire kissed him on the cheek very quickly. "You'll love them William. I know you will. Everyone does. As Dad said, just ignore Hayley."

You could tell William was quite tall, even when he was sitting down, and he had large, dark brown eyes – not dissimilar to Richard's. William was Claire's boyfriend, there was no doubt about that from the way she looked at him and touched his arm on any pretext. Claire was quite obviously bowled over by him, her usual independent streak tucked neatly out of sight. He looked older than Claire, possibly in his early thirties, but that may have been due to his lack of hair, any hair. I wondered if he had shaved his head, or whether it was the result of an illness. But he had retained his eyebrows, so it probably wasn't an illness.

I moved round the table, past Claire and William. The calendar showed that I'd only missed three days. When I turned around I saw Claire fumbling surreptitiously under the table. Were they holding hands or… Not being one to resist temptation I knelt down and tried to see through the gap between their bodies – slightly apprehensive at what I might see, but compelled to look nonetheless.

My immediate fears were unfounded when I realised she was trying to slide a ring on her finger – the third finger of her left hand.

"Dad, Hayley, we have something to tell you. William and I have some good news, well I hope you'll think it's good news – and no, I'm not pregnant, before you start wondering."

"What Claire is trying to say…"

"No William," Claire said. "We agreed I could tell Dad." She cleared her throat and sat a little more upright. "William and I are engaged."

Claire held out her hand to show the ring. Hayley covered her mouth with both hands smothering a little shriek.

"Congratulations," Richard sounded genuinely pleased and a grin spread across his face making his eyes crinkle at the edges. "I couldn't be happier for the two of you."

He must have met William before and approved of Claire's choice.

"I'm sorry Richard," William said. "I was planning to ask your permission, but things got a little out of hand when Claire found the ring."

"There's no need for that sort of formality these days," Richard replied, preparing to top up their glasses. Claire had to remind him that she was on apple juice.

Hayley still had her mouth covered, either in shock or excitement. I couldn't tell which or maybe it was both. Richard was much more composed.

"I take it that you haven't told Lydia and Anthony yet?"

"We've not even told my parents," William said. "Claire insisted that you should be the first to know."

Claire thought it would be nice if they could have a small party, so that William's parents could meet everyone properly and suggested the bank holiday weekend in two weeks' time.

"Perfect," Hayley agreed immediately, her voice still muffled by her hands, which she finally let drop. "William's parents can stay here can't they Richard?"

"Er, I should think so, but isn't Andrew also coming that weekend?"

"I haven't seen Andrew for ages," Claire sounded excited by the news. "It really will be perfect because then everyone I love will be here."

"Everyone except me," I added. But, as usual, nobody took any notice.

"Would the Saturday or Sunday be best for you two?" Richard asked.

The smile faded on Claire's face. I wondered what had crossed her mind.

"It would have been so nice if Mum was here wouldn't it? We should be sharing this with her."

"I am here Claire, but obviously not in the way you mean."

"She is still with us," Hayley said quietly. "Every time we think about her, or mention her, she's here."

She looked at Richard, but he avoided eye contact – William broke the awkward silence that ensued. He must have sensed some undercurrent between Richard and Hayley over me.

"Sunday might be easiest if that's okay with everyone else. I doubt my father can be dragged away from his Friday bowls match, so they probably won't get here until Saturday sometime."

The discussion turned to practicalities of where everyone would sleep – William's parents in the attic bedroom, Andrew sharing with Martin and William and Claire would come over for the day but sleep at her place.

I turned to the calendar again. The bank holiday weekend was two weeks away, fourteen days. I decided that I should be able to judge that quite easily if I put my mind to it. Focussing on the calendar I repeated 'fourteen days' to myself a few times and let my eyes gently close.

It was like a magic trick, when I opened my eyes a whole new set of diagonal lines had been struck through every day up to and including the twenty-fourth of August. I checked the year, just to make sure life, or death, hadn't played a trick on me, but it hadn't. Two weeks had passed, or thirteen days if you were a pedant like Richard.

Saturday 25th August 2007

I'd resurfaced a day earlier than intended, but that was better than a day late. It was so quiet that I wondered for a moment whether everybody had gone out somewhere, but the clock provided the answer – it was only five in the morning – everyone was still in bed.

Outside the garden was already awake. A low sun cast sharp shadows on the lawn and a bird arrowed across the grass, just a few inches above the longest blades. Through an open fanlight on the kitchen window I could hear birds chattering to each other, organising their day. I wondered who was in the house – not having lingered to hear all the arrangements confirmed. With no activity that early in the morning it was safe to explore, but when I got to the upstairs landing I found all the bedroom doors were firmly shut, even the attic bedroom.

There was nothing for me to do but wait. Of course I didn't really have to wait in the traditional sense so I went back to the kitchen. The wine rack had a box on top of it with the lid half open – it looked too precarious even for me, but there weren't many options available where I would be safe when there were maybe eight people bustling around.

I climbed on the kitchen table, pictured everyone having breakfast with me in the middle, and decided I needed some-where I would feel less conspicuous. I sat on the work surface by the sink, lifted my feet onto it, slid around and stood, grabbed the top of the wall cabinet, wedged a foot in the open window and managed to half crawl, half push myself into the space between the wall cabinets and the ceiling. I couldn't sit, the gap was too small, but I managed to recline on one elbow, my head cupped by my hand – I felt almost Greco-Roman in style, but without the suitable attire and possibly not quite so elegantly posed. Closing my eyes I counted to three.

Richard was pouring milk into two mugs of tea – again. Hayley had him on a piece of string. I should have learnt more from her when we were younger. I could have followed him upstairs and snuck into their room, but it would only have depressed me to see them together, in my bed – and it was my bed, I chose it. A slow blink, no more than a count of one, and Martin was there below me.

He was in a pair of long pyjama bottoms, blue tartan. When did they come into fashion for young people? It was nine-fifteen and nobody was having breakfast yet. Martin was still half asleep, spooning instant coffee into a mug while the water boiled and steam billowed up towards me. I had always been an early riser, Richard had too, was this laziness Hayley's influence again?

The letterbox rattled and, after half closing his eyes Martin inhaled the vapour rising from his mug to wake him up. Only then did he wander slowly out into the hall.

He returned with a small handful of post, sifting through it as he leaned on the work surface. His hands froze as he got to one particular item. From my elevated position I couldn't make out the embossed logo on the top edge of the envelope – but it looked significant. I wriggled back towards the window and discovered that getting down from my eyrie was much harder than climbing up. I felt around with my foot until I found the window latch and braced myself against it, but then I couldn't get a good grip with my hands on the top of the cabinets. My foot slipped, my hands lost their grip and I fell, landing bottom down, wedged into the sink. It was not the result I had anticipated, nor was it elegant, but fortunately I was perfectly positioned if I stretched a little to look over Martin's shoulder.

"It's from the hospital Martin." I whispered in his ear.

He methodically unpeeled the flap without tearing it, slid out the folded letter and then stopped as though frozen. I wriggled my bottom out of the sink and half fell, half slid off the work surface. Martin had his eyes closed.

"Just open it and read it," I hissed, both impatient to hear his news and infuriated by the fact that I couldn't do anything to encourage or support him.

"What's the letter Martin?" It was Andrew. I recognised his voice even before I turned round and saw him. "Why have you got your eyes shut? It's not bad news is it?"

"Please read it for me?" he whispered, holding out the letter.

Andrew smiled, unfolded the sheet of paper and read it, silently, to himself.

"Okay, I've read it, what now?"

"Tell me what it says you idiot," Martin snapped.

"For heaven's sake Andrew." I was so angry with him. "Stop mucking about."

"It just says you've got a job if you want it, nothing to get emotional about."

Martin opened his eyes, grabbed the letter, scanned it quickly and hugged the grinning Andrew. Unfortunately, I was standing in between them when they embraced.

The sensation of being squished between my grown up son and his now quite tall, quite well-built, friend was not so much a physical discomfort as an emotional trauma. My whole body got crushed and squirted out, reforming so close to them that when Andrew whispered in Martin's ear he was also whispering in mine.

"Much as I would have welcomed this sort of intimacy a few years ago, you have remembered that I now have a partner?"

"What?" Martin said, laughing, and pulling away. "I'm not that desperate."

"Well, that's the last time I read out your good news for you."

"But it is such great news isn't it? I have a job, a real job."

"It's not my idea of fun, pawing away at old injured people all day. I still don't see why you didn't become a sports physio – you could have been massaging beautiful fit bodies instead."

"It doesn't work quite like that. Anyway, it's good to help people. Isn't that what you're doing?"

"I am travelling the world on behalf of our generous bene-factors and making them feel good about themselves."

"I didn't think it was put quite that way in the charity's mission statement."

"You can't help people on a global basis unless you go and see them and understand their needs – that's my defence and I'm sticking to it."

"But business class on those long haul flights?"

"They need me refreshed and alert when I arrive. But enough of my glamorous lifestyle, when do you start at the body processing plant?"

"Er, September, I think it said." Martin scanned the letter again. "Yes, the third of September, but I have to contact them to confirm I'll take the post."

"So what will you be? You know, like your official title."

"Physiotherapist, Band Five. Wow, I can't believe it's actually happening. It's quite scary." Martin looked almost dazed, then sparked into life again. "I've got to tell Dad and Hayley."

He sped out of the kitchen leaving Andrew to pick up the

abandoned mug of coffee, sniff it and take a sip. After adding two spoonfuls of sugar, Andrew sighed and leaned back against the counter. I followed Martin upstairs. By the time I caught up with him Richard was already on the phone and Hayley was out of bed and hugging Martin.

"Hello Lydia. Sorry to call so early but I thought you two would want to know that Martin got that job at the hospital..."

"So," Hayley said. "Does this mean you're still going to be living at home?"

"I guess so, as long Dad's okay with that."

"I'm sure he'll be glad of the company and with me going away again, at least he won't be rattling around all by himself."

Richard was off the phone very quickly.

"Apparently I woke Lydia, not a good move. Dad said he'll bring champagne tomorrow and we can have a double celebration."

"I'd better get up I suppose," Hayley sighed. "What time are Deborah and Joseph arriving?"

"After lunch Claire said – and she promised to be here before they came."

"They sound like two books in the bible," Hayley mused. "Such dull names."

"Don't pre-judge them," Martin chimed in. "They'll probably be perfectly normal."

"But I don't like normal – apart from your father."

"What does it matter to you Hayley?" I snapped. "You'll be gone soon."

"Anyway, I'll be gone soon, so it doesn't matter to me."

Sometimes I could have strangled Hayley – and the good part would have been that, as things stood, she wouldn't have felt a thing.

It sounded like it was going to be a busy day and that I

would have to be dodging people all the time – and it wasn't like anyone was going to personally introduce me to William's parents.

I wandered back downstairs to the kitchen and through the open door to the garden. Andrew was sitting on the bench and nursing Martin's empty coffee mug. His face was angled up to catch the heat of the morning sun. I slumped next to him.

"If you ever get married Andrew, first be sure to check how your partner gets on with your best friend."

I realised immediately that Martin was probably still Andrew's best friend and a complicated picture congealed in my head. I sighed and closed my eyes. As they were planning a barbecue tomorrow, the garden was as good a place as any to resurface.

Chapter 25
Sunday 26th August 2007

When I opened my eyes it was early morning. Dew sparkled on the grass, scattered like small diamonds across the tips of the longer blades. Only birdsong broke the silence that still lay peacefully over a sleepy suburban dawn.

There was no sound spilling from the house, no cat flap swinging to announce the arrival or return of a night-time prowler. I hadn't thought about Willow or Angel and wondered what might have happened to them. In the handful of days that I'd been around since my death, some sixteen years had passed – time for my children to grow up and maybe longer than the lifetime of the average cat.

I had never been the type to flip to the back page of a novel, to see who died, who survived, or who the murderer was. It was the story that intrigued me – the twists and the turns. The destination was simply the end of the journey. I was living life on fast forward, racing towards whatever conclusion was written for me.

If I was here because people remembered me, needed me, wanted me to be here, that was okay. It was much better than being forgotten, unmentioned or discarded. And it gave me a certain amount of satisfaction, although it was rather petty, to be a constant reminder to Hayley that she could be a better person.

The back door was closed and no windows were open. I thought of walking round to the front garden, but I had missed the date of my tacit agreement to meet Jeremy. With so much going on in my family I confess that I hadn't even thought about him. It would have been easy to stop off a few days earlier, to check if he was passing by and if he wanted to talk.

The click of the back door opening made me start, but nobody came out. Had someone opened it to let me in? Probably not, Martin appeared bright in the sun against the dark interior. The light glinted off the glass in his hand – it contained an effervescent white foam of health salts, bubbling to the brim. He looked down at it and drank it in one long draught.

Martin was clad in a calf-length dressing gown of blue tartan, the toes of his bare white feet stubbed against the threshold. His hair was tousled and eyes looked as though he was barely awake. There must have been a preliminary celebration last night.

Before I reached the door Martin's shoulders shivered, he turned and closed it on me. Standing outside, my face pressed to the glass I saw Andrew enter the kitchen wearing only a pair of boxer shorts. They spoke, but I couldn't hear what they said. When Martin left the kitchen, Andrew picked up a mug of coffee from the table, sniffed it, spooned sugar into it and retreated, stirring as he went.

Martin reappeared with an old photograph album in his hands. I recognised it because it was one I had painstakingly put together myself. He sat at the table, opened the album to the first page and reached for his coffee. It had of course gone and he realised immediately that Andrew was the culprit – he shook his head in exasperation. Andrew smiled and shrugged innocently.

By the time Martin made another coffee and was back at the table, Richard had joined them. He looked over Martin's shoulder and pointed at photographs as the pages turned.

Richard stood straight and stretched with his hands in the small of his back. He looked straight at me and for a brief moment I thought he could see me. I looked behind to see what he was looking at but there was just the garden, nothing unusual or noteworthy. Had he seen me in his imagination?

He moved to the door and rested his head against the glass – maybe he too was suffering from the previous evening and the cool of the glass was soothing on his forehead. I stretched up on my toes and kissed his nose where it touched the glass. Richard closed his eyes, a simple pleasure I was now denied if I wanted to remain in the moment. I hoped he was thinking of me.

I was so close to Richard, with just that sheet of glass between us, I didn't see him reach down to the door handle. He suddenly stood back, opened the door and I fell into his arms, or would have done if he hadn't turned towards Martin.

"I'll leave the door open shall I? It's a lovely day out there."

I had thrown my arms round his neck, to save myself falling on the floor and being trampled, and Richard was now effectively giving me a piggyback. When he walked out into the garden I clung on, only dismounting when he turned to sit on the bench - I didn't fancy being squashed.

I couldn't remember the last time I'd had a piggyback. It was probably at some drunken revel at college. I half fell, caught my arm on the back of the bench, twisted and banged my head on the armrest at the end. I was on my knees, face down and, although nobody could see me, I tried to rearrange myself into a sitting position as though my performance had all been by design.

Without giving any conscious thought to clothes, my subconscious had presumably been hard at work. I was in grey-denim shorts, with raw edged hems, and a bright mustard t-shirt tucked into the high-waisted shorts. It was what I'd been wearing the day I died.

"August burns the life from trees and scorches summer flowers."

It was something I'd written during a crazy period when I aspired to be a poet and attached verses to every illustration I made. I was surprised that Richard remembered those words. I turned to look at him but his head was tilted back and his eyes were closed.

"The crest of summer before autumn breaks, tumbling leaves like seashells on sand."

I looked up at the canopy of a sycamore tree shading the end of our garden. The leaves had long lost their youthful gloss and their colour was already transforming to the mellow tones of autumn.

"A final hurrah before the dying of the year."

"I died in summer too didn't I? My final hurrah."

I wanted to lean back, close my eyes and feel the warmth of the sun on my face. But closing my eyes would have unwanted consequences and I could enjoy neither warmth nor cold.

"Dad?" Martin called from the kitchen door. "I'm making toast, do you want some?"

"Are Deborah & Joseph up?" he answered without opening his eyes.

"Yes, everyone's surfaced, even Andrew."

Richard sighed, pushed himself up off the bench and looked around the garden as though searching for something he had misplaced or forgotten.

"I'm here," I whispered.

Martin had disappeared back inside the kitchen. Richard's head dropped for a moment, then he straightened up and walked slowly to the back door, he glanced towards me, or rather looked in my direction before he went inside.

I decided not to follow. The room would be too crowded and I didn't know William's parents and didn't feel I belonged. But I couldn't stay on that bench all day and I didn't want to leap into the future just yet. There had to be a reason I was here, now.

I closed my eyes and counted to three, there was more activity. The barbecue had been set up but not yet lit, glasses were on a table and people looked to be busy in the kitchen.

Claire and William would be arriving at sometime, probably quite soon, so I decided to walk round to the front garden and wait for them. As soon as I turned towards the driveway down the side of the house I saw him. Jeremy was leaning against the wall, staring at me, half smiling. I had no idea how long he'd been there. I walked close by him on my way to the front garden, not ignoring him, but not pausing.

"You coming?" I asked.

The front garden was neutral territory, a more public space, it wasn't littered with the memories of my family in the way the back garden was. He didn't reply but I assumed he was following me.

"Did you come back on the same day again? The seventeenth of August?"

"Yes, and you're back too. To see me?"

His question caused me to frown, but he was behind me, he couldn't see my face. Had I subconsciously planned to meet Jeremy? If so then I had overshot the date by several days.

"I've walked past every day for the last nine days," he said quietly. "Twice on some days."

"How's your brother?"

We were at the low wall separating our garden from the neighbours – our usual resting place. I heaved myself up onto it, aware that my shorts were tight and my legs exposed. My flip-flops hung from my feet – important not to let them fall because they would disappear.

"He's fifty-seven. He seems ancient. I suppose I'd have

263

looked pretty much the same if I'd lived. We are identical twins, or I mean we were identical twins."

"Do you think that's the pull, the reason why you come back on the anniversary of... Anyway, I mean that as twins you probably have that special bond?"

"Maybe. I'm out of theories at the moment. Doesn't seem any point in trying to work it all out. It won't change anything."

He went quiet, his head hung and his shoulders had rounded. I hadn't seen Jeremy like that before, he'd always been so positive.

"My daughter's just got engaged."

"Nice guy?"

It was a simple enough question, but I didn't know how to answer because I realised I knew absolutely nothing about William.

"He's tall..." I said vaguely. "And bald."

Jeremy was nodding slowly when I turned to look at him. Absorbing these very important facts.

"Richard likes him, so I assume he's okay."

There was a roar from the end of the street as two motorcycles accelerated towards us. The sound had more effect on me than Jeremy. I felt my shoulders tense and muscles, which I wasn't sure I really had, tightened in my whole body. The motorbikes slowed, the engine noise stuttering as they turned into the drive and stopped right in front of us.

"Anyone you know?" Jeremy asked.

I didn't answer even though I recognised Claire's crash helmet.

"Nice bikes," he said. I could hear the admiration in his voice.

"What's nice about them? Isn't that why you're here with me now?"

Jeremy looked at me steadily.

"Look, I was an idiot. I wasn't wearing a skid-lid. Motor-bikes are safe enough – if you're sensible."

Claire and William had dismounted, removed their helmets and kissed briefly on their way to the front door. Before they got there it swung open and both Martin and Andrew emerged. Andrew headed straight for Claire and hugged her.

"How's my hero? Still doing good deeds?" Claire asked.

"I'm very well – and you appear to be the only one who thinks my work is important."

"Oh don't listen to Martin, he's just jealous."

"I am not."

"You sure about that," Claire asked, giving him a hug too.

"Well, I wouldn't mind some of the travel perks."

"But it's always to disaster areas," Andrew whined.

William was introduced to Andrew, who had stood a little back from the reunion. I listened carefully to learn more about this mystery man my daughter was planning to marry, but all I discovered was that he was in marketing – I wasn't even sure what that was.

"He is tall…" Jeremy said as the front door closed, "…and definitely bald."

"Anyway, how are you doing? Is your brother well, you said he's fifty-seven now?"

I know he was only about a year or so younger than Richard, but it was difficult to imagine what it would feel like to be nearly sixty, and I was never going to find out.

"He's fit as a fiddle. He runs, eats well – I nag him a lot about that. I reckon he'll live forever, much as I'm doing but in a more active way."

"We're both in a kind of limbo aren't we? Waiting for something, but not really sure what."

"I was quite good at that, we did it every Christmas."

"What?"

"Limbo dancing."

Jeremy pushed himself off the wall, arched his back, and shuffled under an imaginary pole, standing up and throwing his arms in the air as if successful.

"You are a prize idiot – you do know that?"

"I didn't touch the pole though."

"It wouldn't move if either of us did touch it."

Jeremy stood beside me and leaned on the wall. I put my hand on his shoulder, but it resulted in a strange tingle, a bit like the after effect of pins and needles, like when you're regaining sensation. I withdrew it slowly, not wanting to make a fuss about it.

"I missed you," he said.

"And me you."

"You don't mind me dropping by when I'm around, just on the off-chance that you're here?"

"I like that you do. I miss talking to people. All I do is listen most of the time."

Jeremy nodded and we stayed silent for some time, simply knowing that we could chat if we wanted to. In my head I was still thirty-six, it was difficult to relate to Richard now that he was so much older than me. I assumed Jeremy had even more of a problem being eternally eighteen – not the easiest age to be stuck at. I know I felt like a perpetual outsider at eighteen.

"You ought to join your family," Jeremy said. "It sounds like their party has started."

There was the sound of laughter and raised voices coming from the back garden.

"Come with me, you can give me a second opinion about William."

"Do you think it's possible that you came back to see me this time?"

Jeremy sounded quiet. His usual enthusiasm had waned

and he wasn't offering any new theories about our existence or our purpose. I was fairly sure I hadn't come back just to see Jeremy or I would have timed it better – and this was my daughter's official engagement party.

"Maybe, who knows?"

"I'll see you soon I hope."

Jeremy put one foot back against the wall and pushed off, turning to face me and smiling. Without another word he took one step back, turned, and sauntered down the path, whistling softly.

"Don't let Elwin hear you."

Jeremy raised a hand, but kept walking and kept whistling until he was out of sight. I slid off the wall, taking my weight on my hands. I didn't think my bare legs would be scratched by the bricks, but didn't want to take a chance.

Andrew was manning the barbecue, a big mitt on one hand and a long fork in the other. My mother had cornered Claire. I moved closer to them to earwig their conversation.

"Why would you want to ride a stupid machine like that – it's bound to kill you one day."

"It won't Grand-mere."

"Try telling that to Jeremy," I quipped sarcastically.

"It's all the fault of that boyfriend of yours. He shouldn't encourage you."

"He didn't, and if I hadn't bought my bike we might never have met."

"Pfft, nonsense."

Anthony joined them, giving them each a champagne flute and holding a dark green bottle.

"Would you like some sparkling apple juice Claire," he held the bottle up. "Or can we tempt you to a single glass of champagne?"

"Apple juice will be fine Grandpa."

"And only the one for you Anthony, you know you have

to be careful."

Richard came across and joined them so I moved away a little, not wanting to be accidentally knocked over. He was carrying a bottle of champagne.

"Okay, gather together everyone please. Andrew, any chance you can leave the barbecue for a few minutes?"

The ten of them assembled in a loose circle. Two families and two outsiders, who were now insiders. Hayley was part of my family now, as was Andrew. Both Martin and Richard had bottles of champagne. They were all smiling and it made me happy to see them all united.

Richard removed the foil and wire from the neck of the bottle – Martin did the same. They both eased the corks with their thumbs and then, as the corks began to free, pointed them safely away from the group. Martin held his high, Richard turned, towards me.

Both corks popped simultaneously. I heard a cheer as the cork from Richard's bottle struck me square on the forehead, not hurting me, but knocking me backwards. I fell awkwardly on the steamer chair, my arms and head tangled in the wooden frame. Without too much trouble I extricated myself and tried to pretend that I had simply distanced myself from their celebration.

It was my mother, once again, who broke my composure when I realised she was about to sit on me. There was no time to get out of her way. I drew my knees to my chest, winced, and instinctively closed my eyes.

Three thoughts flashed through my mind. Why did I keep doing that? How long were my eyes closed? When did I really want to come back?

Fate or some other power would make those decisions for me.

Chapter 26
Monday 31st December 2007

When I opened my eyes again the steamer chair had disappeared and I was sitting on the lawn, in the dark. Light spilled from the kitchen and from a half moon in a clear sky, silhouetting the trees and shrubs, stripped bare of leaves. The grass was wet, glistening in patches of light and looking dark and colourless in the shadows. Instinct caused me to shiver, hunch my shoulders and hug my knees even tighter - even though I couldn't feel the cold and damp. Months must have passed, possibly years.

It made no sense to me why I had reappeared in the middle of the night. At least in daytime I might have had a better chance of getting into my house. I checked it anyway, but the back door was closed. The kitchen light was on, suggesting somebody was in, but when I peered through the glass there was no movement, no sign of activity.

The front door proved just as fruitless. Curtains were drawn tight across the lounge windows with only a chink of light escaping and no possibility of seeing who was inside, but the faint murmur of a television suggested that somebody was home, presumably Richard.

A car drove past, all of it's windows were closed, but the loud drumming baseline of a song escaped into the peaceful night. As it faded the silence was even deeper.

I could have easily shut my eyes again and skipped to the next morning. The street lights distorted colours, unnatural pools leaving deep shadows where they failed to reach. I sat in the porch and leaned my back against the door while I considered what to do.

A stray cat prowled along the opposite pavement, almost invisible in the shadows and luminescent ginger under the lights. It crossed over the street and paused at the end of our drive, nose raised, whiskers twitching. It looked directly at me then turned, half crouching when another cat jumped onto the wall dividing us from next door. My ginger cat, he reminded me of Ronnie, fluffed up his tail and hissed. The tabby responded in a similar voice, but sounded much more aggressive and louder.

"Can't you just get on with each other?" I pleaded. "Even Angel managed some sort of restraint and she was evil."

Both looked at me for a heartbeat, but it was merely a lull in the war. The tabby meowed loudly, the sort of wail that could bring the hairs up on the back of your neck. I was about to intervene when the door opened behind me and I rolled backwards into the hall.

Richard stepped forward, a bright orange and lime green contraption in his hand, and a jet of water shot towards both cats, catching the tabby full on its face.

"Thank you," I whispered to them, but the ginger one had slunk away and the tabby was looking warily at Richard. A second stream of water sent him on the way too.

I rolled to the side, not wanting to get caught when Richard closed the door, got up and brushed off my jeans out of habit. I was wearing those red cords again, they were my default choice, but now with a thick, brightly coloured jumper bearing a pattern of snowflakes knitted into it – my half-joke Christmas present from Richard in 1982.

"I think that's got rid of them for the minute."

Richard went through to the kitchen and I poked my head into the lounge. Hayley was there, sitting on the sofa, feet propped up on a low table.

"I could drink another coffee," she called after Richard.

"You could make one yourself couldn't you?" I sniped.

"Or have your legs stopped working?"

"I'd make it if I could," Hayley whined in a sad little voice.

She leaned forward to pick another chocolate from an open box and I saw her right wrist had a plaster cast on it.

"Oh, okay, sorry," I apologised. "I didn't see that."

I followed Richard into the kitchen. He was staring out of the window while the kettle boiled. I couldn't imagine there was much to see and wondered what he was thinking. I glanced at the clock. It was gone eleven. It seemed quite late to be making coffee until I noticed that it was New Year's Eve. I had jumped five months.

"What are you thinking Richard?"

I heard him breathe out, almost a sigh, but he didn't answer. I followed Richard back into the lounge. It was a very staid celebration, just the two of them with a box of chocolates. Selfishly I was pleased to see that it wasn't the same box that we had bought as an indulgence every Christmas.

"How is the wrist?"

"Not that bad to be honest. The plaster is mostly just a nuisance now."

A chirruping sound startled me. Hayley reached forward to pick up her phone – they were so much smaller now that I hadn't noticed it on the table.

"Hello..." She held it out to Richard. "It's Lydia for you."

"Hi Lydia, bit early for New Year..." There was a long silence while Richard listened, a frown forming on his forehead. "Is he conscious?"

Richard covered the mouthpiece and put a hand on Hayley's arm.

"Dad's had a heart attack. Lydia's called an ambulance."

"Yes Lydia, I was just telling Hayley... Okay, don't let him talk you out of going to hospital, I know how stubborn he can be."

271

He turned to Hayley again. "The paramedic has just arrived. Lydia's asking him what they're going to do, I can just hear them."

"Hello... Of course I'm still here... Yes, sorry Lydia, just a bit on edge I guess... Okay, that's good..."

Are they're going to take him?" Hayley asked.

"Okay, we'll meet you there... Don't worry Lydia he's a tough old bugger... I'll see you as soon as we can get there... Don't apologise, I'm glad you called... Okay, bye, be there as soon as we can."

"How bad is it Richard?"

"He's conscious, whatever it was has gone away for the time being. They're taking him in to run checks at the hospital. Are you okay to drive?"

"Thanks to those bloody antibiotics I'm stone cold sober."

"That's probably a first," I was being bitchy, but in my defence, I was worried about Anthony.

"I meant with your wrist?"

"The plaster's coming off on Thursday – I'm unlikely to do any damage to it now."

Richard grabbed his coat and forced his feet into shoes, not bothering to lace them, stuffed a phone and a wallet into the pockets and then stood stock still for a moment. I knew he was trying to remember where he had left the car keys.

"They're in the kitchen, by the back door," I said, having noticed them earlier.

"They're by the back door Richard. You left them there this morning."

I followed them out to the car, wondering how easy it was going to be to hitch a lift. They moved so quickly I didn't have a chance to get in, but then Hayley's door opened and she hurried back indoors – returning seconds later with her handbag. She had left the car door open and I crawled into the back seat.

"Do you think we should tell Claire?" Hayley asked.

Richard shut his eyes and breathed out hard to calm himself. He took out his phone and pressed a few buttons.

"Hello Claire... Yes, I know it's not midnight yet... Listen, Grandpa's had a turn, probably a small heart attack... Yes, I know, but he's okay, they're taking him to hospital now."

Richard nodded and made agreeing noises.

"I'll ring you back as soon as we know more, but probably best not to crowd him... Yes I promise... As soon as we know."

"Claire can't drive, nor can William, but I've said we'll ring them as soon as we know more."

"Martin is on duty tonight isn't he? In A&E?"

"I'd forgotten that."

"Can you ring him? Will he have his phone with him?"

"I've no idea, but I'll try."

Richard did call, but there was no answer. Both Hayley and Richard fell silent for the rest of journey. I climbed onto Richard's lap when we got to the hospital – I wasn't going to be left in the car. When he did open the door I fell out as soon as he moved.

Only Richard was allowed through to see Anthony – and me of course. Martin was already there. He said he'd update Hayley and then he had to get back to his shift duties, but it didn't appear to be a STEMI – a problem with a major artery. They were just about to do another ECG and run a blood test to make sure.

"I don't understand," Lydia said quietly.

"Basically it doesn't look too serious," Martin reassured her. "Although any heart attack has to be taken as a warning."

"I'm fine," Anthony protested. "I don't know what all this fuss is about – and stop talking about me like I'm not

273

here."

"Sorry Grandpa. I'm glad you feel okay, but they are going to run those tests anyway."

Anthony harrumphed and folded his arms in a defiant gesture quite typical of him. I smiled. Anthony hadn't changed.

I followed Martin back to reception, casting glances around me to see if there were any other ghosts. How would I recognise them? I stared and smiled at anyone suspicious. If they smiled back it would be a bit of a giveaway. He reassured Hayley that everything was okay and that she could probably go in when the tests were completed. Richard joined us saying that Lydia was staying with Anthony, but that the nurses said they thought it better not to crowd him.

It all took ages, but eventually the three of us were called back in to see Anthony. The hospital would keep him in for a few days observation and possibly an angiogram. Lydia apologised for ruining everyone's New Year celebrations. Anthony told them all to go home and give him a good night's rest, getting quite angry when nobody wanted to leave.

Richard agreed to take Lydia back with him and that they would all return in the morning – much to Anthony's protests. I decided to stay. I wouldn't really be in the way and nobody was going to object to my presence.

It was almost two in the morning when Martin managed to drop by again. Anthony hadn't been transferred to a ward, but was sleeping soundly behind the curtains – despite the constant flow of new patients, buzzing phones and chatter of the nursing staff. While he was there a man put his head through a gap in the curtains.

"Martin?"

"Yes."

"I'm Peter – I ran the blue call for your grandfather, with

Maggie of course, she was driving."

"Thanks. I mean really, thank you."

"How is he?"

"Okay I think. It was a Non-STEMI so there's no imme-diate danger."

"Your grandmother said you worked here?"

"Physiotherapy, still pretty new to it all. I've only been here five months so still on rotation."

"Cool. We should catch up for a coffee sometime. You can let me know how your grandfather gets on."

They both looked at each other for a few seconds before Martin replied. I was convinced that there was more in that meeting of eyes than in the words they had exchanged.

"That would be good."

Martin scribbled something down on a piece of paper and gave it to Peter.

"I haven't got my phone with me."

Peter smiled, looked at the slip of paper and put it in his shirt pocket.

"I'll text you," he said. "But right now I had better get back on duty. Maggie will be wondering what's happened to me."

"Me too," Martin replied.

They walked away together and I stayed sitting on the end of Anthony's bed – he wouldn't mind.

"You're not supposed to sit on the bed."

The voice came from behind me and I turned quickly, almost losing my balance. There was a nurse standing looking directly at me. Her uniform was slightly old-fash-ioned – a sort of white bib over a blue dress.

"You may be a ghost, but that doesn't mean the rules don't apply to you as well," she said.

"I'm sorry. I didn't think. But you're a ghost too?"

"Of course I am," she straightened her shoulders and

stood tall with her arms folded tightly across her chest. "Otherwise how would I be able to see you and talk to you? But I'm still a nurse and you shouldn't be sitting on that bed."

I slid off and was about to straighten the covers when I realised it would not only be impossible but wasn't necessary. I settled in one of those serviceable armchairs that you only ever see in hospitals and nursing homes.

"Sorry." I mumbled.

She looked at Anthony, screwed her nose and mouth sideways and turned back to me.

"He's in good hands here. Is he your father?"

"No my husband's father." It was my turn to look puzzled. "And maybe my step-father I'm not sure?" Had there been a wedding? Would it have been in a registry office or a church? Had I missed it?

"We were married on the fourteenth of July two thousand and four."

We both turned to look at Anthony, but he was asleep.

"The Glendale Hotel," he mumbled, his voice gradually trailing off. "Lydia said religion was all stuff and nonsense."

"So, yes, my step-father and my father-in-law?" I confirmed. "Is that allowed? It's not like first cousins marrying is it?"

"As far as I can tell almost anything's permissible nowadays – including sitting on beds."

The nurse made a pronounced tut sound with her tongue, just once, turned and walked away. She had only taken six or seven paces when she disappeared. Presumably she had closed her eyes.

"Well she was a bit rude wasn't she?"

"Just doing her job," Anthony voice was faint and faded away as he spoke.

"What do I do now?" The question wasn't really directed

at Anthony and he didn't answer.

I slumped in the chair, sighed and followed the course the nurse had taken by closing my eyes, but I only jumped a few hours into the future.

Anthony was in hospital for four days and I stayed with him throughout that time. My path intersected with that of the nurse on occasions – I never learned her name. She was, I suspect, not overly in favour of patients or visitor's rights and preferences. When Anthony was discharged back into Lydia's care I stayed with him.

12th February 2008

Everything appeared to be going well. Lydia demonstrated cooking skills of which I was completely unaware, keeping Anthony on a low fat, healthy diet – I presumed that those years in Paris contributed to her culinary knowledge. Every day they walked in the park and I accompanied them. By February I had decided to return with Richard after one of his frequent visits – Anthony appeared back to normal and my presence was unnecessary – not that there was much I could have done in an emergency anyway. On my last stroll in the park with them Anthony stopped at a bench.

"I need to rest a moment Lydia."

"Are you all right?"

"Bit breathless," Anthony whispered and put a hand to his chest.

He winced as he sat down, his shoulders rounded and his head dropped.

"Anthony? What is it? Talk to me, please."

"Bit of a pain," he mumbled, putting a clenched fist to his chest. "I'll be okay in a minute." But he groaned under his breath.

Lydia fumbled in her bag for a phone and then shouted at

it to turn on. I was of no help at all – there was nothing I could do. A passing couple stopped and, when Lydia told them her phone battery was dead, the man handed his phone to his wife to call for an ambulance and eased Anthony onto the ground to start CPR. I kneeled next to Anthony's head and put my hand on his shoulder, talking to him, telling him to hang on, that help would be there soon. I hoped somehow he could hear me.

It felt like forever before we heard the siren and a paramedic was jogging towards us. It was Peter.

He took control and his partner, Maggie, helped calm Lydia at the same time as unpacking a defibrillator. It all looked so clinical and practised, but I suppose it was their training.

"I've got a rhythm," Peter said and Maggie double-checked Anthony's pulse.

"Is he going to be all right?" Lydia asked.

"We'll take him to hospital," Peter said.

"I need to phone his son," Lydia panicked. "But my phone's dead and I don't know his mobile number."

"I can phone Martin once we're under way if you want me to."

Lydia looked confused, but I wasn't at all surprised having seen Martin and Peter exchange glances at New Year. Peter and Maggie worked quickly and efficiently, with no hesitation as they moved around the ambulance. There was no opportunity for me to squeeze into the back with Anthony and Lydia, but I did manage to get into the cab as Maggie had left the door open.

When Anthony was being wheeled into A&E he moaned again and his body curled up into a ball. I guessed it was another heart attack even without the number of people clustering round him and rushing him into a cubicle.

I stood with my arm round my mother, wanting to

comfort her, but knowing my efforts were of no avail. Her tears and small gasps to stem her crying blended with the calm but urgent voices around Anthony's bed. A nurse took my place, her arm around Lydia's shoulders, and gently guided her out of the cubicle – she said it was better to let everyone do their jobs. I stayed. I couldn't leave Anthony alone.

When they stopped CPR and all stood back, I saw Anthony's body glow briefly. They agreed to stop treatment and the doctor looked at the clock and announced the time of death. He was a minute late by my reckoning.

"Good heavens, that was all a bit sudden."

I turned to see Anthony standing behind me. I had recognised his voice.

"Alison, how surprising to see you here. Why are…"

He burst into a bright light, which then faded like a firework in a clear night sky.

"Goodbye Anthony, good luck," I whispered and closed my eyes.

Chapter 27
Friday 10th June 2011

When I returned I was still in that same hospital cubicle, but Anthony had gone – his bed now occupied by a large woman who was fast asleep – a single white sheet pulled up to her neck. Her lank dark hair, flecked with grey, had a yellow ribbon, half untied, draped over the pillow to one side of her.

The curtains were pulled around the cubicle. To me they might just have well have been made out of sheet steel. There was no way I could move them and no way I wanted to stay with this comatose woman any longer than I had to.

At the bottom of the curtains was a gap, maybe eight or nine inches deep. I felt confident I could crawl under them and knelt down on the floor, but as I ducked my head down, I saw a teenage girl cowering under the bed. As soon as our eyes met I knew she could see me and that she was a ghost – so much for Jeremy's assertion that you don't get many ghosts in a hospital.

"Are you okay?" I asked, not knowing what else to say.

"I don't know really. Am I dead?"

"Hang on a moment."

I stood up again and looked more closely at the woman on the bed. Her chest wasn't moving and her skin was quite pale and waxy, even her lips were unusually pale and had a faint blue tinge. I was no expert, I couldn't check her temperature, but I was fairly sure she was no longer with the living world. The girl under the bed bore no resemblance to this woman – apart maybe from the colour of her hair. I ducked down again. The girl was looking pleadingly at me, frowning and biting her lower lip.

"Um, given that you can see me and we can talk to each other... you probably are dead. Sorry."

She didn't say anything, didn't move and kept staring at me as though I might have another option to offer her.

"Unless you're a cat of course, or a bird, which obviously you aren't."

"What do you mean?"

"I'm sorry," I apologised. "I wasn't trying to be funny, it's just that cats and birds do seem to be able to... well, never mind that for the time being."

"What am I supposed to do?"

She had me there. I'd been dead for... I wasn't sure that I knew exactly until I found a calendar."

"How long have you been here? Not under the bed, but here, like this."

"I don't know, I don't remember. Not long I think."

"What's your name? I'm Alison."

"Melanie – Melanie Sparks."

I smiled at her and asked her if she wanted to stand up. It was a bit cramped and awkward chatting with her under the bed and me bending down to see her. She hesitated, but crawled out on her side and stood at the end of the bed, facing the curtain, not looking at the body under the sheet.

"What do you remember? Like do you know where you live and do you want to go home?"

"Twenty-five Warner Terrace," she said, sounding confident for the first time.

She looked no more than seventeen and was dressed in a short yellow dress, white tights and red shoes with a low heel and a bar strap. There was a double string of beads round her neck and Melanie was wearing very dark eye make-up. She was the epitome of a sixties fashion plate.

"When were you born Melanie?"

"The second of March – I'm a Pisces."

For a moment I was confused, I thought she meant she was a vegetarian who ate fish, but I quickly realised she meant it was her star sign.

"But which year?"

"Oh," she giggled. "Nineteen-fifty."

I glanced back at the shape of the body under the sheet. Melanie followed my gaze.

"That's me isn't it? I'm dead."

"I don't know. Does it look like you? I mean does she look like you. Sorry."

Melanie nodded and turned away from the bed. She smoothed her dress, her hands pausing as they moved over her flat tummy. She spoke, but addressed the curtain not me. I don't think she wanted to see her old body again.

"This was my favourite dress, but someone spilled red wine over it. I couldn't get the stain out."

Melanie was flattening the material over one hip – presumably looking for traces of that stain. I tried to explain about how this worked, how she might not appear as she was when she died. As I talked I could see her yellow dress getting slightly lighter and glowing - in fact all of her was glowing, her hair, the beads she wore. Her tights were almost blindingly white. In a sudden flare, like a flash bulb going off, she was gone.

There was no way I wanted to stay near her discarded body any longer than I had to. I needed to get out of the hospital. I dropped to floor, rolled under the curtain and bumped into a trolley being pushed by a hospital porter.

There followed a crazy ten minutes, dodging nurses, patients and doctors, waiting for doors to be opened so that I could slip through them. Eventually I made my way to the main entrance where I saw the last person I wanted to meet.

That grumpy nurse was just outside the doors, leaning on a railing, smoking a cigarette and staring straight at me.

"They've banned smoking in the hospital," she said. "Load of do-gooders."

I didn't feel the inclination to argue with her - especially as the smoke she blew out disappeared instantly and wouldn't have affected anyone. You couldn't passively inhale smoke from a cigarette that didn't exist.

"I know," she mumbled disconsolately. "I could smoke inside, it wouldn't do any harm. But it's a rule isn't it? When I started here everyone followed the rules."

I gave her one of those conciliatory smiles, stiff lipped but hopefully looking sympathetic and set off away from her – anywhere away from her.

"See you sometime," she called after me.

"Not if I see you first," I mumbled.

It was a long walk home, but I had nothing better to do and didn't fancy trying to get on a bus, I could get trapped on it. At least the weather was fine. No rain to pound a thousand holes through me. The walk took me almost an hour, but I didn't get tired. I even ran for part of it and found the exercise exhilarating – which was strange because I never ran unless I had to when I was alive.

When I got back home I stopped at end of the drive expecting to have to get my breath back, but I wasn't puffed at all. There was a small car in the drive that I didn't recognise. Having no idea how much time had passed I walked cautiously round the side of the house to the back garden.

The kitchen door was open and I could see the back view of a man in a morning suit. His black, tailed jacket and slate grey trousers would have looked smarter had he been wearing shoes rather than bright orange socks. He was on the phone and it was only when he turned around that I recognised Martin. He was dressed for a wedding with a silver-grey waistcoat, wing-collar shirt and violet cravat. His hair was longer than I remembered, which is what had thrown me at first.

At the hospital I had been in such a hurry to escape that I hadn't even looked to see if I could establish the date, so I had no idea how much time had passed.

Martin was nodding and saying uh-huh every few seconds, he could have been talking to anyone. I turned to where the calendar was hung, relieved to see a new one in place. It was June two thousand and eleven – I had skipped four years.

Was Richard marrying Hayley at last? Was Claire marrying William? Was Martin a best man for somebody's wedding that I didn't even know?

"Wait until you see me," Martin laughed. "I look like a ringmaster in a circus... Look I better go and change my clothes, I was just trying this suit on for size. I need a coffee but I can't risk getting anything spilt on it – Claire would murder me."

Martin laughed at something his caller said.

"Wear your grey suit... Listen I'll see you there tomorrow... Absolutely, I'll be the one showing you to your seat – you won't be able to miss me."

Martin smiled with a small quiet laugh. "I miss you too."

Then he mumbled something I couldn't hear because he turned his back to me again. I looked at the clutter board. Something had caught my eye before, but only just registered with me – an invitation.

Richard Walker & Hayley Byrd
request the pleasure of your company
at the wedding of
Claire Walker and William Duncan

It went on to say that it was to be held at St Mary's Church – where Richard and I were married – and it was tomorrow, at eleven o'clock.

Martin had put the phone down and was in the doorway to the hall when I turned back towards him. The front door rattled open and Hayley screamed. It was the same elongated yelp of delight that I remembered from our teenage years, but now coming from a woman in her mid fifties.

"Martin you look a-ma-zing," Hayley exaggerated the three syllables. "Except maybe for the socks."

"My thoughts entirely," I said.

From the way they hugged like long-lost relatives I assumed Hayley was still flitting around the world.

"I am going to have to protect you from all the single girls tomorrow. They will definitely want a piece of you."

"I'll have Peter to protect me Hayles."

"When did you start letting people call you Hayles? You hated it when we were young."

"Don't you start calling me Hayles. I cut Peter some slack because he'd been drinking, but I don't want it getting to be a habit."

"Just teasing Auntie Hayley."

"And not so much of the Auntie please – it makes me feel ancient now you're a fully grown man."

Hayley looked past Martin, directly at me. I took a pace back thinking for a second that she could see me.

"Where's the blushing bride then?" she asked.

"She just popped out with Jacqui," Martin whispered conspiratorially. "Said they wouldn't be long but they were very secretive about it."

Richard slipped past Hayley and Martin.

"I'll put the kettle on. Who wants tea, who's for coffee?"

They both chorused 'coffee' and Martin said he'd pop upstairs and change. Hayley came into the kitchen and sat at the table.

"I haven't seen Jacqui for years," Hayley said.

"I don't think I've seen Jacqui since the year I died. I hope her ghastly little brother isn't coming – assuming he isn't under lock and key somewhere?"

"What happened to her horrible little brother?" Hayley frowned. "Thomas wasn't it?"

Richard carried three mugs to the table and placed them down carefully before replying.

"Ah, you must have been away when we heard."

"Heard what."

"He died," Richard raised his eyebrows and his lips set firm. "It was a car accident, or to be precise, a stolen car accident."

"Why didn't you tell me?"

"Well, we didn't really know him that well by then. I hadn't seen or heard of him for years. I don't think Jacqui ever talks about him either."

Hayley offered a thoughtful, but sad "Hmm."

The conversation ground to halt – even I had mixed emotions about that news. However much of a problem he might have grown into, Thomas was still a small boy in my memory.

"Right, that's me out of my pantomime outfit," Martin said as he slid into a seat and drew a mug of coffee towards him.

"I thought dressing up was a big thing in your community," Hayley teased.

Martin poked his tongue out at her.

"Don't stereotype me you globe-trotting cougar."

They broke into laughter, but Richard looked a little uncomfortable. "I never know when you two are joking," he said.

"It's nice to be back." Hayley ignored Richard's grumpiness and ruffled Martin's hair.

"Get off me, I hate you," Martin whined.

They both burst out laughing and Richard was compelled to join in. I was still wondering what a cougar was.

It was a good hour before Claire and Jacqui returned and the biggest shock wasn't seeing how tall Jacqui had grown, but how pregnant Claire was. She must have been close to her third trimester.

"You're having a baby?" I don't know why I asked when it was so obvious.

Hayley and Jacqui gave each other a tentative hug, Hayley having to reach up as Jacqui was now several inches taller than her.

"You haven't changed at all," Jacqui enthused, now holding Hayley's shoulders at arms length – and they were long arms.

"Nor have you, except that you've... grown up a bit." Hayley screwed her lips sideways and then carried on, blunt as ever. "Exactly how tall are you?"

"Oh I don't know exactly. Six foot two?" she replied uncertainly.

"Six foot three," Claire replied for her. "Stop pretending that an inch matters."

"Shut up Shorty." Jacqui punched her playfully on the shoulder.

They both broke into giggles. It was obviously a joke between them, even though Claire must have been five foot seven herself.

"How is your... mother?" Hayley asked hesitantly.

"She's fine. You'll see her yourself tomorrow."

"Yes, of course I will."

There was an awkward silence. Questions about her father and brother left unsaid.

"Do you want to feel?" Claire asked Hayley, who hesitated. "Everyone seems to want to. It's not like my body is mine any longer. But you're my second mum, not like some random colleague at work."

Hayley gingerly laid a palm over Claire's tummy. After only a second or two she suddenly jumped and withdrew her hand as though Claire's tummy was a hotplate that she had just been testing for temperature. She giggled nervously.

"One of them kicked me. Did I disturb them?"

"Them? How many are there?" I demanded.

"I think she's letting him know who's the boss already."

"Sounds familiar to me," Martin laughed.

"You're having twins?" I said, both excited and apprehensive for Claire.

"Have you settled on names yet?" Hayley asked.

"I have but William doesn't know so I'm not telling anyone what he's going to choose."

"So, come on Sis, what did you and Jacqui go out to get that's so secret?"

Jacqui clutched a brown paper bag to her chest defensively. Both of them exchanged glances, giggled and Claire grabbed Jacqui's hand and rushed her upstairs – just like they did when they were little.

"Nothing changes around here does it?" Hayley laughed.

"Not really," Richard said.

"Except that my daughter's pregnant with twins," I reminded them all. "And she's getting married tomorrow."

Martin offered to take Hayley's bags upstairs and Richard said to put them in his room because Claire and Jacqui had taken over the attic for their dresses. As if they were going anywhere other than Richard's room.

"You're right Hayley," I sighed. "Nothing does change for you does it?"

Looking at the clock I decided to skip about twelve hours. If the wedding was at eleven, I didn't want to end up trapped in the house and miss it.

Chapter 28
Saturday 11th June 2011

It was light when I opened my eyes and the house was silent. The buzz of an alarm clock somewhere upstairs, even though muffled by a closed bedroom door, suggested imminent activity. A sigh of relief escaped my lips and my shoulders relaxed. For a moment I thought I had misjudged the time and they had already left for the church. A glance up at the wall confirmed that it was still only seven o'clock.

With some caution, listening for movement, I started to climb the stairs. Half way up I saw Richard walk along the landing on his way to the bathroom. A click and another door opened.

"Morning Dad," Martin yawned. "Just going to make tea, you and Hayley want a cup?"

"You know Hayley, she never says no."

Martin was heading towards me and I rapidly retreated, making it to the hall and flattening myself against the wall to let him pass. Claire's door must have opened as she called after him in a faux little girl's voice.

"Make a cup for us too Martin – please little brother?"

Martin raised his eyebrows as he passed by me.

"Okay, tea for everyone," he called back.

"Coffee for me please," a distant voice added.

I wasn't sure if it was Hayley or Jacqui, but Martin appeared to know.

The house went from quiet to busy in the space of a few minutes with Claire banging on the bathroom door asking Richard how long he would be in there and Hayley adding, "Me after you please." I retreated to the kitchen and watched as Martin made tea and coffee and loaded it on a tray. I followed him up the stairs and sneaked into the attic bedroom.

Claire's wedding dress hung on a short, chrome clothes rail – a new addition since I'd last been there. Already small, the room was now even more cramped for space. There was also an electric blue full-length satin dress, very simple and with spaghetti shoulder straps. Jacqui was going to raise a few eyebrows wearing that.

Beside the sofa there was a convenient, out of the way, corner. I sat there on the floor, knees drawn up, waiting for the girls to make an appearance – it was far too busy in the house for me to keep dodging people and nobody was going anywhere while those dresses were still on the rail. The doorbell rang and I heard Richard direct someone upstairs.

"Claire," he called. "Barbara is here."

I crept to the top of the attic stairs on my hands and knees and saw Claire greet this new arrival with a hug. Barbara was carrying a large, pink, aluminium box – it had to be for makeup. Over the next hour I sat on the top of the attic steps watching people cross on the landing below as they trooped back and forth to the bathroom and Claire's bedroom.

"I'll go get your dress."

It was Jacqui's voice. She was climbing towards me up the attic staircase, two steps at a time. I scampered back beside the sofa and watched her as she stooped slightly because of the slope on the ceiling. Jacqui took the wedding dress from its hanger, still in a clear protective cover, looked at it for a moment, draped it over her arm and went back downstairs.

I had assumed Claire was going to dress in the attic bedroom, but the narrow stairs would have been tricky for her to descend in a full-length wedding dress.

After following Jacqui back to Claire's room I realised

there was no spare corner in there for another body, even one as malleable as mine. I watched from the door until Hayley came along and I had to press myself against the wall at the end of the corridor. She took up the doorway, blocking my view. I thought about climbing on her back so that I could see over her head, she wouldn't have noticed, but it would have been a less than dignified way to watch your daughter prepare for her big day, and tempting providence in terms of another accident for me.

I gave up and went back downstairs to the lounge, where Richard was sipping a coffee. He was still in a pair of chinos. I watched him, impressed by how cool and composed he was – until I realised that his newspaper was upside down.

"Not really that relaxed then Richard? But I suppose it is the day our baby girl is getting married?"

"Anything interesting in the paper Dad?" Martin asked, appearing in the doorway.

"No, not really," he answered vaguely.

Richard realised his mistake with the paper and let it fall to the side of his chair.

"To be completely honest Martin, I was thinking about your mother. This should have been her day too."

"I know Dad. But I like to think she's here, in some way, sharing it with us. If we think about her and talk about her it keeps her real for us."

"Thank you Martin," I whispered.

"Do you think about Mum often?" Richard asked

"Quite often I suppose."

"Do you remember her? You were very young when she died."

I held my breath.

"I remember her perfume." He looked down, speaking quietly. "Sometimes, when I'm walking along the street, or if a patient comes in and I catch a hint of the perfume Mum used to wear... it's like I'm a child again. I can't explain it properly."

"Opium, Yves St Laurent. I used to buy it for her every birthday. Claire said something similar years ago about remembering it."

Without thinking I found I had the familiar bottle in my hand. Unscrewing the top I dabbed a little on each wrist. I could smell it too – or maybe it was just the power of memory.

"I could almost believe it's in the air now," Martin said, shrugging. "In my imagination it lingers sometimes."

"Claire is wearing it today. It must be drifting down the stairs."

"Maybe it's me," I said quietly.

"I hope she doesn't overdo it," Martin smiled. "We don't need William's hay fever kicking in at the altar."

I glanced at the glowing numbers on the box under the television. It was only a ten minute drive to the church and it showed 08:53. I did a slow blink, the numbers jumped to 09:27. Richard was back behind the newspaper and Martin had gone.

Another blink and Martin had taken Richard's chair. He was dressed for the wedding now but without a jacket. The clock read just after ten.

Not wanting to take any risks I went back upstairs, careful to make sure nobody was loitering on the landing. The last thing I needed was to be tumbled down the stairs again and miss my daughter's wedding. The door to Richard's room was closed. Claire and Jacqui were sitting in their underwear by an open window in her bedroom, sharing a cigarette. Claire's dress was hanging from the top of the wardrobe door.

"I never really got into cigarettes," Claire said, coughing a little.

"Mum said they would stunt my growth when she caught me sneaking one of hers."

"Oh god I remember that. She went bananas didn't she?"

"She only encouraged me with that threat – but it never worked did it – I still grew into a lamppost."

"How do you know it didn't work?" Claire giggled.

"I'll let you off that one as it's your wedding day. It's hard enough to find a bloke when you're six foot two – how tall might I have grown if I'd been a good girl and taken her advice?" Jacqui raised her eyebrows and was staring at Claire, challenging her to answer.

"You look amazing Jacqui. And you'll find the perfect man and have loads of children – you could even form a basketball team."

"If I didn't love you I'd take William away from you for that one."

"You couldn't. He's in love with these."

Claire cupped her hands under her breasts and pushed them up.

"I'll give you that. I don't have much to tempt him in that department."

"Oh god," Claire sighed. "Am I doing the right thing? I mean William is the right one isn't he?"

"Of course he is. You're mad about him, he's mad about you. I'm mad that you got to him first."

"I know, I've just got the last minute jitters."

Jacqui leaned out the window, stubbed her cigarette out on the window ledge and flicked the butt into the garden – it looked like a well-practised manoeuvre. She took Claire's from her and did the same thing before delving into her makeup bag for a tin of peppermints.

"Can't have you smelling like an ashtray for your first kiss as a married woman."

I sat at the foot of the bed with my knees tucked under my

chin and watched them dress. Claire looked perfect in her wedding gown, Jacqui looked like a model in that figure-hugging blue dress. All the times I'd missed, all the memories Claire and I should have shared were like dreams that slip from your grasp as you wake. I didn't even know where they had been on their holidays, my only clues coming from a scattering of photos on the walls. My self-pity was interrupted when Richard called up the stairs.

"The car's here Claire. How are you getting on?"

"Be down in a minute Dad."

The girls descended the stairs with Jacqui holding up Claire's dress and I followed.

"Come on Jacqui, we should have left ages ago," Martin urged.

Jacqui gave Claire a quick kiss and half ran out of the open front door after Martin. I wondered whether to chance getting in the car with Claire and Richard. It was cutting things a bit fine if I failed, so I slid past Claire in the hall and out into the drive. Luck was with me as Martin, in an unfamiliar car, managed to wind down all the windows at the same time. I dived through onto the back seat, not caring how I got in the car but determined to do so. There were bouquets and a tray of red roses for buttonholes that I was convinced I was going to crush, but I didn't harm a single petal. I simply lay, not too elegantly, on my bed of roses. Martin drove with a sense of urgency, Jacqui telling him to slow down more than once.

"We should have been there twenty minutes ago. I'm supposed to be an usher."

"If people are bright enough to find the church I'm sure they will be bright enough to find a vacant chair."

"They're pews," Martin mumbled. "And that's not the point – I have the buttonholes."

We arrived at the church and I scrambled out of the back

of the car when Martin opened the door to pick up the flowers. Hayley was standing in the porch, alone. Her dress was knee length, a deep blue heavy cotton with startling abstract birds in yellow and red. It must have come from one of her work placements because it looked more South American than European. She was talking to someone I didn't recognise, but I had expected that there were going to be lots of people I didn't know. I hadn't been part of Claire's everyday life for the last twenty years.

I peeked inside the church, but didn't take a seat – not sure what was the correct etiquette for a dead mother. The church filled, Martin took his place and a song began to play that I recognised. Richard and I had danced to it at our reception, it was Etta James singing *At Last*. My eyes filled with tears that Claire had chosen it too. Richard must have told her it was my favourite song. My tummy trembled with emotion and I looked down to see that I was in my own wedding dress from that day, a bouquet of Calla Lily and Baby's Breath in my hands. Richard and Claire appeared beside me and, without thinking, I moved next to Jacqui and walked down the aisle with the three of them. The tears spilled from my eyes but never reached the floor.

When Jacqui took Claire's bouquet and stepped to the side I touched Claire's arm with my fingertips, running them down to her fingers, lingering on the one that would soon have a gold band on it. Claire looked down at her hand. I didn't know whether she was thinking the same as me, or whether she could somehow sense my presence. When she glanced back over her left shoulder she looked directly at me – I smiled, even though I knew she couldn't see me.

I remained close to Claire throughout the service, but when they went to sign the register I sat on the altar step – it would have been too crowded in the vestry. Even when Claire and William were walking up the aisle, as husband

and wife, I didn't follow immediately.

There was a voice behind me that made me jump. For a second I thought someone was talking to me, but it was the priest, mumbling a prayer that was over almost before it had begun. I walked up the aisle of the now empty church, trailing my fingers along the edge of the pews, smiling at the pretty bouquets of flowers on the end of each row.

Outside, the photographer was already organising the formal groups. I stood behind him, along with several guests with cameras duplicating his work. I felt a gentle touch on my shoulder and turned, shocked that someone might be able to see me.

"I never got the chance to get married," Jeremy said.

"What are you doing here?"

"I quite like a wedding," Jeremy shrugged. "They cheer me up."

The photographer called for the bride's parents and I turned back to look at Claire and William, almost starting to walk towards them myself. Hayley was being ushered in as the bride's mother.

"That's your friend isn't it?" Jeremy asked.

"Yes."

"It is nice that your daughter has someone with her."

I nodded in agreement.

"You going to the reception?" Jeremy asked.

"I don't know, I suppose so. I'll have to try to get in a car. I don't even know where it's being held."

"You don't have bother with all that nonsense. I'll get you there."

"How are you going to do that?"

"We are going to car sledge. It's fun, you'll love it."

"I have no idea what you're talking about."

When the photography had finished and people started to drift away into smaller groups, Jeremy led me to the car park. He pointed to a particular vehicle.

"That one's perfect," he said.

Taking my hand, a strange, but not entirely unpleasant, tingling sensation running up my arm, he pulled me towards the car he'd selected. Jeremy let go of my hand, climbed on the bonnet and then onto the roof.

"Come on, get up here."

I had no idea what his plan was, but followed him anyway.

The car had a roof rack, which made it difficult to find my footing. He lay down on the bars on his tummy and smiled up at me, nodding his head sideways for me to join him – which I did.

The owners arrived and, oblivious to our presence, started the engine and began to pull out into the road.

"Hang on tight," Jeremy laughed, his mood infectious.

"This is madness," I said, grinning and frowning at the same time. "It's got to be so dangerous."

"What's the worst that can happen?" he laughed. "We're already dead."

Chapter 29
Saturday 11th June 2011

Jeremy was right, there was something exhilarating about clinging onto the top of that car as it sped along country lanes. Ever since I'd died my life had been watching, hiding, keeping out of people's way – car sledging was fun.

After about twenty minutes on a car roof-rack in my wedding dress, the novelty had worn off. I was relieved when the driver turned into a tree-lined gravel drive. The house itself wasn't majestic, more the faded gentility of a country residence. The lawns however were immaculate, three terraces of impossibly green manicured grass with gentle slopes and stone steps between each level. Two small marquees were located on each side and huge picnic blankets sprinkled with scatter cushions were dotted over the lawns. Cream canvas director's chairs were clustered at intervals and the bride's picnic blanket was at the centre of the top terrace, shaded by a white awning. We both stared in silence until Jeremy summed up the scene before us.

"Bloody hell, what if it rains?"

"But it's not going to," I said, looking up at a perfect pale blue sky, broken only by high wispy ribbons of cloud.

"But what if it did?"

"I don't know."

As people arrived, catering staff in white polo shirts and black shorts greeted them, offering a variety of drinks from small round trays. Jeremy imagined a glass of beer into his hand and I upstaged him with a glass of champagne.

"Ooooh, very posh," he cooed.

"It is my daughter's wedding reception."

I was scrutinizing the guests, trying to identify anyone I knew, when Jeremy tapped me on the shoulder.

"Look at that."

He was pointing down over the lawns to a small adjacent field. Two winding paths led to the centre where a hot air balloon was tethered. It was white with stems of flowers curling up the sides as though growing from the wicker gondola slung beneath it. We walked down for a closer look, clambering over a gate at the entrance to the field. A man was in the basket slung underneath, dressed in black shorts and a black polo shirt. He was firing a burner into the body of the balloon. Jeremy nudged me.

"Come on, let's go for a ride."

"We can't."

"It looks like he's taking it up for a test flight."

Jeremy grabbed my hand, sending a slight fizzing sensation up my forearm. He scrambled into the gondola and held both hands out for me just as the balloon started to lift. I grabbed his other hand and he hauled me in quite easily – I suppose I didn't weight very much at all.

"Wow," Jeremy said. "I never thought I'd get a go in one of these."

The people on the lawns got smaller and smaller as we rose and the symmetrical fan of the picnic blankets more obvious. Claire's train stretched out on the grass behind her, children ran zigzag paths through the scene like pin balls rebounding in an arcade game. Silence enveloped us except for the occasional distant happy scream of a child and the burner whooshing flames and hot air into the canopy above us. I looked up into the cavernous balloon that was holding us up in the air.

The man flying the balloon burped, the long rumbling release of someone secure in the knowledge that nobody could hear him. "Better out than in," he declared. The spell broken, I looked back down at the wedding party and could see the serving staff distributing picnic baskets with guests clustering around the blankets. I wanted to be back amongst them.

"How do we get down?" I asked Jeremy.

"We wait I suppose."

"But we're missing it – my daughter's wedding reception."

"I don't fancy sliding down one these ropes," he said. "Hang on, it's okay, I think we're going down."

The people on the ground looked slightly larger. Jeremy leaned over the edge of the basket and agreed with me. As we watched the ground slowly rose. It definitely seemed like we were stationary and the world was coming up to us. It took far too long, the pilot being in no hurry. We clambered out as soon as the gondola touched down. I brushed off my wedding gown and Jeremy straightened his bow tie. By the time we had wound our way back up the cut-grass path, hauled ourselves over the gate and clambered back up to the lower terrace the speeches were already well under way. Claire stood and a microphone was passed to her. A ripple of clapping and a couple of whistles greeted her. One of the loudest whistles came from right next to us and I looked find Andrew there. His mother Sarah was in a chair next to him. Thankfully there was no sign of his father.

"Don't panic I'm not going to sing," Claire announced.

She looked and sounded so comfortable and so happy that I felt a tear form in the corner of my eye.

"First I'd like to thank you all for coming and I hope you enjoyed the picnic hampers that my wonderful sister-in-law arranged."

Claire applauded towards a woman to her left and everyone joined in with more whistles and hoots. I couldn't help but think of the contrast with our more traditional reception – a cold buffet in a hotel that was past its prime.

"As many of you know my mother died when I was eight. But I wrote to her. I wrote so many letters, telling her how I missed her and what was happening in my life. I also told her that when I grew up I would marry a handsome man." Claire looked at William and made a tick mark in the air. "That I would dress as a princess." She did a small curtsey. "And become a famous author - well, I'm still working on that one. I hoped to make my mother proud of who I am and what I'd achieved, and I think she would be happy for me and William and..." she patted her tummy and looked down at it. "We haven't chosen names yet, or rather I haven't told William which names he is going to choose."

"I am so proud," I whispered. Jeremy took my hand and gave it a gentle squeeze. My arm tingled, but not unpleasantly.

"I missed my mum then – and I still miss her now. But... " Claire paused and cleared her throat. "Today I felt she was with me, and she always will be with me in my heart. And I'm pretty sure she would have approved of my second mum, Hayley."

Claire blew three kisses with the fingers of both hands to Hayley, dropping the microphone in the process, which was caught by William and handed back to her.

"Hayley told my mum when they were little girls that she would travel the world and learn how other people lived."

Claire made another tick mark in the air and a ripple of laughter ran across the lawns.

"I'd like to think that my first mum is here with me today, watching all this and smiling at me – and I'm sure she is in some sense. So, I'd like you all to join me in a toast to my very special family, my dad, my brother and especially to my two mothers."

Everyone stood up. The hairs on my neck prickled and my whole body tingled with love and pride – not just because

301

Jeremy had his arm around my shoulders. Claire repeated 'To my special family' and everybody joined in. I couldn't swallow.

I don't think anything went in after that. The best man, whom I didn't recognise, obviously performed to the expected standard, reflected by raucous laughter from some clusters of picnic blankets. Only the last words sunk in because they signalled the end of his toast.

"Now honoured guests, and Stephen..." there was raucous laughter from one group, but I had no idea what the reference meant. "There will be no cutting of the cake, because there isn't one - although we wouldn't have had to wait long for the top tier to fulfil its traditional function."

He pulled a humorous face and indicated by curving his hand over his own tummy that another event was due not long into the future.

"What we have instead is a cornucopia of cup cakes for your delight – unless you're counting calories that is, and who counts calories at a wedding reception?"

He raised a hand as he said this and beckoned towards both the marquees. Six of the waiting staff appeared, three from each side, with two cake stands each, hanging from their fingers. They circulated the picnic blankets, placing one stand at the centre of each blanket.

The remainder of the afternoon turned into a casual garden party with bottles of wine and soft drinks continually refreshed by the caterers. I picked my way up the steps to where Claire and William were posing for more photographs and stood to one side feeling their happiness radiate with every smile and laugh.

The sun shone, there was a light breeze and every so often the hot air balloon would rise above the event with the sounds of laughter and raised voices from those on board. Jeremy and I sat at the edge of the top terrace, deep in the shade of a large oak tree. We only had to move when children played chase around the tree trunk.

It was almost mid-summer so the sun didn't set until after a band had started to play in one corner of the garden. Claire and William were alone on a temporary dance floor of wooden panels, everyone else standing around the edge. Fairy lights, scattered throughout the trees, had been lit the moment before they started dancing and flashes from cameras caught their every move and turn. I stood to one side, swaying to the music. Jeremy stood behind me, I knew he was there but he left me to my own thoughts, not intruding on the moment.

"I'm going to leave you to it Alison," he whispered. "Thanks for sharing this with me."

"You don't have to go," I said, turning to him. "And thank you for coming, for bringing me here."

"I'm going to hitch a ride with someone. Take a chance that they're going in my direction. There's a car I think I recognise from near my street – one of the benefits of late night walks. Will you be okay to get back?"

"I'll be fine. I might try to get a lift back with Richard and Hayley."

"Okay. See you again soon I hope."

He waved as he sauntered across the lawn, dodging people, smiling at me, pulling faces and laughing. When he disappeared around the corner of the house I turned my attention back to the dance floor. Richard and Hayley were close to Claire and William, chatting while they danced. I couldn't help but feel that I should have been there, not Hayley. I shouldn't have died. I sighed, it was no use being jealous – my premature death wasn't her fault. I imagined a glass of champagne in my hand and sipped it slowly. I could taste it so clearly, the bubbles tickling my tongue. It was a trick of memory I suppose, but it felt so real.

I wandered around the guests, some having gathered chairs into small circles, some sprawled on the picnic blankets studying the evening night sky. The sun had almost set into a misty horizon, the balloon flaring into light and life each time the burners coaxed it higher. Richard was chatting to Peter and Martin, another couple in my uniquely structured family. As I moved next to them, curious about their conservation, my mother joined us. She was seventy-six, twice widowed and looking at least ten years younger than she should do.

"What are you men talking about then?"

"Just saying what a great day it's been," Martin replied.

"And that I could murder a hot dog," Peter added.

"You boys and your stomachs. I couldn't squeeze a grape past my lips after that picnic."

Lydia could however manage a sip from the wine glass that had been superglued to her hand all afternoon.

"Not for me," Richard said.

"You sure Mister Walker? I could bring you one back with all the trimmings."

"I don't eat sausages Peter and do please call me Richard, I feel like I'm at school when you called me Mister Walker."

"See you in a bit," Martin said as they walked away.

I was caught for a moment between staying with Richard and my mother or following the boys.

"Such a shame that Alison wasn't here to see Claire today," my mother said, looking up at the balloon.

Richard raised his eyebrows. He knew the history of my mother and me and I wasn't keen on hanging around to hear my mother reinvent my childhood. When I caught up with Martin and Peter they were each juggling a hot dog, a burger and a glass of beer.

"Has your Dad never liked sausages?"

"Its a long story, maybe not one for tonight. It's to do with

304

my mum and the day she died."

I couldn't believe that Richard might have blamed my stupid brain haemorrhage on him forgetting to defrost those sausages. He'd told Claire when she was young that it was just one of those things waiting to happen, that it was nobody's fault.

They sat on a deserted blanket, propped on pillows, facing each other and munching through their late night snack.

"I was going to ask you something about your dad," Peter said, wiping his fingers on the napkin provided with the food.

"I promise you Peter I'll tell you all about Dad and the sausages another time – not tonight."

"No, it wasn't that, although I confess I'm curious now you've made such a thing about it. It was something else." Peter paused and discarded the napkin behind his back. "I was wondered about asking his permission for something."

"What do you need his permission for?"

Peter produced a small ring box from his pocket.

"It was to do with this."

"Is that what I think it is?"

Peter opened the box. I leaned in to get a closer look. It wasn't as though they would begrudge my interest if they knew I was there. The ring was simple white metal with a band of deep blue running around it, making it look as though three rings had been joined together.

"I thought it was the sort of thing you'd like. Maybe to wear for me, for us?"

When they kissed I made a hasty retreat. There's taking an interest and then there's downright intrusion. Even though they couldn't see me, I could see them. I made my way back to Richard who now had Hayley by his side. She had her arm round his waist and her head resting on his shoulder.

"They've just got engaged," I told them.

I was desperate to share my news. I'd been playing catch-up for years and now I was ahead of the game. They ignored me, but within seconds of my blurting it out Martin and Peter joined us.

"Dad, Hayley," Martin looked at Peter. "We've got something to tell you."

Hayley screamed, in a good way. She had spotted the ring on Martin's third finger.

"You're engaged," she shrieked and threw her arms round their necks, almost banging their heads together.

"That was my line Hayley," Martin mumbled, laughing into her neck.

Peter was laughing too and Richard was trying to shake his hand and congratulate him, but Hayley refused to let go. Eventually Hayley settled down, tears streaming down her cheeks. I was just as pleased. From what I'd seen of Peter he was a really nice man, perfect for Martin – caring, thoughtful and kind. But once again I was an observer, unable to communicate my feelings, unable to join in the celebrations when they told Claire and William.

My family was complete, together that night in a way I could never have imagined.

The band played a last dance, then another last dance, and a gibbous moon cast night time shadows of the remaining guests on the baize lawns.

Claire and William had left, Richard and Hayley were among the last there, a few straggling bachelors and raucous girls clustering on the top terrace. The balloon had been packed away at some point, leaving the lower field empty and cold.

Martin called from the corner of the house. "Dad, your taxi is here. You ready to go?"

Richard looked around. The catering staff had packed up their belongings, leaving only a couple of occupied picnic blankets.

"Yes, we're just coming."

I sped round to the front of the house ahead of Richard and Hayley. There was only one taxi there and my luck was in, all four doors were open. I climbed into the front passenger seat and automatically reached for the seat belt. I never learned.

On the trip home there was no noise from the back seat. I hoped they were just exhausted and that nothing else was going on. To distract myself from the images in my head I told the taxi driver a potted history of my life and after life. He took no interest at all in my story.

According to the digital clock on the dashboard it was just before one in the morning when we arrived home. I scrambled into back seat, sitting bent double on Richard's lap – I couldn't see any reason for the driver to get out or for the front passenger door to be available for my escape. My logic was justified and I tumbled out of his door as soon as Richard opened it.

Neither Hayley nor Richard spoke very much once we were in the house – both were exhausted from their busy day, but I was still wide awake. I followed Hayley upstairs, while Richard went into the kitchen to get a glass of water. I sat on the floor in a corner of their bedroom, still wearing my wedding dress – and it was in perfect condition, unaffected by the balloon ride, traipsing through the grass or even climbing over gates. I pulled my knees up under my chin, arranged my dress neatly around my feet, rested my chin on my arms and waited.

Hayley had gone into the bathroom. Richard came into the bedroom first, sat on the edge of the bed and wearily undressed. My chosen location was somewhat voyeuristic, but we had been married for twelve years so there was nothing that was exactly new to me. Hayley appeared and Richard went to the bathroom – I averted my eyes, studying the framed picture of the knight and a lady on a horse, which was still hung on the wall.

When, a few minutes later, the light went out I was surprised to hear Richard's voice.

"Do you really have to leave tomorrow?"

"I do Richard. I've delayed my flight already so that I could be here today."

"I thought you might change your mind."

"I can't and I have to go to sleep, I'm so tired, I can't discuss it now."

There was a rustling of bedclothes as they both settled and, before I had a chance to decide what to do I heard the first soft notes that preceded one of Richard's snoring bouts. When it reached full volume it could wake the dead – although the dead were already awake in the person of me.

"Richard," Hayley mumbled. "You're snoring again."

There was a moment's intermission before he resumed sawing logs. Hayley must have nudged him in the hope that he would roll onto his stomach.

"I give up," she mumbled. "I'm going to sleep in Claire's room,"

The moon gave just enough light through a gap in the curtains for me to see my way to Hayley's side of the bed. I lay next to Richard, who had finally turned on his side and stopped snoring. Snuggling up behind him I draped my arm over his body.

"Goodnight Richard, sleep well," I whispered and closed my eyes.

Chapter 30
Sunday, 4th September 2011

I opened my eyes and I was alone, the curtains were drawn back and it was light outside. A shower of rain spattered against the window. The bed I was on had been made, pillows fluffed, everything in place except for a suitcase – open on the end of the bed, clothes spilling out from it. I sat up, still in my wedding dress, which felt inappropriate. I concentrated and replaced it with red cords jeans and a baggy sweatshirt.

"Okay, that was easy," I muttered under my breath.

Richard called up from the bottom of the stairs.

"Are you ready? We really need to get going soon."

There was a muffled reply from the bathroom. It sounded like Hayley's voice.

"We're supposed to be there by twelve," Richard added.

Not knowing how far into the future I had skipped caused me to panic, scramble across the bed and check the clock on the bedside table – it was just gone eleven in the morning. Hayley had been leaving the day after the wedding – maybe Richard was dropping her off at the airport.

The bathroom door opened and Hayley called out as she headed back to bedroom.

"So we might be a little late Richard – it's not the end of the world."

"Anything I can do?" he called, sounding frustrated.

Hayley spoke quietly, not for Richard's ears. "Yes. Stop hassling me." Raising her voice and in a totally different, more friendly tone she added. "Almost ready. Just got to find my other shoe."

Hayley was on her knees by the bed. "Gotcha," she said.

I beat Hayley to the bedroom door and scuttled downstairs in front of her. She strolled down after me – her shoes hanging from her fingers. Richard was jingling car keys in his hand and the front door was open a few inches.

Wanting the option of staying in the house or going with them, I took a deep breath, looked up to the ceiling so as not to close my eyes, and slipped through the narrow gap and onto the porch steps. I was so good at the procedure by then that I didn't feel a moment's discomfort.

There was a new car in the drive, new to me at least. Hayley's suitcase was still in the bedroom so I assumed this wasn't a run to the airport. She must have just come back from somewhere. I had jumped more than a night.

There had been no time to check the calendar, but at least neither Hayley, nor Richard, looked significantly older. I dithered by the car, not sure whether to dive back indoors while I had the chance or cadge a lift to wherever they were going. I decided adventure was the spirit of the day and climbed on the bonnet and then onto the roof of the car. It had no roof rack, but it did have bars running along each side of the roof. I lay there on my tummy, arms stretched out, fingers gripping far harder than was necessary while the car was stationary.

The decision having been made, I ran through the possible reasons for their trip. The leaves had turned colour on the tress and some were already falling. It was most likely the autumn term. It was also probably a weekend, as Richard wasn't wearing a suit.

Hayley was buckling herself into the car before she closed the door.

"Did you pick up a bottle of wine Richard?"

"Of course I did, and I've got the present for Claire, and the camera."

Hayley's door slammed, making me jump. The car didn't look very old and I doubt it needed that much force to secure the lock.

"Here goes nothing," I murmured through gritted teeth, as we rolled down the drive and silently offered a prayer to the saint of ghosts that they didn't go too fast.

The journey was mostly through suburban developments and towards the city centre. I was surprised by how much green space had been lost in the past twenty something years. There was also a lot of traffic and it was more stop-start than roaring along empty roads.

We arrived at a leafy inner city street and Richard was driving slowly, obviously looking for a parking place. Residents only signs were prominently displayed, but Richard wriggled the car into a gap that hardly seemed big enough.

William appeared by the side of car waving a small piece of paper. Hayley got out and gave him a big hug.

"Congratulations," she said with her head still on his shoulder. "And I'm so sorry I couldn't get here any earlier, this is the first chance I've had to get back."

"No problem," William replied, disentangling himself from her and leaning in through her door to put the paper sign where it was visible through the windscreen.

Richard had walked round the back of the car and was shaking William's hand. I edged myself forward, leaning down over the windscreen to see what the piece of paper said. Reading upside down is a slow process and I had to concentrate. It was a guest, parking permit, dated by hand for the fourth of September 2011. I had only jumped some three months into the future of my family.

Realising that Claire must have had her babies, my grandchildren, I forgot were I was, lost my grip on the roof rails and slid headfirst down windscreen, over the bonnet and wedged myself against the car in front of us - just to

311

complicate matters I was also upside down.

Fortunately for me Hayley and Richard had gifts to retrieve from the backseat, which gave me time to reach out, grab a convenient lamppost and pull myself onto the pavement.

Feeling more like a vagrant than a grandmother, I crawled to the bottom of a flight of five slate capped steps leading up to a wide front door. There was a stained glass panel in the door depicting a farmer ploughing with horses. The image extended into the sidelights on either side. Using the wrought iron railings for support I hauled myself upright and brushed off my clothes – an automatic and unnecessary response. The front door was ajar and, wits restored, I managed to slip through before anybody else.

The ceiling in the hall had elegant decorative cornices. A black, cream and red tiled floor stretched down the hall in an intricate pattern. The staircase was cream painted wood – the newel post having a fantastical bird carved on the top. The house was obviously very expensive and I wondered how a newly married couple, albeit in good jobs, could possibly afford a place like that. Claire pattered down the stairs wearing an ankle length loose cotton dress.

"Hi Dad, Hayley, how are you?" She called to both of them. "The terrors are both asleep right now, but it won't be long before they're screaming the house down to be fed again."

Because only a single night had passed for me and three months for everyone else, it was like missing several episodes of a soap opera and having to work out who'd done what with who, never mind where and why. The answer to most of my questions would be found upstairs.

"Don't mind me everyone," I offered, half in anger, half in frustration. "I need to go and check something."

I weaved my way between the bodies in the crowded hall,

dodging coats being hung up and snatched hugs between Claire, Hayley and Richard. It was lovely to see Claire again, but I had pressing business to attend to.

The family reunion seemed destined to remain in the hall while I sneaked upstairs. I looked around trying to guess which way to turn.

"Come on, there's drinks in the kitchen," William said. "We don't want to wake the twins earlier than necessary. Red for you Richard?"

I heard Richard saying 'just a small glass' as their voices receded. The house was spacious, even on the second floor. I doubled back along the landing towards the front where another large window overlooked the street. The doors to the rooms on both sides were closed so I retraced my steps, turning right where I could see light spilling onto the corridor through an open door.

Inside a large room, painted in soft white tones, was a cot, a nursing chair and a long sofa. At least I was fairly sure it was a cot even although it resembled some mad designer's fusion of a cot and a four-poster bed. There were even delicate cotton curtains falling from a top rail, gathered with ties to each corner post.

Although I was fairly sure that I wouldn't disturb them, I tiptoed across the carpet and peeked over the side of the cot. Two tiny babies, both dressed in white, lay snuggled together. My beautiful twin grandchildren who would never know me, who I would never hold, never breath in their warm powdery smell, never have fall asleep in my arms. I sank to my knees on the carpet, hands still gripping the rail of the cot, but I was now looking through the vertical bars, wanting to cry equally with joy and an overwhelming sense of loss.

I wasn't aware that I was making any noise. It didn't really matter as nobody could hear me, but one of the twins was awake, staring straight at me.

"Hello baby. I'm sorry I don't even know your names yet."

It was then that I noticed the embroidered script on his outfit – his name was Anthony.

"Hello Anthony. Were you named after your great grandfather?"

He gurgled, his arms moved in excitement and I was sure that he could see me. I stood up slowly, not wanting to disturb him too much as I knew I couldn't pick him up to comfort him. Without thinking, I reached into the cot, wanting to touch his face and feel the warmth and softness of his skin. It shouldn't have been a surprise, but it was – he felt the same to me as everything else in the world. Anthony was like a mobile bronze sculpture, patinated to look real, but offering no sensation of either heat or cold on my fingertips.

He was a happy little baby though, gurgling away, not old enough to really laugh or even giggle yet. His movement woke his sibling who stared at me wide eyed. Her name was now visible, also embroidered. She was called Alison. My namesake. I dropped to my knees again. My legs, and in fact my whole body, reduced to a jelly-like quality.

Contenting myself with watching them through the bars and murmuring small words of comfort, I didn't notice William enter the room. But I did notice when his knee knocked me sideways into the sofa. Not with as soft a landing as I might have hoped for, because the sofa too had the resilience of bronze.

"How are my beautiful little babies? Mummy is going to be here any minute with her lovely boobies so you can both have a nice..."

I started to sing, very loudly, realising that you should never spy on your son-in-law when he thinks he's alone. Both my grandchildren studied me with wide eyes and raised eyebrows, they looked like they were both about to cry.

"I'm sorry," I whispered to them. "But believe me, that was absolutely necessary."

Claire arrived at the door, smiling.

"You do know the baby monitor was on William?"

"Oh fuck," he looked round at the device on a coffee table by the sofa. "I mean fudge."

"I turned it off downstairs, but not before my father heard about how nice his daughter's boobies were."

"Ah," he said, looking embarrassed.

"Well at least you've made Hayley's day. Probably not the cat's day though as she spat her wine all over him."

"Is it safe for me to go back down?"

"Well you can't stay up here all day can you? Come on, let's brave your audience."

Claire picked up Alison, William took Anthony and I followed them both downstairs. Richard and Hayley made a fuss over them, Hayley taking Anthony from William while he went to get a bottle.

The lounge was large, located at the front of the house, but with a bay window high enough above the street for it to still feel private. The walls were deep brick red and the alcoves to each side of an ornate Victorian fireplace were filled with bookshelves from floor to ceiling. The house was larger and decorated in a more conservative fashion than I would have expected of Claire and William.

I sat on the floor by the side of the hearth, my back against a shelf of books. I ran my finger along the spines. They were predominantly on art. Where I would have expected a television was an antique rocking chair. The whole room had the feel of someone older, more established, even the armchairs and sofa were carefully mismatched and had been recovered in an expensive-looking heavy cotton in

315

an abstract pattern of cream, brown and gray. I drew my legs up and rested my chin on my knees.

Claire sat back on the sofa with Alison and started to breast feed her, Hayley fussing over Anthony to distract him. William returned from the kitchen with a bottle.

"Do you want to feed Anthony?" he asked, holding the bottle out to Hayley.

Hayley shook her head. "Um, maybe not today," she said and kissed Anthony's forehead before handing him over to his father.

William sat next to Claire so the babies' heads were almost touching.

"I don't envy you Claire. I know I couldn't have coped with one, let alone two babies." Hayley puffed her cheeks out as though exhausted by the mere thought.

"Oh you get used to it, and William does his bit when he can."

She smiled at William but continued to concentrate on the task in hand. Without looking up, Claire casually asked Hayley what her plans were and whether she was going to return to Spain. There was no immediate response. Hayley looked at Richard before replying.

"I don't think I'm going back."

Richard reached out and took Hayley's hand.

"She's going to be a kept woman from now on."

"About time," Claire said, still without looking up. "I knew you'd win her round in the end Dad."

"I've hardly whisked her off her feet – it's taken me twenty years."

"I was scared," Hayley screwed up her mouth and frowned.

"Of me?" I whispered.

"Alison was always such a presence. I never felt I could live up to her memory."

"You never had to Hayley," Richard said softly. "The two of you are so different – and it was never a competition."

"It was in my head. She was my best friend."

"I still am," I assured her.

"I could never replace her either as a wife or a mother."

I pulled my knees closer to my chest, my hands bunched into fists. I never realised I was, never meant to be, an obstacle in that way. I only wanted to be remembered.

The conversation turned into a distant murmur as I looked around the room. There were three people present that would never know me, not properly. I would only ever be a name, a handful of photographs and the subject of a few second-hand reminiscences. I understood why Jeremy was so eager to get to the end of his vigil, whatever it might entail. I now understood his frustration at coming back the same day every year and the emptiness of not belonging. I wanted to see him again, to tell him I understood, that he wasn't alone.

To my grandchildren I would be no more real than a character in a book or a film. They would never know the sound of my voice, the touch of my hand, the softness of my laughter or the warmth of a comforting hug when they had fallen over or were upset.

I squeezed my legs even closer to me, turning my feet in, making myself as small as I could – and I closed my eyes, tight shut. I wasn't even sure I wanted to open them again, not ever again.

Chapter 31
Saturday 19th June 2021

Of course I did open my eyes again, I had no choice in the matter, but I had momentarily forgotten where I was. The room had changed. The dark walls of the lounge were now painted a soft pale gray and there was a television screen next to me, wafer thin, hung on an arm extending from the wall.

"Ali, Ant, come on you lot, get a wiggle on. I'm not going to be late for my little brother's big day."

It was Claire, shouting from another room her words echoing through the hall. I stood up slowly, taking my time to cross to the door.

"I'm ready Mum." The voice was from a girl who was sauntering down the stairs. First her feet appeared and then her body and then a perfect replica of Claire from when she was about seven years old. I gasped and covered my mouth with a hand. Anthony and William followed close behind.

"All present and correct Captain. First Mate William and deckhands Ali and Ant reporting for duty."

William was wearing a pale blue blazer, cream trousers, a white shirt and a striped blue and green tie. Claire was in a pale yellow cotton dress with dark blue polka dots. The children were dressed to match their parents' outfits. I wasn't keen on the shortening of their names to Ant and Ali, but it wasn't my choice to make. It looked as though they were off to a regatta or in fancy dress for some summer garden party.

"You look gorgeous," Claire said, brushing her cheek against William's. "But I mustn't ruin my lipstick."

William patted Alison's behind.

"Don't start all that stuff," Ant complained and reached up to the latch on the front door.

"Do you think Martin will have children?" Ali asked. "I'd like a cousin, maybe three, all girls. They would be more fun than a brother."

"Maybe they will adopt." William suggested.

"What does adopt mean?" Ant asked from the front door.

"It's when you give a home to a baby that nobody else wants," William explained.

Was Martin getting married? It was the only explanation to the way they were dressed and the questions being asked. Men couldn't marry of course. Had Martin decided that he wasn't gay or was I confused?

"Men can't have babies," Ali said, "They haven't got boobies so they can't feed them."

"That's just stupid," Ant snapped. "You can feed babies with bottles."

"I think we'll stop there for today," William suggested.

So who was Martin was marrying. Could men get married? Because if he was marrying a woman, why would they have to adopt.

"It's a good point Ali," Claire said. "But it's a bit more complicated than that. Now where is that car?"

From out in the street there were three short toots on a horn.

"It's here," Ant shouted.

I managed to squeeze past Ant and saw a driver opening a sliding side door to a smart, modern minibus. "Thank you," I said as I climbed in. He took no notice of me. It would seat seven people and I didn't know if they were picking anyone else up. I headed for the back, sitting in the middle of a bench for three.

Claire and William took seats at the front, Ant and Ali

headed my way and I made myself as small as I could. They took a window seat each. There were only two places to spare if you included me.

"You have my grandmother's address?" Claire asked the driver. "Because I'm a bit worried about time."

"I'll get you all there in plenty of time, don't you worry," he assured her.

Claire slumped back in her seat. "I thought this day would never come," she sighed.

"But what day is it? Come to that, what year is it? And what's happening?" I leaned forward hoping to get some clues.

"It has certainly been a roller coaster," William said. "I always thought Peter was the one."

"God no," Claire muttered. "He turned out to be a real bastard didn't he?"

"Language," Ali called from beside me

"What did he do?" I begged.

"He always came over as such a nice guy, sensible, caring, honest," Claire sounded puzzled.

"And I suppose his wife thought so too."

"I know, it's still difficult to believe."

"Little ears are listening William."

"No I'm not," Ali piped up grumpily.

"But I am – and thank you for at least giving me a clue. Now, who is Martin marrying?" I demanded.

"Water under the bridge thank goodness," Claire said quietly, closing the subject.

We pulled up outside a town house. My mother was already standing on the steps waiting for us. The driver got out and she climbed in with the help of a hand offered by William. She barely acknowledged the driver. My mother was at least consistent.

Winding out of the city and into countryside, I realised

that the scenery was familiar. My suspicions were confirmed when we turned into a tree-lined gravel drive that I
recognised from Claire's wedding venue.

"Brings back memories doesn't it William?"

"I suppose we've been here before as well," Ant added
seriously.

"Yes, you're right, all five of us," William laughed.

"Six if you count me."

The house had been smartened up significantly since
Claire and William's wedding, but that was about seven
years ago if I'd guessed the twins ages correctly.

There were twenty or more cars parked along the drive.
Ours pulled up to the main entrance. The driver leapt out
and almost ran round the vehicle to open the sliding door.

Martin was on the steps leading up to the house, dressed
in a candy-striped blazer. Andrew, his childhood friend, was
next to him in a blue and green striped blazer, both had
matching white cotton trousers and similar tan coloured
brogues. They even had identical ties in deep, almost fluo-
rescent, green and blue stripes.

I assume Andrew was acting in the role of best man. He
hardly looked any different from the last time I'd seen him,
tall, slim and boyishly good-looking. As everyone got out of
the minibus, my grandchildren remained by the door,
blocking my exit.

Ant whispered, but rather too loudly, from behind his
sister. "Which one is the bride?"

"Neither," Claire hissed, bending down to straighten his
tie. "They are both grooms. Now, no more questions until
we get home."

Of course my mother had to chip in with her usual lack of
tact.

"One of them is always the bride," she mumbled.

William leaned close to Claire. "You really are going to

have to have a word with your grandmother Claire. I know grew up in a different era, but she can't say things like that in front of the children."

"I've tried, but she doesn't listen or doesn't care, or she does listen and still doesn't care."

I managed to slip out of the car before the driver slid the door across, slamming it into place. I jumped at the sound, not wanting to think what would have happened to me if I had got caught in it. I shuddered and my body sort of rippled like a jelly on a dish.

Claire was hugging Martin, William shaking hands with Andrew. My mother had taken charge of my grandchildren, looking like a paragon of virtue from a bygone age. Even she was dressed in the same style of extravagant garden party chic. I was impressed by how well she carried her age, but then my mother always had style.

"The front row is reserved for you. Dad and Hayley are already here," Martin said, and for a moment I thought he was talking to me. When I turned around he was holding both Claire's hands. "We'll be there in a few minutes, just waiting for a signal that they're ready for us."

I followed Claire, William and her family, my family, into the house and down a central aisle between rows of chapel chairs. They paused every now and then, exchanging a few words with guests they obviously knew well. Nearly all the men in the room were dressed in colourful blazers with trousers ranging from white to bright red.

Richard and Hayley were already seated on the front row on the right hand side, a vacant chair to Richard's left. Lydia sat next to Hayley. I tried to calculate how old she was, but couldn't be certain. She was definitely at the top end of her eighties.

Lydia leaned in towards Hayley. "One of my lovers turned out to be gay – it certainly explained a lot." She pursed her lips and nodded knowingly. I squeezed in next to my grandchildren, wanting to hug them, to gently rake my fingers through their hair. Ant pulled out a small plastic figure from his pocket.

"Put that away Anthony," William hissed at him. "I told you not to bring it today and I'll confiscate it if I see it it again."

It didn't go back into his pocket. Instead Ant hid it in his hand on my side, out of sight of his father. Every so often he made it walk along the edge of his chair

A single reedy note sounded to one side and an *a cappella* group launched into a song I recognised from the very first line – *How Sweet it is to be Loved by You*' was a favourite song of mine. It always brought a lump to my throat. How that happened when I didn't really exist in the conventional sense, and didn't have a throat or a lump in it, always remained a puzzle to me.

I turned at the same time as everyone else did, to see Martin and Andrew walking down the centre aisle of the room side by side. For the first time I looked across to the front seats opposite me. I recognised Sarah, Andrew's mother, she was older now – everyone was except me. It all fell into place, I realised Martin was marrying Andrew.

My mouth was probably hanging open during the whole ceremony. I had so many questions nobody was going to answer. A voice shocked me back into reality.

"I thought I might catch up with you here. It's been a long time."

It was Jeremy, standing so close that his whispered words in my ear made me jump. I slapped him on the shoulder.

"You could have given me a heart attack."

"Hardly likely in our situation," he laughed. " Where have you been all these years, or have we just missed each other?"

"Long story," I said.

He was wearing a school blazer with a badge on the breast pocket. It had a Latin inscription embroidered under a shield. I couldn't read Latin, but he noticed me looking at it.

"Closest I could get to the dress code," he explained.

"How did you know about Martin's wedding?"

"I like your family, they're fun, much better than my boring brother's lot. I usually pop round to see if you're there and try to keep up with what's happening."

While we were talking a loud cheer rang round the room, followed by applause, and the a cappella group broke into an old Stevie Wonder song *For Once in My Life*.

I had never really listened to the words before, even though I'd sung along to it countless times, adding la las to the phrases I couldn't remember. But now I was joining in and, buoyed by the occasion, crying as I listened more carefully.

The reception was in a marquee on the middle lawn of the three terraces, and I, with everyone else, watched as Martin and Andrew took to the floor for the first dance. They were hilarious, hamming it up to *Dancing Queen* in front of everybody. The joy on their faces was wonderful and the guests were clapping and cheering at every pose and obviously well rehearsed dance move. I couldn't stop laughing and crying at the same time.

Jeremy dragged me onto a corner of the dance floor when everybody else joined in. I was my seventeen-year-old self again, wearing a ridiculously short dress and dancing barefoot. It never struck me at the time how odd this was as Martin and Andrew must have been in their mid thirties..

The party went on until midnight when the last dance was announced. Both Jeremy and I knew that it wouldn't be right to be falling into each other's arms in some tingling embrace. We drifted, slightly awkwardly, back to a table covered in half-empty glasses, party streamers and remnants of wedding cake. Abandoned blazers were slung over the backs of chairs with handbags and shoes lying on the seats.

"I might leave you to it," Jeremy said. "Think you can find your way home by yourself?"

"I'll be okay. I've done it before. What about you?"

"I'll hitch a ride somewhere. I'll take pot luck on where I end up."

"You do like an adventure don't you?"

Jeremy shrugged and smiled at me.

"Life should be about adventures, why should death be any different?"

Jeremy blew me a kiss and wandered away towards the front of the house. Later I saw him on his back on top of a car, waiting to be taken to wherever destiny chose.

I sat near the exit to the tent in order to keep eye on Richard and Hayley. I assumed they would have a taxi to pick them up and planned to hitch a ride with them. It turned out to be quite simple, nobody was in any rush and I had plenty of time to crawl into the car and extricate myself at the other end of the journey.

"I'm whacked Richard," Hayley yawned as soon as they were in the hall. "I'm going up to get out of these clothes."

"I'm just going to sit down here for a bit, let the day settle in my head."

"Don't be long then."

Richard eased off his shoes, leaving them scattered with Hayley's in the hall, and went into lounge. He looked around as though he wasn't sure what he was doing there. Walking over towards a tall wooden bookcase, he knelt on the floor and pulled out an old photograph album. It was the one of our wedding. He sat on the sofa with the book on his lap and opened it it up.

"You've kept it here all these years," I whispered and sat on the arm of the sofa, looking with him as he turned the pages.

I felt connected again, content, my body relaxed against Richard, leaning on his shoulder. But then I heard him wince and a take sharp breath. He clutched at his chest and the photograph album fell to the floor, breaking the spine, the pages laying at odd angles to each other. I couldn't help. Only Hayley could save him. I ran into the hall shouting at the top of my voice.

"Hayley, quick, come down here."

She was already wandering down the stairs in a silk dressing gown, but in no great hurry.

"Quick," I practically screamed. "Richard is having a heart attack."

"Richard," she called. "Are you coming to bed?"

Hayley walked into the lounge, half asleep already, nonchalant, yawning. I was still screaming at her. When she saw Richard collapsed on the sofa, a taut grimace of pain on his face and his hands clenched to his chest she reacted immediately. I leaned against the wall, unable to help, my words of reassurance and comfort falling on ears that were deaf to me.

Chapter 32

Hayley grabbed the phone and dialled emergency services. She was calm and precise, giving the address, Richard's symptoms and the fact that he was still breathing, but that he couldn't talk easily.

I had no real sense of the time it took for the ambulance to arrive. It felt like forever, but was probably only a matter of minutes. Hayley remained on the phone relaying any changes and trying to keep Richard comfortable.

Blue lights flashed through window as soon as the ambulance turned into our street. Hayley rushed to open the front door and immediately returned to Richard's side. The paramedics were calm and efficient, more than could be said of me. I was babbling at them to get him to hospital as fast as they could.

Fortunately neither of the paramedics was Peter, who I hoped had been thrown out by his wife and was now living in a cardboard box in a shop doorway. One of them took down both Richard's and Hayley's names and details, the other started to check Richard's condition.

"How is he? Is he going to be all right?" Hayley asked.

"You're his partner are you Hayley?"

She looked confused and distressed, but nodded vigorously.

We both rode with Richard in the ambulance, blue lights and an intermittent siren breaking the peace of the early hours of a Sunday morning.

Hayley rang Claire from the hospital. I looked at the notes sheet of the paramedic and learned his admission was recorded as one-fifteen on the Sunday morning. Claire arrived thirty minutes later, was allowed into the cubicle and gave her father a hug.

"You are going to get better Dad. I refuse to let this sort of thing happen to you."

Richard smiled at her. He was out of pain, but his eyes were sunken and his face ashen.

"These things happen Claire. We know that better than most families."

This was my husband and my daughter, but I felt like I was eavesdropping on a personal moment. I left them for a while and sat in the waiting room. When Claire and Hayley came out I asked them what was happening. They hugged and Hayley said she would phone Claire if there was any news, but what Richard needed was rest. Both of them looked exhausted.

None of this applied to me. I hadn't disturbed anyone's sleep in decades. I dodged through a door when it opened and managed to slide under the curtains surrounding Richard's cubicle. I lay on the bed next to him my arm draped over his chest.

I talked, hoping it might calm him even though he couldn't hear me. I reminded him about our early days at university, about the dreams we shared, the afternoons we spent in bed together, our honeymoon, our holidays, the joy of Claire and Martin's births. I don't know how long I talked, or how I didn't close my eyes when I tried to recall all the special moments we had shared. Somehow I kept them open, not wanting to leave Richard, not thinking of anything but our life together.

When I felt a hand on my shoulder I turned, surprised, not sure who it could be. It was that nurse again, the abrupt, unsympathetic nurse that I had avoided when I was here last. Her voice was now soft and caring.

"He's gone Dear."

I heard the pinging of the monitor, saw lights flashing on a panel, heard the nursing staff and a doctor burst through the curtain and I was brushed aside. Hitting the floor in a sobbing, curled up ball.

That nurse I despised was there, cradling me in her arms, talking quietly to me, comforting me in the way I had been trying to comfort Richard.

Jeremy
Wednesday 14th July 2021

Jeremy sat cross-legged on a font at the back of the church. It gave him a good view of proceedings and he was safe from being jostled by the mourners whey filed in and out. He had always liked funerals, almost as much as weddings. He thought the crying could be a bit intense sometimes, but at the back of the church he was less bothered by it.

Funerals were also closer to the family services he had attended as a child, at least in the way people dressed. Men were not so formal these days, but there was always a good smattering of suits and ties. Women dressed smartly too, but not so often in black. Jeremy approved of that. Funerals should be a celebration, but then not everyone shared his perspective and understanding.

He had long since stopped fretting about why he was still here, what he was waiting for. He knew he was waiting for his brother – it was just taking a very long time. It would happen soon, but he was in no hurry.

Occasionally, as today, Jeremy would hope to witness a reunion. These things were usually brief affairs but brilliant nonetheless – in more ways than one. He had never been married, never had the opportunity, but could appreciate the bond that was formed when people did get married – sometimes forever, sometimes not.

The couple at the front of the church looked to be in their mid thirties, but Jeremy knew that appearances meant nothing. He also knew that Alison had died at the age of thirty-six so maybe that was why she appeared to be about that age, as close to Richard's age as she could manage.

Printed in Great Britain
by Amazon